# MEMO TO THE LEADER

WILLIAM WALLING

Strategic Book Publishing and Rights Co.

Strategic Book Publishing and Rights Co., LLC
USA | Singapore
www.sbpra.net

For information about special discounts for bulk purchases, please contact Strategic Book Publishing and Rights Co., LLC Special Sales, at bookorder@sbpra.net.

ISBN: 978-1-950015-81-8

*"The future ain't what it used t'be."*
—Yogi Berra

# FOREWORD

The most hideous aspect of perpetual confinement was isolation. His keepers treated him with neither respect nor disrespect, neither kindness nor unkindness—an Olympian aloofness that refuted his existence, as if living burial was a lame substitute for eternal rest. Random sleep-deprivation sessions garnished by deftly applied psychological pressure before medication-enhanced interrogations were the only interruptions to the great pains his unseen captors took to deny him the solace of oblivion.

Guards with opaque Asian features wearing baggy tan uniforms regarded him as an object, not a person when food trays were deposited or retrieved from a shallow slot in the barred-steel door of his damp, jackhammer-scored limestone cell. He was infrequently marched to a natural gallery in the caverns, and urged with rude gestures to perform shuffling calisthenics.

The vacuous days and invisible nights dragged past in sunless solitude, strung together like evil beads in a necklace of anonymous weeks and months. He had all the time there was, or all that might remain, to examine, reexamine, reflect upon, evaluate, and reevaluate the confluences of circumstance, situation, and human activity that culminated in The Great Mistake. Everlastingly, elliptically, he revisited the complex jumble of personalities, actions, encounters, conspiratorial schemes and endeavors leading to the fully fleshed out, world-changing scenario in which he had played the principal role.

*Take care what you ask for!*

The caveat resonated in his mind like a clarion bell, and circled there, spinning round and round until he could not stop second-guessing his part in the charade's triumph, or tragedy, and then second-guessing his second-guesses until the riddle had neither beginning nor middle, only an end, and reflexive hindsight crowded his mind into shadowy labyrinths. What multiplied his torment tenfold was a nagging dread that if captivity proved as everlasting as he thought it might he would eventually find himself no longer *himself*, just a half-remembered stranger bent upon vainly trying to pick shadows off the damp wall of his cell.

Perhaps if he had firmly declined the mission, had adamantly refused to go on the fateful evening Dean Omsley appeared unannounced at the chalet, subsequent events might have taken a more laudable course. But that was wishful thinking, the essence of futility. Bernard's visit had made an abrupt beginning of sorts, yet there had been more, so much, *much* more.

# ONE

## *Colorado-Provinz, Monat Mai*
## *Deutsches Weltreich Jahr 142*

As a youngster, Jamie had been told how some *Aculturazation Ministerium* bureaucrat intrigued by the potential evident in the edited, anonymous genome-engineering chart issued to newborns, had decided his first language should be German.

Three decades later Professor James Silverthorne, endowed with linguistic fluency untainted by any hint of a provincial *Amerikanischer akzent,* leaned forward in a soft leather armchair and began to earnestly describe the historical imperatives he hoped to unveil if vetted to undertake retro-temporal research in what he considered an exceptionally interesting period of antiquity. Surviving Roman records had skimpily cited the events, personalities, circumstances and situations culminating in a pivotal twenty-century-old battle possibly responsible for inspiring a major change in the peoples dwelling in northern Europe.

*Kanzler von Colorado-Provinz* Ernst Hoffmann lifted an imperious hand, silencing his visitor in mid-sentence. "Your command of German is admirable, Doctor Silverthorne. But would you mind helping me brush up on my nodding acquaintance with English?"

*"Natürlich, Herr Kanz …* Certainly, sir." Uncomfortable over the unexpected invitation to visit the chancellor in his palatial Provincial Seat of Government chambers, or his aristocratic stature in the *Deutsches Weltreich* hierarchy, James construed the erudite official's

reference to an "acquaintance" with English as pure sham. It was second nature for his host to disarm lesser mortals with false modesty, yet he also sensed Hoffman's real reason for wishing to abandon the mother tongue. It had to be the black-uniformed *SS Untersturmführer* seated rigidly nearby, his body language denying Silverthorne's very existence. A political attaché blood-sworn to remain forever loyal to the memory of Adolf Hitler, the junior *SS-*officer's assignment was to shadow Hoffmann during his daily conduct of government affairs, and if necessary report any act or spoken word officialdom might judge contrary to *Nationalsozialismus* doctrine.

Reclaiming his train of thought, James continued his explanation. "Opinions differ widely, sir. Most of my colleagues believe the successful ambush and annihilation of three entire Roman legions created a turning point in Rome's imperial growth. Others consider the battle, known in Roman records as *Varusschlacht,* was no monumental historical milestone, just another of many legionary versus barbarian conflicts that pepper antiquity."

"And your personal view … ?" At ease behind his massive desk, Hoffmann toyed with the honorary Order of Teutonic Knights signet ring bestowed by *Reichskounzel.*

Though his conviction was visceral, not historically fact-based, James didn't hesitate to voice his firm belief that the massacre in *Teutoburger Wald* had ignited a catalytic change in the societies of at least four barbarian tribes in the *Germania Magnus* region. "You see, at that moment in time Rome had barely finished putting down a massive, drawn-out uprising in what are now ———"

"Tut, Professor," said his host. "I have no wish to be inundated with historical data. What is your, um … gut feeling about the battle, if that's the appropriate Americanism?"

"My interpretation, shared by many historians, is founded on passing inferences in a few Roman chronicles. Neither Caesar Augustus nor any of his successors in the principate seemed interested in reviving an ambition to conquer and subjugate the tribes in that region after it was aborted due to the loss of three irreplaceable legions. It freed the peoples in question from Roman hegemony, allowing them and the neighboring tribes to develop their own language and culture. If the Cherusci warrior-prince Roman literature identifies as Arminius had failed to organize and lead a huge, allied barbarian army into battle, or the struggle gone the other way, I seriously doubt whether the —"

"Hermann!" declared Hoffmann, a disagreeable burr sharpening his diction. "You surely meant *Hermann der Cherusker,* rather than the hero Rome bastardized in the Latin tongue as *Arminius.*"

Feigning chagrin over his purposeful gaffe, James said hastily, "Forgive me, sir. But I fear either identity is equally suspect. His indigenous *Cherusker* name is one sidelight I hope to learn."

Less than wholly mollified, his host nodded. "Do go on, Professor."

"Speculation," pursued James, "has been rife for generations. Many historical quandaries are rooted in *clades variana,* yet another Latin term for the major setback to imperial expansion. For instance, what if the victors had become the vanquished? Would Emperor Tiberius have resumed the conquest, and perhaps extended Roman provincial rule all the way east of the Rhine to perhaps the Elbe? If so, would the western empire have later fallen into eclipse with both the Gallic *and* Germanic peoples under the thumb of one or more latter-day Caesars? Later still, would a barbarian coalition known as the Goths have successfully marched on Rome? Or very much later, how would a revised European populace have affected Charlemagne's attempt to resurrect *Imperium Romanorum?* And of far greater modern significance, lacking a German nation, what of today's *Deutsches Weltreich* empire?"

A refractory glint invaded the chancellor's dark eyes. "Provocative questions indeed, Professor! Yet referring to *Tausendjahr Weltreich* as an 'empire' strikes me as rather tactless. Should our noble *Reichsführer* or *Reichsleiter* overhear our modern community of nations labeled an 'empire,' I daresay they would take umbrage."

As if humbled by the chastisement, Jamie said, "Your pardon, a slip of the tongue, sir."

Hoffmann's manner softened. Thoughtfully fingering Silver-thorne's dossier on the desk beside a red-leather-bound folio edition of *Mein Kampf,* he nodded. "All well and good, Professor! We asked you here this afternoon to discuss your proposed junket to antiquity, and so we shall. Absolutely no one would think to belittle your amazing accomplishments, or your expertise and outstanding qualifications to undertake such a daring venture. Your most recent book electrified historians and literati everywhere, especially the intelligentsia in the capital, *Welthauptstadt,* who praised your work to the skies. By the way, refresh my memory, if you will be so kind. What was the nickname his subjects bestowed on their beloved monarch?"

*"Der Alte Fritz,"* supplied James, his suspicions aroused by the abrupt change of subject.

A dry chuckle. *"Der Alte Fritz, ja, ja!"* Ignoring his earlier request for aid in "brushing up" on English, the chancellor had subconsciously reverted to German. "One glaring omission in your Potsdam narrative still piques my curiosity. How in the world were you, a friendless stranger, able to infiltrate *Schloss Sanssouci* and actually stand in the presence of Friederich der Grosse? I was tremendously impressed by your remarkable insights, especially by the superb word-picture you painted of the era's preeminent ruler clad in his faded Prussian military uniform, shuffling about the summer palace using a silver-handled cane."

"Friederich was a most accomplished flutist and composer, *Herr Kanzler.* He devoted his waning years and energies more to music than statesmanship, or command of the Prussian military."

*"Ja, ja, sehr wahrscheinlich ... "* The chancellor broke off, and again reverted to English. "You've been enormously privileged, Doctor Silverthorne. I confess to having greatly enjoyed your

Potsdam book, but readers like myself are still owed an explanation. How in the world did you, a perfect stranger, manage to worm your way into a position as household servant?"

James forced a self-effacing smile. "Looking through servants, not directly at them, was a habit ingrained in the late eighteenth century's Prussian elite. My pose as a provincial from southern Germany, doubtless enhanced by my peculiar modern accent, enabled me to talk my way into duty as a footman. Later, a friendly equerry helped me obtain posting as a bewigged usher. The only glitch in the entire junket took place when my locket and snuff box went missing."

"Glitch . . ?" Hoffmann's brows contracted. "I fear you've lost me."

"A colloquialism for a problem of some sort. Dean Omsley had an old pawn shop locket reworked in the institute's nanotechnology lab. Outwardly a cheap trinket on a tarnished silver chain any servant might wear, it enclosed a nanorecorder. The snuff box held all the unprocessed digital images I had snapped in secret, plus snatches of eavesdropped conversations. I've often wondered what the thief—another servant, I'm sure—thought when he or she pried open the locket and tried to make sense of the sub-molar device. Both items were probably discarded as useless."

The chancellor clicked his tongue. "A dreadful loss! Capturing tangible glimpses and actual, spoken words from that rich era of our past would have added enormously to your book."

James was forced to agree.

"Still, daring a visit to antiquity seems, well … Shall we say a touch overzealous?"

"Quite a long jump," admitted James, hoping to deflect what he thought might come next.

"A major understatement." As if to subconsciously reassert his authority, Hoffmann touched the Heidelberg scar marring his left cheek. "More than two millennia, twice the length of any retro-temporal transposition thus far contemplated."

Upon being introduced to the chancellor, James had intuited the scar to be a product of inner Party surgery—an elite "signature" meant to remind lesser individuals of the "fair-haired" status bestowed on young *Herrenvolk* deemed eventual candidates for high government service.

His professional politician's smile clicking on and off, Hoffmann said, "Win or lose, permit me to congratulate you and Professor Omsley for pleaded a winning case. After all, it is *your* neck you seem willing to risk by courting unknown ancient dangers. The submitted prospectus was taken under advisement weeks ago. I invited you to drop by today due to a call from the Reichsleiter's executive assistant about another matter. Before signing off, she hinted broadly that your junket to antiquity would shortly either be sanctioned or denied."

"Wonderful news! Thank you ever so much for letting me know, sir."

"Oh, waste not your gratitude on a public servant, Professor. It is I who should be thankful for owning a front-row seat on each of your brave, fascinating research ventures into our common past."

Pushing back his high-backed executive chair, the chancellor rose and turned to the stone-faced *SS* junior officer. "Dieter, I find myself in need of a breath of fresh air. Relax and have coffee while I walk our celebrated visitor to his car."

The *Untersturmführer* responded with a solemn blink, an uncertain nod.

* * *

Nattily attired in a fashionable smoke-gray tunic replete with wrap-around collar, *Kanzler* Ernst Hoffmann emerged from the massive building with James in tow. Donning rimless anti-glare shades against the brilliant sunshine outdoors, he acknowledged with a regal head-dip the salutes of uniformed *Ausland Staatspolizei* sentinels braced to attention on both sided of the columned entry.

Razed decades earlier along with all neighboring structures, the old Denver Civic Center had given way to lush parklands and widely spaced public buildings. On earlier visits to the Provincial Seat, its overt grandiosity had impressed James as obnoxiously pretentious. To him, the neoclassic, columned architecture was reminiscent in style and scale of celebratory spectacles such as the annual Nuremberg Nazi rally depicted in grainy, cataloged black-and-white films he had studied which dated back to pre-War of World Liberation years. Descending the broad-risered marble steps, the unfolding vista reaffirmed his prior conviction that all the surrounding architectonic monstrosities had been designed to satisfy only those already megalomaniacal.

Larger-than-life, the polished bronze figures of Nazi demigods Adolf Hitler and Erich Lustmann gazed fondly at one another across the still waters of a kilometer-long reflecting pool. Lesser statuary groupings featured secondary and tertiary *Reichshelden.* The sightless metal eyes of *Generalfeldmarshal* Erwin Rommel, the lionized *Afrika Korps* "Desert Fox," and mastermind of the stubborn defense of *Festung Europa* which had so frustrated the massed Allied forces bravely attempting to invade the continent, were fixed on the adjacent *Panzer Schrein,* its centerpiece a nostalgic, weatherproofed *Königstiger II* heavy tank that had wreaked havoc on more than one continent during "The War of World Liberation." Beneath the gigantic killing machine's turret-mounted 8.8-centimeter cannon, the bronze effigy of *Waffen SS-Hauptsturmführer* Joachim Peiper, once commander of *Panzergruppe SS-Leibstandarte Adolf Hitler,* knelt down holding a map flat-pressed to the ground while pointing out a salient ripe for attack to his immediate superior, *Waffen SS-Oberst-Gruppenführer* Josef "Sepp" Dietrich.

Huge red-and-black swastika banners rippled along the divided, tree-lined boulevard, where buses had pulled up curbside to disgorge clamoring files of schoolchildren bound on a field trip to the nearby *Weltreich Museum.* Chatting and posing for digital and holographic snapshots, flocks of tourists strolled the riparian esplanade branching off on either side of the reflecting pool. Somewhere in the sprawling adjacent parklands, band music played in erratic counterpoint to the faint, rhythmic wheezing of a giant carousel.

A uniformed chauffeur lounging at the entrance to the underground garage noted Chancellor Hoffmann's approach in company with the passenger he himself had dropped off earlier. Hurrying to the polished electric limousine, he stood rigidly beside it, prepared to open the passenger door.

Halfway along the shaded walkway leading to the garage, the chancellor took Silverthorne's elbow with unexpected familiarity, and drew him to a halt. Head lowered, he said softly, "Jamie, I do hope you understand why formality was mandatory there in my office. One minder or another loafs forever in my chambers, making it necessary to limit all conversations to generalities."

*Minder!* Jarred by a Briticism the other had doubtless acquired during his previous tenure in Cambridgeshire Province, James said, "Don't give it a thought, sir."

"I would pain me to have you think me unsympathetic to your proposed junket to antiquity. My outward standoffishness is due to, well … Every brainwashed, self-important young *SS-Überwachung* loafer who follows me about like a *verdammt* puppy dotes on reporting any overt familiarity I might show a civilian visitor, or a single unconscious slip from political doctrine when conversing with a distinguished academic such as yourself. In my world, government is not the simple straightforward occupation the uninitiated may believe it to be."

"I understand completely," said James, taking the other's "my world" reference at face value, not rhetorically. It *literally* was their world!

\* \* \*

A matter of professional courtesy, Hoffmann had ordered a government limousine dispatched to fetch James from the institute. The chauffeur ushered Silvethorne into the rear seat, inquiring in German where he wished to be taken.

"Back to Goebbels, *bitte.*" Despite the fancy uniform, he thought the smarmy fellow should have had *Ausland Staatspolizei* stenciled across his forehead, or maybe *Sicherheitsdienst,* one of the snoopers from Colonel Jürgen Müller's *SD* stable, not some *Polizei des Provinziellen Zustandes* street thug.

The silent electric limo eased up a curling access ramp, slowed to a crawl at the crest, paused briefly to automatically insert itself into the regulated flow of autobahn traffic, de-energized internally and began drawing power and guidance from an induction strip embedded in the roadway.

James had no desire to converse with the driver. Depressing a rocker switch, he raised the tinted privacy window between the front and rear seats, reclined against the cushions, eyes closed, and pretended to doze until the vehicle left the autobahn and the Flatirons came in view.

With auto-guidance deactivated, the chauffeur took his time negotiating the Boulder community. He swung the limo into the former University of Colorado campus, where bold, arching letters proclaimed it institut josef paul goebbels, and crawled along the broad, divided thoroughfare, then turned into Zehnte Strasse, where it had to stop and start to let haphazardly jaywalking students cross. James lowered the partition and asked to be dropped off in front of the high-rise Humanities Center. Where he got out, and bent to thank the chauffeur. But the fellow's billed cap never turned a millimeter as the limousine surged away from the curb.

In a reflective mood, his thoughts centered on the potential ramifications of being summoned to an impromptu audience with the province's lord and master, he returned the nods of several passing students, entered the building and stepped on the escalator, riding up to the third level. A glance at the antique Seth Thomas analog office clock tick-tocking on his wall informed him only ninety minutes or so remained in his academic day. He considered chucking it, reclaiming his two-place commute 'copter from the Humanities roofpark and heading home to the mountains, then changed his mind and decided to review a few odds and ends before leaving.

A brusque verbal command woke the computer. The integral flat-panel display slid up out of its nest in the desk, and illuminated. James opened the Postwar Enlightenment 230 folder, and scanned his own notes for an upcoming lecture just as an uninflected digital voice announced, "New news is good news, Boss!"

James eyed the blinking "Eyes Only" icon listing the originator's identity, and said, "Open!"

A cryptic phrase lit up the display: birdwatching time, jamie.

"Reply to sender," he instructed. "Think I'll beg off, Bernard. Too late in the day."

Seconds later the screen read: better late than sorry. spotted a nice purple finch creekside. birdwatching time, I tell you. don't let me down!

Tiny hairs lifted at the nape of Silverthorne's neck. "Don't let me down!" amplified the request for his presence twentyfold. It translated as: "Hie your arse over here now, now, *now!*"

James put the computer back to sleep, collected his topcoat and left the office in a rush.

# TWO

## Goebbels Institute
## May, DWJ 142

James spotted the dean of Goebbels' History Department prowling near the bank of Boulder Creek. Carrying a tripod-mounted monocular with a shoulder-slung camera bobbing at his side, Omsley halted and peered up into a copse of yellow pines, ostensibly searching for birds.

Silverthorne knew better. His senior colleague was checking for concealed surveillance devices in the layered branches. Conventional wisdom espoused by ultra-paranoid officialdom had it that inherently rebellious students, not to mention a cadre of liberal-minded professors and teaching assistants, were prone to social unrest in general and political dissent in particular. Therefore, with frustrating regularity, night-prowling technicians relocated about the campus all varieties of nano-vid cameras, pinhead audio pickups, and sub-miniaturized motion detectors.

Approaching within earshot, James called, "So where's this prize finch of yours, Bernard?"

In late middle age, Omsley's smile might have looked welcoming to a casual observer, but it never got past his lips. "Must've taken wing," he confessed. His eyes bright with an excess of nervous energy, he asked about James's visit to the chancellor's office. "Any resolution?"

"No, way too early, Bernard. The wheels of *Reichskounzel* may grind slowly, but they grind exceeding fine." Worried without knowing why due to the other's imperative summons, James tried to respond in an offhand manner, finding it no easy task when he knew every word, gesture, and nuance of body language was being viewed and recorded for evaluation. "As always," he said, his statement laden with an exaggerated dollop of respect, "Chancellor Hoffmann was sympathetic, but it isn't his decision. We're damned fortunate to have him on our side, Bernard. He makes that extra, extra effort to understand what the retro-temporal junkets are all about, if not completely how much they affect all historians."

"A major understatement, Jamie! Nor is he chary about throwing his full weight behind each of our prospective proposals." Omsley decided against any further need to butter up Hoffmann for the benefit of an invisible audience and gestured toward a nearby pine. "Look, my finch flitted to a higher branch!" Erecting the tripod, he planted the legs, swung the monocular around, and bent from the waist, looking directly down into the right-angle eyepiece, a posture intended to make lip reading impossible. In a stage whisper, he said, "Henny's cell went down last night."

James flinched. Forcing a cough as a pretext for covering his mouth with a tissue, he softly murmured through the cloth, "Henderson was *taken?*"

"No, thank God!" was Omsley's sibilant reply. "A bachelor, he felt the pip coming on and went over to the infirmary. His encrypted e-mail reported that Müller's *SD* bloodhounds had broken in and triggered his apartment alarms, barely giving him enough minutes to bolt.

To conceal his acute distress, James said calmly, "There, I see the finch. Give me a peek."

Omsley relinquished the monocular, and James bent over the eyepiece. "Whole damned cell?"

Omsley assumed an affirmative response would be taken for

granted. He gestured at a tree where the phantom bird had supposedly alighted. "Look a bit higher, off to the left."

Obediently canting the monocular, James whispered, "Where the hell *is* Henny? Lacking his expertise, we haven't a prayer of, um … getting the job done."

Complaining that the bird had flown again, Omsley brushed James aside and reclaimed the monocular. "Can't tell you for obvious reasons. The Lebe device and thorium isotope are safely stashed and a new scheme's in the works. Afraid it's our last shot at getting you off."

His emotions roiling under the cascade of godawful news, James reacquired the monocular. "They're getting too close, but we don't dare react in any way to Henny's cell going down."

"That," affirmed Omsley, "is an absolute certainty."

To keep up appearances, they attached the digital mini-camera to the monocular's eyepiece adapter and snapped pictures of nonexistent birds, all the while exchanging whispered suggestions that might lead to solving a dilemma threatening to cast desperately unwanted suspicion on them and their subversive cell.

\* \* \*

In a basement of the institute's utility complex, *Grösseres Denver Gaus Sicherheitsdienst Direktor* Jürgen Müller punched an alphanumeric code in the cipher panel beside an unmarked stainless-steel door. Admitted into a small antechamber, he nodded to the armed guard on duty and gazed into the eye cups of a security scanner long enough for his iris patterns to be read and recorded. Deadbolts retracted, admitting him into a long, indirectly lit gallery, its walls lined with tiered banks of flat-panel displays. Handpicked overachievers in the *Grösseres Denver Gaus* Senior Hitler Youth deemed politically reliable were stationed before each dual tier of monitors.

Hands clasped behind his back, Müller strolled down the narrow center aisle at a leisurely pace, pausing now and again for a cursory glance at a displayed scene. "Anything of interest, young gentlemen?" he inquired of the gallery at large. "Any bloody fistfights, juicy seductions, scurrilous graffiti artists doing their day's work? Anything above and beyond the ordinary?"

An adolescent youth with a tousled cowlick of dark hair swung around, a mischievous grin in evidence. "Just the usual losers smoking dope on the green, sir."

"Really? My, how pedestrian!" exclaimed Müller. "No, don't look at me," he remonstrated. "Keep your attention focused on campus goings-on."

"Those bird-happy nuts are at it again," informed a stocky youth farther down the row.

Müller ambled onward, stopping beside the youth who had spoken.

"Ah, Dean Omsley and his time-jaunting colleague. It never ceases to amaze me how, or for what ridiculous reason noted educators willingly devote their precious leisure hours to the filthy activities of birds."

"That pair, they're famous in here," assured a stocky youth. "Wander around the campus a couple of times every week they do, checking out what might be in the trees."

"Not surprising," declared Müller. "Both are distinguished professors. I doubt if either will ever do or say anything not according to doctrine."

"Guess not, sir. But that isn't what's strange. They chase birds at all hours, rain or shine, icy wind or snow. Last winter I had the duty when the whole campus was white, and there they were, toting a camera and telescope, stomping around ankle deep in slush with nary a bird in sight."

"Hmmm, that does sound peculiar. Yet a hobby is a hobby; mine's fly fishing. I know nothing of birds, nor care to learn. But in winter, well … who knows? A few of our feathered friends may be white, making them difficult to pick out on video against a snowy backdrop."

"S'pose so, sir. Mind if I ask what you meant by time jaun … Just now, you said, uh, time something …"

Müller watched the images of Silverthorne and Omsley exchange places over the monocular eyepiece. "The ornithologist bending over is Professor Silverthorne, a celebrity. He's earned a degree of fame by doing remarkable research in several eras of our past."

The lad tripped over "ornithologist," but let it slide. "You saying he's gone back in time, like Herr Lustmann?"

"Not once, on several occasions, though of course not to the War Years, but elsewhere, and elsewhen. He's written several fascinating books, including an account of his venture to eighteenth-century Prussia. He's also the institute's foremost authority on the War of World Liberation. I sat in on his lecture about the vicious fighting in and around Stalingrad, where a brave maternal ancestor of mine was unfortunately a casualty. Studied the War Years in Gymnasium, didn't you, *Jugend?*"

"Oh, yessir. But Stal-something … Name doesn't ring a bell. Where is it?"

Müller smiled. "You'd go blind searching for it on a modern map as either Stalingrad, or its original Russian name, Tsaritsyn. *Der Führer* took to heart a harsh lesson taught by the ancient Romans. At the conclusion of hostilities, Stalingrad's fate was sealed in the same manner as that of Moscow, Kiev, Leningrad, and other Soviet cities. The sizable industrial center once situated along a bend of the Volga was reduced to a barren wasteland devoid of anything living."

"The whole city?"

"*Jeder Stock und Stein. Wehrmacht* engineers razed Stalingrad, then poisoned the rubble with radioactive salts so nothing could live there for a century or more."

"Hey, that is really wild!" exclaimed the youth. "And, your, uh … ancestor?"

"A Sixth Army *oberleutnant,*" said Müller. "I have a faded snap-shot of him in uniform. During the long, bloody siege, *Generalfeld-marshal* von Paulus was awarded the *Ritterkreutz* First Class for what Professor Silverthorne claimed was our outstanding military triumph during the Barbarossa Campaign ..." Sensing his tale of minimal interest, Müller broke off and strolled onward, now and then glancing at the paired video displays, stopping twice to speak briefly with one youthful watcher or another.

Upon exiting the surveillance gallery, he slowed his pace, preoc-cupied by rolling around in his mind something the *Amerikanische Jugund* had touched upon: the tidbit about two learned history professors birdwatching while the campus was snowed in and quite likely bereft of birds. His training and experience had attuned Mül-ler to seize on anything that struck him as an outlier, anything fall-ing beyond the Party-defined parameters of conventional behavior.

Although most likely of little or no significance, the youth's men-tion of the professors birdwatching in winter caused him to file a mental note and later order a deep background investigation of both academics he privately considered pretentious intellectual poseurs.

\* \* \*

Two days later, Dean Omsley returned from the lecture hall in late forenoon to find *SD Direktor* Müller lolling in the chair behind his desk. From long force of habit, he larded his greeting with excessive bonhomie. "Ah, Jürgen, there you are! Good of you to drop by."

His stoic nod at odds with a vapid smile, Müller said, *"Guten tag, Herr Doktor."*

Dr. Omsley had made it a habit to cultivate the *SD* official, believing it a necessity due to the revolutionary conspiracy in which he was deeply embroiled. Strict adherence to the dictum of holding one's friends close and one's enemies even closer adhered to a political philosophy shared by all his patriotic, disingenuous fellow conspirators, not to mention the firebrands among his current crop of graduate students. He and other highly placed revolutionaries in America's *Deutsches Weltreich Provinzen* categorized *all* foreign-born officials—good, bad, or indifferent—as the enemy. Atop the current local queue, the *SD* colonel lounging arrogantly behind the desk, reared head and shoulders above the others.

"You've turned your office into an avian shrine," remarked Müller, eyeing the plethora of flat photos, holographic reproductions, and paintings gracing the walls with feathered images. "I've been admiring your picture gallery."

The avian reference raised Omsley's hackles. "Why, glad you like it, Jürgen. May I show you a new pic, a fine purple finch I snapped yesterday afternoon?"

"Finch, a rare bird?"

"Quite the opposite, but an exemplary specimen of the common chaffinch. Would you care to see it?" Not waiting for a response, Dr. Omsley woke the computer. "Open *Fringillidae,*" he said calmly. Soft orchestral music played as the display panel rose from the desk and lit up.

"*Fringil* … an odd sounding term. Why the accompaniment, Professor?"

Dean Omsley held his fixed smile. "Another minor conceit of mine, Jürgen. It's the cuckoo section from Respighi's 'Ornithological Suite.'"

Outwardly unimpressed, the *SD* officer merely nodded. "Do cuckoos belong to the same, er … bird grouping as the … Fringiwhatever?"

"No, the *Cuculidae,* a different family order,*"* declared Omsley. "The *Fringillidae* belong to the passerine suborder—songbirds, including a variety of finches." Hurriedly surfing through five or six images, he settled on a stock shot. "There! A beauty, isn't it?"

"To me it looks like an ordinary sparrow."

"Similar, but slightly larger. Note the pastel purple-orange coloring behind the eyes and mixed in with the cape feathers."

Müller studied the full-color display. "Professor, you say this picture was taken late yesterday afternoon?"

"Why, yes. Down near Boulder Creek."

"Think back and you may recall how a thundershower scrubbed the sky clean yesterday afternoon. Distinct bands of high cirrus are visible above your bird's perch."

Omsley's breathing quickened. "Well, for the love of … Right you are, Jürgen. I've called up the wrong photo, a silly mistake." His hands palpitating slightly, Omsley sifted through the file of finches. "Ah, here we are!"

"Yours is a most interesting hobby." Müller studied the new digital image. "Tell me, must you abandon birdwatching in winter, or do snowbirds perhaps frequent this locale?"

The oblique direction taken in the other's fishing expedition froze Omsley's smile. He forced a tongue-in-cheek, jocular manner, saying, "In a sense, Jürgen, snowbirds do visit this region in winter, but only if you count the skiers who flock to the mountain resorts."

Müller's lips curved in a reluctant half smile. "Snowbirds, *ja*. A good one, Professor!"

"During the cold months," Omsley added hastily, "Jamie and I … that is, Doctor Silverthorne and I keep a sharp lookout for woodpeckers."

"In the snow season?"

"I'm sure it can sound odd to the uninitiated, but in the fall, woodpeckers often bore holes in tree trunks, cram them with nuts, then return in winter when food is scarce to peck them out."

*"Nüsse?"* Müller revolved the notion. "I suppose that makes sense, at least to birds." Rising slowly, he stepped around the desk. "Well, I must be running along." Sensing the approach of a warm body, the office's pocket door obediently slid into the wall. The *SD* officer hesitated. "Oh, I nearly forgot why I stopped by, Professor. Tell me, has your time-traveling fellow birdwatcher's proposed junket to

Germania's distant past been approved?"

Taken aback by the query, Omsley said, "You're aware of our prospectus?"

"Why, yes. Does that surprise you?"

"I'm sure your realize *Reichskounzel* insists that all prospective retro-temporal ventures be held in the strictest confidence. A research junket is never announced prematurely before being formally sanctioned. May I ask how you learned of it?"

"Oh, we have our sources," Müller said airily. "If and when approved, a visit to antiquity strikes me as a frightfully long jump— more than twenty centuries. Yet having enjoyed his most remarkable book on late-eighteenth-century Prussia, I'm certain Professor Silverthorne has the sand, as well as the experience and ability to undertake such a daring venture."

"Never doubt it, Jürgen! Daring it certainly will be, if and when approved. An exceptional degree of risk is inescapably attached in a retro-temporal transposition of such enormous length. Yet Doctor Silverthorne is incredibly adept, resourceful, and experienced. More than simply knowledgeable about the distant era, he's steeped himself thoroughly in its known history."

"I am sure it is so, Professor. Your programs aimed at first-hand clarification of happenings in the social and military milieus of past eras are awe-inspiring. Keep up the good work, eh?"

"Thank you, Jürgen. We shall continue to do our best."

An electric actuator whined faintly, and the pocket door slid closed behind Müller. Slumping into the chair behind his desk, knees fluttery, Omsley clasped his hands together to quell their minor palpitation. Only too aware that his office, and every closet, lavatory, classroom, and auditorium on the campus and its outskirts were under perpetual surveillance, he tried hard not to let Müller's inquisition unnerve him, for that was *precisely* what his fishing expedition had been all about.

Even so, the bastard's unheralded appearance and less than subtle way of posing leading questions had struck a false chord. The *SD's* intelligence chieftain had no more interest in birds than did he himself, or for that matter Jamie, nor was he prone to indulge in idle conversation about birds, let along remark on a supposedly confidential prospective junket to antiquity. That aspect of his visit was totally out of character.

*SD* Director Müller's suspicions had been aroused somehow, but aroused by *what?* Had he, Jamie, or another member of their campus cell made a misstep along the way? It was difficult to believe a gaffe significant enough to be attract Müller's personal attention had been committed by any of the individuals who came to mind.

Closing his eyes, he reconstructed what he could recall of their conversation, and he ended up still clueless. Despite Müller's obnoxious superior manner, he was by no means slow-witted. His remark about how the office resembled a museum's aviary gallery had been a purposeful off-center prelude to cloud his questions by a blunt statement of his "real" reason for dropping by. Still and all, what possible motive could be attributed to baiting he himself with comments about winter and snowbirds?

*Snowbirds!*

A tentative answer flashed before his mind's eye. Had surveillance reported his and Jamie's practice of birdwatching in all seasons, even deep winter, when few if any birds were about? If so, would something so ordinary be able to squeeze the hair-trigger of Müller's suspicion?

The notion seared him! Jamie had been correct in saying they were getting close.

*Too damned close!*

# THREE

## *Santa Fe, Argentina*
## *May 1960 CE*

The rains had come with a vengeance to the humid state of Paraná Pampas. Commuters among several hundred thousand denizens of Santa Fe, at the confluence of the Rio Salado and Rio Paraná, and also those dwelling across the water in Santa Fe's twin city, Paraná, were leery of venturing to the opposite shore with the rivers roiling at or near flood stage.

The nightlong downpour had drenched an enclave of ODESSA-refugee Nazis in the northwest suburb of Esperanza as well, where the tempest continued unabated in murky dawn. Frothing drain-pipes discharged runoff from the red-tile roof of a sprawling, two-story mansion in a compound behind a high stone wall, making it blind to the street, where gutters and storm drains overflowed as multi-channeled runnels sought paths to the raging river.

A broad-brimmed rain hat obscured Erich Lustmann's masculine features as he stepped out of a leased, four-seat Fiat 500 Topolino. Tall and forceful in bearing, clad in a thigh-length yellow poncho, he trotted through the downpour, unlocked and drew wide one of the double gates, and dashed back to the Fiat. Driving into the compound, he parked under the third carport in a line, hustled back to close and lock the gate, then splashed across the courtyard's rain-cratered paving, ducking into an outbuilding isolated from the mansion by a breezeway.

Doffing the rain hat and slicker in the entry mud room, he shook off the droplets and hung the garments on pegs. Inside the recreation room, beyond the green swath of a billiard table, the previous evening's round-robin of chess and card games had abandoned a half dozen tables and left a number of chairs scattered in helter-skelter disarray. Neither the fortyish man hunched on a barstool with his back turned or the stocky former *Waffen SS Feldwebel* polishing glassware behind the bar acknowledged the newcomer's arrival.

Lustmann brushed back a damp, unruly wheat-colored forelock and crossed glances with his rival candidate in the mirrored wall behind the bar. "Well, if it isn't Mig-gu-el," he greeted in German, purposely mangling his pet Spanish name for the other. "Elbow bending at this hour is precocious, even for an Irishman."

"Mig-gu-el" neither turned around on the barstool or looked up. "Once a Scot," he said, returning identity mockery for mockery, "always a Scot, Eee-rr-ich. Try remembering that." A century-old migration to Germany had inspired "Mig-gu-el's" proud highland forebears to change the spelling of McCall to Mackall. "Where the hell have you been?"

"Across the river, getting soaked."

"Soaked in the wallet by some diseased Paraná tart, I'd wager."

"A sound bet." Lustmann's wolfish grin bared near-perfect white teeth. To the barman he said, "Hans, fix me one of those tootie-fruity rum concoctions with a colored parasol in it, *bitte.*"

The ex-*Feldwebel* left off polishing glassware. "Sir?"

"You know, a gargle like one of the fancy layered Technicolor drinks they serve in Buenos Aires tourist traps. Oh, never mind! If it's too much trouble, I'll settle for *Dunkel Bier.*"

Unfazed, the bartender pulled down the polished wooden handle of a beer engine, laid a paper napkin on the polished mahogany bar, and set down a foam-topped stein of dark brew.

"The colonel," remarked Mackall, "has had people out searching for you half the night."

Lustmann sipped brew. "I was unavoidably detained. The rivers are still rising, flooding the bridge approach. I had to wait for the ferry. Tell me, why the dour face on this damp, filthy morning, Mig-gu-el? What's troubling you?"

Again, their glances crossed in the mirror and locked there. The glare Mackall awarded his rival's image should have cracked the glass. "While you were getting your ashes hauled in Paraná, the colonel briefed us on ..." Mackall paused, smacked his lips. "Best, I think, for the bad news to come from Manfred. By now he may be calm enough to soften the blow."

Lustmann patted dry his beer-foam mustache with a paper napkin. "Thanks, but no thanks! I can do without another of his long-winded orations. Come on, don't be snobbish, Mig-gu-el. What momentous tidings does the colonel wish to impart?"

Knowing himself the bearer of grim tidings, Mackall's countenance brightened. "Eee-rr-ich," he drawled in a cheerless parody of his rival's name, "it's a news item that will cause you deep and lasting heartburn. A distinguished country squire who insisted on foisting himself off as Ricardo Klement vanished yesterday with only the slimmest of slim traces."

Lustmann almost knocked over his beer stein setting it down. Openmouthed, he rocked back and cried, *"Grüssgott!* Eichmann, gone?* You can't be *serious!"*

Mackall shrugged. "Manfred's almost certain he was taken."

"By *Argentinos, die Mossad, Amerikaner Dummköpfen,* who does he think it was?"

Mackall shrugged. "Good question. Manfred thinks it had to be the *verdammt* Israelis. A suspicious group was reportedly seen last week arriving at *Sauce Viejo Aeropuerto.* If he was right, Herr Ricardo Klement has probably been flown out of the country."

Lustmann swore a vile oath. "The stubborn, self-centered idiot! If the Jewish swine do have him, there's no question Otto will hang.

Manfred warned him time and again, *pleaded* with him to come live here with us. But the conceited jackass only listened to an inner voice he alone could hear. Believing it safer not to hide in a crowd, he stayed holed up in his lonely country shack."

A former battle-hardened *SS Panzeroffitzier,* Mackall could think of nothing good to say about his rival candidate. He finished his drink in silence, a faint smile tickling the corners of his mouth. It was common knowledge among the expatriates of *Organisation der ehemaligen SS-Angehörigen,* ODESSA, that Lustmann had commanded an *SS-Einsatzgruppe* made up of Special Section IV B4 thugs engaged in rounding up Jews, mental defectives, Gypsies, homosexuals, cripples—any and all victims ripe for deportation to Auschwitz-Birkenau or another of the numerous slaughterhouses. "Close to *lieber* Otto, weren't you, Eee-rr-ich?" teased Michael Mackall, sarcastically drawing out the syllables to provoke his rival.

Deeply disturbed, Lustmann's attention had strayed while he digested what to him was a crushing calamity. "Um, yes ... close." Angrily pushing aside the beer stein, he said, "We shared duties in Hungary, later in Warsaw, later still in Lvov, Kiev, and, yes ... Kharkov."

"Ah, Kiev! I take it your 'sworn duty' in combat was sharing with infamous Otto the brave assaults undertaken by you and your fellow *Schutzstaffeln* warriors to win the blood-soaked Battle of Babi Yar. You and your grandstanding *Totenkopfverbände* butchers were no doubt indecently proud of your triumph over all those helpless civilian men, women, and children."

Lustmann stiffened. "Mock our duties all you wish! Otto Adolph Eichmann was and is a great man who will be sorely missed. But, what now? Lacking his support, we shall have to—"

"Support!" hooted Mackall. "Exactly what brand of support might that be?"

"Don't play dumb with me!" declared his rival. "You know damn well what I meant."

"Ah, the *treasure!* How could I have overlooked your meaning when it had all the clarity of a fall of cinders. I sincerely hope and pray," Mackall said hoarsely, "that whatever is left of our looted *SS* hoard remains safely buried in some upcountry cave."

The pirated gold from *SS* coffers, recast dental fillings, melted jewelry stolen from countless Holocaust victims, and a residue of other personal effects had been smuggled to Argentina years earlier, and offloaded from a riverboat carrying the illicit treasure trove upriver from Río de la Plata. Also on board was a principal architect of the genocide, former *SS Obersturmbannführer* Otto Eichmann, who had been warmly greeted by *Dictador* Juan Perón, his Fascist officials, and a herd of accompanying *descamisados*—"shirtless" working-class laborers and ruffians making up the strongarm squads and much of the *Perónista*-controlled police force. Argentina had more than welcomed the contingent of fleeing Nazis who offered a portion of their treasure to help finance the social welfare and public works programs trumpeted by Perón as *justicialismo*.

\* \* \*

Mackall tilted back and drained the dregs in his glass. Idly watching the barman tidy up behind the bar, he lit a cigarette, and ordered another schnapps.

Lustmann roused from the dark ruminations wracking him and broke the lengthy silence. "What I meant by support was … with Otto gone, the future of our enterprise may be in jeopardy."

His response laden with naked contempt, Mackall said, "For God's sake, Eee-rr-ich! At least *try* and come back into the real world. All your hero of heroes ever did for ODESSA was keep both blood-soaked hands on the money spigot. Other than that invaluable service, how will his absence make a whit of difference to our future, supposing we actually *have* a future?"

"Hearing you spout negative dreck," accused Lustmann, "makes me certain you have never considered the matter in depth. Five years ago, a junta overthrew Perón, forcing us to weather one crisis after another under not merely one, but *two* military dictatorships. Now, with Perón in exile and Eichmann gone, when the money runs out, our pitiful remnant of ODESSA had also best run out. If only Lebe would step up the pace of his experiments. If and when he manages to fit all the puzzle's pieces in their proper places, we may at last prepare to—"

"Insert the muzzle in our collective mouth," sneered Mackall, completing his rival's statement for him, "and squeeze off a collective round in unison."

It was Lustmann's turn to sneer. "Some defeatist bastard you are, Mig-gu-el!"

"Most willingly do I accept that role," rebutted Mackall, "but not entirely. Let me return your left-handed compliment by explaining what an incurable naïf *you* are. Do you really place a gram of credence in the ability of our resident mad scientist to pull a single meaningful sliver of success out of his bag of magic tricks? If so, my defeatist nature assures me fervent, frequent prayers must be sent up to Saint Jude, the patron of lost causes."

Lustmann bristled. "Permit me to correct my most recent accusation, Mig-gu-el. You're not capable of defeatism, only cynicism, which is even worse. What is in Doctor Lebe's bag of magic tricks is the sole reason one of us candidates may someday become ODESSA's savior."

Mackall shot back, *"Ach,* what a gullible, snotty son of a bitch you are! Dare to call *me* cynical, but you can never bring yourself to admit that then was then and now is *now!* Sailing back in time is a fifth-rate fairytale fit to tell small children at bedtime. A full decade and a half has been ripped from the calendar since the war ended, and only a little less since you helped Eichmann escape from that Yankee internment camp. For most of fifteen miserable years we've been marooned in this godforsaken hellhole, withering away slowly, patiently dying on the vine."

His rival's vitriolic diatribe caused Lustmann to recall Eichmann's prophetic words on the eve of their escape. They had been playing the colonel's favorite game, Skat, when without preamble Otto had thrown down his cards and cried, "We shall either fail gloriously, Erich, or survive to help put Humpty Dumpty back together again, *nicht wahr?*"

"Given a choice," replied Lustmann, "I wholeheartedly prefer the latter course." He thought bitterly about how sloppy America's toy soldiers had been, how careless about everything except their Lucky Strike cigarettes, Hershey chocolate bars, and bubbly Coca-Cola. "Those American fools had no inkling who Otto was, nor were they a bit interested in finding out. Even the intelligence brass who interrogated us wasted no time or energy trying to learn some connection between Otto's name, rank, and career."

"*Career!*" jeered Mackall. "The chief *Einsatz* butcher's *career* certainly endeared him to your poultry farmer boss, and did so with twice the heartfelt emotion of your dearest of dear departed colleagues, Himmler's journeyman butcher, Heydrich."

Lustmann fumed in silence. "You're drunk, Mig-gu-el."

"A possibility," admitted Mackall. "And why not? Viewed through the bottom of this glass, the soggy outside world takes on a richer, far better appearance."

"Let me offer you a word of warning, my friend."

"I'm *not* your friend."

Tight-lipped, Lustmann's glare raked the other. "Friend or foe, deprecating the efforts of *Herr Doktor* Lebe—in every respect a much better man than you—is a grave mistake. He has worked with demonic persistence to ensure the survival of National Socialism, and one fine day his brilliance may afford one of us a unique opportunity to rectify a great wrong. Lebe and Colonel Stoltz make no bones about favoring you over the other candidates, including me, and so be it. Don't bother with a denial, Mig-gu-el! You've been Manfred's fair-haired favorite ever since Lebe began his crazy experiments. Yet as the prime candidate to undertake the mission, should there ever be a mission to undertake, I cannot for the life of me understand why it's so terribly difficult to appreciate the *extremely* difficult task Lebe has been struggling to accomplish."

Mackall barked a short, brittle laugh. "Hah! Prime candidate to be locked in a padded cell of some asylum! I can't believe how deeply deluded you and the others are regarding our private mad scientist *and* his childish ambition."

"Now hear me, Mig-gu-el!" bellowed Lustmann, raising his voice for the first time. "Stiffen your spine and at least *try* to be a true believer. Or if that's too much to ask, why not step out of the competition? I'd be delighted to take your place at the head of our short queue."

*"Anyone* but you!" scoffed Mackall, slurring his words. "If by some miracle Lebe's otherworldly efforts were to culminate in a happy ending, a murderous, lowlife toady like you wouldn't *begin* to fill the bill. As for being a true believer, try turning your forefinger around and aiming it at your own breastbone. You'll find it the most difficult exercise ever invented."

Lustmann said bitterly, "Brave talk!"

"What do *you* know of bravery?" demanded the other. "While my crewmen and I were engaging Soviet or British armor in our Tiger panzer, your *SS Totenkopfverbände* death squad was bent on staying well out of harm's way in order to eagerly and efficiently commit mass murder between stints of rounding up helpless civilian men, women, and children to dispatch to your collection of *Vernichtungslager* slaughterhouses. You know what that makes you, but you refuse to admit it."

In a low, dangerous tone of voice, Lustmann said, "I am what I am, and you are what you are. Some time ago each of us swore a blood oath, pledging our lives *and* honor—our *souls!*—to the service of *Der Führer's* sacred person. You might keep that in mind."

"What *you* might keep in mind," mimicked the other, "is a

separate but equal truth. Some fifteen years ago, our brave, noble *Führer* sent a bullet crashing into his brave, noble brain."

Lustmann choked back the feral rage rising in his throat. Only partially successful, he said tautly, "Tomorrow, the progress of Lebe's childish ambition will again be tested, and to the chagrin of you and others of little or no faith, tomorrow we may learn how deluded I really am."

"Ah, tomorrow and tomorrow and tomorrow," declaimed Mackall, tipsily exaggerating his Shakespearean elocution. "Indeed, on the morrow, ODESSA's resident mad scientist will once again try to pull a live rabbit out of his parlor magician's hat. Ask yourself this: except for consistently slaying rabbits in one silly *experiment* after another, and between times boring the rest of us with technical babble, exactly *what* has ODESSA's scientific genius accomplished?"

A grimace of clear quill hatred evidenced Lustmann's disdain for Michael Mackall, and a torrent of loosely chosen words erupted. "That remark is unworthy of the *Dritte Reich* you claim to have served! It's all I can do to keep from smashing your face with this stein."

"Well, smash away, Eee-rr-rich! A mighty *SS* warrior like you should never shirk from doing whatever he's convinced himself *must* be done. Go ahead, get on with it! You'll provide me with one more excuse to smash *your* face, as if I needed one."

Indifferent to his own safety and well-being, the burly former *SS-Feldwebel,* no longer a young man, stepped between the glowering antagonists. "Gentlemen, you've both had enough. The bar is closed."

Lustmann turned on his heel, stalked out of the recreation room without a backward glance, and punctuated his exit by slamming the door behind him.

\* \* \*

Near dawn, the rain had tapered off to scattered showers, then later to brilliant midmorning sunshine eclipsed from time to time by a scurrying procession of cloud remnants promising a warm, steamy day in suburban Esperanza.

Before noon, ODESSA's half dozen mission candidates were reposing in chaise lounges and unfolded lawn chairs on either side of *Herr Doktor,* Alfred Lebe. Seated next to him, former Wehrmacht *Heer Oberst* Manfred Stoltz, by unspoken agreement the ODESSA group's nominal leader, wore a pensive expression. Everyone present seemed preoccupied with keeping watch on the sky above a three-meter-square fish net suspended on thin rods above a shallow pit filled with loose wood shavings.

As Lustmann knew he would, the theoretical physicist had grown more and more fustian as the crucial instant drew closer. Yet, for whatever reason, his agitation was more obvious than during prior experiments. The noon hour passed without the specimen's appearance, doubling Dr. Lebe's disquiet. The elderly, chain-smoking scientist's arthritic knees creaked faintly when he strained to rise from a lawn chair, clasped his hands behind his back, and began to nervously prowl back and forth behind the semicircle of candidates and a few standing watchers, the focus of his attention never straying from the rain-washed sky directly above the net.

Seconds passed, wore away into minutes. Low-voiced murmurs, grumbles, and comments from several candidates began to erode Colonel Stoltz's patience. "Alfred," he inquired, posing the question delicately, "about how much leeway in your calculations?"

The physicist's tiger-pacing slowed. "A question difficult to answer. Plus or minus a quarter hour, perhaps a fraction more considering the longer transposition interval."

Someone in a lawn chair uttered a low-voiced remark that all three previous specimens had punctually appeared within seconds of the designated tick.

Lebe frowned upon overhearing the comment. "Young man," he said in the manner of a savant stooping to correct a child's erroneous impression, "my estimate for the twenty-four-hour transposition was relatively straightforward, whereas the current specimen was to be, er ... that is to say *will be* dispatched an entire calendar week hence.

"Grammatical tenses," he clarified as if resenting the necessity of doing so, "tend to become confusing. Transposition should occur precisely one hundred and sixty-eight hours before the fact, or to use a simplified term: *now.*"

Lustmann took advantage of the brief silence. "*Herr Doktor*, several facets of your experiments continue to puzzle me. How is it possible for the specimen to be nibbling lettuce in the hutch over there, when at any instant the selfsame rabbit is due to arrive from ... some future hour?"

Dr. Lebe said scornfully, "Selfsame rabbit indeed! You voice arrant nonsense, Herr Lustmann. Think about what you just said, really *think!* Then, now, and forevermore, duality of existence is too absurd a concept for any living organism. A single unique specimen was, is, and shall be involved in *each* of my retro-temporal transposition tests. You ask how this can be? For the most basic of reasons, neither animate nor inanimate objects can simultaneously occupy identical spacetime loci in the classical continuum. That would, you see, amount to an illogical—nay, impossible—paradox, a matter of mutually exclusive incompatibility, *nein* impossibility!"

"Please forgive my backwardness, *Herr Doktor,*" prodded Lustmann, "but a pair of identical rabbits do seem to be the case in point."

"Bah! Your simplistic assessment ignores time tagging. The specimen over there in the hutch has endured, now endures, and will continue to endure on our *present* timeline until it's dispatched one hundred and sixty-eight hours from this very moment, whereupon it will undergo retro-transposition and instantaneously return to our 'now.' The retro specimen has retained its 'then' time tag, you see, and merely *appears* to subjectively coexist with its temporal replicate for one entire calendar week until the divergent timelines coalesce, and what you so loosely term 'that selfsame rabbit' will instantaneously reunite with its apparently selfsame doppelgänger."

Purposely ingenuous, Lustmann asked if that meant a transposed candidate like himself could shake hands with his younger self during the early months of a war prosecuted with his aid that might well be destined to culminate in an all-conquering German victory.

Lebe frowned. "More muddy thinking! You are infected with a virulent case of very imprecise terminology, Lustmann, so it may be futile to try and formulate anything like a meaningful response. Tell me, what was your age in the estimated target year?"

"Nineteen thirty-nine? Umm, I turned twenty in late nineteen forty and spent the early months in the Breslau *SS* academy training for—"

"*Sehr gut!* Therefore, in the Gregorian 'now' of our common era, nineteen sixty, you have escaped demise despite a penchant for muddy thinking and reached the approximate age of forty. If you should be selected for the mission, what you envision would amount to an *extremely* unlikely happenstance. Once one has been retrotransposed into some past era—presently a one-way venture, since I have not yet devised a method of retrieval—your 'then' time-tagged self would continue to exist along the temporal progression of that particular timeline until you reach the present moment, whereupon the timelines would automatically coalesce, unity would be reestablished, and you would live out your remaining years in straightforward fashion.

"However," he qualified, "if by an astounding coincidence of time and place you should meet your 'then' time-tagged unique and youthful doppelgänger, he might mention the remarkable resemblance you bear to one another, and that would be the total upshot of having crossed paths on his native timeline. No paradox could possibly occur, yet should either of your separate time-tagged selves lose his life while *seemingly* sharing co-existence, well …"

Lustmann's interest peaked. "What then?"

"Why, were such a happening to take place," replied Lebe impatiently, "and it was your 'then' time-tagged self who expired, it would be considered a natural consequence, since he had lived until the specific time-tagged 'then' instant of losing his life."

"And I, my real self, would I also be ... extinguished?"

"No, certainly not! Never leap to some faulty conclusion, Lustmann. Instead, reason out the matter for yourself. You have lived in the 'now' timeline until the present moment, and as a visitor to the 'then' timeline you would simply continue to live out your normal lifespan."

Confused by the physicist's 'then' and 'now' babbling, Lustmann caught a sharp glance from Colonel Stoltz and returned an all-but-invisible shrug. *"Viel dank, Herr Doktor* Lebe. Now all becomes clear," he lied. "But in referring to the present experiment, you spoke of a week-long, uh ... retro-transposition. How does one account for the interval between what you called the time-tagged specimen's dispatch a week hence and the present moment?"

*"What* interval?" demanded Lebe. "Past and present timelines coexist simultaneously within multidimensional spacetime continua. Think of other timelines as blank slates upon which nothing had yet been written—or *could* be written—until my breakthrough. When the current specimen reappears—at any instant I'm sure—it will confirm that one hundred and sixty-eight hours from now, as gauged along the natural, immutable progression of our timeline, I shall once again write indelibly on that figurative blank slate."

Colonel Stoltz regarded the physicist with a troubled squint. "Alfred, are you telling us zero time passes while the specimen is shifting from a week in the future to ... er ... the 'now' timeline?"

As if he enjoyed talking down to a military-minded layman, Dr. Lebe's pedantic response proved grossly irritating. "Dear Manfred, your attempt to define something in its own terms renders the query meaningless. Transit time in relation to *what?* Time is a total imponderable, a classic, unknowable phenomenon, or was until the advent of quantum physics.

"The advent of ... what?" Lustmann wanted to know.

The physicist shook his head rather sadly. "It's futile to try and explain the, um ... are you at least conversant with Einstein's revolutionary nineteen-ought-five Relativity thesis, or Planck's quantum hypothesis, or better still Niels Bohr's marvelous advancements?"

"Uh, no. Afraid not."

"No matter. Einstein's inspired breakthrough spoke of weaknesses inherent within classic physical models, and then went on to brilliantly conceive underlying ... call them a string of innumerable, existing building block principles, for want of a better definition, all of which depend upon quantum-based theory to explain photoelectric effects. Common sense tells us the lounge chair you were sitting in, while a physical, measurable object, is in essence a specific, unique outcome of classic applied physics involving the assembly if component elements, while quantum. . . Oh, dear! This grows too abstruse for generalizations to make any sense at all. Explaining my breakthrough to a lay person," he continued, "involves the fact that quantum theory itself defies common sense. Schrödinger's famous equation uses symbolic logic to define quantum physics the way quantum wave functions generate the evolution of a quantum state and quantum time—*time*, Herr Lustmann!"

"You've lost me a little, but I'm very interested."

"All quantum physics allows us to do," declared the physicist, "is define and describe various probabilities, including randomly probabilistic quantum time resulting from interactive wave functions. I seized on the model intuitively created by a Danish physicist, Niels Bohr, to describe the quantum milieu, where jumbled particles repeatedly turn into waves, then back into particles, which apparently communicate in a way that defies all normal conceptions of time and space. If something called coherence occurs—a concept difficult to comprehend that I will not delve into—where wave functions produce only random probabilities, including quantum time. After years spent struggling with the complexities of multiple research methods, most soon discarded, I totally eliminated randomly probable outcomes in a manner analogous to obtaining specific results via classical physics, and was thus able to—"

*"There!"* cried one of the seated candidates.

A splotched brown-and-white object fell in a long arc, missed the stretched-out net and pit of wood shavings by a scant half meter, rebounded from the turf, and lay still.

Alfred Lebe loosed a fulminant curse. Charging across the lawn in an arthritic half trot, he knelt with obvious difficulty beside the specimen. Colonel Stoltz, Mackall, Lustmann, and several other candidates crowded around the fallen rabbit.

*"Coriolis!"* exclaimed the physicist. Angrily glaring up into the unoffending sky, he performed a self-deprecatory headshake. "The temporal locus of exit was far higher in altitude than I had calculated. Coriolis force, a function of the planet's axial spin, no doubt induced lateral impetus that affected the specimen's post-transposition vector and velocity."

Colonel Stoltz scrutinized the rabbit, the blood oozing from its mouth and pink nose. "Alfred, your estimate called for the specimen to appear roughly three meters above the lawn."

A snicker issued from the group of candidates. "More like three hundred."

"Really, Manfred!" said Lebe, his attitude peevishly defensive. "Once again you and the others snipe at the experiment's undesired conclusion, and again as usual take issue with the myriad inconsequentials but fail to acknowledge another resounding success. The specimen before us underwent retro-transposition across a gulf of one hundred and sixty-eight real-time hours. Whether or not the specimen survived is immaterial. Doctor Klinghoffer will perform a necropsy to determine whether tissue damage occurred during transposition or upon impact—two vastly different, yet important reasons for what has occurred.

"Of equal or greater significance," he pursued, typically launching into one of his educational lectures, "is that I shall now be able to further define and refine my retro-temporal algorithms. The extremely useful data deriving from this fourth overtly successful experiment, performed over a greater span of quantum-time than the preceding, will enable a spectrum of far more precise extrapolations, leading to the establishment of a profoundly more definitive basis for calculating future transpositions. It also means infinitesimal variances can be further reduced between all previous test data and those obtained from the current success ..."

Having heard it all before, Lustmann lost interest. He stepped away from the candidates trying to make sense of Lebe's rationalization for the rabbit's demise, and paused at the lean-to, inspecting the now-empty hutch with a jaundiced expression.

"Ho-hum, Eee-rr-ich! Another uneventful day in Esperanza, and another dead rabbit."

Lustmann pretended to ignore the taunt. Turning toward the mansion, teeth gritted, he suppressed an urge to rearrange Mackall's lean, self-satisfied features, marched up the steps, yanked open the screen door, and entered the verandah without a backward glance.

# FOUR

## *Estes Park Village, Colorado Province*
## *June, DWJ 142*

Silverthorne and his dinner guest, Chancellor Hoffmann, were taking their ease before a cheery blaze in the study's arched fieldstone fireplace. Sipping Green Chartreuse *digestif,* the chancellor gazed at a panorama framed by French doors opening on the flagstone terrace, and distantly beyond, silhouetted against the azure twilight sky, the snowcapped peaks of the continental divide. "Jamie," remarked Hoffmann, "the view from your aerie is magnificent."

"And also a magnificent distraction when I'm sitting here trying to write. The light changes hourly, and the mountains seem to change with it."

His guest chuckled drily. "How can you endure such awful suffering?"

Having dealt with few *Herrenvolk* in his thirty-eight years, and never before with a highborn aristocrat of Hoffmann's stamp, Silverthorne's opinion of the official was ambivalent. An eminent panjandrum of the Aryan Master Race, were Nazi balderdash to be taken literally, the chancellor symbolized everything James despised, while remaining an unwanted benefactor. The sense of indebtedness stemmed from his guest's unflagging support of the retro-temporal research program established under Dean Omsley's guidance, but due more to the unanticipated bounty for which the official was mainly responsible. Atop a spur of the mountain above the eastern gateway to Rocky Mountain National Park, the picturesque chalet where he and Emily made their home had been gifted by *Reichskounzel* shortly after the publication of his book on late-eighteenth-century Prussia.

While enjoying his DWJ 138 sabbatical in Welthauptstadt Germania, the Deutches Weltreich capital renamed by *Der Führer* after the War of World Liberation, Dr. Hoffmann had apparently lavished praise on Silverthorne's retro-temporal venture in Potsdam, a junket capping all his prior research visits to bygone eras past, an impromptu testimonial that must have impressed the aged co-chiefs of state, who were modeled on Hitler's *Richtungweisend* tract that praised the logic of dual consuls elected by the Senate to govern the Roman Republic in antiquity. In the wake of a surprising stroke of serendipity, James had been forced to work hard to overcome his wife's reluctance to entertain the couple she regarded as "a typical bloodsucking Nazi overlord and his social butterfly *frau.*"

James had repeatedly explained why his unique Chair of Retro-temporal Research made hosting the Hoffmanns a political necessity that had *nothing* to do with observing the social amenities. His gentle, continuing persuasion had finally convinced Emily of how mandatory an informal invitation to dinner would be, if only to reciprocate for the memorable occasion when they themselves had been wined and dined in the executive mansion, plus of course an occasion for tendering grateful appreciation for inspiring the award of their chalet.

Their distinguished guest sat forward in the leather armchair. "My compliments to your wife, Jamie. Please tell Emily the dinner was superb. But satisfy my curiosity about something, if you will. Where in the world does one obtain fresh venison this time of year?"

"For bow hunters, it's year-round deer season." Silverthorne gestured toward the laminated steel bow and the quiver full of broad-point arrows slung beside the fireplace. "When the weather warms, deer migrate back up to the high country. I caught a six-point buck in a timberline meadow, dressed it out up there, and had the devil's own time hauling it downhill on my back."

Hoffmann wagged his head. "Is there no limit to your prowess? Celebrated educator and historian, time traveler par excellence, bestselling author, birdwatcher extraordinaire, yet until this moment you hide your competence as a bowman. What next, Professor? I'm beginning to think of you as a dedicated overachiever."

The other's "birdwatcher extraordinaire" citation tripped Silverthorne's main circuit breaker. Pretending humility, he clothed his urge to dissimulate by a change of subject to one supposedly nearest his heart. "Using a bow could become an advantage if … that is, if and when I've been sanctioned to visit early first-century Germanorum."

"Oh, *that* again!" Looking pained, Hoffmann said, "Jamie, being who and what you are, it's no surprise to hear your one-track mind speak up. Why are you so eager to be off on the upcoming venture? The ancient barbarian triumph over three entire Roman legions you're so fixated on is frozen in time. *Varusschlacht* will patiently await your arrival, never fear."

"I don't know. Lately I find myself going through the motions, making it difficult to give my students the attention they deserve. I tend to slough off their questions with short answers, lecture with less than total concentration. I suppose the root of my frustration is—"

"Please, no more," urged his guest. "I already know what you were about to say."

"Ernst, you cited my credentials a moment ago, but neglected to mention a prominent one. It's flattering to be known as the institute's foremost authority on the War of World Liberation, the reason waiting lists for my undergrad courses grow longer each quarter. What bothers me deeply is … to ask bluntly, why is there no hope of sanctioning someone with my experience and background to visit the War Years and do some truly meaningful research?"

The chancellor sighed. "Yes, I smelled it coming. Your remarkable achievements have not gone unnoticed by our leadership, nor unrewarded." To illustrate his remark, the other gestured theatrically toward the snowcapped peaks looming in the gathering dusk. "Just this once, try and view the problem through leadership's eyes. Your expertise and experience should make you the very first to acknowledge how ultra-conservative retro-temporal research must remain. Above and beyond research, our leaders have pledged to never, for any reason, relax their unrelenting guardianship of the portal to the era comprising the crucial War Years.

"I realize why you resent that proscription," he added, hoping to forestall a response he did not wish to hear. "It's perfectly natural for an eminent historian to desperately yearn for a chance to further the fund of hard-earned knowledge acquired to date through normal here-and-now research. How could an enormously gifted professional historian feel otherwise? Why, your most recent book offered an incisive critique of Goebbels' ponderous chronicle of the War Years, and I assure you it has gathered no dust on my bookshelf."

"And if you'll forgive my overused response," said James, his frustration no longer entirely a sham, "the sheer volume of half-truths, disinformation, and outright falsehoods clouding Goebbels' pretentious 'historical' tomes are enough to confound any historian worth his salt."

A sharp look. "How can you possibly know of such lacks?"

"Goebbels, or whoever penned the volumes credited to his authorship," asserted Silverthorne, as if trying to recover from his intentional slip, "blithely reminds us of the dire straits the adolescent Reich was mired in when Red Army hordes crashed into Berlin and took hostage every member of the scientific community it located, including noted physicist Alfred Lebe. After longwindedly iterating and reiterating supposed facts, *Reichsminister* Goebbels pens a lucid explanation of how, by virtue of a plethora of American forces, arms, and military materiel flowing across the Atlantic, were used in concert with the so-called Allies to destroy the Luftwaffe, devastate *Kriegsmarine*, and overwhelm Wehrmacht forces in every theater of war.

"What disturbs me most," pursued James, now on a roll, "is that Goebbels harps on the fact that with Germany's major cities bombed, burned out, and in ruin, and the global conflict all but lost, the Allies were warned of secret weapons under accelerated development—functional ballistic missiles, jet-propelled aircraft, nuclear, chemical, and bacteriological advances, and so forth. Then he figuratively takes a deep breath, glosses over what subsequently transpired, and leaves his readers hanging by intimating that in their wildest dreams the Allied powers never suspected a lurking postwar secret weapon like the Lebe technique, and lets it go at that."

When at last James fell silent, a shadow smile was teasing the corners of his guest's mouth. Switching languages, the chancellor began quoting a passage from one of Goebbels' volumes, and then broke off, his brow creased. "I can't quote the phrase verbatim, but the gist of it went roughly like this: Complacent in victory, the barbarous Soviet tyrant released Alfred Lebe from captivity, permitting his return to a conquered, plundered, sundered Germany."

*Sundered!* The word startled James. He couldn't imagine why the chancellor had irrelevantly injected such at term into the text of his half-remembered message. Hoping to learn the answer, he improvised with a white lie. "I remember that too, Ernst." Having steeped himself in the pretentious 'history' credited to Goebbels' authorship, he was certain the ponderous, multi-volume *War of World Liberation* shad beyond doubt alluded to 'a conquered, plundered, Germany,' but *sundered* made absolutely no sense.

Noting his host's reaction, Hoffmann hastened to say, "We must be realistic, Jamie. Sanctioning a civilian retro-temporal venture to the War Years Era would be considered an act of clinical insanity by *Reichskounzel.* You of all people should understand why superb vigilance is mandatory to keep that door tightly closed and tightly sealed."

"I wholeheartedly agree," lied James. "Nevertheless, it's galling for a professional historian not to be trusted when so many varied details scream for investigation, and so very many obscure events and situations cry out for in-depth research and reconciliation and cause."

"Trust?" The chancellor's hard stare disconcerted James.

Realizing he had broached a topic not merely distasteful to the *Weltreich* hierarchy, but so far off the table as to be inviolate, James confessed with solemn intonation that certain events and circumstances of the past were indeed too crucial to entrust to *any* individual, no matter how knowledgeable, competent, or otherwise acceptable.

Hoffmann nodded. "You and your counterpart at the University of Leipzig went through an agonizing series of deep background investigation, psychological interviews and tests before *Reichskounzel* would consider vetting you to visit selective eras of our common past, but *only* to learn, never to touch, disturb, and potentially mutilate. As I've heard you say yourself, Jamie, the reflexive dangers involved in promiscuous time travel would be immense. A single misstep in the past, no matter how slight, innocent, and in no way malicious, could easily engender or ignite some unforetold, utterly catastrophic consequence."

Sensing how irritated the other had become by even discussing a visit to the War Years, James was framing a conciliatory remark when the official suddenly rose from the armchair. "Shall we rejoin the ladies? It's late, perhaps time to call it a night."

"Ernst, if my questions have offended you, let me apologize. Please try understand why—"

"Tut, say no more!" denied the chancellor, his manner now

decidedly cool. "It is *you* who must understand what a waste of breath it is to belabor your less-than-sensible ambition to research during the War of World Liberation. Hoping to be vetted for such a junket was as hopeless yesterday as it is today and will definitely be tomorrow and forever!"

Chagrined at the unanticipated spinoff resulting from his intentional gaffe, James ushered the chancellor out of his study, all the while kicking himself mentally.

\* \* \*

The chancellor's polished political persona resurfaced upon rejoining his *frau* and their hostess. All smiles, the departing couple thanked Emily and James for the wonderful evening.

The chalet heliport, carved into the mountainside ringed by forested slopes, was too confined for the huge, long-range government jetcopter parked below at the village air center. A small electric runabout airborne aboard the craft, meant to serve in the manner of a ship's boat, had shuttled the guests up the twisty mountain road to the driveway, where a uniformed chauffeur stood beside it.

After a final round of farewells and good wishes, James and his wife saw the couple off. Emily hurried back indoors to escape the evening chill, but James hesitated in the entry, pensively watching the runabout's taillights disappear downhill. Regretting his error in handling the official, he joined Emily, who had donned an apron and was loading the dishwasher. Glancing at James, she pulled a face and held her nose with two fingers. To Emily, *Frau* Gerda Hoffmann was no more than a self-centered fashion plate and trophy wife, but she knew better than to say so aloud even in the "privacy" of their chalet.

A moment later, the clicking of dinnerware ceased in the kitchen. Emily called to James in the beam-ceilinged living room, asking why he'd left their commute 'copter parked on the helipad.

"Not guilty," he called back. "I folded the rotary wings, rolled it into the hangar by hand."

"Then why's it still sitting out there?"

Puzzled, James rose and went to the kitchen window. "Whups! That isn't our bird." He ducked through the study, grabbed a hooded jacket from the entry closet, and emerged in the crisp mountain air.

His head lowered beneath the two-place 'copter's drooping rotary wings, Dean Omsley held a forefinger to his lips and beckoned James to the helipad. Taking his colleague's elbow, he leaned close, and in a stage whisper asked if there was a safe place for them to talk.

"A safe place is mythical," was Silverthorne's whispered response. "Brrrr, cold out here!" he said aloud for the benefit of omnipresent surveillance. "Let's get inside by the fire."

"It will really be frigid when you hear what I have to say," whispered Omsley, then said in a normal voice, "Apologies for bursting in on you like this. I started to call you, then decided to fly up and pass on the good news. The Reichsleiter's executive assistant called to say *Reichskounzel* has sanctioned your venture to ancient Germania Magnus." Tugging his stunned and speechless colleague backward, Omsley whispered, "Walk with me up the trail. It's the best we can manage and too little time left to do otherwise."

"Chancy," whispered James, taken aback by the puzzling change in Omsley's demeanor. Hesitant to follow him in starlight along a narrow walkway bisecting the chalet's miniature rear garden, they groped their way in tandem up a narrow, winding footpath leading to the crest of the forested ridge. They halted when Omsley believed them beyond earshot of the chalet, and he whispered, "There was no call, Jamie."

"What?"

"Shhhh, keep it down! I was having supper in the Fifth Street Hofbrau when my silent alarm began vibrating. It was Henny calling to say, "Run, Bernard!" He's fairly certain Müller's *SD* bloodhounds had broken into my apartment. I rushed to the institute roofpark, spooled up the 'copter and never looked back. I knew you were entertaining the local royalty and orbited a distance off until his big bird cranked up and took off down in the village. Two local cells have gone down in as many months, announcing loudly and clearly that someone has talked. No surprise; they have both devious and brutal methods of loosening tongues."

Again rendered speechless by the disclosure, James flinched, eventually found his voice, and whispered, "Means we're both under the gun, Bernard."

Omsley ignored Silverthorne's distress. "There's no time to worry about it. You're going now, Jamie, tonight! Henderson has it arranged. Hate to say it's now or never, but that it is."

"*Now?* But it wasn't penciled in until I returned from Germanorum. When and how did Henny manage to—"

"Everything's fallen apart," whispered the other. "I gave it some thought and can only hope my 'good news' charade was overheard. They'll scoop me up shortly, but in light of your notoriety and high regard in high places, it may force Müller to touch base with the chancellor before he dares to order your arrest and possibly goad your dinner guest into gaining *Reichskounzel* approval, which could take hours, even days, and I doubt if Hoffmann would sign the warrant on his own initiative. Whether or not that thesis holds water, minutes count, so listen closely."

Omsley outlined his clandestine method of staying in contact with Henderson via innocuous e-mail messages sent "in the clear," yet encrypted via the unbreakable one-time pad system. "Henny's one wise bird! He used an ironic cipher base: the official English translation of *Mein Kampf* no one reads but displays prominently on every desk, bookshelf, school, hospital, and public building in America. You'll go as planned," Omsley concluded, "with one glaring exception: retro-temporal transposition has to take place onorbit."

"*Orbit!* Jesus, Bernard! How the hell do I get into space, or for that matter *down?*"

"Shhhh, you're all but shouting! What worries you so may be the easiest part of the junket. We're damned fortunate," assured Omsley, "to have friends in low *and* high places. You'll pass yourself off as a working steward aboard a *Raumhansa* shuttle due to lift off late tomorrow afternoon from the Pacific. Henny's already aboard *Walküre,* but don't ask me how he got into space, because I can't risk telling you. His encrypted e-mail described a reconfigured, ablative pressure suit rigged by a tech specialist who converted it adequately for atmospheric reentry."

"It's *that* desperate?"

"Desperate is too pale a term," said Omsley. "This police state they've built in America makes all others seem permissive by comparison: monolithic, iron-handed domination of damn near every human being everywhere. You *must* go back, and you *must* succeed! Fortunately, the jump's less than a century and a half. I can't begin to guess how Henny managed to smuggle the Lebe device out to *Walküre,* let alone the ultra-precious grams of enriched thorium isotope we paid such an exorbitant price in pain, careers, and lives to obtain."

His head spinning, James whispered, "So I'll come down where and, just as importantly, when?"

"Somewhere in Europe is all Henny promises, in late spring or early summer nineteen forty of the Gregorian timeline. Premature, perhaps, but *you* chose the target time frame yourself."

Silverthorne's uncertain nod was lost in the darkness. Heartbeats of silence ensued. "There is no way no way to pin down a meaningful calendar window. Arguments have raged about aiming for a particular period during the War Years, but the only firm answer to that is in their sealed archives. There's damned little to go on except for Goebbels' pretentious drivel and the works of those other Nazi bores. Who can say how much is valid?

"I'm convinced the alliances with Italy and Japan can be taken for granted," he continued, "but reclaiming the Saar Basin, Sude-tenland, and annexing Austria prior to invading Poland to start the main event, and then swindling England and France out of their pledged military aid to Czechoslovakia, all strike me as less than probable. But it's that lightning assault through Belgium and Holland leading to France's rapid collapse I've always thought too pat for belief.

"We're told the legendary Nazi hero of heroes was sent back," pursued James in a musing whisper difficult to hear, "to contrive some unknown way of coaching the Nazi hierarchy on how, by some miracle, to stop Britain from rescuing an entire allied army stranded on Belgium's beaches; or successfully counseling the *Luftwaffe* to pound Britain's ports, industrial areas, and ships into submission rather than raining destruction on the civilian population; or downplaying the staggering *Kriegsmarine* losses to British sea power before mounting the Channel crossing; and then pressing Wehrmacht *Heer* forces to win glorious victories on England's southern beaches. Goebbels spends an entire half volume commending Hitler's patience for pausing to consolidate the conquered territories of western Europe before turning his ground and air fury eastward to decimate Byelorussia and the Ukraine, devastate Kharkov, Kiev, and totally obliterate Moscow, Leningrad, and Stalingrad, victories he labels a long, drawn-out prelude to the conquest of North America. How can anyone with the most trivial knowledge of the War Years swallow those idealistic scenarios?"

"Once on site, you'll be separating the grain from the chaff and making decisions."

James shivered in the brisk mountain air. "Decisions about how to change all that! How? *How?*"

"Since there's no choice, you'll have to play it by ear. You are overqualified for the mission, due to your prior time junkets, especially after immersing yourself in *their* version of the War Years. At any rate, you've been judged the sole trump card left in our hand.

Fail to play it now, however unfavorable the odds, and we could lose the chance forever."

"Hoffmann upset my digestion by toying with me after dinner," muttered James. "He misquoted a tidbit from Goebbels' epic narrative, with an account of physicist Alfred Lebe being freed from Soviet captivity and returning to a conquered, plundered, sundered Germany. *Sundered!* I've racked my brain trying to guess where he came up with such an odd, inappropriate—"

"Speculation is a waste of time and energy, Jamie. You'll have to unearth the truth, the facts."

"Get real, Bernard! This junket is … what I'm being tasked to do falls somewhere beyond ludicrous. What the hell! Their efficient propaganda mill never tires of boasting how Lustmann was sent back and, by whatever means and methods, played marionette master of the Nazi ruling clique. And why not? He enjoyed an enormous advantage by carrying back definitive knowledge of the *actual* War Years he himself had experienced in part, and doubtless used that twenty-twenty hindsight to stage-manage and direct the war redux in order to drastically alter the outcome. I'll wager our favorite chancellor is aware of *exactly* how it was accomplished."

"Forget about guessing what a Nazi politico of the first water and his superiors know and don't know," advised Omsley. "Warring cultures collide, and neither the victors nor vanquished can escape without being changed in a number of ways. The chancellor may well be the most Americanized official governing any province. Viewed objectively, he's been a valuable asset."

"Granted, but I—"

"Enough!" Omsley said aloud. "In the final analysis, Erich Lustmann succeeded. If it was done once, it can be done again."

"Can it really?"

"Never *dare* to think of your mission as hopeless," declared the other. "Lustmann and Hitler are demigods in the Nazi pantheon, sacred icons school children are taught to venerate. Huge throngs attend the *Heldengedenktag* commemorating Lustmann's triumphant return to the then-present timeline, which often surpasses Hitler's annual birthday celebration. We were forced to infer to the best of our ability where Lustmann was and approximately when."

James groaned. "Come on, Bernard! He was *somewhere* in Europe, *sometime* between nineteen thirty-eight and forty-nine, and all of those archaic Gregorian dates are speculative, based on few genuine facts. My task will be a search comparable to seeking the proverbial needle in a monstrous haystack. And suppose I *do* luck out and find the man. What then?"

"I'm certain ODESSA wanted him in Berlin prior to the eruption of hostilities." Bernard pulled up his tunic's sleeve and glanced at the luminous dial of his wrist chronometer. "Let me finish quickly and be on my way. Henny's cell had rounded up every authentic twentieth-century *Reichsmark* that could be begged, borrowed, or pilfered, plus a handful of jewelry to aid you in scraping by until you can steal or earn more. Duplicate sets of forged documents identify the bearer as a freelance Austrian correspondent or Milanese history professor. Once you're ready, choose the most suitable ID. Your German's near perfect, your Italian passable. Either cover should suffice."

"The Austrian seems best, assuming the *Anschluss* took place as reported."

"Good, good! Now listen! Henny's provided for ninety-six kilograms of transposable mass, you and everything inside or equipping the special ablative pressure suit. Once on the ground in Europe, wear *Lederhosen* hiking about on an extended *Wanderjahr* to atemporize. On your last junket, you roamed Berlin for only days before going to Potsdam, but that was merely research. This jump is *very* different."

Omsley checked his wrist chronometer again. "I really must be off! By now Müller's bloodhounds have no doubt been dispatched and the hunt is underway." Embracing his younger colleague in the darkness, he said with a catch in his throat, "You can do it, Jamie! I *know* you can. We're counting on you, *millions* of us. *Hals und Beinbruch!*"

James muttered, "Sounds like I may break my fool neck as well."

"Someone will come by in the wee hours to collect Emily," said Omsley. "She'll be safely sequestered, though neither of us can be told where, so don't worry about her. Your first move will be to get down to the bakery shop in the village before sunrise, between four thirty and five at the latest. Sven Carlsen will meet you, see you on your way."

"Sven is one of us?"

"For years, yes; his drivers begin deliveries around five thirty. He'll hide you in one of the vans. Once away from the village, head straight to the airport, but stay clear of the passenger complex. Go to the Lufthansa building and ask for Harrison Brughley. Harry will arrange to sneak you aboard the first flight to Raketenflugplatz Pacific, so dress accordingly, not like some tourist off on a Hawaiian holiday. You'll be met at the airport in Lahaina and conducted to the shuttle."

"What if I'm ... recognized?"

"Don't let it happen!" warned Bernard. "Shave the beard, neatly trim the mustache, then appliqué this fake Heidelberg scar a cosmetologist provided; instructions on how to make it look real are in the packet." He handed over a fat envelope. "The scar will label you a Lufthansa executive and hopefully draw attention away from your features. Wear dark glasses only in daytime. If you are stopped for questioning, throw an indignant fit, get up on your high horse and talk down to whoever accosts you."

"What about you, Bernard?"

After a brief silence, Omsley said, "Hate to say its endgame time, but there's no place to hide, and I wouldn't enjoy being interrogated. All the luck there is, Jamie! You're the very best there is, but you'll still need every smidgen of good fortune that comes your way to succeed."

James trailed his colleague, stumbling back down the footpath in starlight. From the chalet's terrace, he watched the dark figure of Omsley climb into the two-place commute 'copter. The glow coils lit, the first-stage turbine spooled up, and the turboshaft engine caught, continuing its octave-by-octave climbing whine. Lightless, the small 'copter rose a few meters vertically, tilted forward, and vectored off into the night sky.

Minutes later, James's premonition of impending disaster ballooned as he pressed his lips against his wife's dark hair and whispered only those details of what was coming she had to know.

Emily wept quietly for a time, stifled her sobs, and helped James clip his beard. He shaved and trimmed the mustache but left it intact. Preoccupied with what was in store, he had difficulty following the handwritten instructions on how to disfigure his cheek by applying the faux Heidelberg saber scar.

# FIVE

*Esperanza de Argentina, 1960 C.E.*
*Greater Denver, DWJ 142*

Well past midnight, the dimly lit street lay still and deserted, except for an occasional passing car or the cantina's habitués infrequently drifting in and out. Fires of resentment and frustration raged in Erich Lustmann, vigilant for an hour in another Fiat runabout leased by ODESSA. He had parked across the street, from where he kept watch on the cantina's shadowed doorway, chain-smoked, and stewed about the betrayal, reviling Colonel Stoltz for his obstinate, single-minded decision to back *his* favored candidate to undertake the mission, asinine Michael Mackall.

Manfred had not been solicitous when summoning him for a "private chat." With neither a milligram of soft soap or painkiller, Stoltz had coldly announced that he, Lustmann, had been designated first alternate for the mission upon which all ODESSA's hopes and dreams rested.

First *alternate!*

Eagerly anticipating election as the Chosen One, he had been enraged beyond all boundaries when informed that naïve, antagonistic "Mig-gu-el" had been chosen to take the place he knew was rightfully his and his alone. Selecting the former *Panzerkampfwagen* battle hero had been the brainstorm of not only the colonel, but also that senile, arthritic fossil *Herr Doktor* Alfred Lebe, both of whom were suffering from ingrown minds when it came to dealing with anything beyond their own narrow spheres of expertise or widely differing fields of interest. In most, if not all, real-world respects, the physicist was about as perceptive as the average twelve-year-old, yet he had managed to convince Stoltz that Mackall was psychologically better suited to undertake the mission than he himself, and most galling of all better qualified!

Despite the ego-shattering letdown, he had done his best to pretend calm acceptance of their joint decision by vigorously praising Lebe's most recent triumph, the miraculous transposition of a living specimen that had vanished from its hutch in the now timeline, only to reappear and fall unharmed into the net above a pit filled with wood shavings at precisely Lebe's predicated instant after two calendar months had elapsed since its dispatch, a trial that incredibly bridged what the half-crazy old man had called a "temporal gulf" of one thousand four hundred and eighty-eight real-time hours. To borrow from the physicist's lexicon of arcane gibberish, this indisputable feat of near-magic had electrified the entire ODESSA enclave by falling into the net and instantly "amalgamating" with its "now" time-tagged, lettuce-chewing doppelgänger.

Spouting a cliché while wallowing in self-adulatory rapture, the elderly physicist had hooted, "Nothing succeeds like success!" Dithering with unbridled jubilation, Lebe had gushed like some over-emotional schoolgirl before launching an incomprehensible monologue that described in endless detail how the upcoming correlation and refinement of empirical data deriving from this latest, greatest, and most impressive success had crowned all his previous successes, and had then made the mistake of announcing how he meant to prepare for a subsequent penultimate trial he had already "penciled in," transposing a specimen over a *six-calendar-month* temporal gulf.

At which point Colonel Stoltz had put both booted feet down. His tone and manner brooking no argument, Manfred had declared that what there was to learn from Lebe's never-ending experiments had already been learned. He insisted that no purpose would be served by further "gee-whiz" experimental transpositions, nor any foreseeable gain realized by wasting another milligram of precious, difficult-to-obtain enriched uranium isotope to power one more unnecessary trial.

ODESSA's leader, or commanding officer as some expatriates thought of him, had convinced himself how mandatory it would be to initiate the mission at once, with zero delay. Eichmann's disappearance, a blow intimating that more than one team of Mossad Nazi hunters might arrive at any moment, had gravely worried Stoltz much more than worsening the already oppressive odds against achieving the ultimate mission objective by further widening the two-decade gap between calendar 1939 and 1960.

Each passing week—each *day,* Manfred had argued—lessened their chances of achieving the desperately needed goal, a conclusion to which Dr. Lebe had naturally objected strongly in a gravelly voice laden with overtones of foreboding, crying that to act prematurely would vastly diminish the overall chance for success.

Never one to be swayed by rhetoric once his military mindset was cast in concrete, the colonel had squelched Lebe's objections with an emphatic declaration that the candidate selected would be dispatched on Thursday, the first day of September, 1960, a truly portentous date corresponding to the fateful moment two decades in the past when a stage-managed border incident had provided Chancellor Adolph Hitler with an excuse to send his Wehrmacht legions and Luftwaffe aerial armada crashing into and over western Poland.

Utterly dismayed, in fact close to tears, the physicist had continued doing his damnedest to out-shout the colonel, a failure Lustmann had witnessed more than once. But when his martial decision had firmly solidified, Stoltz was no longer merely a stubborn ex-Wehrmacht *Oberst,* but an adamant, unstoppable force of nature immune to any and all counterarguments.

At midmorning the following day, Lustmann had been bitterly forced to endure an infamous "penultimate briefing," during the course of which his emotions had again segued from outrage into vindictive fury. Barely able to contain himself when Stoltz had announced that his detested rival was the chosen one and he himself relegated to the role of "designated backup," Lustmann had nevertheless steeled himself and undergone the supreme test of sitting on his hands through the remainder of that humiliating, demeaning session with all the other candidates present, all the while suppressing a wild urge to seize Stoltz by the throat and wring the life out of him. Worst of all during this emotional trial, when his burning gaze had been fixed on him, jubilant Michael Mackall had refused to so much as acknowledge his rival's presence.

Fuming silently, Lustmann clicked his gold-flashed lighter, touched the flame to the tip of a fresh cigarette, and only then noticed a half-consumed butt smoldering in the ashtray. He chucked the butt out of the Fiat's rolled-down window just as Michael Mackall emerged from the cantina with a blowzy young woman on his arm, a cantina fixture known to dispense mediocre sexual favors in exchange for mediocre sums.

*A shame,* thought Lustmann, *but there it is!*

It had to be made to look like an ordinary, after-hours street mugging gone wrong, the sort of crime any of the *descamisados,* ruffians, and lowlifes who frequented the cantina might pull off without a blink. Wearing sneakers, he got out of the Fiat very slowly, left the door unlatched for silence, and padded across the street.

Trailing the chatting couple along the darkened sidewalk toward Mackall's parked Fiat, he unbuttoned his linen jacket, tugged the silenced Walther automatic pistol from under his belt, slipped off the safety and quickened his pace, and brought the weapon up in a two-handed isosceles grip. His single round took the waitress squarely at the base of the skull, pitching her forward into a face-down sprawl on the sidewalk.

Mackall whirled, stared at Lustmann in shocked, open-mouthed disbelief.

*"Falscher Hund!"* accused his former rival, squeezed off two quick rounds, and went down on one knee to rifle the pockets of the man designated to usurp his place in history. He found it difficult to pull the *Panzergruppe Fier* signet ring from Mackall's finger. Hastily stuffing the ring, keychain, wallet, and money clip securing a wad of folded pesos in his jacket pockets, he rose to a semi-crouch, and turned around, scanning the street in both directions. Other than Mackall's nearby Fiat and his own vehicle parked across the street, only one other auto was visible at a distant curb. No pedestrians were in sight.

Studying his rival's still, crumpled figure, he breathed, *"Adieu, Mi-gu-el. À bien tôt."*

Crossing the street at a leisurely pace, he started the Fiat and drove six blocks toward the river, stopping only once to toss Mackall's belongings in a refuse bin, except for the ring, money clip, and currency. Driving back to the enclave, he couldn't imagine what had inspired him to bid farewell to his detested former rival in French.

\* \* \*

"Urgent call, *Herr Direktor.* Channel six."

In the staff limousine's rear seat, *Ausland Sicherheitsdienst* Colonel Müller punched his satellite phone. "Do you have him in custody?" he asked without preamble.

*"Herr Direktor,* the suspect's 'copter was intercepted departing the vicinity of Rocky Mountain Park. The pilot ignored every radioed command and warning to ground the vehicle, and despite all efforts veered toward—"

"Don't make me ask again," interrupted Müller. "Is he in custody or not?"

"Indeed, *Herr Direktor,* if only in a manner of speaking. The aerial pursuit ended when the suspect's helo flew straight into the face of Mount Evans. An air ambulance hovered and dropped paramedics at the site. The remains are being recovered, although making a positive identification may, um … forensic procedures may be required, in view of—"

"*Danke!* Carry on, *Herr Leutnant!*" Müller switched off and swore a vile oath.

"He had to be the ringleader," remarked one of the other officers.

"*Ja,* I'm certain that is so." The *SD* director cursed again. "Pompous Dean Omsley was apparently flying the 'copter himself and took the easy way out, but his birdwatching colleague will not be permitted to tread that safe path. Mertz, where the hell are the 'copters?"

"Overhead any moment now, *Herr Oberst.*"

Müller reached forward and chucked the driver's shoulder. "Step it up!"

The electric limousine surged approaching Estes Park Village, then had to slow again to negotiate the first sharp curve in the road. Tires screeching, a pair of unmarked black vans also swept around the curve, one leading the limo, the other following close behind.

\* \* \*

Shielded from the dim glow of a distant streetlight, Silverthorne watched the procession of vehicles zip past from the mouth of an alley and turn uphill. All three sets of front and rear lights winked out as the leading van entered another of the switchbacks leading up to his chalet.

Bernard had imagined Müller might be reluctant to order the arrest of a celebrated educator and time traveler without Chancellor Hoffmann's approval. He should have known better. *Ausland Sicherheitsdienst* was no fainthearted organization, nor would its shrewd, self-confident director stand idly by and wait for authorization to arrest a suspect he did not guess but *knew* to be a member of in a revolutionary conspiracy cell. It was *SD's* practice to collar and viciously interrogate anyone who fell under even mild suspicion, no matter how well connected or favored, then worry later about potential repercussions.

James anxiously shot the cuff of his tunic. The phosphorescent dial of his antique analog wristwatch told him only minutes had passed since he had last checked the time. The *SD* team would reach the chalet in minutes, but a half hour and more remained until five o'clock, and it was too soon to approach the bakery.

In the wee hours, with all inside and outside lights extinguished, he and Emily had crouched in darkness until feeble scratchings announced someone was at the entry door. Holding his wife in a final embrace, he had breathed an unspoken prayer that the underground railroad set up by Omsley was still intact and functional. Kissing Emily goodbye, he wondered if he would ever see her again before hustling her and three items of haphazardly packed luggage into an unlighted electric minivan, handing her sight unseen into the care of a dim figure with whom he had not exchanged a single word. Brimming with deep misgivings, he had watched in starlight as the blacked-out vehicle cautiously felt its way downhill.

At 0350 by the brass naval chronometer on his desk, he had panicked at the thought of staying in the chalet a second longer than seemed necessary. Preparing to leave on foot, he was struck by a notion to drag a red herring across the path of the inevitable pursuit. Switching on a table lamp in the family room and the banker's lamp on the desk in his study, he had abandoned half a mug of lukewarm coffee after purposely spilling a little to indicate a hasty departure, scattered a few manuscript pages, snatched his briefcase, and bolted from the study by way of the terrace, leaving the French doors ajar to invite pursuit in the wrong direction.

The faint thrash of distant rotary wings snapped his attention back to the present. Flying in a widely separated vee, a trio of government jetcopters coming in fast from the south made him glad he had abandoned his own two-place commute 'copter on the chalet helipad to prevent the much larger rotary-winged official aircraft from landing.

The mountainside above the village burst into actinic brilliance. Orbiting like three giant vultures, the helicopters illuminated what he hoped that bastard Müller would consider the logical upper mountain search area. Caught in a momentary time bind, he thought it best to move out briefcase in hand, cautiously peeked around the corner of the building in either direction, took a deep breath, sauntered unhurriedly across a side street toward the bake shop—to a casual observer just another early riser off on his usual business day—and turned right at the first intersection. Halfway down the block, with the darkened bakery sign and front windows in view, he paused on the sidewalk, made a careful item-by-item survey of what little was visible along the dark street, and slowly walked up the driveway leading to the rear parking lot.

"Here!"

Startled by low-spoken hail from the shop's foundation shrubbery, James halted. An indistinct shape looming in the predawn darkness, said softly, "This way!" James felt his arm taken and led down the driveway and around to the rear of the bakery where the overhead floodlights were unlit. Silhouetted against the sky glow, four delivery vans were backed up to the loading dock.

"Had no idea you were one of us," whispered James.

"Weren't supposed to," was the other's all-but-inaudible response. "By now they have every downhill road blocked. Get in this van and go down on the floor between racks. My driver's first stop is Phantom Valley Ranch. He'll drop you off up there."

"Sven, I'm heading for the airport, not *into* the park."

"Shhhh, don't argue," whispered Carlsen. "The early whirlybird picks up Missus Kilpatrick's guests, dumps a few downtown, then flies the rest on to the airport. Missus K's an old, dear friend. I went to see her minutes after Omsley called me. A half dozen or so guests will be riding the 'copter, so invent a cock 'n bull story and mix in with 'em."

Painfully aware his options ranged from slim to none, James whispered, "No way can I thank you enough, Sven. You're taking one helluva risk."

"All our prayers go with you, Professor!" The van's rear doors were wrenched open. "Get in now; first light's coming soon."

Silverthorne clambered inside and crammed his lanky frame prone in the narrow aisle between racks filled with fragrant, fresh-baked bread and pastry.

Seconds later, floodlights drenched the loading dock vans in brilliance.

* * *

"The single most egregious error you can possibly make," warned Dr. Lebe, "will be to neglect or ignore the carryall's fail-safe protection." Lebe pointed. "Here, see this off-color rivet on the lower rear corner of the aluminum case? It's also an electrical anode. Should you fail to apply voltage before undoing the latches, unseating and lifting the lid, a pyrotechnic charge will instantly turn to ashes every nitrocellulose flash-paper document inside, as well as incinerating the bundled currency. Were that to happen, your capsulized account of the War Years and the scenario of prescribed, suggested military and civil corrections to specified wartime efforts, plus instructions and redirections, not to mention the funds needed to sustain you, will be lost forever. Hence, it will be vital to rigorously adhere to the procedure I have outlined, or the precious papers you carry into the past will be become charred reminders of your stupidity. *Verstehen Sie?*"

Lustmann detested being talked down to. He inquired sharply, "Direct current, or ...?"

"Does not matter, either will do," replied the physicist. "A minimal amperage jolt will open the redundant fail-safe switches and disarm the igniter, then automatically rearm it when the lid is closed again and latched. Easiest, I should think, will be to touch the anode with wires stripped from, oh, a table lamp, toaster, whatever is handiest. But lock this in memory, Lustmann: I can't overstate the importance of opening the carryall *only* after applying voltage to the subject rivet."

Lustmann's affirmative nod was slow in coming.

"Nonsense! How could something so important be forgotten?" scoffed Colonel Stoltz. "Erich, let me remind you of something equally vital. When preparing to open the carryall, make sure you won't be disturbed. Isolate yourself before delving into the account of the War Years, removing funds, or whatever else you deem necessary. Should anyone from the visited retro-temporal era glimpse the exposed contents, it would mean—"

"*Ja, ja!* I'm really not quite *that* dull, Manfred." Though eager to be off, Lustmann had fallen into a mild funk over the prospect of actually diving headfirst into the unknown. He changed the subject by complaining about his inexperience as a parachutist.

"For everyone and everything there is always a first time," was Lebe's dismissive retort.

Displeased by the physicist's cavalier attitude toward his safety, Lustmann sniffed and said crossly, "What I fail to understand is the necessity to jump at such a low altitude. I realize drifting down from on high would increase the risk of exposure by someone on the ground—"

"*Nein!* Always try to *think* before you speak," interrupted Lebe. "I've told you more than once that the safety margin for deploying the parachute at an absolute minimum altitude of one thousand meters cannot be ignored. Low hills exist in Mecklenburg, but none loftier than a kilometer."

"What," inquired Lustmann, "would be so awful about coming down on a low hill?"

The physicist smacked his lips irritably. "Young man," he

declared, "the danger is not a question of landing *on* a hill, but retro-temporally emerging *within* a hill."

"Within? That's ridiculous!"

"Ah, there I beg you to bend a trifle and allow me to differ." His above-it-all-manner coming to the fore, Lebe asked stridently, "Can you begin to imagine what might occur if the molecules making up your organism, plus the inanimate materials you carry, simultaneously try to coexist within the physical structure of a *hill?* In truth, I am unable to hazard a guess about what might occur, but I should *not* wish to be close enough to learn that particular lesson."

Lustmann glanced uncertainly at Colonel Stoltz. "All right! A minimum altitude of one kilometer. You also mentioned latitude as a secondary quintessential factor."

Vexed by the statement, the physicist wagged his head sadly. "Must everything be explained to you ten times over? Berlin circa nineteen thirty-nine is a major metropolis situated at fifty-two minutes, thirty degrees north, while your immediate destination, Calgary, lies at fifty-one degrees, one minute north. After overnighting in Canada, you and Manfred will be flown north to a latitude corresponding to the Mecklenburg-Schwerin lowlands north of Brandenburg. The bush pilot, a stalwart former Luftwaffe courier shot down twice behind Soviet lines, received the lat and lon coordinates in a coded transmission after I had used exquisite care to calculate, check, recheck, and triple-check the precise instant of retro-temporal initiation in relation to two-plus decades of earth spin, then went back and *again* rechecked all calculations.

"At or near high noon, September first, Herr Lustmann, you shall leave the aircraft in flight, hopefully above the minimum altitude, and immediately key my device. I guarantee your emergence in midair above the Mecklenburg countryside on Friday, the first day of September in Gregorian calendar year nineteen thirty-nine of the Common Era. *Guarantee,* do you hear? The sole problem you might encounter would be for some farmer, pedestrian, or whomsoever to glimpse your descending parachute and report it. If so, you must invent a plausible explanation."

"What if I jump out of the aircraft and strong winds sweep my parachute for a good distance and I ... well, emerge and splash down in the Baltic instead of—?"

"Never, Herr Lustmann, not from that low altitude," insisted Lebe. "Yet it would be wise to try *not* landing in any Mecklenburg stream, river, pond, or bog. I targeted the area between the communities of Pritzwalk and Rheinsburg, where only a minor river flows, the Dosse."

"Erich, we really should board now," urged Colonel Stoltz. "Refueling stops add hours to the long flight to Canada, and you should get all the rest you can in the air. Sleep will come more easily if you take it for granted that all preparations have been made."

"*Alles ist in der Ordnung,*" chimed Dr. Lebe, eager to see them on their way.

Colonel Stoltz turned around slowly, searching the near and far reaches of *Aeropuerto Sauce Viejo*. He made a point of solemnly shaking the physicist's hand. "I should be back in a week, ten days at most. Until then, Alfred ..."

Lustmann nodded farewell to the physicist, followed Stotz across the tarmac, and up the rear loading stair lowered from the ventral fuselage of a leased Martin 202 airliner.

Rife with misgivings about the replacement candidate, Lebe stationed himself behind a chain-link fence, cupped his hands as a megaphone, and strained his vocal cords calling Glückauf!" He watched the passenger ramp retract upward and nest in the ventral underside of the aircraft's aft fuselage. A propeller turned slowly, and engine number one belched exhaust, roared to life, then the other engine started, doubling the roar. An attendant in coveralls unplugged a cable from the receptacle above his head, closed and secured the access panel, and backed out, wheeling away the battery cart that had supplied auxiliary cranking power to start the engines.

The aircraft swung about toward a taxiway, its propeller wash blowing Lebe's sparse gray hair in disarray. Gripping the chain-link fence with white knuckles, he succumbed to the fatalistic misgivings that plagued him, then chided himself for lapsing from a self-imposed rule to never allow emotion to cause any deviation whatever from a guiding principle of long standing to maintain an attitude of rigorous scientific pragmatism. Nevertheless, the prayer formed again in his mind, a distant echo of his Catholic upbringing.

*Herr Doktor* Lebe capitulated, letting go of the fence and crossed himself.

* * *

*It's too easy,* thought James, piqued by the imagined, lurking disasters born each time the bakery van turned a corner. Scrunched awkwardly between racks of fragrant bakery goods, he survived a nervous wait until the silent electric vehicle halted, then backed up to the Phantom Valley Ranch delivery entrance.

The driver de-energized the vehicle, left the driver's seat whistling a tuneless melody in a less-than-convincing show of going about business as usual. Opening the van's rear doors, he purposely aligned them with the van's sides to aid in screening the interior from view.

A woman in late middle age James assumed to be Mrs. Kilpatrick emerged from the rustic building. She began needling the driver, criticizing the moderate staleness of certain items in the previous day's delivery. Her salty comments continued unabated as she gestured for James to clamber out of the van, led him into the building, and shoved him into a storeroom lined with shelves stacked with china, utensils, and kitchen bric-a-brac.

"Stay put! I'll come collect you," she whispered and closed the door behind her.

James relaxed his grip on the attaché case, flexed his fingers, and

eased down on the lid of a sealed metal container. Too nervous to
sit still, he rose to brush off the delivery van dust clinging to his
jacket and trousers. Shifting his weight uneasily, he hoped for the
best, fearing the worst, and waited through an eternity that must
have lasting six or seven minutes.

Mrs. Kilpatrick opened the storeroom door. Looking harried, she
summoned James with a crooked forefinger. "Early 'copter's due
any minute now," she whispered. "I'm leery of two guests waiting
for pickup, both supposed German businessmen. Sven wanted you
to mingle with the guests, but I mean to introduce you as a visiting
family friend. What name's on your papers?"

"Geist, Raumhansa Operations Manager, Wilhelm Geist."

Taking his arm with maternal familiarity, Mrs. Kilpatrick was all
smiles, chatting amiably while escorting Silverthorne along an
extensive hallway. She uttered a little laugh in response to some
unspoken comment while ushering him into the expansive lobby,
where two women and a trio of departing gentlemen reclined in
lounges beneath the rough-hewn ceiling beams. At first glance, his
prospective fellow travelers appeared to be as advertised: strangers
thrown together by chance. Casual introductions were made all
around.

"*S'tut sehr gleich, Herr Geist,*" a gentleman said politely. Displaying more than casual interest in the scar marring James's cheek, he
added, "Flying with us this morning, sir?"

"I wish it were so. I'm here to attend a business conference in the
local Lufthansa Business Center, but actually I serve in the North
American Provinces Division of Raumhansa."

Mrs. Kilpatrick intervened, offering a reprise of her sunny smile.
"Herr Geist and my nephew, Dolph, are old friends. I look forward
to Willi's visit whenever business brings him to Denver."

"Adolphus and I," said James, "were gymnasium classmates in
Stuttgart."

The flight to the heliport atop a metropolitan Denver high-rise proved uneventful, but flying onward to outlying *Flughafen* forced James to engage in a meaningless conversation with his seatmate, another of Mrs. Kilpatrick's guests. Adroitly fielding queries about himself and his work, he gently corrected the lady's misconception that he was with Lufthansa, not Raumhansa, the cartel's spacecraft operations affiliate. Speaking rapidly to forestall further questions, he described a synthetic current joint project and his varied duties contributing to it.

His first glimpse of a saturnine individual obviously waiting to meet the arriving jetcopter at the *Flughafen* Denver helipad raised his hackles. Clad in a thigh-length black leather coat, for all practical purposes an unofficial Gestapo uniform, the expressionless gentleman unobtrusively scanned each deplaning arrival. "Ladies and gentlemen," he said, "before sending you on your way, may I trouble you for a look at your travel papers, *bitte?*"

His pulse racing, James said in the most authoritarian manner he could muster, "Your pardon, sir. I won't be leaving Denver until late this evening."

"So?" Inspecting Silverthorne more closely, the greeter reacted to his air of importance, his eyes narrowing at sight of the status symbol on James's cheek, the expensive looking attaché case he carried. "Might I have a peek at your credentials, sir?"

Being "sirred" encouraged James to flip open his calfskin wallet and display the artfully forged plastic card featuring an embedded rainbow Raumhansa hologram that identified him as Wilhelm Karl Geist, an employee of the government transportation cartel's space division.

"*Viel Dank,* Herr Geist."

His florid features crowned with a flowing mane of silvery hair, a nattily attired older gentleman approached the group uninvited. "Ah, there you are, Willi! Good to see you. Why're you dawdling out here? We've been anxiously awaiting for you to arrive."

"The 'copter grounded only moments ago, Herr Brughley." James hoped he had guessed correctly.

The man in the black leather coat spoke up. "You pardon, sir. Is Herr Geist known to you?"

"Quite well. He's a business colleague." The Lufthansa executive's response, while amiable, was in no way subservient, making it obvious that further explanation was unnecessary.

"Are you prepared to vouch for Herr Geist's bona fide employment with Raumhansa, sir?"

"Well, now, let me see ..." Something of a showman, the Lufthansa executive pursed his lips as though pondering the question. He asked James if he had recently engaged in any criminal activities, earning a giggle from the gossipy woman who had interrogated James in flight.

James forced a smile and said glibly, "Not lately, Herr Brughley."

"Good! Come along, we've much to discuss and little time in which to do so." Voicing non sequiturs, Brughley led his "business associate" to the nearby slidewalk, where they each took two quick steps in the direction of movement, boarded the moving walkway, and were carried sedately around sprawling Terminal D toward an adjacent office complex. Despite the brisk morning air, James was perspiring slightly as they entered the building, where he and Brughley were the sole occupants of an elevator compartment going up six floors to the offices of Lufthansa's regional headquarters.

Brughley's meaningless chatter resumed as he escorted James away from the elevator bank, their presence attracting only a few incurious glances as the executive conducted his guest through the antechamber of a large, well-appointed corner office, where his executive assistant was talking on the phone. Brughley sat down at his desk, motioned James to a chair, put a silencing forefinger to his lips, and whispered an instruction for Silverthorne to wait in his private executive washroom, then in a normal voice he said, "Would you like coffee, Willi?"

*"Nein, bitte.* I'm fine, Herr Brughley." Leaning across the other's

desk, James whispered, "How long until the, er . . ?"

"Less than two hours," was the other's hushed reply. "You'll be taken down through the service area, boarded ahead of the other passengers, then met in the Lahaina arrival lounge."

Without another word, Brughley rose, offered James a brusque nod of reassurance, and left the office, closing the door behind him.

In the washroom, afflicted with more angst than he had experienced since childhood, James snapped over the lock on the door, set his briefcase on the floor, and sagged down on the lid of the commode, beginning a seemingly endless wait for whatever might happen next.

# SIX

## *Low Earth Orbit, DWJ 142; Northern Germany, 1939 CE*

Predawn darkness shrouded Calgary when Colonel Stoltz and Lust-mann left the hotel and found the taxi Manfred had ordered the previous evening idling at the curb to keep the driver warm in the chill night. They endured the twenty-minute drive to Springbank Airport in a western suburb of Calgary, Colonel Stoltz stoic, wholly self-contained, Lustmann consumed with unspoken dread of what he knew was in store. Arriving not long after first light, they were greeted by the sober pilot and conducted out to the hardstand next to a public hangar, where the driver of a fuel truck was servicing a high-wing Cessna monoplane.

Several uneventful hours later, the aircraft's port wing dipped in a shallow bank, and the Cessna began to lazily orbit in a wide circle. "Dead reckoning says we're on target," intoned the taciturn pilot, pointing to the instrument panel as if to confirm his statement. "Altitude just above eleven hundred meters, lon one hundred and fourteen degrees, four minutes west, lat fifty-two degrees, thirty-two minutes north, or thereabouts."

*Thereabouts!* Unnerved by the connotation of potential inaccuracy coupled with the ex-Luftwaffe airman's soft-spoken, above-it-all attitude, Lustmann peered apprehensively at the Canadian snowscape unreeling beneath them, a sight that made him feel a dozen times more fearful about what was in the offing than he

71

could have imagined. He was preparing to tell the pilot what he could do with his loosely stated "thereabouts" destination, when Colonel Stoltz asked loudly enough to make himself heard above the throttled-back buzz of the light plane's engine. "Bare minutes until noon, Erich. Have you readied yourself?"

In lieu of an answer, Lustmann squinted at the instrument panel. The three-pointer, sensitive altimeter was impossible to read. He swallowed with difficulty and uttered a weak-voiced, "Er, yes … prepared."

"*Ganz gut.* Now, for one last time please give me your full, undivided attention." Staring hard at Lustmann, the picture of sincerity incarnate, Stoltz instructed him for the fourth or fifth time to key Lebe's device the instant he fell free of the airplane, but not to so much as *think* about touching the D-ring. "Pull the ripcord in the here and now, and you'll find yourself in yesteryear without a parachute and plunge to your death. Are you perfectly clear on that?"

"*Ja, ja!*" In no way reassured, the repeated question struck Lustmann as offensive due to the other's gruff way of restating the obvious. His throat incredibly dry, he faltered, then said slowly, "Promise to watch, Manfred, and make sure I don't drift down into the snow."

"Get hold of yourself, for God's sake! Relax, and breathe deeply," counseled Stoltz. "Steel yourself for the effort mentally but let yourself go limp as a dishrag just before you jump. *Hören Sie, was ich sage?* We've all prayed so long and hard for this historic moment to arrive, making it unseemly for you to show squeamishness about carrying out the sacred duty you've pledged to undertake. Lebe's final experiment proved conclusively that his ingenious device will perform *precisely* as specified, and I'm supremely confident you will successfully accomplish your duty."

"I feel, uh …" stumbled Lustmann. "I mean, I know how … indebted I should be for this honor conferred on me, Herr Oberst. But while I vastly admire Lebe efforts, I'm much bigger than …

well, than a rabbit."

"What foolishness! You just said you were prepared, so stop mouthing nonsense and, for the love of God, get your thoughts in order!"

A bleak grimace was the only reply Lustmann could come up with. Despite the cold of western Canada, a film of perspiration beaded his forehead beneath the goggles pushed up into his hairline. He literally sweated through the stretched-out minutes passing at glacial velocity as the Cessna droned on, continuing its lazy orbit above a timbered snowfield. Now and again the pilot turned to glance back expectantly but said nothing to his passengers.

"Time!" announced the colonel. He clapped Lustmann's shoulder a lusty blow, his manner abusive, his frigid stare persistent, accusative, and declared coldly, "I know it was you, Lustmann! I had to play dumb when those detectives came to interview us about Mackall's murder, but all along I *knew* you were responsible. It was not a guess. I *knew!*"

The prospective time traveler was speechless.

"If you are half as eager," rasped Stoltz, "to capture the prize we've handed into your care as I had hoped—no, *prayed* you were—and chose to prove it by yearning for it strongly enough to do murder, you should assuredly have the stomach, grit, and heartfelt *desire* to undertake the immensely important task we've laid before you and vetted you to perform. Now the time has come to get on with it in every sense of that term, time to perform, to accomplish the task you have *pledged* to undertake. Leave us now!"

With the colonel's unanticipated verbal assault skittering around in his mind like a hot coal, Lustmann was blinded by a sudden, desperate urge to get as far away from Stoltz as possible. He frantically groped to unlatch his safety belt and cranked the Cessna's passenger door handle with spastic urgency. Encumbered by the parachute chest pack and the bulging rucksack hung on his shoulders, he pulled the goggles down, adjusted them over his eyes, and inserted a gloved hand into the heavy quilt coat's slash pocket, feeling for the stud Lebe had blithely referred to as "the retro-temporal trigger." Straining with his free hand to push open the Cessna's door against the slipstream, he thrust his right boot outside; the rushing airstream threatened to tear his leg away before his boot found the projecting "step" used to board and deplane from the high-winged aircraft.

Clutching the door in a death grip, eyes tightly shut, jaw clenched, he drew a deep breath, tensed to launch himself into the thin, frigid air streaming past, and froze, paralyzed by the thought of actually diving out of an airplane in flight. One terrified glance at the white terrain slipping past a thousand meters below brought all further thought to a sudden halt.

Manfred Stoltz erased the last vestiges of his reluctance by applying the soles of his boots to Lustmann's backside and shoving him energetically, extending both legs.

Screaming hoarsely as his violent exit overcame the door's slipstream resistance, opened all the way, and he tumbled into space totally disoriented, too terrified by the inborn fear of falling to scream again as the wind ripped his hand from the coat's slash pocket. He desperately tried to relocate the pocket by feel, but it was made difficult by his glove and the hurricane streaming past. He panicked, tried again unsuccessfully, then in sheer desperation pressed his gloved hand firmly against the coat, slid it down into the slash pocket, contacted the stud, and pressed it hard enough to all but break his thumb.

A vile, gut-wrenching sensation twisted his bowels. The up-rushing snowfield vanished, and he found himself falling inside a cloud, unable to see anything other than the damp mist streaming past. A second, stronger surge of panic overwhelmed him, driving him to fumble for the chest pack's D-ring. His gloved fingers closed around it, and he gave a lusty tug. The chest pack came open, the chute unfurled, and the canopy snapped open with a harsh jolt conducted through the risers that made his testicles ache. Blind inside the mist fogging his goggles, he drifted downward until the parachute dropped clear of the low cloud ceiling, and there below, coming up faster than seemed natural, was …

*Magic!*

Releasing the chute's risers with one hand, he tore the moisture-beaded goggles from his head and let them fall away. In abject disbelief, he ogled the gray-green countryside he had never again expected to see. Gentle slopes covered here and there with brakes of low-growing timber were off in the distance to the left. Beyond a pattern of farmlands bisected by the string-straight incision of a road, and directly ahead as near as he could tell, there was a low-lying area that from high above had the look of a bog that grew larger as he drifted down toward it. Farther off were what might be farm buildings, and in the middle distance the silver sheen of a stream or small river.

The gray, weepy overcast made it difficult to decide where he and the ground, now rising faster, and coming closer, would meet. What from on high had seemed a swampy area transformed itself into a wetland sump littered with large and small boulders. He tugged the risers gently, clumsily, trying to steer clear of the boulder-strewn patch.

His boots hit, splashed in puddled groundwater, and his legs buckled. He instinctively tucked up, felt himself being dragged through puddled ground between rocks by a stiff breeze that made the parachute resemble a billowing spinnaker sail as it dragged him deeper into the soggy, rock-strewn pasture. Digging in his boots, he yanked hard with both hands on the chute's risers to spill air, struggling to collapse the parachute, then collapsed himself.

Breathing in convulsive gasps while sprawled unmoving in the mud, he watched the low clouds scud past overhead until his rapid breathing slowed. Clambering erect with difficulty, he unbuckled the harness and let the parachute blow away to become entangled in boulders downwind. Manfred had advised him how necessary it would be to bury the chute. It did seem the wisest course, although in wet ground it could turn into quite a chore. Searching his surroundings for a drier spot in which to scoop out a shallow pit with his knife, he was startled to hear someone call, *"Halloo!"*

A boy in a padded herringbone twill coat with the collar turned up against the chill breeze had emerged from a nearby fringe of woodland. A shotgun was draped over his forearm, broken open for safety, and his catch, a pair of water birds, was tied to his belt. "I saw you float down from high above, sir. *Wer sind Sie?"*

"The most important individual you're ever liable to meet, *Jugend.* Come help me fold up this parachute." Lustmann's knowing smile was meant to be disarming but proved insufficient. The circumspect youngster stayed where he was.

Lustmann unbuckled the straps, shrugged out of the backpack, and laid it on the slanted crest of a boulder. Gathering the risers, he pulled the muddied nylon chute to his chest and squeezed and compacted it into a muddy bundle. "Are you aware," he asked, wondering if the question held any meaning, "that today is Friday, September first?"

Puzzling over the question, the boy's affirmative nod was slow in coming, but mind-blowing to the world's first time traveler. "Been off hunting and missed hearing the news on the radio, eh?"

The boy squinted uncertainly. *"Jawohl, mein Herr. Ich habe nicht der Radio gehört."*

"Then be of good cheer! On this auspicious day, *Der Führer* sent a number of Wehrmacht divisions smashing into Poland. I just returned from flying over the front taking photos near the border town of Gleiwitz. Flying back, the pilot had engine trouble, forcing me to bail out."

"Germany is … you say we are now at *war,* sir?"

The youth sounded more incredulous than Lustmann had anticipated. "Oh, yes. But not yet the real war, just what people will soon joke about and call the *Sitzkrieg*. Still, the true shooting war will begin soon enough, but not until after the cautious French and British declare war on the Reich. Our enemies are much too spineless to dare firing anything at us but threats and bad words during this, er … twilight war. You may take that as gospel, *Jugend.*"

Hearing unfamiliar terms caused the boy to restlessly shift the shotgun from one arm to the other.

Lustmann smiled again. "As for myself, have you never before met a *Schutzstaffeln offitzier?*"

The boy blinked. "You are of the *SS, mein Herr?*"

"At your service." His manner crisp, Lustmann said, "Enough chitchat. I would be most grateful if you direct me to the nearest telephone, *bitte.*"

The bird hunter said he would be happy to oblige.

\* \* \*

Unnerved by the risky service she had agreed to perform, Raumhansa's wary roving safety inspector could not hide her deep concern. Heart in her mouth, she had taken James's arm in the *Flugplatz* concourse minutes after his jetliner touched down in Lahaina, hustled him into the not-very-clean washroom of an airport service building, and breathlessly urged him to discard his travel garments, don a rumpled tan jumpsuit replete with the Raumhansa logo, and a half-size-too-large pair of soft, Velcro-shod microgravity boots of the type worn by working space crewmen and women.

While James was changing clothes, she explained that he would be replacing a Purser Feuerbach on the shuttle soon due to lift off. Using liquid hand soap and a safety razor, Silverthorne shaved his pencil mustache, peeled the faux Heidelberg scar from his cheek, scrubbed his face, and toweled off vigorously to rid himself of excess nervous energy.

"I know Rosty Feuerbach," confided the inspector. "He's … to be polite, he's the pet of *Hanseatic's* Chief Steward Dries, who'll be most unhappy to hear his … friend's been taken ill."

"How was that arranged?" asked James as they headed toward a large jetcopter on the helipad.

A woman of few words, the inspector seated herself beside James and tossed her head unhappily. "A taste of doctored coffee. He'll soon be fine."

They had been airborne no more than ten minutes when the inspector pointed to the helo's forward transpex bubble. "Raketen-flugplatz Pacific's come in view."

A floating metal island gradually emerged from a nacreous haze softening the seagirt horizon. Rimmed with low-lying structures, the space terminal featured a half dozen launch pads, including a pair supporting ogive-prowed ground-to-orbit shuttlecraft. Seeing their point of departure gave James pause. He had never ventured into space, nor had he any past or present inclination to do so. "How long until the shuttle, er … takes off?"

Stress affected the woman's speech. *"Hanseatic?* Oh, close to … call it ninety minutes."

The jetcopter descended to a bull's-eye helipad cantilevered over the sea on the terminal's western perimeter. Although on what to her was familiar turf, the woman's feeble attempt to mask her agitation infected James as she escorted him to the launch pad. Deathly afraid of what might go wrong, she took him in through the service entrance, where they boarded the aerospacecraft through an open hatchway by dodging beneath a conveyor belt carrying a procession of large- and medium-sized containers from the automated weigh station into a branching passageway.

James decided his benefactress had accurately gauged Chief Steward Dries's reaction when she informed him Purser Braun would replace Feuerbach due to his "pet's" incapacitation. Visibly displeased over the substitution, Herr Dries regarded Braun with narrow-eyed suspicion. "And you, an American from the look of you, how much space experience do you have?"

"Very little, sir."

Puffing his cheeks, the chief purser said, "Wonderful, just wonderful! After liftoff we'll find something you may be able to do. Stay out of the way until I tell you to strap in."

"*Jawohl,* Herr Dries."

\* \* \*

Seeing reborn Berlin, Lustmann told himself, was like *being* reborn. No, *better* than being reborn—marvelous! Seared by the sights and sounds crowding into his senses as he strolled Ku'dammstrasse, his elation was unbounded. He exulted in the row of red-and-black swastika banners rippling farther down the thoroughfare, reveled in the sidewalks crowded with Berliners going about their daily lives. A sense of purpose prevailed, elevated for his personal enjoyment by a sprinkling of *Erdgrau* military uniforms worn by numerous passersby in either direction.

The farther he went along the boulevard, the stronger, more genuine was the blissful, nostalgic euphoria welling up inside him. It was an experience literally beyond belief, a magical return to the lost city he had witnessed as a metropolis destroyed from the air, but now again the capital of youthful memory. Berlin struck him as … It was useless; there was no adjective adequate to describe the intense sunburst of emotion that racked him.

Having always believed himself an unsentimental, coldly logical pragmatist, the bare fact of re-experiencing Berlin redux as an intact, orderly city was a thrill he could never have imagined awake or dreaming. As a candidate to take part in Lebe's harebrained time-travel scheme, he admitted viewing the factuality of what might take place as not merely fantastic, but surreal. Yet here he was, his lust for life rejuvenated in living, breathing call-it-what-you-will Berlin in the wake of decades spent in traumatic, nightmarish absence. Lebe's miraculous, innovative device had instantaneously thrust him back into a once familiar timeline, well-remembered

Berlin redux, and feverishly reignited his ambition to accomplish the sacred mission he's been assigned to undertake.

Supremely excited, all his senses intact and deployed, he aimlessly roamed the rhythmically beating heart of what in retrospect had been a bombed-scarred, burned-out skeleton of a great city ruined and then abandoned by the Russian, American, French, and British swine. He examined every item of his surroundings while pacing along the sidewalk, inhaling Berlin's heady life and vibrant energy, tasting it, rolling the texture and flavor of the city around on the palate of his mind like a heady draft of champagne.

He relished beyond measure the sheer joy of feeling the pavement beneath his boots in the once lost, miraculously restored late summer of 1939. It no longer mattered whether fuddy-duddy *Herr Doktor* Lebe was a certifiable lunatic or the most accomplished scientific genius in human history. He'd invented a means of allowing him to actually arrive alive and well two decades short of his later existence on the same timeline he could not bring himself to accept as the redundant future. Lebe had assumed monumental stature in his eyes, and had in fact become his personal patron saint, as well as a potential beloved savior of the Fatherland.

He had cleaned most of the mud from his clothing and boots at the Mecklenburg farm, while halfheartedly fending off the fawning attentions of the bird hunter's stodgy parents, who were delighted to aid an elite *Schutzstaffeln* officer who had fallen out of the sky into their midst. His fanciful word pictures of screaming *Stuka* dive bombers wreaking havoc, *Panzerwaffe* columns rolling into Poland ahead of surging tides of mechanized infantry, had been received with wide-eyed, patriotic enthusiasm. Yet, once the bird hunter's parents had begun to contemplate the potential hardships, travail, and other dangerous situations war might bring with it, coming as it did hard on the heels of the Great War to End War, with all the privations that had drastically shredded the quality of German life, he had detected overtones of apprehension.

Frustrated and impatient to be on his way but inhibited by a lack of a readily available way to disable the fail-safe device and open the carryall still in his rucksack, he had solved the quandary, not to mention mystifying his hosts, by requesting a short piece of wire and a moment of privacy. Handed a half meter of baling wire snipped by the bird hunter from a roll in the barn, he had isolated himself in the bathroom, unscrewed a light bulb, inserted one end of glove-insulated wire into the socket, and touched the other end to the off-color rivet, producing a small but satisfactory spark. Unlatching the carryall with a degree of trepidation and apprehensively inching up the lid very slowly, he'd loosed a heartfelt sigh of relief. Stacks of banknotes bound with paper straps and the irreplaceable half ream of nitrocellulose flash-paper had arrived from two decades in the future visibly intact and undamaged.

Rejoicing over the prescient visions of a successful mission crowding his thoughts, he had fingered the condensed, encyclopedic account of the "real," well-remembered war not too distant in calendar years on this same timeline, complemented by a corollary, thinner flash-paper bundle containing comprehensive advice and counsel about to how to affect various ways and means of coaching correctable, redirectable, and or deletable events and situations pertaining to specific, crucial wartime military and political events, happenings, policies, and above all else "misguided" Führer decisions and directives. Taken as a whole, the separate stacks of flash-paper went far beyond being priceless, especially the varied "blueprints" prescribing or proscribing definitive courses and changes of action intended to not only portend a glorious future for Nazi Germany, but to make Adolf Hitler's *Tausend-jährig Reich* dream a reality.

Magnanimously handing over a large-denomination banknote to his host and hostess, he had graciously overcome their objections with a casual remark about the SS never failing to pay its debts. Afterward, he had condescended to accept the farmer's offer to drive him to the town of Ganzlin at the southern end of Plauer See, where after profusely thanking his benefactor he had purchased a ticket and smoked impatiently on the station platform waiting for the train.

An overpowering sense of unreality he wasn't able to shake off for most of the day had gripped him and literally taken his breath away upon stepping down from the railcar in Berlin's Zoologischer Garten Bahnstation. Hatless, the rucksack strapped on his back, he had strolled block after block in an ecstatic daze, straying from the main thoroughfare several times to take in the sights on neighboring streets, once halting in his tracks at an intersection, transfixed by something starkly unbelievable only he himself would appreciate. Across the way, the Kaiser-Wilhelm-Gedachtniskirche reared resplendently intact, not the bombed-out shell he recalled from a brief visit to Berlin during the dark days prior to Germany's long-drawn sigh of defeat.

Strolling onward, he resisted an impulse to enter the first haberdashery he passed and purchase a few items of respectable apparel, then later put aside a desire to phone and reserve a hotel suite in order to get directly to the task at hand. Instead he ambled onward toward Einemstrasse while absorbing the pace and vitality going on all around him.

Tiring from his long stroll, he thought of hailing a taxi and asking the cabbie if he knew a good place to spend the night, then dismissed the notion and strolled onward. His mission labors could wait. At the moment, he decided to wallow in the reborn milieu of Berlin, a sumptuous feast he couldn't bring himself to abandon on impulse, or for that matter *any* reason.

\* \* \*

"Braun, you slow-witted sluggard! I want that manifest reconciled before we dock at Walküre."

"*Es wird, Herr Dries getan.*" Grasping the shuttle's freefall safety line, James tugged himself along the companionway per regulations. The close-mouthed, breathlessly nervous safety inspector had not informed him the chief steward was not a revolutionary, merely someone with a natural for bullying underlings who'd kept "Purser Braun" hopping ever since liftoff.

Compounding the strangeness and uncertainty of being under microgravity freefall was Silverthorne's intense dislike of the cargo bay's close confines and faint, unappetizing odor. Aware that *Hanseatic* would soon begin maneuvering to match *Walküre Raumstation's* orbital vector and velocity, he wondered if he would be able to hear the acceleration warning while floating about in the ship's utilitarian bowels. Clipping the safety tether to a stanchion, he activated a handheld recorder and began checking off coded container labels against an electronic manifest while worrying about Emily. There had been no safe way to tell her the truth, but she had gamely pretended to believe his vaporous tale of unspecified, yet serious trouble in the wind and feigned acceptance of how mandatory the need was for "temporary" separation.

The distant honking of a klaxon warned him to hurry and finish logging the cargo waybills ASAP. Minutes later, a mild surge of weight on his Velcro-shod boots accompanied the low, conducted rumble of the shuttle's thrusters, shortly succeeded by milder surges, and finally a faint jar, a sighing chuff of air and a subtle pressure pop in his ears that announced docking. He untethered and busied himself recording the final items of freight manifest entries.

Sounds of movement in the companionway cued him that stevedores had already come aboard to offload *Hanseatic,* or possibly that the mean-spirited chief steward was sneaking in to continue making life difficult for his substituted whipping boy.

Then the hatch of his cargo bay was opened, and a softly spoken voice said, "Jamie!"

Silverthorne clumsily whipped himself around. "Henderson!"

"Shhhh, keep a lid on it." The redhead had grown a wispy auburn beard. Clutching the handle of a black medical valise, he closed the hatch. "Scheme's gone sour. We're in a foot race."

"To … get me off?"

Henderson's grimace confirmed it. "Be nip and tuck, Jamie. They must've backtracked you to the Denver airport and on to Raketen-flugplatz Pacific. We're still in the ball game, but …"

James glanced anxiously at the closed hatch. "Listen, the chief steward's liable to—"

"Uh-uh," denied the other. "He got sleepy sudden like, won't bother anyone for hours. Hate to say it, but it's the bottom of the ninth with two outs and only one runner left on base. You, my good and dear friend Professor Silverthorne, laying down a sacrifice bunt won't buy us a thing other than the third out. It's either Hail Mary time or go for a longshot home run. Now listen close, okay?"

Talking fast, Henderson outlined what James was to do right after entering *Walküre Raumstation.* "Thorium's in convenience locker four twenty-nine, third tier on the left as you go in the tran-sient passengers lounge." He opened the medical valise, handed James a plastic keycard. "We're docked in a zenith berth, so you'll have to lug the shielded, heavy-as-hell lunchbox down into the nadir berthing stack and ask for Chris Faigele, a maintenance tech well known to everyone down there. Tell him a dirty joke so he'll know you aren't a ringer. He'll install the thorium, prime the Lebe device, fit you into the special ablative vacuum gear he's rigged, attach your thruster and the other paraphernalia, and take you to the airlock you'll use. Bernard's last encrypted e-mail said your false molar was in place, so here's your return ticket."

Rummaging in the black bag, the redhead handed over a small capsule. "It's pre-tuned to a specific Gregorian calendar date on another timeline, so insert it in the phony tooth ASAP. The come-back drill matches all your other jaunts: twist that tooth while pressing down hard and your accumulated temporal potential will snap you back into Carlsbad's reception chamber like an unleashed rubber band." He felt for something deeper in the valise. After a barely audible click, his stern expression gave way to a rueful grimace.

"No, Henny!" James cringed at sight of the timer, a pair of wrapped-together gelignite bars.

"Afraid it's the way she falls out, Jamie. I'll try to buy you ten, fifteen minutes—more if I can figure out how to do it. A major distraction's badly needed to keep the all the uniforms guessing and maybe hold off a bit before combing this orbiting tin can to try and run you to ground. Don't fret about me. I've got an arm-long list of scores to settle.

"One last word, then I have to scat. Far as I know, you have zero space experience, but the size and purpose of what you've got to do is … Try hard to pretend you're an experienced space hand, and do what Faigele tells you. Suited-up out in vacuum, lower the p-suit's headpiece reticle—Chris'll coach you on how to use it like a horizon sensor—and align your attitude either feet-wet or feet-dry, with Walküre's orbital vector facing directly toward the planet's distant, blue-tinged limb. Their hoity-toity Raumstation's in a fairly low orbit, so transfer injection from this perigee should phase you in with earthspin nineteen-forty, or close as the number crunchers could calculate. From what I saw while *Hanseatic* was in ascent boost, the timing looked pretty good, but you could have a short wait until Europe rolls over the horizon.

"Pray for no dense cloud cover," he continued. "Soon as the British Isles peek over the limb, rotate your backside to the line of flight, but make sure to stay vertical relative to the substellar wet- or dry-feet point beneath your boots, and chin the red lever. If there *is* cloud cover, you'll have to interpolate the substellar point from whatever distant terrain you can spot. Clear so far?"

Having grown more nervous with every spoken word, James nodded mutely.

Henderson's grunt of approval was no more than marginally

reassuring. "The retrofire sequence," he warned, "will kick hell out of you despite your low relative mass. This big bucket's orbital velocity equates to beaucoup kinetic energy, and that's what has to be nullified to a point that allows you fall almost straight down into the atmosphere. The yellow chin lever's a backup in case the red switch bilges. But it won't, so don't sweat it.

"Then comes the reentry heat wave," added Henderson. "Don't let it scare the liver out of you. In freefall, an aneroid switch will auto-trigger the suit's drogue chute to keep you below terminal velocity, then retro-temporal transposition will take you out of the p-suit at about six klicks altitude and automatically pop open your chute, hopefully over Germany, Austria, Hungary, or somewhere in between. The ocean is no problem, but f'Chrissake, steer the chute away from any lakes, rivers, or streams you may be dropping into, or more importantly mountains. Come down over the Alps, Dolomites, or whatever, and you'll have to do some fancy riser work to change direction. Try and get your bearings terrainwise while still on high. Got all that?"

"I ... think so, Henny."

"Terrific! Shake my mitt, then hang out here in the cargo bay until the passengers are offloaded. We're betting the whole damn farm on you, Jamie. Let us down and I promise to come back and haunt you." Medical valise in hand, Henderson opened the hatch and vanished in the passageway.

* * *

Standing on an elevated pallet in the haberdashery fitting room clad only in briefs, an undershirt, and gartered calf-length stockings, Erich Lustmann condescended to let a clerk take, one at a time, tape measurements and call out figures to an assistant.

The establishment's elderly chief tailor fussed inconspicuously behind the employees and client and regarded the tall, distinguished looking customer with frank curiosity. "Your pardon, sir, but If I recall correctly, you also mentioned a need for undergarments?"

From his high stance, "Herr Klasse" looked down at the tailor literally as well as figuratively. "A half dozen undershirts and briefs should suffice. I also require several white linen dress shirts. My luggage, you see, was dispatched by the railroad fools to some unknown destination."

The tailor clucked sympathetically. "Most regrettable, sir."

"I would be the very last to argue," said Lustmann, disgust written plainly in his aristocratic, clean-shaven features. "Without the prompt assistance of your excellent establishment," he added, "I would be traipsing about Berlin in travel garments."

"It is our distinct pleasure to be of service in any way we can, sir. Please allow me to verify your original wishes." The tailor consulted a note pad. "You expressed a wish for—"

"A pair of worsted woolen business suits," supplied Lustmann, "tailored precisely per the sample I tried on, one dark brown, the other dark gray. I should also like a pair of summer-weight linen suits, one tan, and a second in pastel blue, also tailored per the sample."

"*Ja, ja,* it shall be done exactly as you desire, sir." The tailor consulted a calendar. "Will it be convenient to return for the fittings in, shall we say six business days?"

"That won't be necessary. I'll be staying at the Adlon. Have everything sent there."

"Your pardon," objected the tailor, "but without proper fittings you run the risk of—"

"I realize you mean well," interrupted Lustmann, "but I want you to honor my request, *bitte.*"

By no means ingenuous, the veteran tailor had provided custom uniform fittings for any number of ranking military and *SS* officers. Early in the present session, while the gentleman's sleeve length was being measured, the tailor had noted the *SS* blood-type tattoo inside his raised left arm. "Perhaps," he suggested, "we can also interest you in a new uniform, sir."

A sharp look from Herr Klasse preceded his stern negative head shake.

"Your pardon, sir. I meant no offense and wished only to inquire. May I also say the briefs you wear are, uh … somewhat unusual. I have ever seen anything quite like them."

Lustmann pursed his lips self-consciously, wondering what the tailor might say if told his jockey shorts had been—that is, *would be* purchased in far off Argentina two decades in the future. "My undergarments were made to special order," he said and changed the subject. "I should also like a few ready-to-wear items. Nothing stylish or custom tailored, just a jacket and two pairs of trousers to make myself presentable until the more formal garments are delivered."

"We shall be delighted to accommodate your every wish, sir."

After the customer had dressed in the off-the-shelf garments he had selected, the haberdashery's owner took it upon himself to personally tender the bill. "Merely a deposit is needed today, Herr Klasse. The balance will become due when you return to—"

"My whereabouts often change on short notice. It will be more convenient to settle now." Riffling a wad of banknotes, Lustmann counted out the quoted sum.

Unaccustomed to accepting payment in large-denomination currency, the proprietor made only a token effort to hide his surprise before ordering a clerk to prepare a seldom-used cash receipt.

Making ready to leave, Lustmann asked to use the telephone. With operator assistance, he placed a call to Hotel Adlon and reserved a deluxe second-floor suite.

# SEVEN

## *On orbit, DWJ 142*
## *Berlin, Autumn 1939, CE*

Knowing his effort to hurry would attract unwanted attention, James slowed his clumsy, hand-over-hand progress by snubbing his momentum on the freefall safety line and halted at the intersection of passageways to peek around the corner. Cargo containers secured on a conveyor belt were being carried down into *Walküre Raumstation.*

What made him jerk back his head under microgravity was what he suspected was a pair of *Ausland Staatspolizei* assets idly observing the offloading procedure. Henny had promised ten minutes of grace, but a slice of that had already evaporated while he'd waited for the last passengers to disembark. He tried to think of some believable way to convince the goons he was a crewman, and quickly settled on Henny's sincerity scenario as the best bet, but only *if* he had the moxie to pull it off. A dead giveaway would be letting the uniforms see his nervousness or offering misfired responses under questioning. Maybe a pretense of scatterbrained, willy-nilly agitation would suffice.

Rounding the corner on the fly, he gave one long-armed tug on the safety line in the manner of a salted spacehand and sailed headlong into the net rigged under freefall. While the net was recovering from the impetus of his plunge, he reached for a lower strand.

"Here now, you! Where's the fire?" asked one of the watchers.

"I'm a steward aboard *Hanseatic,* sir. I want to—"

"Your ID, *bitte."*

When he came closer, James noted the small round *Sicherheits-dienst* medallion crowned by a *Deutschen Adler* clutching a swastika in its talons gleaming above the chest pocket of the questioner's neatly creased gray tunic.

*SD pros!* The discovery was chilling. *And worst of all,* he thought, *they have been posted on the lookout for a fugitive named Silverthorne!* Hooking an elbow through the rigging, he tugged the wallet from the Raumhansa jumpsuit's slash pocket.

Appraising the forged ID with a neutral expression, the *SD* asset who'd accosted him relayed the information to his partner "Braun, Heinrich G., RH employee 792054."

His companion scanned an electronic *Hanseatic* crew roster, then looked James over. "Where were you born, Heinrich?"

"Düsseldorf, sir."

"A fair city. Why the big sweat to get inboard?"

James hesitated, feigning embarrassment. "This, uh ... young lady, a passenger ..." He glanced sheepishly from one *SD* asset to the other. "Never before have I seen such a *Schatze!* We'll soon be prepping for the return flight, so I thought to, uh ... try and catch up, get her number."

The other asset grinned crookedly. "You know crewmen aren't supposed to chase passengers, Braun. Anyhow, short tryst seems hardly worth the effort, so—"

"Lute!" The *SD* man was tapping his left ear. "Condition Red, Zenith docks!"

"What's the story?"

"No details, just a red-alert summons!" James was rudely poked. "You, back aboard ship now! Enter the station and we'll collar you later, and it won't be a pleasant time, *verstehst du?"* The agents swarmed in tandem down the rigging, out of view.

*Look for me later,* thought James, *and you'll have some search!*

Letting a few seconds slip away to make sure the *SD* assets were out of sight, he hurriedly pulled himself down the rigging and entered what appeared to be a spin elevator compartment and fretted anxiously until the compartment matched rotation with the torus ring housing *Walküre's* counter-rotating, pseudo-gravity segment. After a brief pang of dizziness, he felt minimal pressure on the soles of the Velcro-shod boots and the hatch slid open.

A touch queasy due to his energetic first bout with microgravity, he followed signs, head lowered, trying to hurry without being overly conspicuous, and joined a sprinkling of others going his way along the midway. Locating the transient passenger lounge, he slipped inside, palmed the keycard Henderson had given him, and reconnoitered. Locker 429 opened to expose an oversized metal lunchbox stenciled with the Raumhansa logo. Remembering to breathe again, he offered Henderson a silent, heartfelt salute.

Under *Walküre's* pseudo-gravity spin, the massive lunchbox was difficult to handle. First he tried to nonchalantly lug the burden against his leg, but it spoiled his gait, turned his clumsy progress into an eccentric, gliding lope. He emerged in the nadir berthing stack when a different spin elevator rotated to a stop and ignored a blinking microgravity warning sign urging the use of freefall safety rigging. Clutching the lunchbox handle, he one-handedly tugged his way along a microgravity safety line, awkwardly heading down into the nadir dock area.

He had barely cleared the interlock chamber when an alarm klaxon's intermittent squall warned of a resilient iris beginning to contract around the hatchway at his heels, notifying users that the hermetic hatch was about to close and seal off the stack. His margin of safety was a few meters.

Pressing onward, he passed curious workers swarming into the corridor eager to learn what and apparent fuss inboard was all about. Crossing glances with a man in a pale-green jumpsuit, he snubbed to a halt and asked where he could find a tech named Faigele.

"Ah, Chris. *Ja, ja, t*ry the maintenance depot, just beyond bulk-head sixty-one."

*"Danke!"*

"Hey," the fellow called after him, "what's stirring inboard? Why'd they seal up?"

"Haven't a clue." James pulled his way along the stack. Bulkhead 56, 57 … He ticked off three more, snubbed the nylon safety line to slow his plunge, and came close to losing the lunchbox when inertia made it want to keep moving. *Can't be much time left,* he thought. *Wait, there it is.* Pushing off transversely, he arrested his flight before an open cubicle where a quartet of men in jumpsuits radiated in all orientations facing a flat-panel video monitor blaring an announcement of some kind.

Before he could pulse any of them, someone grabbed his free arm. "Skip the joke; I've heard them all. Didn't think you'd make it."

"Neither did I," admitted James.

"Pass me the freight," urged Faigele, "and come this way!"

* * *

The portly, middle-aged bellman made a feeble effort to conceal his surprise over the amount of Lustmann's gratuity. On this drizzly, overcast Berlin morning, all the suave guest in Suite 204 had requested was a pair of ordinary flashlight batteries and the early bird editions of *Berliner Morgenpost* and *Bild-Zeitung.*

"Most generous of you, sir. Thank you very much." A quick, practiced bow. "If you wish, I will be happy to insert the batteries in your flashlight."

"That won't be necessary." *Or possible,* thought Lustmann, who owned no flashlight.

"Should you require anything else, sir, I remain at your beck and call. Perhaps you would also like a copy of *Völkischer Beobachter,"* he added, referring to the Nazi Party organ.

"An excellent suggestion. And you are . . ?"

"Hans, sir."

"I mean to commend your thoughtfulness to the management, Hans. In addition to *Beobachter,* a bit later in the day you might also bring me the afternoon edition of *Tageblatt?*"

"Delighted to be of further service. Thank you again, sir."

At a dismissive wave from Herr Klasse, the bellman performed an obsequious parting bow and eased the door shut behind him.

Lustmann dialed the hotel operator and requested room service. Though less than palatial, the second-floor suite suited his needs. The parlor featured a balcony overlooking Pariser Platz, and in the near distance the landmark Brandenburger Tör. The suite's amenities included a kitchenette and small refrigerator. In addition to a light breakfast of fresh fruit, Danish pastry, and coffee, he ordered a half case of *Dunkel bier,* caged the phone, and unfolded *Bild-Zeitung.* Skimming the front page, he found it almost as newsworthy as the stone tablets brought down from Mount Sinai by Moses, but he also had a premonition of his mission's impending success. Unsurprisingly, the lead column was captioned by a wire photo of the stern, dark-eyed Führer, his iconic toothbrush mustache intact, and a billed, braid-adorned *Schirmmütze* cap hiding his combed-over cowlick.

The morning edition revived in broad strokes what little he could recall of what he and he alone on the current timeline subconsciously regarded as the "real" Polish campaign. Von Rundstedt's Army Group South had reportedly overrun the Warta River in several places, with Krakow not far ahead of the rampaging Wehrmacht *Heer* forces. To the north, Kluge's Fourth Army had begun linking up with Kuchler's Third Army Group coming in from East Prussia, their combined aim to encircle the Polish defensive forces while howling Stuka dive bombers and JU-88 *Schnellbombers* decimated the rear. *Bild-Zeitung* went on to report how the Poles had mistakenly stationed their defensive units too close to the German border, a tactical error allowing the main Wehrmacht juggernaut to sweep past and grossly disrupt desperate Polish troop and cavalry movements. A pair of enemy divisions was cited as having been shredded as they pulled back through the resulting corridor to hopefully regroup.

He paused, refolded the newspaper. Once again, the front-page wire photo of Hitler struck him as oddly wrong in miraculous, for him, second-time-around Berlin, as he couldn't stop thinking of the capital. The photo made him realize he had not shared a reverence for *Der Führer* with his *SS* compatriots during the pre-redux wartime era he had experienced, but privately characterized the Austrian corporal as a malignant narcissist randomly endowed with a talent for bombastic, inflammatory demagoguery. He vividly remembered how, at the start of this same-yet-other war, he of the mustache, drooping forelock, hypnotic dark eyes, and rehearsed gesticulations had stridently talked his way into leadership of a splintered collection of street thugs and radical misfits who had audaciously labeled their movement the German Workers Party.

Not until serving months incarcerated in Landsberg Prison for instigating a reckless, premature overthrow of the government in some *München Bierstube* had Hitler's polemics begun swaying the wise heads of government led by elderly Chancellor Hindenburg and proceeded to hypnotize the vast majority of Germans with his volcanic rhetoric, then convincing many business and professional military leaders how marvelous it would be to view the world through *his* eyes.

Unbelievable as that was in the resurrected now of 1939, it remained hardly possible to believe a shrewd, lowlife toad like Adolph Hitler had managed to talk his way into the leadership of all Germany, and thus ensure the birth of *Dritte Reich*. Yet in what he simply could not stop thinking of as the first-time-around time-line, *Der Führer's* virulent anti-Semitic hatred had been the sole virtue to which he himself had subscribed and had been reborn in the now. After all, the global struggle he had earned the supreme honor of revising had been a direct result of the global Zionist conspiracy coupled with the economic debacle that had befallen the Fatherland and most other nations in the wake of the outrageous French and British reparations demands to which Imperial Germany had succumbed in the wake of the Great War to End War. His temper flared, an emotional spike marking his usual reaction to the injustice of all that had devolved from the obscene armistice in France.

Opening *Morgenpost* brought a thin smile of approval. After day-long discussions in Parliament that encouraged bitter public opposition to the pacifist line taken by Chamberlain's government regarding the invasion of Poland, England had decided to present the Reich with an ultimatum.

An *ultimatum!* Lustmann chuckled. *The mice,* he thought, *again seek to bell the cat. Morgenpost* also reported that the National Service Act passed in Parliament called for conscripting all able-bodied men between the ages of 19 and 41. The French Council of Ministers had vowed to do something similar, issuing an addendum declaring that *La Belle* France had every intention of fulfilling its obligation to Poland. In another column, he learned that ten squadrons of Royal Air Force Advanced Air Strike Forces had been flown across the Channel and were now investing French aerodromes. In Rome, it seemed fascist *wunderkind* Benito Mussolini had declared Italy a neutral nation and then immediately called for a five-power peace conference.

Herr Klasse laughed aloud after reading the Mussolini tidbit. If Hitler was a malignant narcissist, *Il Duce Fascismo* had years of study ahead of him before he could contemplate such lofty status. Forever a hindrance, never an aid, the alliance with Italy brought to mind the defamatory joke circulating among *SS* trainees in the aftermath of Mussolini's febrile military disaster in Abyssinia. Some entrepreneur, according to the jocular tidbit, had for some reason invested in several boxcar loads of surplus Italian military rifles, for which the posted sales advertisement read, "Never fired, only dropped once."

In an unanticipated flush of good humor, Lustmann chuckled again and rose to answer the door chime. He admitted a pair of waiters bearing a breakfast tray and a half case of beer. They reacted to his extravagant tip with even more surprise than had the pudgy bellman, Hans.

After a Spartan breakfast, Lustmann set the tray out in the hall for pickup, locked and chained his suite's entry door, and carefully taped the flashlight batteries together end-to-end. Taking down the aluminum carryall from a high shelf in the bedchamber's walk-in closet, he carried it into the sitting room, grounded the lowermost battery per instructions, and touched the exposed positive terminal of the upper battery to the off-color rivet doubling as an anode. He repeated the process to be on the safe side, unlatched the lid, cautiously swung it up, and breathed a sigh of relief. Lifting the top half dozen sheets of nitrocellulose flash paper, he sank into an armchair beside the French doors leading out to the balcony. He intently burned the compressed, crisply edited text into his mind.

Feeling disgruntled minutes later, he replaced the documents, closed and latched the lid, and replaced the carryall in the bedchamber. The rampage into Poland had taken *Heer* Wehrmacht forces all the way to the Vistula, where they had been reportedly halted to keep faith as signatory to Foreign Affairs Minister von Ribbentrop's prior feat of arranging a non-aggression pact between Germany and the Soviet Union. The Polish *Blitzkrieg* was soon to be succeeded by far greater triumphs, specifically incursions into Belgium and the Netherlands, leading to the subsequent conquest of France, and culminating in the dual occupations of Norway and Denmark. Yet reading the capsulized account of the war's early phase had driven home a singularly displeasing fact: he had arrived in 1939 Berlin prematurely, so much so that there would be little or nothing to proactively do in the coming months. Mid-1940 would have been a much more appropriate period to be snapped back into the current timeline, since no conceivable reason existed to tamper in the least, most modest way, with military successes piled atop one another.

His first major redirection appeared to be attempting to influence the outcome of a crucial event about which Colonel Stoltz and the ODESSA brain trust had lectured the candidates to near distraction, a matter of rectifying Hitler's inexplicable desire to hold back defensive forces to hinder the evacuation from the continent of Allied forces stranded near the Belgian port of Dunkerque. Yet that momentous gaffe would not take place until late May and early June of the ensuing year, months ahead in the now timeline.

What that fat, brandy-swilling pig Churchill had called "a miracle of deliverance"—Operation Dynamo—that resulted in the rescue of several hundred thousand British and Allied military personnel stranded on the beaches by a huge flotilla of large and medium ships and small watercraft, had been such an utterly illogical blunder by *Der Führer* that the cited schemes counseling methods to correct a "reprise" of Hitler's monumental judgment error would warrant his total concentration. Many other, more subtle homework items would also require study and staying atop the news before finalizing an introductory letter to some as yet undetermined destination.

Once a much-medaled field-grade Wehrmacht officer, Manfred Stoltz had possessed a more comprehensive overview of WWII than any other of the ODESSA expatriates. In describing what he believed had gone right on the battlefield, at sea, and in the air, former *Oberst* Stoltz had often emphasized what had indeed gone wrong on the battlefield and in Berlin, and why. Between times, he had incessantly drummed his lessons into the half dozen assembled candidates, listing various means, methods, and avenues by which military and political leadership opinions and decisions simply had to be funneled into the Nazi hierarchy by blatant or subtle sermons aimed at overcoming the bureaucratic failures and inefficiencies that had continually plagued the military and the nation's leadership and exacerbated both types of mistakes, such as the one affecting the fiasco at Dunkerque, as well as numerous others further downstream.

The lag and hiatus in jet-propelled aircraft and rocketry development, not to mention aircraft mass production, were prime examples of precisely what had to be eliminated or minimized. Heavy bomber production simply *had* to be strongly encouraged, especially after some pea-brained, self-satisfied Luftwaffe official had insisted, like a true Nazi bureaucrat, that all heavy bombers would be limited to two engines, not the four needed to provide long-range operations and significant bomb-load capacity. Even more asinine had been the way another official had dictated that all medium bombardment aircraft must also incorporate dive bomber capability, an idiotic dictum. Yet, dealing with such esoteric matters would have to be addressed later.

Lustmann opened the glass-paneled French doors and stepped out on the balcony. The drizzle had ceased, but a gloomy gray overcast lingered over Berlin. Leaning on the balustrade, he lit a cigarette, smoking hungrily with a chill morning breeze on his cheek, and idly studied an attractive *Fraulein* ankling past on the sidewalk below.

Thousands of times the funds any normal individual would consider ample were locked away in the carryall, a gross understatement, really. ODESSA had supplied him with a fantastic cache of large denomination *Reichsbank* notes that in the now timeline were no longer worthless stacks of paper. In addition to flash-paper accounts of the course then-WWII had taken in all military or political theaters, not to mention the step-by-step corrective flash-paper "blueprints" suggesting means and methods of carrying out his mission, it was reassuring to realize more cash than anyone could ever spend was bundled in the carryall. It was a treasure he intended to deposit in increments as a safeguard against theft or being charred, should he forget himself and open the carryall in an unsafe way.

His mood changed suddenly. He looked forward to the months of fall, winter, and spring, a period better filled with good times instead of languishing in the doldrums. His eyes moist, he hungrily followed another *Fraulein's* high-heeled progress along the sidewalk. Who could fault his notion to enjoy himself during the ensuing hiatus in his mission?

Smiling, the future *Deutschen* hero of heroes concluded, *No one!*

\* \* \*

Silverthorne found it difficult to keep up with the fast-moving technician. Toting the all-important heavy lunchbox, Faigele pulled himself into a nearby airlock service compartment, where racked tools and a pair of slack, matte-silver pressure suits were stowed on the curved bulkhead. He battened the hatch behind Silverthorne. "What do you mass?"

"Just under eighty kaygee, stripped."

"Good, good! Henderson's calculations pegged you a few grams heavier. Stay put until I call you. I have to do a quick job installing the thorium, then arming the device." Lugging the shielded lunchbox, Faigele pushed off and disappeared headfirst in the airlock chamber.

Hour-long minutes evaporated with glacial velocity before something seemed nudged *Walküre Raumstation* and a barely audible low-frequency rumble rattled loose equipment.

Frowning, Faigele appeared in the airlock chamber. "Henderson?"

Silverthorne's constricted throat did not seem to be working properly. He nodded bleakly.

"News of a zenith stack bomb scare blew through the dock just before you showed up. Hurry now! The topside hubbub might cause traffic control radar to miss you altogether. Strip to the skin and get into these things."

"How about the instructions on how to—"

"I thought Henny had given you a blow-by-blow game plan. Not to shove the risk off on a greenhorn, but no minutes are left to go through the drill item by item. Do your best to remember every word Henny had to say, but get busy now!"

James ripped open the Raumhansa jumpsuit's closure strip. Clumsy under microgravity, he got out of the garment and briefs, and then fumbled to don clean, old-fashioned woolen underwear, a tan cotton shirt, well-worn lederhosen and calf-length woolen stockings. Floating topsy-turvy in midair, he let Faigele tie the leather thongs of both scuffed hiking boots and unfold a worn tweed jacket with leather patches at the elbows. He helped James don it and shoved a tightly folded Tyrolean felt hat with a feather in the band in the jacket's side pocket.

Next came a faded canvas rucksack. "Strap it round your middle," urged Faigele. "The parachute's a backpack." The technician's nimble fingers mated the paired, quick-disconnect aluminum bands supporting the Lebe device and tightened them under Silverthorne's arms. "Not what could be called comfortable, but it'll have to do."

James let the other help cram him, gear, chute, rucksack and all into an overly bulky, oddly configured silver pressure suit. Only a small peephole was left in the convex headpiece lens, with the remainder thickly sprayed with some sort of hardened, white gunk. Moving behind him, Faigele attached a pair of slender, unconnected thruster bottles to mounting pads on the rear of the suit's utility belt.

"Chin the blue test circuit lever on the left side of your headpiece," instructed Faigele.

James glanced up into the prism viewer, craned his neck, and depressed the lever.

"*Ganz gut!* You have juice to the squib." Warning James to keep his chin clear of the lever, the tech twisted home and mated the thruster bottle's electrical connectors. "In a nutshell, your drill goes like this: green's for transfer orbit, but re-rigged for this usage, and red's the backup. Your mass is fairly low, so the thrusters should prove adequate to null all but a smidge of your orbital momentum."

"Velocity?"

"Close enough to not argue about. Retrothrust should null most if not all the orbital kinetic energy stored in your small mass and p-suit, which is teensy compared to that of *Walküre,* and allow your descent only a red hair short of falling straight down into the atmosphere. When you sense the first fringes of air tearing past," added Faigele, speaking fast, "a reddish glow will build around your suit. Don't let the flaming re-entry bath scare you; the heat shield will slide down over your headpiece lens. I'll seal you now and you're on your way. *Gluckauf!*"

Swaddled like an infant in heavy outdoor clothing, and enclosed and sealed in an unfamiliar pressure suit, with the cumbersome rucksack and bulky parachute pack hindering his every movement, James nodded his thanks to the technician. Faigele returned the nod, left the airlock chamber on the fly, and commanded the inner hatch to cycle closed.

Feeling like an ungainly teddy bear, his vacuum gear began ballooning around him as air pressure fell in the chamber. His own unnaturally loud breathing tended to drown out the faint, conducted sound of pumps scavenging air that gradually dwindled and then died when the egress hatch light winked green and the outer hatch automatically cycled open.

Heart in his throat, James cautiously stretched his right gauntlet out into vacuum, felt around for the handhold Faigele had described, touched it, then convulsively seized the slim bar with both gauntlets. Drawing a deep, agonized breath, he clutched the bar in a death grip and slowly pulled himself out into space.

The endless night formed a circumambient, star-flecked back-drop to the immensely curved, glowing planet that, for whatever reason, looked as if it was out rather than down beneath his suit's boots. Three vessels limned in reflected earthlight were berthed in *Walküre's* nadir stack—a pair of bloated, stub-winged aerospace shuttlecraft identical to the *Hanseatic,* and a blunt-ended, wingless space-to-space lunar transport known irreverently as a "boxcar" by military personnel. Below him, whether or not it looked like that was the proper direction, the rumbling, cloud-draped face of Earth struck him as incredibly beautiful.

James clumsily wrenched his p-suited self about per Henny's les-son until he faced downward, then planted both boots against *Walküre's* metal skin, squatted with the help of the handholds on either side of the hatch, flexed the pressure suit's knees to their articulation limits, drew an agonized breath that sounded overly loud in his own ears, let go of the handholds, and drove hard with both legs.

Sailing headfirst through vacuum, he waited until his modest momentum had hopefully carried him far enough away to at least lessen his p-suit's backscatter in *Walküre's* traffic control radar mon-itors. He threw out his left arm and leg the way Henderson had coached. The resultant gradually rotated him about the suit's short axis. Several tries of experimentation taught him the headpiece reticle could be adroitly used. After two more tries, he managed to orient his attitude toward the distant, ethereal pale-blue limb of Earth, a task made difficult by the small window in thermal protec-tion compound surrounding a clear circle in the p-suit's faceplate lens.

Correcting his slow, residual minor-axis tumble by throwing his head back against the quilted padding of the headpiece, he semi-stabilized his line of flight. Stars forming the Dipper's curved handle swam into his limited field of view. Moving his arms and legs in unison, he turned himself one hundred and eighty degrees about the long axis of his p-suit. The Earth's limb again crept into the reticle and he awkwardly restabilized. Tolling the passing seconds, he began a "Thousand and one, thousand and two …" countdown. There was absolutely no sensation of motion, though he'd been told that relative to the planet's surface, the momentum of his minute mass compared to that of gigantic *Walküre Raumstation* was taking him into a higher orbit.

In minutes, the toe and lower ankle of the Italian boot, plus a fringe of Sicily's northern coastline, appeared through a gap in the cloud cover obscuring most of the Alpine region. What had to be a slice of Europe was faintly discernible and what might be a short, fuzzy portion of the French coast as well. If the British Isles had already rolled over the limb, they were invisible beneath dense clouds.

After experimentally extending and retracting his arms and legs, he managed to rotate clockwise about the suit's long axis, stabilized, and found himself flying backside first toward the planet's cloudy limb, his long axis orientation roughly normal, that is perpendicular to the planet beneath his feet.

With a surge of apprehension, he closed his eyes tightly and chinned the green lever. An exceptionally loud conducted roar threatened to rupture his ear drums, and a strong, continuous shove kicked him so hard in the small of the back that his lungs emptied explosively.

# EIGHT

## *Berlin, Spring 1940*
## *Fall 1939 CE*

Impeccably clad in a double-breasted gray business suit, Lustmann checked the contrasting four-in-hand knot of his red-and-blue paisley tie. He admired his appearance in the walk-in closet's floor-to-ceiling mirror, then tried on the black felt homburg, adjusted the curled brim, turned left, turned right, and decided it made him look like a pompous politician. Doffing the hat, he used both hands to smooth back his overlong crop of wheat-colored hair and decided to ask at the desk if the hotel could recommend a local barber.

Taking up his new ebony walking stick, he stepped into the hallway, made sure the door of his suite was securely locked, bypassed the elevator, loped downstairs two risers at a time, and made his way across the lobby looking neither left nor right. Handing over his latch key at the desk, he casually inquired if there were any messages for Suite 204.

"Let me see what the night attendant left, sir." The youthful clerk made a project of consulting a sheaf of spindled notes. "*Nein*, Herr Klasse. Nothing for you."

"*Viel Dank.*" His ridiculous-though-necessary query had confirmed his pose as a transient Swedish business executive. In the unlikely event of a positive response, he would have dashed back upstairs, abandoned everything except the carryall, and fled from the Adlon in sheer panic.

The uniformed doorman touched his billed cap at sight of the tall, distinguished looking gentleman who emerged from the Adlon, briefcase in hand. Having paid a premium to ensure the leased car and driver would be on dawn-to-midnight call twenty-four-seven, he found the black Mercedes-Benz Saloon occupying curb space nominally reserved for taxis. Standing beside it, the driver held the rear door for his passenger.

"Reichsbank," Lustmann said tersely.

The building's monolithic, sparingly windowed façade had been designed to impress passersby. A former *SS* officer, Lustmann knew Reichsbank had been, and in the miraculously resurrected now was certain to be, the repository of untold millions in confiscated *SS* wealth. The main chamber's vaulted ceiling and ultraconservative décor enhanced its solemn atmosphere of rock-solid integrity, while sustaining Prussia's love affair with regimentation, and featured a proper place for everything, with everything in its proper place.

Lustmann refused to make eye contact with the well-tailored clerk who came forward to welcome him. He looked through the fellow as if his existence was superfluous and paced along a row of offices in leisurely fashion. Conscious of the eyes following his stroll, he glanced in passing at the nameplate beside each door and halted outside the office of a comely brunette with an elegantly coifed, upswept hairdo he judged to be in her mid-to-late thirties. A polished brass nameplate identified the occupant as: G. L. SHARPE, NEW ACCOUNTS MANAGER.

G. L. Sharpe's gray-blue eyes widened with interest at sight of the debonair gentleman leaning on an ebony walking stick just outside her door. Cutting short a phone conversation, she caged the handset and rose gracefully behind the desk. *"Wie kann ich Ihnen helfen, mein Herr?"*

"Good day to you, er ..." He glanced again at her nameplate. "Fraulein Sharpe, is it? I am Herr Klasse. I should like to discuss opening a special account."

Soft-spoken yet businesslike, she smiled and gently corrected him. "I am *Frau* Sharpe, sir. Reichsbank will be delighted to try and accommodate to your every need, Herr Klasse. Won't you come in and have a seat?"

Lustmann accepted the invitation, hesitating upon noting the miniature replica of a Knight's Cross pendant on a gold chain against the woman's stylish dark-green dress. "Your pardon, *Frau* Sharpe." Seating himself in a straight-backed chair, he stared at the facsimile medal. "I hope you will excuse my forwardness, but I assume it was a loved one who earned the signal badge of honor you're wearing."

Her manner unselfconscious, Frau Sharpe said, "A posthumous award, I'm afraid"

"Oh, do forgive me! Surely such a tragedy did not take place during the current campaign."

"No, it was ... It happened some time ago. My husband was an airman, a pilot assigned to the Kondor Legion in Spain."

"Please overlook my indelicacy for reminding you of such a terrible loss, Frau Sharpe. Unless memory fails me, wasn't that the Luftwaffe air wing sent to support Franco's struggle against the Communist riffraff daring to call themselves Spanish Loyalists?"

"You are most considerate, Herr Klasse. It was just as you say." Frau Sharpe blinked. "You spoke of opening a special account?"

"Indeed. I was told Reichsbank offers private numbered accounts."

"Absolutely confidential accounts, of course, but not coded numerically," she explained. "Swiss financial institutions used to provide that service, including BIS in Basel, with whom we work closely. Our private accounts are keyed to a client's restricted data and unique background information, with access via a codeword or short phrase of the client's choosing."

"Ah, restricted. Excellent! It's an operative term of paramount interest to me, since it will be necessary for all my financial transactions to be conducted with utmost discretion."

"On that you may rest assured, Herr Klasse. Discretion is a Reichsbank speciality."

"Oh, I'm certain of that." Without asking permission, Lustmann rose and closed the office door. "You may also believe it a peculiar demand that each of my transactions be conducted on a cash-only basis. I represent a certain highly placed executive who insists upon anonymity, and for whom I act as a trusted agent in all of his financial dealings …"

Herr Klasse glibly spun his rehearsed tale, explaining how deposits and withdrawals would occasionally involve international wire transfers of significant sums. He assured the attractive accounts manager how it would ordinarily be unthinkable to take a stranger into his confidence, but had decided it needed to be done in order to avoid any curiosity that might arise regarding certain unusual but necessary procedures and arrangements, believing it best to achieve mutual understanding right at the start.

"In your case, Frau Sharpe, I can't imagine the widow of a fallen warrior who's made the ultimate sacrifice for the Reich being less than worthy of implicit trust."

A slight frown deepened the cleft between Frau Sharpe's brows. "Significant cash transactions of large amounts are quite common at Reichsbank. I see no problem."

Lustmann's warm, disarming smile erased the accounts manager's expression of mild concern. With the urgency of a confession meant to ease her mind, he described being burdened with the task of aiding to ensure the continuing availability of the finest grade of Swedish steel the Reich was procuring for the armaments industry, adding as a corollary endeavor his duty to assist in encouraging Sweden's ongoing neutrality as a principal supplier of superior carbon-steel in great demand during wartime. He told her in passing that he would be staying at the Adlon for weeks or months but would occasionally travel home to his estate near Malmö. He concluded by saying he sincerely hoped Frau Sharpe realized how vital it would be to sustain the clandestine nature of all prospective financial dealings.

"Your confidence in Reichsbank," said Gerda Sharpe matter-of-factly, "will not be misplaced, Herr Klasse. I see no obstacle to satisfying your stated requirements. May I ask the amount of your first deposit?"

"A million and one-half in large-denomination Reichsmarks," he declared, his manner purposely offhand. He reached down and meaningfully hefted the hand-tooled leather briefcase.

Frau Sharpe did not react to the stated sum other than telling him there were several forms he had to fill out with information the bank guaranteed to be held in total confidence in their vault. "Afterward, you may select the private codeword or phrase that will permit access to your account. Nothing too common, yet easily remembered, but not written down anywhere."

Lustmann dipped his head. "Thank you, Frau Sharpe. I am entirely at your disposal."

* * *

For Silverthorne, the atmospheric reentry fire bath had been ten times more terrifying than Chris Faigele predicted. The preset barometric switch commanding the Lebe device had keyed automatic retro-temporal transposition at what he had assumed was the proper altitude. His prior research junkets had made him all too familiar with the brief, gut-wrenching sensation that once again had wracked him upon being precipitately flung backward from one quantum timeline to another. Falling free of the scorched custom vacuum gear the instant transposition had taken him out of it bodily, he'd yanked the parachute's D-ring hard. The canopy had deployed, unfurling partway before it popped open, rudely jerking him to what felt like a sudden stop in midair.

From on high, only scattered portions of the countryside below had been visible through a patchwork of drifting clouds. Laboring to breathe as he descended through the rarefied air on high, he had scanned the surrounding terrain, randomly searching for a relatively open, lightly wooded area. Snowy peaks indistinct in the bluish haze of distance had loomed above a faintly cloudy undercast. The sheen of what might have been a far-off body of water had been visible nestled among the distant the foothills.

A novice parachutist, he had sensed the ground coming up faster than anticipated, the impression due more to proximity than velocity. He'd almost been swept across an unpaved cow path of a dirt road, but the breeze had not carried the chute as far as it might have. Instead of coming down boots first in an inviting plowed field, he had dropped into a patch of shaggy firs bordering a patch of denser forest. Instinctively crossing his raised arms to protect his face, he'd felt fragrant boughs whip past, then a ripping jolt that left him dangling in the risers, with the breeze soughing through the layered branches around him and either the mid-morning or mid-afternoon sun warm on his cheek.

Overhead, the parachute's torn canopy was impaled on the tree-top, the ground directly below hidden by spreading fir branches. Judging from a stretch of plowed field he could see beyond the rutted dirt lane, he estimated dangling no more than three meters above the ground. He could either hang suspended by the chute's risers and wait for what might happen next, or take a chance, unlatch the harness, and shove aside the limbs as he fell past to the ground. Still, anything could be under the tree—a fence, a farmer's bull, anything.

A childish voice startled him by calling, *"Dort ist er!"*

A pair of teenage boys came dashing along the lane toward his tree. The shout in German had elated Silverthorne; it meant he had come down in Switzerland, Austria, or, best of all, somewhere within the German borders.

A third, younger boy halted behind the first two and waved to James excitedly.

"Are you able to get down, sir?" The two older boys were standing in the lane, gazing up at him.

"Yes, I believe so," called James. "Is there anything beneath me under the tree?"

"Patches of grass, sir, and patches of muddy ground."

"*Ganz gut!* Stand back, *Jungen!*" Undoing the chest catch, he lifted his arms and slid out of the harness. Fir limbs drooped under his weight, but his feeble effort to push them aside proved futile. Thrashing the air for balance, he twisted aside, landing canted sideways, and rolled on his left shoulder. "Whew, that last step is a crusher!"

"Are you injured in any way, sir?"

"No, not at all." James gained his feet stiffly and brushed off the forest debris clinging to his tweed jacket. "Good thing you three happened along when you did."

"Where did you drop from, sir? No balloon or aeroplane was in sight when you drifted down."

Lacking a chance to open the backpack and examine the forged papers, James could not remember the cover identities Omsley had invented for him. He fell back on his role as a Raumhansa purser. "My name is Braun, Heinrich Braun. What are you fellows called?"

The boys introduced themselves as Karl, Stefan, and Heinz. Knowing his stock of believable tales was limited, James explained that he'd been soaring in a glider. "Caught in a strong updraft with no way to lose altitude, it then became a question of jumping or being carried higher and freezing to death or suffocating from lack of air to breathe."

"*Wundershöen!*" exclaimed young Heinz.

Karl was persistent. "Your craft was too high to be seen, Herr Braun?"

"I was very high indeed," assured James, which was certainly true enough.

"What is that odd, er … shiny belt thing around your waist?"

"Oh, part of the apparatus that holds one in place while soaring." He fingered the retro-temporal generator's shell, now bereft of the Lebe device and thorium isotope power source. "I jumped too quickly to think about disconnecting it."

"I shouldn't wonder that you were very frightened," said Heinz.

"Oh, I certainly was!" admitted James. The flaming atmospheric reentry had not induced ordinary run-of-the-mill fright, but a siege of naked terror that lasted much too long. James stretched and stamped his boots to settle the rucksack on his shoulders. "I must be more careful in the future. Tell me, how far away is the nearest town?"

Karl grinned. "Winterlingen is only about three kilometers down this lane, Herr Braun. Yet, until now I have never heard anyone call it a town."

James returned the boy's grin. *"Danke.* I really should be on my way. By the way, my parachute looks torn beyond mending. You fellows can have it if you figure out how to get it down."

The notion excited the youngsters, who began arguing about ways, means, and methods of recovering the ruined chute.

Swinging a leg over the split-rail fence, James set out along the rutted dirt lane. It *had* to be Germany, no borders to cross! He congratulated himself for surviving the crisis at the chalet, the unseen-but-nerve-wracking chase that followed, capped by the ordeal of descending from orbit. He was *here,* striding along a rural lane in the spring sunshine of Adolf Hitler's adolescent *Dritte Reich.* In the best of spirits, he thought of how Henderson had worked wonders paving the way for him to reach the ground alive and well, still in one piece. Recalling Henny's sacrifice caused his euphoria to wane. The redhead's martyrdom had affected him deeply.

Once the parachute retrievers were out of view, he stepped behind a copse of roadside trees to relieve himself. Undoing the straps, he eased the rucksack from his shoulders, unclipped the aluminum shell that once secured the Lebe device, thrust it into a thicket, and pulled loose brush over it. Opening the rucksack, he pocketed the meager wad of currency, stowed the handful of jewelry in an inside jacket pocket, and sat down. Resting his back against the bole of a fir tree, he examined the forged documents.

Omsley had wisely concocted dual mythical identities, and either fictitious individual would do, since both were purported citizens of nations allied with Nazi Germany's cause. The photos of Vittorio D'Agati, a Milanese history professor, and Hans Steyr, a freelance Salzburg journalist, were identical digital shots lifted from the *Vergangenkarte* he had applied for in *DWJ* 134, an invalid, meaningless date in the now of what he was almost certain southern Nazi Germany circa 1940 of the Common Era.

One slip-up that compromised the Austrian cover he had chosen to use might also undermine the atemporization process, something he more than anyone knew to be a prerequisite for visiting any past era, and doubly so in the crucial now of what he had always thought of as the War Years. The question he asked himself was whether he was enough of an actor to pass himself off as an Austrian journalist. Austria had been reportedly annexed to *Dritte Reich* circa 1938 in every tome he had studied. Wondering if the *Anschluss* had already taken place, he figuratively kicked himself. Fact or fiction, swallowing Austria might be, and possibly … He decided "might, is, was, and would be" were grammatical tenses to be used with care. The pretentious, multi-volume chronicle credited to Goebbels' authorship had been advertised as a meticulous, detailed insider's account of the War of World Liberation, yet here in the redundant reality of what was almost certainly Nazi Germany, the wordy volumes supposedly penned by Goebbels could neither be a history or awarded even minimal credence.

Staring at the forged credentials, he firmed his decision to pose as an Austrian journalist as much simpler to pull off than a cover as an Italian educator. Opening a slim waterproof container from the tweed jacket's inner pocket, he tried to imagine where and how

Bernard's team had unearthed archaic rarities like wooden kitchen matches. Striking one, he consigned the Italian forgeries to the flames, clambered to his feet, and smeared the ashes around with his boot, then redonned the backpack and resumed the hike.

A kilometer farther along the lane he met a lone farmer coming the other way driving a one-horse cart, with whom he exchanged pleasant nods in passing. Another quarter hour of vigorous walking brought a church spire in view above the gentle rise not far ahead. At the crest of the knoll, the community of Winterlingen revealed itself as a picturesque village nestled among rolling slopes. Descending the shallow grade, he entered the narrow main street and moseyed past a half-timbered hostelry, a cobbler's shop, a bakery, a *Bierstube,* several more shops, and a small square of green labeled "Keinath's Park." Uphill on either side, dozens of neat, half-timbered houses were ranged around a steeper rise topped by the church.

Thirsty after the excitement of arrival and exertion, he turned back and entered the wood-paneled taproom. Other than a group of elders clustered around a card game in the rear, he and the barman were the only occupants. The malty, heavy-bodied stein of lager served by a taciturn *Barkellner* exceeded all expectations.

"Ah, that's what I needed!" He ordered a refill. "Do you by chance have a map of the region? High time I found out where my *Wanderjahr* is taking me."

The bearded proprietor left off reading a folded newspaper, rummaged under the bar, and unrolled a dog-eared sheet of parchment, slapping it flat on the polished wooden surface. "You are here, in Winterlingen." Making change for Silverthorne's Reichsmark, the *Barkellner* punched the pads of mechanical cash register, loosing a loud *cha-ching!*

James learned that, purely by chance, he had landed a short distance north of the Danube and east of the Rhine in Württemberg. From on high, it had been the far-off Alps he had glimpsed, with the sheen of Boden See—Lake Constance—agleam in the far distance. Stuttgart, the nearest city of size, lay fifty or more kilometers to the northwest, while Berlin was over six hundred klicks to the northeast. He could adopt an easterly route and work his way toward Munich, and from there head directly to Berlin by rail. Deciding against that course, he chose to strike for Stuttgart on foot—not the most direct route—yet traveling at a leisurely pace would allow him an ample opportunity to begin atemporizing thoroughly.

"Tell me, does this road lead all the way to Stuttgart?"

"*Ja*, from Hechingen, after an easy hike to Tailfingen," said the bartender, pointing out that destination on the map. "Once there, take the footpath over the hills to Hechingen, which is here. Go on and you'll cross the Neckar on the Reutlingen bridge, then its straight on to Stuttgart."

James finished his second stein of beer, thanked the bartender, reseated the backpack on his shoulders, and set off with a will toward Tailfingen.

\* \* \*

Prompt as ever, Hans delivered the morning papers minutes after a truck dropped off the bundles at the intersection of the hotel's service alley and Wilhelmstrasse. Accepting the extravagant tip with profuse gratitude, the bellman bowed and beamed as he exited the suite.

Lustmann yawned, eased open the door to the bedchamber, and peeked in. Gerda Sharpe was still asleep, her long brown hair draped across the pillow, the dim aureole of one fulsome breast peeking at him amidst the rumpled bedding. He had made love to her twice the previous evening … Had it been three times? Twice, thrice, what did it matter? It was too early in the day to keep score on incidentals.

Gently closing the bedroom door, he sat down over coffee and the newspapers. Once again, *Völkischer Beobachter* proved unfolding it was a waste of time and energy. The NSDAP Party organ featured adjectives galore, interspersed with glowing phrases and endorsements of military victories, forests of exclamation points, and little else. The lead column described in lurid propagandistic detail how the Reich's "magnificent, valorous, dedicated, indomitable" Wehrmacht had gone about the business of "scorching" Poland. Impatiently crumpling *Beobachter,* he let it fall to the carpet.

As far as he could tell, the sole aim of *Der Angriff,* an agitprop rag published by the Goebbels' Reich Ministry of Public Enlightenment and Propaganda—a classic, all-time misnomer, that!—was to suborn and redirect the collective mindset of German workers and their soon-to-be effectively castrated unions. The content of *Angriff* was even less informative or appealing than *Beobachter's* published "news."

A major irony of the era had been Hitler's demagogic takeover of the aggregate misfits, street thugs, and miscreants making up the so-called German Workers Party, then remolding it to fit the template of his personal world view. A joke lacking any vestige of humor was that the Nazi hierarchy had no more interest in German workers than in the beasts of the field, treating both as consumables to be used by the leadership for its own purposes, then casually discarded. The German workers, Lustmann knew, would learn a harsh lesson when droves of slave laborers began pouring into the factories, farms, and businesses.

Once an eager young *Hitlerjugend* stalwart himself, his sole reason for going to all the trouble of researching and documenting his untainted Aryan bloodline had been to earn the privilege of later petitioning for membership in the Nazi Party, also a stern prerequisite for admittance into the *Vogelsang SS Akademie* and his eventual ambition to aid in every conceivable way what had been bruited about and rumored as a "satisfactory" Final Solution to the Jewish Question. He consoled himself with the definite knowledge that Able Adolf, supported by Himmler and the coterie of other criminals and self-important, more or less demented, windbags drawn into his inner circle would be an unswerving drive to implement just such a truly *final* Solution.

Crumpling *Der Angriff,* he dropped it to the carpet, unfolded *Bild-Zeitung,* and noted the date caption: Wednesday, 26 September 1939. Here at least he discovered a smattering of reportage, if only a tongue-tip taste of genuine, meat-and-potatoes news, not the airy soufflé printed in the pair of so-called newspapers he had just discarded.

French resistance forces had apparently advanced eight kilometers or so into the Saarland Basin along a wide front, in Lustmann's opinion a Gallic misadventure akin to whistling in the dark. The French claimed their military incursion had forced a partial withdrawal from Poland and the subsequent redeployment of a half dozen Wehrmacht divisions. British observers, however, were said to have expressed serious doubt about that. The advance had apparently established French forces within hailing distance of the Siegfried Line, but General Gamelin, said to be in command of the bastion, must have realized a frontal assault on Germany's defensive fortress was out of the question and had called a halt to the mislabeled French "Saar Offensive."

In Poland, elements of General List's army group had reportedly met with pockets of stiff resistance near Lvov. Elsewhere, Wehrmacht *Heer* motorized infantry detachments driving across the Polish plains had successfully swept north and taken multiple bridgeheads on the eastern shore of River San. The Polish army in and around Poznan had been cited earlier in one of Hitler's propaganda scare bulletins for having "ambitiously invaded Germany with plans to march on Berlin," only to unexpectedly turnabout and attack the Eighth Army's flank, igniting a vigorous battle near River Bzura.

Polish troops had also managed to not only slow the advance but push back Wehrmacht forces several kilometers south of Kutno and then temporarily recapture Lowicz, while Gdynia had been evacuated. The Luftwaffe had bombed Krzemieniec in eastern Poland, declaring it an open city after Warsaw's diplomatic community sought refuge there. In Bucharest, former salesman and current foreign minister Joachim von Ribbentrop had issued a vigorous demand for Romania to refuse asylum to any Polish officials who dared to flee across the border, then proceeded to issue empty threats of a military reprisal for noncompliance.

In France, the Anglo-French Supreme War Council had reportedly met for the first time in Abbeville, where a Czech army-in-exile was said to be forming. *Even louder whistling in the dark,* thought Lustmann, fascinated by reading of unfolding, dimly recalled events, the accuracy of which he could check in the irrefutable, capsulized account of what to him was and would always be *authentic* World War II. Everything currently taking place along Lebe's second-chance timeline automatically magnified itself a thousand fold when viewed through the lens of the encyclopedic flash-paper document safely locked in the carryall.

Gerda Sharpe emerged from the bedchamber wrapped in a sheet that indifferently covered her nudity, mumbling a sleepy request for coffee.

"Surely, my love." Lustmann poured for her. "Did you rest well?"

A groggy affirmative nod. "I should get home and on to the bank. What time is it?"

"Early," he said. "Sevenish, thereabouts."

Gerda sipped coffee, regarding him over the cup's rim, her gray-blue eyes clouded from sleep. "Erich, I had a dream, and you were in it."

"How romantic!"

"No, there's something about you that ... well, bothers me."

"Really? Can't have that, can we? What may I ask do you find bothersome?"

"Exactly who the hell are you? And every bit as importantly, *what* are you?"

Lustmann laid aside the newspaper. "Rather odd direct questions."

"Did you honestly believe me gullible enough to swallow that fish story about fronting for some highly placed Nazi bigwig, or that froth about your swank Swedish estate?"

"Froth, dear one? Whatever is it that causes you to doubt me?"

"Oh, come off it! In my modest, but now and then important position, I deal on practically a daily basis with dandified, nose-in-the-air second- and third-echelon Reich executives, all of whom stage a grand entrance worthy of some exotic strain of royalty, and all are escorted by an entourage of mindless know-nothing heel-clickers. But never—not *ever*—do any of them remotely resemble a sophisticated gentleman like yourself."

"That is absolutely the most fascinating left-handed compliment of all time." He punctuated the utterance with a disarming smile, adding, "I have it! Let's return to bed, discuss it further?"

"Oh," she said airily, "you're a demon lover, and obviously more than simply well-off. It makes you a valuable client of the bank, yet something about you is … I don't know. There's something about the way your fish story struck a false note moments after you appeared in my office doorway."

"How disappointing!" Lustmann made an effort to keep the saucer and demitasse in his hand from chattering as he hastily set it down. He radically changed the direction of their conversation while striving to keep his voice level, asking Gerda if she belonged to the Party.

The query earned a puzzled blink, the hint of a frown. "Exactly what made you ask *that?* Are your *SS* gorillas coming to arrest me?"

Lustmann forced a chuckle. "Not at all, it's just that … Gerda, you weren't supposed to learn of my … affiliation, though as things stand, I see no reason to deny it."

Gerda shrugged. "Oh, I noticed your tattoo the first time we … came together. My father," she added, "was an ardent Nazi, but I …" She sipped coffee thoughtfully. "I grew up in Berlin when a wheelbarrow full of Rentenmarks bought a loaf of bread, *if* there was any to be had, and helped serve customers in my parents' Wilmersdorf bakery. Every month like clockwork, a pair of Communist loudmouths would drop by and explain to my father how the store's front window could be 'accidentally' shattered. Father paid up, and so did every other merchant on the block."

"Threatening a one-store *Kristallnacht,*" remarked Lustmann, "limps minus the starring Jews."

"Extortion, plain and simple, it was. One fine day a truckload of *Sturmabteilung* huskies arrived in the street. Two Brown Shirts strutted into the bakery and bluntly demanded to know if we were on the Communist protection list. They left a phone number for Papa to call the next time we were bothered. He called, and shortly thereafter there were a few broken heads in the street. We never saw the Communists again, and in my father's eyes the *SA* had transformed itself from a gaggle of crude, insolent bullies to a legion of heroes, and he petitioned for Party membership."

Lustmann nodded. "The *SA* replaced the old *Freikorps* rebels who battled agitators after the Great War. Then after the *Röhm Putsch,* the *SS* replaced the *SA* as a far greater, more truly dedicated Nazi organization."

"Then you really *are* an *SS* officer? Despite what I said earlier, I'm impressed."

"Gerda," he said earnestly but also dismissively, "you're much too perceptive for any more fish stories. My lagging truthfulness stemmed from a single fact: knowledge of my affiliation would have placed you in harm's way, and since I … since I've been exposed, you force me to explain how my vital undercover assignment requires me to report directly to the office of Reichsführer-Schutzstaffel Himmler—" He broke off, unnerved by Gerda's doubting stare.

"It also forces you," she drawled, "to change the subject, Herr Klasse."

"I won't have you think ill of me."

"Oh, forget it! I promise to believe whatever you tell me. Unfortunately, there's more."

"More ... what?"

"A more profound reason for ..." Gerda trailed off uncertainly, her disconcerting gaze locked with his. She cleared her throat. "Your original cash deposit of a million and one-half in serialized, large-denomination notes ..." Pausing again, her brows contracted, she said, "One of the watermarked *Tausend-Mark Reichsbanknoten* in a bundle struck us as a very strange bedfellow for the other currency. Minute engraving variances and serialization indicating the date of issue ... Your pardon, the date experts tell us it *will be* issued."

"*Will be?* I fear you've lost me, Gerda."

"It has also 'lost' everyone who's seen it, including me. Expert analysis firmly establishes the fact that the issue date is a very questionable calendar year, nineteen forty-two. Unless I've been grossly misinformed, we're here in your suite in late autumn, *nineteen thirty-nine.*"

Lustmann felt his heart skip a beat. Colonel Stoltz had personally vouched for the germane quality of each and every item of treasure he had carried into the past, including then "useless" *Reichsmarknoten* unearthed hither and thither by ODESSA search teams prior to his departure from 1960 Argentina. More than once Manfred had spoken of the exquisite pains taken to ensure that such an anachronistic disaster could *never* take place.

"Ridiculous!" he exclaimed, his voice cracking. "A foolish mistake like that has to be the work of a counterfeiter or some dimwitted clerk."

Gerda's headshake negated both possibilities. "High denomination banknotes are routinely checked by Reichsbank specialists, and occasionally monetary experts who are called in, all of whom in this instance discounted your theory at first glance. The clerk who counted out and catalogued your first deposit recorded the peculiar banknote, but instead of sending it to the vault with the remainder, he brought it into my office. Under a microscope, the note shows minor wear and tear, indicating that it was not, *could not have been* a pristine issuance, but had quite likely been in circulation. Nor do any of the experts summoned by Herr Funk believe it to be the work of a counterfeiter. The ink, paper, engraving, watermark— every feature—had been verified as authentic. One of my associates has checked the likelihood of a serialization error and similar details. He's certain such an off-brand answer is improbable—or for that matter impossible."

Lustmann nervously drummed his fingers on the coffee table. "I'm at a total loss to explain such an outré occurrence. All I can say is … Gerda, be assured that the funds I deposited are all legitimate, since all derive from *SS* holdings. Where else could such sums have been obtained?"

Her accusative stare weakening, Gerda looked away. Draining her coffee, she rose without a word, clutching the bed sheet around her, and went into the bedchamber.

Silently cursing the ODESSA's carelessness, he decided bedding the widow Sharpe had been an egregious unanticipated error. Lovely playmate or not, she would have to go—a regrettable necessity, but there it was. Not quite yet, however. The "misdated" banknote might have come to light with or without their romantic connection. More to the point, should something untoward happen to Reichsbank's accounts manager, their liaison would inevitably be discovered, and the lantern of suspicion would immediately shine brightly in his direction.

He toyed briefly with a notion to abandon the Adlon forthwith, register at another hotel, and transfer the remaining funds to a different bank, but quashed the impulsive idea. Fleeing would only contribute to any potential suspicion by the authorities, while doing nothing untoward might obviate or allay it. His sole recourse for the time being would be to stand fast and bluff it out. During the months to come, he meant to redirect all his energies from idle pleasure and focus every waking moment on the monumental task before him.

Gerda Sharpe dressed hurriedly, primped, and left the suite with only a parting wave. Lustmann dismissed all thought of her and her bogus banknote. He sat down and tried to imagine how to begin searching for a fitting place to send the all-important introductory letter he had thus far put off beginning to so much as draft.

* * *

Silverthorne's atemporization trek took him through Ebingen, a larger community than Winterlingen, where he rested on a bench outside the church, but did not tarry. When his worn boots had marched their weary way to the community of Tailfingen, the sun had fallen behind forested hills, and a ruddy sunset glow painted ominous bronze and saffron clouds along the western horizon.

He found shelter before the rain came, allowing a cloddish inn-keeper to persuade him the best food and softest beds in all Würt-temberg could be found beneath the hostelry's gabled roof. In the paneled dining room, thin slices of flat unseasoned "veal" were served with dumplings called *spaetzle* and the youthful waiter's wink and nod. The entrée, James realized, chewing his first bite, was venison. He imagined that an unwary stag had probably wandered too near the inn. Washing down his first meal in Nazi Germany with two steins of absolutely delicious lager, he climbed the stairs to his room, undressed, gratefully crawled into bed, pulling the eiderdown comforter up to his chin, and listened in drowsy contentment to rain drip from the eaves.

Outside the downstairs dining room, he had resisted an urge to buy what passed for the local newspaper, dismissing the notion because trying to read it bone tired as he was would have been a lost cause. Gothic numbers on the foyer calendar had revealed the current day as *Donnerstag, den 11 April 1940*. If any "factual" information he had ever obtained proved valid in this other timeline, Germany's military juggernaut had just fallen on Denmark and Norway.

Approaching the outskirts of Stuttgart at mid-afternoon the next day, he was beginning to have serious doubts about the wisdom of taking the train to Berlin. During a rest stop at the rail station, he firmly resolved to forgo travel by rail in favor of hiking, the rationale being that atemporization on foot would prove more valuable in the long run than spending a portion of his limited funds riding to the capital in a comfortable wagon-lit.

Stuttgart to *Aalen,* northwest through Ansbach, all the way to Nuremberg, most times he overnighted beneath roadside trees, enviously remembering that first luxurious night at the inn, and either hitched rides or hiked the lightly trafficked country roads. A talkative truck driver picked him up and bent his ear for fifty kilometers, then treated him to a *Wurst und Bier* lunch in Bayreuth. The loud-mouthed trucker insisted that the war currently turning some fainthearted Germans into "Nervous Nellies" would be over in a month, two at most. After all, hadn't the Reich been waging war since the previous September? And what, the driver asked himself, had mighty Great Britain and France done after proudly declaring war? Not a thing, he answered himself, other than making threatening noises.

The trucker insisted that the so-brave French snail-gobblers and tea-sipping British snobs had rested fearfully behind the silly French Maginot fortifications, or stayed safely at home across the Channel and sweated little green apples instead of daring to fight. All either enemies of *Das Reich* had done, or for that matter *could* do, was watch Germany's mighty forces enjoy military success after resounding success, overwhelming regions of Poland, stealing away the bastardized nation calling itself Czechoslovakia without a shot being fired, and having the sand to take back what were rightfully Germany's anyhow, the Saar Basin and Sudetenland.

James proved himself such a rapt listener that the truck driver invited him to wait while he ran an errand— an errand of the flesh, as reported later in lurid detail—and then faithfully carried him all the way to Leipzig, where he rested for an hour after an atemporizing walkabout of the city, came across a day-old newspaper left neatly folded on a park bench, and found that General von Falkenhurst was sharing the headlines with Admiral Raeder in *Weserübung* triumphs, the codeword designating the Danish and Norwegian blitzes and subsequent occupations.

"Your papers, *bitte?*"

Alarmed, James stumbled to a halt. Lost in thought, he had been ambling along the sidewalk in some nameless Brandenburg town and had failed to notice the *Schupo*'s approach. Mumbling, *"Natürlich,"* he forced a smile.

The uniformed policeman was short in stature, with pinched, arrogant features. In handing over his forged credentials, James let the *Schutzpolizist* glimpse the wad of Reichsmarks in his wallet.

"Austrian, eh? And how are things in Salzburg, Herr Steyr?"

James added an extra dollop of warmth to his reply. "I'll find out in a week and a half, when my *Wanderjahr* takes me back home."

"You are a reporter employed by some Salzburg newspaper?"

*"Nein,* a freelance journalist here to gather background material for a series of articles I intend to write about the wartime mood in Germany. With Austria now a part of the Reich, there is a great deal of interest in the topic at home."

The *Schupo* had apparently taken James for a vagrant, not surprising in view of the "journalist's" lederhosen, backpack, and rumpled Tyrolean hat. "Ummm" was all the officer had to say when he returned the forged documents and nonchalantly strolled away.

The incident, his first bad moment, made James realize his

*Wanderjahr* togs, while appropriate in the back-country byways of Württemberg and southern Germany in general, would never do in cosmopolitan Berlin. Arriving footsore in Wittenberg, he combed the side streets, then spent an hour sorting through heaps and racks hung with castoff clothing in a secondhand store. To stay in character, he haggled with a clerk over the modest price difference between his hiking attire and the items he wished to purchase, emerging in a worn but not threadbare dark-gray business suit, a pair of rundown-at-the-heels black shoes, and a much more optimistic outlook.

Nostalgic on April 19, 1940, he once again stood in Pariser Platz, gazing at the nearby Doric columns of the Brandenburger Tor monument topped by an equine quadriga driven by the Greek Goddess Eirene, a personification of peace. In 1784, the retro-temporal junket in Potsdam had shortened his visit to Berlin, when the site featured only one of numerous gateways in the ancient wall enclosing the original Berlin fortress.

Walking west on Ebertstrasse, he watched a yellow tandem streetcar roll past, bells clanging. Vehicle traffic and pedestrians passing through Pariser Platz partially obscured his wistful gaze down Unter den Linden. During his retro-temporal junket to Potsdam, Frederick the Great had been enjoying his declining years in the Summer Palace, Sanssouci, and Berlin's broad Unter den Linden thoroughfare had been lined rows deep in magnificent old lime trees. In the now of 1940 Berlin, several rows of puny, two- or three-year-old saplings stood, planted after major excavation for a subway beneath the thoroughfare had removed all first-growth trees.

Overwhelmed by his first glimpse of a much more modern city than he recalled from the older era, James had to remind himself he was strolling in modern 1940 Berlin, not Welthauptstadt Germania as Hitler had renamed the capital after the War of World Liberation.

He skipped lunch in favor of taking in the capital hour after hour, finding many streets still village-like, still partly devoted to bicycles as well as autos, trucks, and buses. Even a few *Pferde Droschken*—horse-drawn carriages—lingered here and there in outlying districts, holdovers from a more slow-paced era. White-jacketed traffic policemen exhibited Prussian authority and dignity regulating vehicular flow with whistles and robotic gestures. In view of Berlin's wartime status, fewer uniforms were to be seen on the street than James had anticipated, though here and there the *Feldgrau*-uniformed rankers mingled with a few Wehrmacht officers wearing tunics replete with red collar tabs. In Friederichstrasse, he halted on the sidewalk, struck by the sight of a dozen *Hitlerjugend* juveniles trooping past. The boys were clad in short black trousers and brown shirts, each with a black neckerchief slipped through a braided leather loop.

Conscientiously adhering to Omsley's repeated urgings to atemporize thoroughly, he rested on a bench for almost an hour, analyzing the traffic flow, watching pedestrian passersby, and subconsciously comparing the street scene with what had been memorable on his former visit to Prussia's more distant past. Atemporization was critical; feeling oneself "at home" in any unfamiliar milieu was an indispensable prerequisite to historical research or any other activity for a stranger in a strange land and timeline. Feeling and acting like a stranger tended to increase the risk of making an unconscious social gaffe and draw undesired attention to oneself—an especially dangerous giveaway for an intruder in wartime Berlin.

Too restless to sit still longer, he rose and went off on a late sightseeing tour, turning away from Pariser Platz, strolling east past the Adlon Hotel to Glinka Strasse, where he went over to the center mall. A block beyond the Charlottenstrasse intersection, he paused to silently salute the statue of King Frederick the Great and returned to the southern sidewalk.

Just before reaching the Palace Bridge over the Schloss, he

learned that King Frederick's old artillery arsenal, the Zeughaus, had transformed itself into a historical museum and military hall of fame. Intrigued, he climbed the steps and roved through gallery after gallery filled with items of special interest, inspecting suits of sixteenth-century armor, the death masks of notables, including a likeness of revered former German President Paul von Hindenburg, and became fascinated by the host of dust-free mannequins ensconced behind plate glass, all clad in resplendent military uniforms from one bygone era or another. He capped the museum visit by stopping to read a placard that informed him the uniformed wax figure of Napoleon Bonaparte was crowned by the actual hat the emperor had worn on the fateful Waterloo battlefield.

Since his visit to Prussia's late-eighteenth century "past," certain sections of the city had undergone extensive sea changes of one type or another. King Frederick's parade ground had transformed itself into the acreage of *Tempelhof Flughafen*. The massive, red-brick façade of Town Hall had been scrubbed clean of accumulated grime, and certain dimly remembered late open fields and woodlands, mostly in western sectors of the city, were now a maze of paved streets lined with relatively new structures.

Ravenous in late afternoon, he treated himself to an early supper in a large, popular restaurant featuring a dozen halls, each with its distinctive theme and décor—sunny Spain, the fabled American Wild West, the Rhineland, and so forth. Choosing the Bavarian Alps bordering Austria, he dined on a so-so serving of pork tenderloin while a noisy thunderstorm raked a not-very-realistic model of Zugspitze, Germany's loftiest mountain peak. Although less than impressive, the surrounding Alpine diorama was enhanced in an artistic if amateurish way when simulated thunder crashed, accompanied by the patter of rain drumming on the roof. In the storm's wake, the sun broke out, and a yodeler strolled about comforting the diners.

With dusk approaching, his immediate interest was, if at all possible, locating shelter, hopefully in a decent, dry, reasonably priced lodging place. Walking about a lower-class neighborhood with that in mind, he crossed the Spree on the arched pedestrian level of double-decked Oberbaum Bridge and continued along Warschauer Strasse toward the railroad yards. Circulating through the mixed residential and small-business neighborhood in semi-darkness, he happened to spot a red-and-black swastika banner prominently displayed in the front window of a moderately run-down two-story house. Drawing near, he slowed his steps at sight of a "Room for Rent" sign in the opposite, more distant window.

A grumpy, sharp-eyed woman in late middle years took her time answering the doorbell, nodded an impatient invitation for Silver-thorne to enter when he mentioned the window sign, and announced herself as Frau Kraven. Laboring ahead of him up two flights of creaky stairs, he was shown into a cheerless, bleakly fur-nished attic room that smelled faintly of mildew. All he wanted or needed was basic shelter, in fact not much more than a place to sleep, and readily agreed to the modest weekly rental.

Curious about what she must have judged to be an unusual accent, Frau Kraven inquired if he was a foreigner. His now-famil-iar tale of being a freelance Salzburg journalist drew a sniff of mild suspicion from the landlady, who seemed to regard the profession of scribbler with little enthusiasm. She treated "Herr Steyr" to a brief, poignant account of her late husband's demise. A conscripted soldier battling in the endless trenches of France during the Great War to End War, neither Herr Kraven nor his remains had returned from the Western Front.

When the door finally closed behind Frau Kraven, Silverthorne dumped his rucksack in the corner, descended to use the boarding-house's second-floor hall bathroom, then got out of his clothes and fell into the narrow, lumpy mattress on what amounted to more of a cot than a bed, and was asleep in minutes.

# NINE

## *Berlin, Winter 1939*
## *Spring 1940, CE*

Waking before daylight, James hustled downstairs feeling well rested, but also half starved. He intended to rush out and find some inexpensive local eatery, and was on his way to the front door when the landlady asked if wanted to join the other lodgers in the dining room. Frau Kraven had not told him when he moved in that her establishment was as much a bed-and-breakfast hostelry as a boardinghouse and invited him to the daily repast included in the weekly fee.

He was wolfing down oatmeal leavened with thick cream and spoonsful of brown sugar, between times spreading freshly churned butter and jam on slice after slice of delicious, still-warm dark bread, when a pair of lodgers came into the dining room chatting about the day's big event. Listening with half an ear, James eventually recognized the subject under discussion.

*Führergeburtstag!*

Figuratively kicking himself for being too weary the previous evening to appreciate the significance of the day after his arrival, April twentieth, he blamed the oversight on his state of excitement over having safely reached the capital. What better method of atemporizing could there be than perchance catching view of the living, breathing megalomaniacal demagogue who had revived barbarism in the same artistic, intellectual social milieu that had produced

Goethe and Beethoven, not to mention a near philosopher-king, *Friedrich der Grosse?*

He finished breakfast and was told that purchasing a day ticket entitled the holder to transfer at will, in any order, from subway to surface to elevated public conveyances. Boarding a tram, he checked connections with the operator, jumped off quickly before the tandem yellow streetcars clanged away, and waited for a pair with the specified number. In a somewhat circuitous route, he rode sardined in with the other standing-room-only passengers for a relatively short distance, twice changed trams, and got off on Ebertstrasse on the eastern edge of Tiergarten. Impressed by Berlin's 1940 public transportation system, he believed it might outdo that of many cities in later eras. During the previous day's wanderings, he'd been equally impressed after visiting a postal substation not far from his new lodgings, and planned to make it his "office," if accommodating customer needs was typical of the small branch station, since others in central Berlin should likewise offer well-lighted public rooms staffed with ink pots and—wonder of wonders!—pens with sharpened nibs with which one could actually write.

Joining thousands of Berliners congregating along Charlottenburger Chaussee to witness the celebration of Hitler's fifty-first birthday, he found the crowd in a festive mood. Congenial smiles were the order of the day, the crisp spring air filled with happy chatter. A number of spectators had equipped themselves with homemade periscopes fashioned of small, canted mirrors fastened to sticks, or affixed at the top and bottom of cardboard mailing tubes.

Forty minutes later, celebrants along the thoroughfare cheered a procession of horse-drawn caissons rumbling past, slowly followed by an armored car preceding a Wehrmacht regiment marching in lockstep. The uniformed soldiers looked as young and inexperienced as they were, likely as not infantry trainees assigned to parade duty since their more experienced brethren were engaged in important business elsewhere in Europe. Rather than carrying weapons, the marchers strode in ranks, lofting tall poles topped by a moving forest of waving black swastika banners. A half dozen warplanes soared over Tiergarten during the parade, while units representing the Luftwaffe, Army, Navy, and of course the *SS* marched past. Standing for so long wearied James to the point of wishing he could retreat farther from Charlottenburger Chaussee and sit down to rest beneath the park trees.

At last, preceded by a military band trumpeting the *Deutschland-lied* anthem, a gleaming armored Mercedes-Benz touring saloon wheeled past at the pace of a walking man. Standing erect in the forefront of the huge auto's rear seat, his dark eyes shadowed by a billed cap, *Der Führer* wore a tan military uniform. A red swastika band prominently encircled his right arm in a sustained, bent-elbow Nazi salute, a pose leaving James with a strong impression the stolid, self-satisfied Nazi icon was celebrating himself more enthusiastically than anyone in the wildly cheering, flag-waving hordes of onlookers.

He shuddered slightly over the physical reality of the one-vehicle motorcade sweeping past and the electric fluid that transformed the air in Tiergarten, complemented by the approving clamor sent up by the crowd. Seated next to Hitler, his ferret-like features serene, Reichsminister Goebbels shared the celebratory atmosphere along with florid-featured Luftwaffe *Reichsmarschall* Göring. In the front passenger seat, Hitler's anointed deputy, Rudolf Hess, wore an indifferent expression, staring directly ahead through the vehicle's windscreen. A half dozen *SS-elite Leibstandarte* officers from Hitler's black-uniformed personal bodyguard—*praetorians in all but name,* thought Silverthorne—walked on either side of the huge, slow-rolling open touring car.

He strained on tiptoes, peering over the sea of heads between himself and the street, doing his best to remain inconspicuous by cheering as loudly as the spectators around him, totally unable to tear his eyes from a scene that struck him as a melodramatic, true-color substitute somehow reproduced from one of the grainy black-and-white films he'd viewed ad nauseam as a schoolboy, then studied later with intense professional interest. Furthermore, the sight provoked the identical reaction he had experienced then on his own timeline: revulsion coupled with abject disbelief. Whether in real-time before his eyes circa 1940, or in a grainy, archaic film projection, or for that matter one of the meticulously preserved still photos on his own future timeline, he vowed to do his damnedest to eradicate the repugnant scene before him for all time to come. It was starkly incredible—no, *impossible*—to appreciate what an indelible, blood-smeared mark the smug, stereotypical face riding past a stone's throw from where he stood had left, or in the present context *would leave* upon the world and everyone in it.

Eyes watering, his emotions roiling, he turned and edged toward the crowd's fringes. The thrill of elation that had swept through him upon learning of an opportunity to actually see Hitler in the flesh had evaporated when he had witnessed the living, breathing Führer and the pomp and circumstance surrounding him, but it had also discouraged him over the sheer hopelessness of performing the unique, do-or-die task his fellow conspirators had worked and died to set before him. What could one lonely stranger do to thwart the strength, purpose, and will so vibrantly on display in Hitler's militant "redundant" *Dritte Reich?* Omsley's encouraging words echoed hollowly in his mind: "Lustmann succeeded, and if it can be done once, it can be done again."

*No reason why it can't, Bernard. No reason except for …*

He reproached himself for allowing a defeatist attitude to surface so early in the game. After all, he had barely put in an appearance in Berlin, hadn't been in the capital long enough to begin atemporizing properly, let alone take a first tentative step in what promised to be an immensely difficult hunt. Barring major miracles, a lengthy, all-consuming effort would be required to even catch a whiff of Lustmann's trail, should a trail exist. Locating his quarry would doubtless mean discovering the world-saving hero's basic intentions, how he planned to accomplish *his* miracle.

Not until then could he dream about inventing reasonable means and methods of reversing any actions by the Reichsheld, whatever he might find them to be. It was self-deceptive, not to mention foolish, to anticipate major, minor, or incidental miracles falling from the sky to aid him in fulfilling his mission, a goal that looked less fruitful now than when he and Bernard and the others had dreamed and schemed in the "vanished" Deutsches Weltreich about some way to accomplish what amounted to a prospective major miracle. The only course open to him would mean assuming Erich Lustmann was alive and well and, according to logic, here in Berlin at this very same moment.

If so, how could he hope to locate the Nazi hero of heroes who had to be every bit as desperate as he was to remain anonymous at any and all cost but had lost himself somewhere in a thriving wartime metropolis of four millions, Lustmann's objective the direct opposite of his own? Startled by a random notion that erased his gloomy, foreboding mood, he wondered if he had been drawn to Tiergarten to perhaps catch a glimpse of Hitler's annual birthday celebration, might not his quarry also be somewhere in the wooded park?

Fired by the prospect of ending his search almost before it began, he began prowling along the still-crowded thoroughfare, scanning faces, quickening his pace when he overheard people in the dispersing crowd gabbling about how regal and triumphant Hitler had looked, how graciously he had momentarily halted the slow-moving Mercedes and the accompanying procession to bend with a smile and accept a nosegay from tiny, blonde twin girls.

He plowed back and forth near Charlottenburger Chaussee, searching the faces and figures around him in the thinning throng. Spotting a tall gentleman briskly striding away who might be worth a closer look, he hurried after him, only to discover he had chased a puffing, ruddy-faced elder who most likely walked his regular few kilometers each day to stay fit.

Turning discouraged steps toward The Kroll, a fashionable open-air restaurant in Tiergarten now doing land-office business after the parade, he circulated around the terrace for a quarter hour, sizing up the diners, and was forced to give up the fruitless search, concluding that Lustmann had to be elsewhere. Crestfallen, he re-boarded the crowded tram and rode for hours, searching the sidewalks for an unmistakable face long since etched in memory, got off feeling desperately frustrated, and walked about a while longer.

In late afternoon, two lackadaisical brown bears on the far side of a moat and the steep-sided wall of their enclosure at the Berlin Zoo ignored James and a scattering of children and gawkers lined up at the railing. He dined sparingly at a sidewalk café, was drenched by an unexpected shower, and ended his roving by leaning on the arching balustrade of the Oberbaum Bridge pedestrian causeway, staring down at the turgid waters of the Spree until twilight's chill drove him to descend from the bridge, hustle to the boardinghouse, and climb the creaking stairs to his cheerless, unheated attic room.

\* \* \*

Leery of several preliminary targets he had researched, Erich Lustmann scratched out a pair of addresses on his list, narrowing his selections to a pair of establishments, one in Wilmersdorf, the Mitte Berlin district where Gerda Sharpe had grown up, and a third farther from the central city in outlying Schöneberg, beyond the Landwehrkanal. He was personally scouting the prospective destinations for the planned but not not-yet-started vital introductory letter he had put off drafting so long that he'd reached the point of putting off the putting-off.

All told, he had paid brief visits on foot to a half dozen addresses gleaned from magazine and newspaper advertisements, often doing so in the rain, and once during off-and-on snow showers, and he had even surveyed other sites lifted from the telephone book. His solitary wanderings for no obvious purpose had bewildered the driver of his leased Mercedes-Benz Saloon, a taciturn middle-aged fellow unimpressed by the extravagant tips he had received for doing little more than waiting in the auto than driving. Following orders to the letter, on more than one occasion the driver had parked the gleaming sedan on a side street and dozed while awaiting the return of his mysterious, yet well-heeled passenger.

Herr Klasse, had the driver only known, was now leaning in favor of the Schöneberg address. Both potential targets in Wilmersdorf fronted on moderately busy streets, whereas the smaller Schöneberg storefront was situated in a narrow lane, lost in a row of shops, older houses, and walkup flats. Any of the selected addresses would do to test the waters, of course, since the principal intent of the pristine letter he was forever preparing to write but had not gotten around to sitting down with pen and paper and actually *drafting* it, while simple to state, was not that easy to compose. Schöneberg had become the slight favorite due its location in a quieter neighborhood, despite the particularly garish display in the storefront's large window.

The end of December signaled that the calendar year of his premature arrival was all but spent. Worse, weeks had passed beyond the date he had promised himself would mark the absolute deadline for composing and dispatching the all-important introductory letter. The task nagged him daily, hourly. Finishing and posting the *verdammt* letter had somehow changed from what could always be done later to a tenuous, if inarguably mandatory, chore demanding immediate attention. It was a nagging duty he simply could no longer shirk.

He winced and thumbed his throbbing temples. Ever since opening his eyes in early morning, an ingestion of aspirin had engaged in a losing battle with a vile hangover doubly compounded by a pulsating toothache. With or without analgesic, the aching tooth troubled him more than the aftereffects of overindulgence. He had vowed to cut down on the champagne, on high living in general for that matter— a distasteful prospect, yet necessary. He decided to make an appointment at some local dentistry parlor, and then, fresh out of excuses and freed from all distractions, he meant to sit down and devote his energies to the long-overdue task.

Gerda had absented herself for weeks after reporting the bank's investigation of a not merely bogus, but "impossibly" dated *tausend* Reichsmark banknote, reducing him to the pursuit of loose women in bars and restaurants, or on one notable occasion the dazzling brunette goddess he had crossed paths with during intermission in a theater lobby. He supposed it was just as well that their intimacy had cooled. Disposing of Frau Sharpe might not be necessary after all.

Absently massaging the gum line above his aching bicuspid, he thought about Gerda. On his next visit to the bank, she had greeted his arrival in the manner of a queen bee exhibiting the above-it-all reserve Reichsbank insisted she adopt with strange clients. That had later changed, of course, when he deposited another briefcase bulging with cash and punctuated the delivery with a casual quip: "We shall pray none of these notes will be minted in the near future." Reminding her of the inexplicably serialized, post-dated banknote nevertheless thought to have been in circulation by more than one expert had earned him a distasteful grimace, but the least hint of a smile as well.

Pleased to see the holiday season folderol over and done with, he made a valiant effort to ignore the aching tooth while skimming the Thursday, twenty-eight December *Morgenpost*. Leafing through the articles and news stories, he was searching for any stray morsels of current news fit to underscore the importance of the introductory letter that *still* had not begun but *had* to be penned and posted. The authorities, *Morgenpost* reported, had announced that

seventy thousand inhabitants of a Polish town, Kalisz, were sched-
uled for deportation in order to make room for scores of ethnic
Germans flocking into Poland from the Baltic states of Estonia,
Latvia, and Lithuania. *It's a start,* he thought, *yet only the tip of the
relocation iceberg to come.*

News of the war in Finland drew less press coverage, mainly
because it involved military aggression by Germany's supposed non-
aggression pact cosigner, Stalin's USSR. Holding a tenuous position
around Suomussalmi, the 163rd Division, an element of the Soviet
Ninth Army, had been surprised and ripped apart by successive,
persistent Finnish hit-and-run attacks. The anticipated reinforce-
ment by the Forty-Fourth Red Army Division, rushing to succor
what elements were still in place, had suffered delays in moving
forward due to constant harassment by the fierce, tenacious Finns,
whose winter tactic was to isolate individual Soviet columns crossing the Karelia Peninsula's trackless, forested snowfields, outflank
them with small groups of agile ski troops, and decimate them little
by little and one by one. The Soviet command had apparently failed
to counter these strikes with less well-trained and equipped cross-
country skiers than the Finns, who, clad all in white, were semi-
invisible against a snowy backdrop. Concerned over the mounting
attrition, Stalin had apparently ordered a coordinated, step-by-step
assault on the Finnish Mannerheim Line.

In Switzerland, industrialist and principal Nazi fundraiser Fritz
Thyssen had vigorously protested to Hitler, insisting that he had not
sacrificed millions to forward the USSR's Bolshevik cause, but
rather was in opposition to it. In the North Sea, a British battleship,
HMS *Barham,* had been damaged by a torpedo attack credited to
Kriegsmarine *U-Boot 30.* In Britain, compulsory meat rationing
had been invoked, while Japanese bombing raids had ravaged the
Chinese military supply base of Lanchow, deemed mandatory to be
held by Chiang Kai-shek's defensive forces.

Dissatisfied with the less-than-sensational news of the day, he noisily crumpled the copy of *Morgenpost,* chucked it in the direction of a leather-bound wastebasket. Nothing in the way of a military or political crisis seemed to be on the near horizon, nor a single newsworthy item to cite in order to underscore the importance of the pristine message he simply *had* to write and post.

The pulsing ache in the offending bicuspid drew his attention back to the source of discomfort. Vigorously rubbing his lip over the sore spot, he loosed a fulminant curse, decided enough was enough, seized the phone, and rang up the front desk. "Herr Klasse here, Suite two zero four. Is the hotel able to recommend the services of a competent local dentist?"

After an impatient wait, he jotted down an address and phone number, curtly thanked the deskman, and requested an outside line from the hotel operator. He explained to the dentist's receptionist that his dental problem verged on an emergency, listened with half an ear, and was angered by a woman's offer of an appointment several days hence. Interrupting irritably, he told her he was in Berlin on very important business, staying at the Adlon, adding that the hotel's management had recommended the services of Dr. Kleinschmidt, saying the constant siege of pain barred any chance of him functioning normally until the much-later appointment she had suggested.

Promptly at two that afternoon, after an additional forty minutes of tooth-pounding misery in the waiting room, a white-smocked dental assistant seated him in a tilted-back leather chair and fastened a cotton bib around his neck. White-haired and stooped, Dr. Kleinschmidt nodded politely to his "emergency" patient, scrubbed his hands at the sink. Using a dental mirror and steel pick, he examined the indicated tooth with the aid of wire-framed bifocals with thick lenses. "How long has it troubled you, sir?"

"Few ... days, week," mumbled Lustmann, tongue-tied by the instruments.

"Also, I believe we can ..." The dental tools came out of Lustmann's mouth. "Only two of your fillings are visible, sir, and both most unusual. May I ask where this work was done?"

Lustmann quailed inwardly, thinking, *Not again!* It had been his lifelong conceit to maintain near-perfect teeth by persisting in the punctilious brushing and flossing regimen drummed into him as a youth. A bearded Argentinian dentist had repaired the caries in question with plastic fillings, a procedure made necessary by the exigencies of wartime, and in his case a decade of foreign exile to follow accompanied by a change of diet.

He mumbled, "Experimental," attributing the work to a Swedish researcher.

"Remarkable!" Dr. Kleinschmidt clucked admiringly. "The material is certainly not amalgam, yet perhaps a touch whiter than your enamel. Frankly, the fillings look so natural they are very difficult to see. Can I trouble you for the name and address of the, er ... specialist responsible for such procedures?"

"Sorry, he's ... no longer with us, Doctor. Can we please get on with plugging that tooth? I have a very important appointment in less than an hour."

The dentist injected Novocaine, numbing his patient's jaw, but Lustmann's pristine exposure to the noise and vibration of a low-speed dental drill circa the current year threatened to make him tear the bib from his neck, bolt from the chair, and dash out of the dental parlor. His eyes clamped tightly shut, he sat through the punishing ordeal with feigned stoicism, all the while wondering from what quarter the next idiotic anachronism would rise up and bite him in the ass, or perhaps seek revenge yet again in the mouth.

\* \* \*

James awoke at sunrise. A dim glow illuminated the east-facing filmed window centered like an afterthought on the end wall between the attic's steeply canted eaves. He was hungry but believed it prudent to pinch every penny and dismissed an urge to go out in search of coffee and a roll. He let his stomach growl until it was time for the insipid boardinghouse breakfast to appear on the dining room table downstairs.

He had begun to appreciate the fact that the inquisitive reigning matriarch of all she surveyed, Frau Kraven, still nurtured vague suspicions about him and his alleged journalistic profession. It was her habit to note the comings and goings of all five lodgers, but for whatever reason she seemed especially curious about the activities of a purported Austrian journalist called Herr Steyr, who'd begun to suspect that more than once while he was out she had gone into his attic room and perhaps poked through his few personal effects and belongings. Finding her nosiness vaguely worry-making, he meant to stop in a few pawn shops and secondhand stores during his search for Lustmann, check for bargains, and squander a pittance of his dwindling funds on a used typewriter, then substantiate his cover story by writing a newspaper article for snoopy Frau Kraven to find.

Determined to get on with the mission, he wrapped himself in the frayed comforter to combat the early morning chill, took several sheets of foolscap from the backpack, and began to list every shred of data he had studied or been told about *DKW*'s hero of heroes, Erich Lustmann, who had been—that is, *would* be—fortyish at the time Lebe's team of ODESSA expatriates had dispatched him from Argentina. In the here and now, his fortyish quarry was every bit as much an intruder in current timeline Berlin as he was and only a few real-time years his senior.

On the past and future Deutsches Weltreich timeline, bombastic published biographies, eulogies, and tributes had glowingly characterized him as a "modern Renaissance man," a patron of the arts endowed with superior intellect and impeccable taste, all in all a rare, unique individual endowed with a golden touch, not to mention being a talented scientific dilettante who had aided physicist Lebe in developing the quintessential details of his pristine retro-temporal process. As an accredited historian, James had intuitively suspected the *Reichsheld* celebrated in song and story to actually have been more a confidence man than hero. Reading between the lines, his studies had amplified the notion that the hero's sleek, egotistical gloss praised in innumerable books, films, poems, and the media—even one opera—possessed no more than moderately high intelligence, but enormous resolve and a treasure of self-esteem beyond measure.

The principal reason for this latent suspicion had been persistently circulating rumors not even a dread of serious reprisal could suppress, a cascade of floating, whispered inferences that Erich Lustmann had been a dabbler in the occult "sciences" and perhaps a fervent subscriber to arcane beliefs and practices. The official published biography had minutely examined, dissected, and cataloged the hero's life subsequent to postwar recognition by the neo-Nazi autocrats who had ruled their new empire for decades in the wake of Hitler's passing.

Several highly placed leaders of the widespread revolutionary conspiracy in which James and thousands of American patriots were embroiled had initiated an in-depth investigation of the "actual" Lustmann. Hence, the tidbits and inferences he'd been unable to unearth in neglected documents pertaining to the then-sixtyish savior of Deutsches Weltreich had hinted that a checkered decline marred by two or more failed marriages, as well as his unsavory involvement with a prima ballerina in Ukraine Province officialdom was never able to squelch, had brought about a half dozen plunging dips and rocketing ascents in and out of Party favor, not to mention being later clouded with scandals that proved difficult to sweep under the neo-Nazi rug. In late middle age, outwardly indifferent to politics, Lustmann had wallowed in his super-celebrity status, sure that his epochal, world-changing retro-temporal escapade had elevated him to Olympian stature.

In the final analysis, official propaganda notwithstanding, Lustmann's lifestyle had probably contributed to his ultimate undoing, a principal reason why the underground insurgency's leaders had elected he himself as the best qualified candidate capable of freeing the America and the world from its Deutsches Weltreich malignancy. Additional rumors and scandalous innuendoes had suggested that the hero's deeply mourned passing had not resulted from the massive stroke of record, but from a thoroughly dissolute lifestyle. His eventual demise, according to the most disparaging if partially believable innuendo, inferred that the hero of heroes had drunk himself to death, all the while conducting séances for affluent dowagers and courting well-heeled distaff members of the lunatic fringe. Should that be even partially true, the final curtain had rung down on a life unlike that of any other scientific dilettante or artist in history.

He finished jotting down his reflections and came full circle, ending up confronted by the same enigma he had started out hoping to solve: How in the name of God Almighty had Erich Lustmann, alone and friendless upon his miraculous return to the same "authentic" wartime Nazi German timeline in which he had later served, managed to gain the attention of one or more ears, hearts, and minds within the Nazi hierarchy? How had he even made himself *heard,* let alone convinced anyone in authority—and yes, possibly *Der Führer* himself—how accurate was his seemingly prescient foreknowledge of things to come? How had his warnings, suggestions, advice, and counsel, or any other way of reaching the ears, eyes, and minds of the Reich's civilian and military leadership, been so much as halfway believed, or yet more incredibly *acted* upon? How had the man gone back and changed history, the nitty-gritty of it, the basic mechanics?

Every fellow conspirator in the hopefully never-to-exist Deutsches Weltreich he had eagerly fled had echoed his own pet theory, and the myriad questions branching from those theories and guesses had been endlessly debated. There was, to cite an extreme example, the fanciful Martin Borman hypothesis, someone's suggestion that Hitler's all-but-unknown close disciple and associate, the shadowy behind-the-scenes figure who had supposedly replaced Rudolf Hess as Hitler's anointed deputy, was actually Erich Lustmann. A number of less extravagant theories abounded, each pooh-poohed as preposterous by James himself and most other conspirators.

At last hunger drove him to dress hurriedly in the unheated attic room, rush downstairs, and indulge in Frau Kraven's ho-hum breakfast. While downing his oatmeal, he decided whatever method Lustmann had devised to aid Germany's victory over the might of the combined Allied forces did not matter a whit. Finding him would have to provide a path to the answer.

*Finding* the man ...

\* \* \*

Warned a dozen times to neither write the letters in longhand nor address the envelopes in like fashion, thus eliminating the efforts of some handwriting expert, Lustmann rigorously adhered to the dictum by laboriously hand printing the pre-scripted message letter by letter, punctuation mark by mark. Each succeeding missive after the introductory letter would also have to duplicate its hand-printed style and theme to prove both had originated from the identical germane source. A secondary rule was that each message had to be limited to one or more briefly stated caveats, notifications of impending errors in military or political endeavors—in some instances an insistence that a certain upcoming decision would ensure calamitous consequences—and then point out valid reasons why that was so, or perhaps add a jeremiad defining some method of thwarting the actions or reactions of the so-called Allies. The ODESSA brain trust had also decreed that editorializing the first, all-important letter might cloud the message itself and had drummed into all six candidates a dictum that the wordage in each had to be the soul of brevity.

Disturbed by the multiple not-completely-understood commandments, he had nevertheless been vain about the Spencerian calligraphy diligently practiced as a schoolboy and further cultivated during his *SS* career. He soon found printing the pristine message one letter at a time inhumanly tedious, vastly unsatisfying, and entirely frustrating.

Completing the handwritten first draft, knowing it less than perfect, he conceded that for some reason the message's erratic nature also enhanced its impact. Colonel Stoltz, aided by a literary-minded ass styling himself a former *Waffen-SS Gruppenführer,* had written, rewritten, edited, picked to pieces, rewritten yet again, and polished the text of the introductory letter. In essence, all that had been required was a verbatim printed transcription, with perhaps here and there a fillip of his own invention. For example, after several tries, he decided to capitalize the entire printed text, his rationale being that since all nouns were capitalized in German, it made the entire task much simpler to do properly.

Snapping his lighter, he lit a cigarette, sat back, and smoked hungrily in triumph while admiring his handiwork for the third or fourth time:

> Upon receipt of this note, I am certain you will believe me under treatment by not one but an entire team of psychiatrists. Nevertheless, I am no longer able to hold back word of certain indelible, recently experienced visions that have awakened me in the night—often night after night— and left me sleepless. I cannot explain the visions, nor how and why the sights and sounds flooding into my mind from nowhere have for days on end turned me into an incurable insomniac.
>
> All I can say is that I know myself to be grossly afflicted with some totally unknown form of preternatural ability or talent, and in truth infinitely more of a fiendish "talent" than any unaffected individual could begin to imagine. What is

worse, this unconscious talent is something I have no absolutely no ability to control, have no desire to be endowed with, and for no imaginable reason wish to be afflicted.

I confess to having suffered since childhood from what may be loosely termed "visions," although throughout the turbulent years referring to my "ailment" in that frightfully lame and inappropriate manner would be exiguous. The visions do not seem to occur due to social or personal circumstances, nor at present are rooted exclusively in the righteous war our beloved Reich is brilliantly prosecuting. As I pen this note, all I can say is that for some inexplicable reason, originating in some outré, arcane, precognitive source, I am able to clearly envision future events and happenings before they morph into reality.

I fully understand how insufferably idiotic that statement will sound to most sane, stable individuals, and I cannot begin to guess what type of negative reaction such a claim is bound to have on whomsoever this letter makes aware of my serious problem. But I have no choice except to self-righteously insist that what I have described, while admittedly beyond the pale of ordinary fantasy, is also accurately described. The clarity, scope, and indelible nature of my most recent vision makes it impossible to remain silent, hence my decision to take a deep breath and refute all attempts to slough off my strange, exotic affliction as delusional. Specific foreknowledge of things to come—my visions—are not symptomatic of the mental illness to which I have constantly dreaded falling victim, and it therefore behooves me to forcefully assert, reassert, and doubly underscore the plain and simple truth, which bluntly stated is that while I am an undeniable visionary, I judge myself to be among the sanest of the sane.

To baldly restate known factual data in order to establish the bona fides of my claim of a form of clairvoyance, our beloved Reich is engaged in waging a justifiable, righteous war destined to avenge the gross severity, excessive unconscionable reparation demands of the English and French to which imperial Germany succumbed in an act of treasonous betrayal by its own leadership, thus preventing our great nation from reassuming its rightful place on the world stage. Not once, but over and over again and again have I "seen" French toy soldiers, reinforced by British regiments, crouched behind the futile Maginot defensive fortifications in eager anticipation of a frontal assault that doubtless would have resulted in drawn-out, stalemated sieges of trench warfare forming a reprise of the horrific, ongoing carnage suffered by all concerned during the great war to end war.

I and I alone am able to confirm the fact that such shall not happen. In my vision, I have "witnessed" a Panzer-gruppe column kilometers in length toil along the narrow roads lining dense, forested hills, preparing for a lightning swift assault on Belgium, the low countries, and France, a crafty, massive thrust around rather than against the extensive fortified Maginot bastion erected by the complacent French. The Reich's conquest of France will cap a series of glorious triumphs the French and British military are woefully ill-equipped to repel or successfully blunt. I have seen Wehrmacht Heer battle victory after victory wrought by our forces. I have seen a conquered France with proud red-and-black swastika banners waving along the Paris boulevards and rippling above napoleon's triumphal arch. I have seen der führer's little hop-skip of joy celebrating the French surrender in the forest of compagnie that will take place in the identical railcar where imperial Germany's

November criminals agreed to prostitute themselves as signatories to the vile, disgraceful armistice bringing about an unjust peace, writing finis to the so-called great war to end war.

More than anyone else on god's earth am I able to enjoy a heartfelt, abiding understanding of how indescribably difficult it will be for anyone to accept my visions as other than the ravings of a lunatic confined in the padded cell of a madhouse. yet believe you must, for I possess neither the intellect nor imagination to account for my gift, or curse, whichever may be the case. All I can hope to achieve is to forthrightly relate the incredible pictures and sounds that flash before my mind's eye of substantial, though unverifiable, before-the-fact events and circumstances that shower me with cascades of inexplicable, unending preternatural visions.

Lustmann paused to search for just the proper concluding catchword or phrase appropriate to illustrate the letter's sincerity. Unsnapping the rubber bands securing the vital documents that accompanied a concise, flash-paper account of the real WWII, he reviewed the first few pages and came across some lines that scholarly ass of a *Waffen-SS Gruppenführer* had urged Stoltz to include back in two-decades-in-the-future 1960 Argentina. The obnoxious know-it-all had come up with a phrase that struck Lustmann as not only obscure, but neither apt nor all that meaningful. He reconsidered, began to appreciate the need for a reference tending to emphasize his repeated claim of possessing unknown and unknowable precognitive powers. Eventually settling on the line credited by the *Gruppenführer* to a poet named Eliot, he shrugged and appended it to the final paragraph:

Time present and time past are both perhaps contained
in time future, and time future contained in time past.

Pleased and satisfied by the result of his effort, he hand-lettered "Heil Hitler!" in place of a signature, and then self-labeled himself as the sender by printing "A Friend of the Reich." With bold strokes, he hand-lettered the envelope's Schöneberg address in green ink, licked a postage stamp, and pasted it on the envelope. Folding the letter neatly, he slipped it into the envelope, sealed the flap, and tucked it into an inner jacket pocket.

He would go out later and post the crucially important introductory missive in an anonymous sidewalk letterbox, or a postal substation if he happened to pass one. Every ensuing letter would likewise be surreptitiously posted in one of the hundreds of red letterboxes, postal drops, and substations situated from one side of *mitte* Berlin to the other, should that prove necessary.

Delighted to have the nagging chore over and done with, he smiled and lit a cigarette.

# TEN

## *Berlin*
## *Early Spring 1940*

*Amt Ausland Abwehr im Oberkommando der Wehrmacht,* Germany's military counterintelligence agency, born circa 1920 despite being proscribed by the Treaty of Versailles, was directed by Vice-Admiral Wilhelm Canaris, a gentleman who disliked wearing his Kriegsmarine uniform, though on certain state and social functions it was obligatory. What he invariably did wear, and seldom if ever discarded, was a stoic mask few of the individuals he dealt with were able to penetrate. Wily and urbane, nattily attired in a dark-brown business suit on this damp spring morning, the admiral considered his work infinitely more important and rewarding than his family, or for that matter a small coterie of personal friends and acquaintances with whom he rarely had much to do.

*Allgemeiner Feld-Marschall* Wilhelm Keitel, *OKW* chief of staff and supreme commander of all *Dritte Reich* armed forces, sat stiffly upright opposite the admiral's desk, tapping an impatient forefinger while awaiting Canaris's reaction to the bizarre letter. Keitel's displeasure became more evident when the admiral looked up from the sheet of unwatermarked stationery and said without the slightest change of expression, "Odd."

"Very," agreed the chief of staff. "Some Hungarian fortune teller, the Great Zoltan, walked into Amt IV Prinz Albrecht Strasse headquarters and informed the Gestapo duty officer that a rather …

strange letter had arrived in the afternoon post, and boldly announced that it had impressed him as worthy of official notice. Heydrich's Gestapo clowns arrest anyone and everyone on sight, no excuses required or permitted," assured Keitel.

"Of course," echoed Canaris, outwardly aloof, offering no clue what a great shock the odd letter had triggered. His first searing thought had been that it was virtually certain that *OKW* general staff conferences in neighboring Tirpitzufer Strasse headquarters had been compromised. The admiral, known for invariably speaking his mind when he judged it wise, had formed a habit of keeping his private thoughts private throughout his naval intelligence and subsequent *Abwehr* careers.

"What do you make of it?" he inquired casually, hoping the query made him sound as disinterested in the subject as he had intended.

A blink of irritation punctuated Keitel's sharp reply. "It has to be the raving of a mentally unbalanced individual who nonetheless believes in his own sanity."

"One might say," observed Canaris, his quip flashing mordant humor, "that all madmen are convinced of their personal sanity."

Keitel smacked his lips. "Surely you aren't suggesting this 'Friend of the Reich,' whoever and whatever he turns out to be, is endowed with supernatural prescience?"

"Surely you aren't suggesting I'm suggesting anything of the kind," said Canaris, his utterance devoid of emphasis, although the underlying sarcasm came through as a subtle rebuke. "If you believe this silly letter was a product of dementia," he prodded, "why bring it to me?"

"Because whoever he is, and whatever minimal degree of mental balance he has retained, I believe you will agree that the message itself is very disturbing. The depth of knowledge this visionary demonstrates goes leagues beyond any rational explanation."

Revolving the wisdom of venturing on a fishing expedition, the admiral eyed his visitor keenly. "How so, Wilhelm?"

"You were briefed on the gist of *Generaloberst* Guderian's revised, refined *Gelb* scenario."

Canaris nodded. *"Der Schnelle* Heinz is forever proud of his tactical masterstroke to initiate the western campaign, but refused to admit cribbing the basics from von Manstein's original scheme of the op codenamed *Gelb,* which was formerly sanctioned weeks ago—" He broke off, unable to sustain his offhand manner.

"Whoever deserves the credit for Gelb, it struck me as a most impressive piece of work. But then Guderian's recent notoriety derived from his penchant for ignoring any order he did not concur with one hundred percent and assaulting whoever and whatever stands in the path of his panzers. He proved himself worthy of field command during the Anschluss and Sudetenland operations, and perhaps more profoundly during the actions in Poland. Do you imply that this visionary letter mimics the Gelb western offensive?"

"No, not actually mimics," said General Keitel, "but it does suggest *far* too much confidential knowledge of *Gelb* for comfort. In my opinion, coincidence played no role in how this strange letter came to be written. General Bock's army group, as you recall, is slated to assault Belgium and Holland in a feint aimed at drawing the French and British defensive forces northward, while Leeb's army group holds the frontier opposite the Maginot defense perimeter to pin down all forces currently investing the fortifications. The western thrust has von Rundstedt leading his *Panzergruppen* through the Forest of Ardennes, skirting the static Maginot positions in a surprise strike through the hilly, forested narrow roads most tacticians, including our own experts, considered in no way negotiable by armor. Rundstedt is then slated to cross the Meuse near Sedan and engage the French and British defenders from the rear ..." Keitel paused thoughtfully. "What troubles me most about the self-proclaimed 'sanity' of this ... modern Nostradamus, is that almost everything is in readiness to launch the Gelb offensive."

His mien serious, sharply focused, Keitel said, "I put to you a firm guarantee of something I know to be true, something I believe with all my heart. As we speak, not a single individual other than a member of the senior staff can be *marginally* aware that Gelb has gained *Der Führer's* stamp of approval."

Canaris nodded reluctantly. "Your inference is plain, and I'm in total agreement," he said, believing none of it in spite of what the "sane" visionary letter writer seemed to know.

"Another feature of this peculiar letter," admitted Keitel, "disturbs me still more. How in our friend of the Reich's vision could he possibly *envision* Hitler doing a little victory jig outside the same railcar in which, to paraphrase his letter, Imperial Germany's November criminals sold out our nation in nineteen eighteen. Not long since you remarked about what a showman *Der Führer* is. Think how like him it would be for him to self-dramatize a Nazi military triumph of such magnitude in the identical historic site where Imperial Germany had acknowledged defeat.

"Try as I might, it was impossible for me to ignore a subterranean conviction that something dire lurks between the lines of this grotesque letter. A subtle, threatening undercurrent runs through it that I can attribute to only one singular fact: whoever and whatever he is, the writer has a frightening depth of knowledge concerning affairs you and I have been duly sworn to conscientiously guard in total secrecy. He *must* be run to ground quickly, and he *must* be, uh … encouraged to talk."

"Ummm, on that we concur wholeheartedly." Canaris had liked neither what he'd read nor what the text connoted, something Keitel had just confirmed. "You referred to the letter-writer as 'he.' You assume it was penned by a man?"

"A reasonable assumption, don't you agree?"

Miffed at having his question answered with a question, a favorite tactic of his own, the admiral asked sharply, "Have you told Himself about this peculiar letter or shown it to him?"

"Certainly not! I thought it unwise to present him with anything so unusual before we had a chance to discuss it. To the best of my knowledge, other than myself, only that *Reichsheini* Himmler, his vicious trained monkey Heydrich, and his ill-trained monkey Müller, no other *RSHA* higher-ups have been made aware of the letter's existence unless someone mentioned it."

"Good! Let's keep it that way for the time being." Canaris glanced at the hand-lettered sheets innocently unfolded on his desk, reminded himself of the missive's content, and revised his original suspicion. The damned letter was not—*could not be*— associated in any way with espionage. The dullest spy who ever drew breath would never consummate an act of sheer brilliance such as penetrating *Oberkommando* staff conferences, then turn about and *mail* his victims a detailed description of the secrets he had ferreted out.

"Our friend of the Reich could be a veteran of the Western Front," ventured the admiral after a moment of silent thought. "Perhaps a retired field-grade officer in the Great War who's possibly versed in reading maps and has analyzed the current situation as a whole. Putting two and two together, he could have intuited the enormous tactical value of a surprise stroke in much the same manner devised by Manstein and refined by *Generaloberst* Guderian."

"It could be as you say," admitted Keitel, privately dismissing the notion.

"At any rate," pursued Canaris, "I share your concern over the last item on our friend's agenda. Describing Hitler doing a victory jig in Paris to celebrate a postulated French surrender perturbs me as much, or even more, than it does you."

"With or without a military background," declared Keitel, "that touch struck me as nothing less than magically insightful for *anyone* to invent. Whoever authored the letter, be he friend or foe of *Das Reich,* would have to be personally acquainted with Adolph Hitler's ... quirks to imagine that an emotional degree of showmanship, let alone invent a self-congratulatory reason for it."

"I'm one hundred percent with you there, Wilhelm." Folding the letter, Canaris handed it to the chief of staff, advising him to either keep it hidden or burn it. "Whether our letter writing friend is an authentic seer or eminently certifiable," he said, drawing out the words as if to invite argument, "I judge his message *not* to be the work of a simpleton. A high degree of sophistication pervades his use of terms, his phraseology. You say it was posted here in Berlin, so if another should be delivered, that might narrow the chase to some district.

"Leave this, er … fortune teller's address and phone number with me, if you will. You say *lieber* Heydrich and his *SS* poultry herder boss are aware of it, so perhaps we should let the Gestapo fumblers handle the preliminary legwork. No one would think to term those idiots competent, but they do know their way around the streets. Once our friend has been collared and pumped dry, I'll order the seer released, along with an official apology for detaining him."

"Sensible," said Keitel. "Once he's been found, the fellow can be shadowed to learn where he goes, what he does, and who he contacts."

"Just so," said Canaris, disdaining the other's penchant for stating the obvious. "Once in custody, he'll be warned of what will happen to him if he breathes a syllable of the letter's contents to another living soul. Innocent, guilty, or falling into the wide crack between, we'll run him to ground, that I can promise you!"

"Put your best people on it," advised Keitel unnecessarily.

Assuring the general he would, Canaris thanked him for privately alerting him to a potentially dangerous breach of security.

* * *

At first glance to most people, the manual Olivetti on a dusty shelf in a backstreet pawnshop would have looked like an obsolete relic, but the only other mechanical typewriter James had ever seen had been on display in Greater Denver's Reichsmuseum. He asked the pawnbroker for a sheet of foolscap, inserted it in the roller, and randomly tapped keys. After a brief haggle, he handed over the modest, agreed-upon sum, carried the machine home to the board-inghouse, and cleaned it up, deciding all it needed was a little oil here and there and a new ribbon.

He'd never given thought or found a reason for learning how to type. The voicewriter on his own timeline had incorporated—that is, *would* incorporate—transliteration, text storage, and retrieval firmware for whatever commonly used language one chose, plus ancillary software that enhanced nuance of meaning, displayed dia-critical editing marks, and an integral spell-check, also in selective languages. In his former future life, inputting the voicewriter had been as natural as breathing. An irreplaceable tool when writing, editing, and polishing his papers and books, the ultra-sophisticated device had seamlessly facilitated the dissemination and assimilation of information to and from students and colleagues whose native tongues were neither German, English, Italian, nor basic Mandarin.

The obsolete but useful Olivetti's QWERTY key pattern was totally foreign to him—round discs protruding in staggered rows, each identified with a Gothic letter, number, or less-than-familiar symbol, leaving him with no choice but to hunt and peck. He also became irritated by the loud, erratic click-clack of type striking a sheet of foolscap wound around the worn roller.

Completed in fumbles, bumbles, fits and starts, he captioned his first op-ed piece "Wartime Berlin," bylined it to his alter ego, Hans Steyr, and sat back, wondering if clumsily typing the paper might have been a waste of time and energy, while acknowledging the chore may have been necessary due to his nosy landlady's curiosity about the foreign "journalist" under her roof whose comings and goings on nameless errands were not really unusual, only that he had demonstrated little in the way of practicing his supposed occu-pation.

An acquired academic foible was his belief that whatever was not written down had never actually taken place, hence committing to paper the impressions gathered in roaming the capital and conversing with anonymous strangers had helped him organize his own thinking. Whether or not the faux article had any other value remained to be seen, but at least snoopy Frau Kraven had heard sporadic typing coming from the attic room, hopefully reassuring her the foreign boarder was as advertised: an Austrian national practicing the profession he was in fact hiding behind.

Reviewing his article, he was mildly surprised by how thickly he had laid on the bombastic optimism and patriotic fervor gained by sampling the opinions of the individuals with whom he had struck up conversations—shopkeepers, laborers, professionals, and in one singular instance a streetwalker whose views he had sampled, only to realize her prompt responses had been in the interest of soliciting trade, not providing information. A basic op-ed think piece, the article was a straightforward paean to illustrate with what enthusiasm Berliners were endorsing the "just and righteous war" Germany was prosecuting, and suggesting with zero subtly that since Austria had been annexed to *Dritte Reich,* all Austrian citizens would be wise to take note of how the German general public was reacting and follow suit. Three and one-half pages of double-spaced, hunt-and-peck prose, plus the laborious, exasperating use of the Olivetti just to get his thoughts on paper, had wearied him, depleted his psychic energy.

Feeling a need for physical activity after battling the Olivetti to a draw, he descended the stairs soft-footed, ducked past the widow Kraven, who was singing to herself off-key in the kitchen, and slipped out of the boardinghouse to resume his random search for Erich Lustmann.

Footsore after hours of fruitless wandering, he decided help was necessary. He stopped at a bookseller's shop in Alexander Platz and purchased a guidebook titled *Berlin Von A Bis Z.* Back in his lonely attic room, he spent the rest of the day plotting and marking the location of every bistro, theatre, restaurant, opera house, and movie theater listed in the guidebook or that he had discovered pounding the streets in various districts of Berlin.

Mornings thereafter were given over to sketching out and writing articles supposedly destined to be sent home to Salzburg for publication, with afternoons reserved for making his rounds, hoping against hope to pick out the unmistakable face in the crowd. Between times he lived a Spartan existence, keeping up with news of the war's progress in day-old newspapers scrounged from park benches or trash bins. At the current rate of expenditure, his cash would be gone in another month, six weeks at most if he watched every pfennig. Then he would have to fall back on his last resort, the scant handful of jewelry to sell.

Thoughts of pawning the jewelry sadly turned his mood back to that of his previous future life and Bernard Omsley, who would have been proud of the thoroughness with which he had atemporized. He began to feel at home among the innumerable working-class Berliners he approached, and using the rich, racy argot of the streets, where money was "wire, moss, gravel, or powder," and Reichsmarks were *Eier*—eggs—or *Emmenchen,* a diminutive of letter *M.* The best linguistic tutors had been the salty-tongued flower vendors in Leipziger Strasser. He stopped there whenever he was in the vicinity and made it a practice to handle the blooms critically while dropping sour comments about the withered look of the bouquets despite their exorbitant cost, and invariably received a fluent dressing-down that aided in building a lexicon of slanderous abuse.

Spending niggardly sums on more than one occasion, he purchased a standing-room ticket and almost developed fallen arches at Staatsoper, arriving when the doors opened to search for Lustmann among the arrivals, then prowled the lobby during intermission to survey the crowd of chatting operagoers, and conscientiously kept vigil after the final curtain call as the massive building emptied, watching for his quarry in the dispersing crowd.

One memorable evening he reveled in *Die Meistersinger*'s contra-
puntal magnificence after having his sense of security jolted by a
momentary scare. Unbeknownst to him, a rumor had circulated
that *Der Führer* might decide to attend the performance. The rumor
proved false, but he had been accosted upon entering the opera
house by a gentleman he assumed to be a Gestapo agent, who probably considered an opera patron's second-hand apparel not fit for
mingling with well-dressed Berliners and demanded to see his
papers. He had also endured an excellent production of *Zauberflöte*,
then weeks later a pompous production of *Aida*.

At last forced to conclude Lustmann was not an opera buff, he
sought his fellow time traveler in less highbrow venues, patronizing
sporting events, open-air band concerts, and reconnoitering the
parlors of a few bordellos, and once on impulse figuratively held his
nose while attending a stage-managed Nazi street rally. All such
ventures proved disappointing. With a sinking feeling, he began to
regard the random searches as wasted effort, uneasily forcing himself to reject the dread notion that Lustmann had yet to put in an
appearance, a notion spurred by the pressure of increasing urgency
as time passed that brought on fits of mild depression. Taking a
firm, resolute grip on himself, he pushed discouragement aside,
steeled his devotion to continuing the quest. Nothing at all in the
early course of what he still thought of as the "War Years" seemed
to vary from the accounts rendered in the tomes he had studied in
school and later immersed himself in after gaining the professional
insight needed to digest and critique records such as the ponderous,
thirteen-volume War of World Liberation history credited to
Reichsminister Josef Goebbels.

He played endless suppositional games, trying to walk in Lustmann's shoes while making his rounds, imagining where the hero
of heroes might be staying, how and by what means he hoped to
get on with his mission, positing how he might occupy his time.
Actually, there were very few differences between the situation of

his quarry and himself. Both were interlopers, strangers in Berlin, although in that respect Lustmann owned a substantial advantage. Not only a born-and-bred German national, he had supposedly lived in the capital as a youth.

If so, it seemed reasonable and logical to assume he *had* to be here in the springtime of 1940. The ODESSA expatriates who were said to have schooled him on carrying out his mission would definitely have wanted Lustmann on site when hostilities erupted. Best perhaps to take his presence for granted, an attitude that should make finding him a matter of sheer perseverance.

Despondently closing the purchased guidebook late one cloudy afternoon, he stopped for supper in a small mom-and-pop café, and then, in low spirits, wearily dragged himself back toward the boardinghouse. Crossing the Spree on the Oberbaum Bridge's upper-level pedestrian walkway, he ambled three blocks farther toward the railroad tracks, turned the corner, halted in his tracks, and shrank back against the fence in front of a neighboring two-story house.

An indistinct figure, his head tilted back, hat brim pulled down over his eyes, was slouched in the driver's seat of a sleek black Audi sedan parked at the curb directly in front of Frau Kraven's boardinghouse.

Staying partially shadowed, James deliberated for seconds, drew a deep breath, and walked quickly past the parked Audi and hurried up the steps. Neither his landlady nor any lodgers were lounging in the parlor. Going up the creaky stairs two risers at a time, he hesitated on the second-floor landing to peer upward through the row of posts supporting the bannister.

The door to his attic room stood ajar. Angered to think snoopy Frau Kraven had again taken advantage of his absence to invade his privacy, he surged upward, meaning to once and for all set her straight on the issue. Gaining the narrow landing atop the stairway, he halted again, feeling the small hairs lift at the nape of his neck.

An unsmiling intruder seated on the edge of his bed was gazing at something between himself and the ancient Olivetti typewriter resting on the battered nightstand James used as a desk. The stranger looked up, calmly inspected James through the half-open doorway, and said, "Come in, Herr Steyr, or would you rather be addressed as 'A Friend of the Reich'?"

\* \* \*

Temporarily a shut-in due to heavier than usual spring snowfall, Erich Lustmann spent the early morning hours reading the newspapers, a practice often inspiring a siege of displeasure. Plain vanilla in every respect except on details previously unknown to him, he was the one and only individual in the current timeline able to dip into a personal treasure trove of factual data relating to what he could not help but think of as the "recurrent" war, and more importantly what future events were soon due to occur. Thus far, the war's course matched to a tee everything chronicled in the flash-paper "script" secured in the carryall.

To date, each item of print or vocal reportage, and especially radio bulletins, used only glowing, sugar-coated terms to relate the manifold major and minor successes and achievements wrought daily by the Reich's military juggernaut. Press attention currently focused on the air and sea rampage aimed at occupying strategically situated Norway and Denmark, yet offered no more that spotty news of the dual operations, a lack chiefly responsible for his sagging spirits. The war's smooth progress, achingly familiar in most respects, left him with little or no ammunition to use composing any fresh letters ODESSA had insisted on to proactively forward his mission.

Having laboriously hand printed a second letter, then weeks later a third, the core message in each had been to remind those in authority of the uncanny accuracy inherent in each and every one of his predictive "visions." As an afterthought, he had also offered a bonus warning of the danger posed by British sea power, reinforcing its accuracy by citing the classified codename *Weserübung* assigned to the Scandinavian offensives known only to *OKW*'s high command. Posting his third letter on the last day of March, he had unobtrusively slipped it into the slot of a sidewalk red public letterbox several blocks from the Adlon.

On the morning of Tuesday, April 9, Hans the bellman, prompt as ever, had delivered the morning papers, then bowed and scraped and voiced undying gratitude for Lustmann's overly generous gratuity. *Morgenpost* offered glad tidings stemming from the Weserübung campaign, but also tidbits not so appetizing, including word of how a pair of Wehrmacht divisions under General Kaupitsch's command had overwhelmed Copenhagen in less than twelve hours. On the opposite side of the ledger, the Norway landings had been much more difficult than *OKW* anticipated. A small flotilla of troop carriers steaming toward Oslo had met increased resistance entering the fjord, and at the Oscarsborg Narrows, a recently commissioned British heavy cruiser, HMS *Blucher,* had been sunk. This setback had compelled troop landings a good distance from the objective, where airborne units were taking serious casualties during a simultaneous paratroop drop at the Oslo airport.

Dense fog had apparently impeded the invasion at Kristiansand, although most Wehrmacht elements had safely moved ashore. The vital Stavanger airfield had been taken via airborne assault, despite losing a preponderance of equipment destined for use by ground assault troops when a Norwegian destroyer sank the vessel transporting it. At Bergen, surprise had won the day after the cruiser *Konigsberg* was seriously damaged by shelling from a coastal Norwegian battery. To the north, Trondheim had fallen almost without a shot being fired.

The most indecisive segment of the Norwegian Weserübung operation, the push toward Narvik, had featured a sharp exchange between British battle cruiser HMS *Renown,* and a pair of Kriegsmarine pocket battleships, the *Scharnhorst* and *Gneisenau.* In spite of a disparity in firepower between the respective opposing forces, *Gneisenau* had sustained sufficient damage to force her captain to break off engagement. A British destroyer force was said to be steaming toward Narvik, while off Kristiansand, the cruiser *Karlsruhe* had been sent to the bottom, most probably by a British submarine. Despite these difficulties and setbacks, *Morgenpost* labeled the Weserübung incursion into Scandinavia a series of resounding successes. Most Wehrmacht units had managed to get ashore and establish control of the crucial Stavanger airport, now a base devoted to aiding the Luftwaffe to not only restrict British operations by sinking a destroyer, but also badly damaging the battleship HMS *Rodney.*

Despondently crumpling the newspaper, Lustmann sipped coffee laced with cognac, flicked his gold-flashed Dunhill lighter, and briefly studied the flame before touching it to the cigarette. He reflected on the upcoming events capsulized in ODESSA's flash-paper scenario, particularly the breach of a nonaggression pact signed by Reich foreign affairs minister von Ribbentrop and that vicious Georgian bastard, Stalin. Grimacing in rancor over the underhanded way the opportunistic Red *Schweinhunden* had demonstrated their Communist-style compliance with the treaty by immediately sending Red Army contingents into Poland from the east, making the pact supposedly in force more worthless than the paper on which it was written.

Worse, more than a year still remained before Hitler would give up on that "other" timeline and cancel crossing the channel to assault England, and in its place ordered the onset of Barbarossa, the *OKW* codeword for invading the Soviet Union. It would be no simple task, he realized, to provide "visionary guidance" to the Nazi mastermind whose demagoguery ruled, and in a pejorative sense often *overruled*, the actions and tactical intentions of competent professional military as well as amateurish Nazi masterminds, in particular the *OKW,* the majority of whose senior officers urged a hiatus in the conflict in order to firm up and consolidate all European territorial gains to date, and thus significantly delay Barbarossa. It would be no straightforward task to organize the coaching suggestions originated by ODESSA, Stoltz, and his confreres on ways and means of changing Hitler's mind and then influencing, redirecting, and rectifying the course of the war by averting as many downstream errors as possible. Delayed or not, the Barbarossa campaign lay months in the future, which meant little was to be gained by making any plans about it at this early stage of the conflict.

One consequential goal had been drilled into the candidates by repeated lessons: the need to compose a stern caveat aimed at turning about head to tail what was commonly known as "the early war's most ridiculous fiasco," when one-third of a million stranded British and allied troops had been successfully evacuated from beaches near the Belgian port of Dunkerque. He meant to throw his heart and soul into composing the Dunkerque letter. An enormous amount of apolitical and international pressure could have been exerted on the British during the "real" war if vast numbers of Tommies and their allied cousins had been annihilated or taken prisoner on the Belgian beaches—and what a superb bargaining chip those irreplaceable troops would have become when peace negotiations began with the government of that brandy-swilling tub of lard, Churchill! Dunkerque would arrive on the eve of a crucial period when coaching the success of Operation Seelöwe, the "Sea Lion" Channel crossing, would become mandatory. This time, he decided, the invasion definitely *had* to lead to a conquest of the British Isles.

Slated to take place in late May and very early June, Dunkerque would occur at a time not all that far off, which meant that if Hitler's incredible, indecisive failure to act were to be reversed or ameliorated, Dunkerque would become the conflict's first turnabout, if not a true military reversal. It was by no means too early to begin drafting that critical letter, but unfortunately, as had been the case with both recent missives, it would necessitate a message he would have to compose from scratch, a devilishly worrisome notion in itself. Moreover, a corollary requirement would be to inject verbiage consonant with the theme and tone of the earlier letters, which would make it not exactly a labor of love, but a prospective task in which he knew himself to be in no way proficient.

Shortly after the Dunkerque letter, two others would come due, possibly a third. The principal objective of each would be to revise the strategic and tactical thinking of egotistic, self-centered Luftwaffe *Reichsmarschall* Göring. Included in the flash-paper précis of the aerial war against Britain was a series of lessons on the various aspects of obtaining positive, practical bombing results, not strewing civilian carnage helter-skelter during the coming summer's all-out aerial assault on the Englanders. It seemed Hefty Hermann's one-track mind had settled on repeated attempts to terrorize the Britishers into submission by decimating the civilian populace in London, Coventry, and other cities, possibly because the *Reichsmarschall* had become an overrated hero by demonstrating his valor after replacing the revered ace of aces, von Richthofen, as commander of the baron's *Jagdstaffel* during the Great War.

According to Colonel Stoltz, Göring had only a fuzzy conception of how obtuse the stiff-upper-lip Britishers really were, or how obstinately and defiantly they had refused to be intimidated by WWII's aerial Blitzkrieg. What the Luftwaffe's master should have realized the first time around was a vital need to attack and destroy every stick and stone of Britain's industrial infrastructure—aircraft production facilities, airports, seaports, armaments factories, shipyards, and every vessel at sea, or for that matter docked in port. If all went according to the master plan formulated under the guidance of Stoltz and ODESSA's self-declared wise men, the Luftwaffe's epicurean leader might be forced to heed the message in the coming letter and abandon the nonregulation, self-inflating uniforms he wore, a stroke of overweening hubris that on occasion had made him a laughing stock.

Lustmann stewed about where his trail of logic was leading and readjusted his thinking. Thus far into the era he was miraculously revisiting, the war had reprised its former course to a tee, which seemed an improper, too subjective way of viewing matters on the now timeline, but he also found it all but impossible to be wholly objective. He had to forget about the former *DWK* air he'd breathed, the sidewalks he had strolled, or the *SS* duties he had performed, and think of this "first time around" conflict exactly as did those now too busy fighting and dying and planning and directing the manifold wartime events, advances, retreats, adventures, and misadventures he hoped to effectively stage-manage, praying that before the so-called Battle of Britain ran its course during the lovely European summer just over the horizon. Hefty Hermann Göring would need to be convinced how mandatory it was to abandon his preconceptions, self-indulgences, conceits, and excesses, and devote all of his energies to take charge of his aerial armada in an aggressive, forethoughtful manner. If such a fanciful, wishing-well change were to actually overtake the *Reichsmarschall,* surely as night followed day it would set the stage for the success of Seelöwe, the subsequent waterborne invasion leading to a conquest of the British Empire's seat, and perhaps even the consolidation of western Europe under the Reich's fierce, forceful determined hegemony prior to invading the immense, near-hemisphere-spanning expanses of the Soviet Union.

\* \* \*

Rooted in the doorway of his dreary attic room, James suppressed a panicky urge to dash back downstairs out of the boardinghouse into the night. But along with the gentleman who had coolly greeted him using some peculiar term, an image of the man slouched in the Audi sedan parked outside flashed through his mind. Heart racing, he tried not to sound indignant saying, "Who are you? What are you doing in my room?"

The expressionless stranger ignored both queries. "Once more, may I ask how you prefer to be addressed? *Als Herr Steyr, oder Freund des Reichs?*"

James did not have to feign perplexity. Breathing raggedly, sustaining his aggressive bravado, he said, "A *friend* of the. . . Listen, whoever you are, I'm patriotic as the next fellow, but I don't, uh … What the hell is this? What do you want of me?"

"Tell me, Herr Steyr, when undertaking your journalistic endeavors," inquired the other calmly, "do you always use this antique typewriter, or perhaps change pace on occasion and hand letter your articles in … oh, for example, green ink?"

The other's ongoing questioning gave James serious pause, but also a chance to frame a reply. He took it for granted the suave, well-dressed gentleman seated on his bed was no Gestapo thug. Whoever and whatever he might be, his cool manner removed any thought of regarding him as other than a self-assured individual, but that also prompted a counterattack.

"You have me at a disadvantage, sir. You appear in my room uninvited, ask meaningless questions, which, frankly, I have no idea what you're talking about. You may be someone in authority, but I do have a right to know who you are and why you have invaded my privacy."

"Please come in and relax, Herr Steyr." The other gestured toward a rickety, ladder-backed chair, one of few other items of furnishing in the stark attic room. "I think perhaps what I needed to know has already been answered. To the best of my knowledge, you are not in any sort of difficulty with the authorities. To save time, may I have a look at your papers, *bitte?*"

His unannounced visitor's abrupt transformation from stern interrogator to cordial interviewer did nothing to reassure Silverthorne. He made a project of extracting and handing over his credentials, then obediently sank down in the rickety chair.

"Ah, Salzburg. Your landlady mentioned that you are Austrian." The stranger returned the forged credentials. Fingering the typed pages of foolscap resting beside the Olivetti with a speculative air, he said, "I hope you won't be offended, but I took the liberty of reading this manuscript while awaiting your return. Truthfully, I was most impressed, Herr Steyr. It struck me as unusual, and more than a touch surprising, to learn in what depth a foreign journalist has assessed the wartime mood of we Berliners, and doing so by using distinctly upbeat terms."

His tension easing only a trifle, on a hunch James paraphrased a statement in the Nazi bible. "*Der Führer* explained to us how Austria simply had to return to the great German Mother Country, not only because of economic considerations."

Although his expression remained neutral, a twinkle of mild amusement invaded the other's dark eyes. *"Ein Reich, ein Volk, ein Führer?"*

James nodded. "United indeed, sir. Ever since the Anschluss, that phrase has become something of a cliché, but it will help rewrite my country's future history. Our border with Germany is merely an arbitrary line on every map. I'm certain most Austrians already regard themselves as integral citizens of the Reich. One might say it has been both a social and a governing marriage."

"One might indeed. Your piece about Germany's wartime mood interested me greatly."

James shrugged. "We Austrians share not only a language, but essentially the cultural and social worldview of most German citizens. I know this to be the case in Salzburg, Linz, and Vienna, especially since *Der Führer* boasts of Austrian roots himself, and he of all people should—"

"Quite so, quite so!" interrupted the visitor. "Tell me, what prompted you to leave Salzburg?"

"It was a spur-of-the-moment decision, sir. A freelancer with limited funds, I opted to spend my *Wanderjahr* in Germany when the editor to whom I plan to submit my articles showed an eagerness to publish a firsthand account of how the war is affecting Germans. I plan to assure him how wholeheartedly those to whom I've spoken are—"

"You have no formal affiliation with a newspaper, magazine, other type of publication?"

"Not at present, but one day I hope to achieve that goal. Having my work published is rather a … I confess to being very ambitious."

"With good reason," said the stranger. "I suspect your ambition will pay rich dividends, Herr Steyr. You write very well, making it simple to foresee future success coming your way."

"You are most kind, sir. Thank you."

"You've lived all your life in Salzburg?" The queries came faster now.

"No, I was apparently born in my namesake Austrian town, Steyr."

"Apparently?"

"I grew up a foundling, an orphan who knew neither parent. To my misfortune, that's why I found myself ineligible to join the Party. There was no way to document my heritage."

"You petitioned to join the National Socialist Party?"

"Twice, sir. But the authorities told me—"

"Yes, yes; I understand. So, you spent your infancy in an orphanage?"

James made up the tale as he went along, informing the other his stay in the orphanage had been no more than a matter of hours. "When I was brought in, a middle-aged couple happened to be visiting, looking to replace the son they lost during the Great War. I was given over into their charge, never formally adopted but afforded a wonderfully good home, renamed for the town of my origin, cared for, loved for myself alone. We moved to Salzburg in my eleventh year."

"And the name of your foster parents?"

"Grundig, sir. Bishop and Klara Grundig. Very fine people, the finest!"

"Bishop, a churchman?"

"Oh, no! My foster father's given name."

"Do the Grundigs still live in Salzburg?"

"It saddens me to say both passed away some years ago."

His gentlemanly visitor smacked his lips and glanced down at the manuscript in front of him. "Your work affected me positively, Steyr. You write directly to the point, with clarity of statement and few if any discursive asides or extraneous comments. If you have no objection, I should like to show it to a professional with whom I'm acquainted. Do you think that might be possible?"

"Why, I'm uh … That's very flattering, sir. I would appreciate having it back afterward to edit and polish, then hopefully interest the Austrian editor I mentioned in publishing it."

"I promise to have it back in your hands within a week. Will that be satisfactory?"

"Why, yes, of course. Thank you very much. Would it be an imposition to ask your name?"

"Not at all. Ulrich Meisinger." The smooth-talking gentleman rose from his seat on the bed and offered his hand. Gathering up the manuscript pages, he said cordially, "Thank you, Herr Steyr. You've been most cooperative." Tall and lean, his purposeful strides carried him briskly from the attic room, after ducking his head a trifle to pass under the doorway's lintel.

Shaken by the visit, his thoughts tumbling over one another, James relived the encounter minute by minute. He descended the stairs and bathed his face in cold water in the second-floor bathroom. Knowing it pointless to try and guess who Meisinger might be, or what branch of officialdom he represented, the responsibility for his surprise appearance was obvious. Nosy Frau Kraven's curiosity about her boarder's comings and goings at all hours must have caused her to alert ... who? The authorities, he was certain, but from what office?

His inquisitor had been no run-of-the-mill Gestapo thug, but a polished, intelligent professional of some kind whose forceful, authoritative manner automatically guaranteed him total control when questioning anyone. Nor had his queries resembled what one might hear from an interrogator bent upon grilling someone under any type of active suspicion. His opening persistence in asking if Steyr wished to be addressed as someone friendly to the Reich was puzzling. James frowned, wondering exactly what *that* had been all about.

He continued revolving the surprise interrogation, trying to imagine what ramifications there might be, if any. Retracing the bouncing ball Q and A session, he slowly climbed back up to his room, sat down on the lumpy bed, and stewed about the encounter for a time. He finally decided that whatever the upshot of Herr Meisinger's visit might be, having his anonymity evaporate in such a totally unexpected fashion was worry-making, yet he was encouraged to think there could also be a positive side. Spending a few precious Reichsmarks on the old wreck of a typewriter had not only allowed him to reinforce his journalistic pose, Herr Meisinger's visit made it beyond doubt the wisest unforeseen move he had made since hiking to Berlin.

He meant to sit down in the morning and, as a matter of insurance, write a backup article.

# ELEVEN

## *Revelation, Berlin*
## *Late Spring 1940*

Admiral Canaris rarely allowed his emotions to surface, yet on occasion exceptions did occur. *"Had* to show the *verdammt* letters to Himself, didn't you?" Smacking his lips angrily, he added, "Heinrich, what the hell prompted you to insist on making *Der Führer* aware of that string of idiotic letters? *Why* must you forever whisper in his ear, just to curry favor, or what?"

Unable to cope with the heat in the Abwehr chieftain's eyes, Reichsführer-*SS* Himmler blinked and looked away. "He insists upon being informed of everything that transpires." Cornered behind his desk, Himmler was accustomed to issuing orders no one dared to question, and utterly detested any and all forms of confrontation. Deeply resenting Canaris's rudeness for bursting into his office unannounced he attempted to imagine what manner of reprisal his belligerent visitor might devise for one who had betrayed a confidence and inquired how Canaris had learned about how the news had upset *Der Führer.*

"A call at breakfast!" Folding his arms, the admiral subjected Himmler to further punishing scrutiny. "He rang me up himself, didn't bother ordering that liverish, errand-running jackanapes Hess to place the call. He demanded to know why we haven't yet collared the letter-writing charlatan, then in the same breath demanded to know why he'd been kept in the dark about this … this Nostradamus.

What choice did I have but to finish telling him the truth?"

Once again, Himmler self-consciously averted his gaze, and light reflected from the banker's lamp on his desk turned the rimless lenses of his spectacles opaque, veiling his eyes. "I shouldn't wonder that he flew into one of his classic rages."

Canaris uttered a disgusted snort. "Not over the phone," he denied, outwardly calm yet seething internally. "He reserves his carpet-chewing, arm-waving tirades for *OKW* staff conferences if and when things do not go precisely according to *his* vision. Have you any inkling what a gross, unwitting disservice you've done, Heinrich?"

"That's totally unfair," objected Himmler. "How could telling him about the letters and giving him one to read possibly do harm?"

"As usual, you ask the wrong question," declared the admiral, his refractory gaze colliding headlong with that of the other. "What you should have inquired was how, in what manner, did it perhaps encourage him to perhaps take to heart and *concur* with the advice and counsel, wit and wisdom, stemming from the visions afflicting our insomniac friend of the Reich?"

"Concur? Please, Admiral! I don't see how you can—"

"Heinrich, for the love of Christ, *think!* Until the deranged individual penning these ridiculous letters has been run to ground and had the truth wrung out of him, making Himself aware of the ongoing lunacy is far, *far* from the useless distraction you may think it is."

"What do you mean?"

"Should our prophetic friend remain hidden much longer," informed Canaris, "have you given any thought at all to what could come from his visionary cascade? What if our noble Führer decides to cash in on the maniac's ability as a seer, a genuine prophet?"

"You can't be hinting that he's—?"

"Hinting I am not! You should realize how gullible our leader is in his dogmatic, self-assured fashion, how oddly fixated he is, has always been and will forever be on Wagnerian fairytales of fate, magic fire, dragons, sword-wielding invincible Aryan supermen, all that sort of childish rot. What if the Reich's mastermind begins to actually take *credence* in our friend's outrageous boast of prophetic virtuosity, gradually turns into a true believer?"

"Preposterous!"

"So is the whole damned thing! What if Himself begins swallowing whole the content of one preposterous vision after another? You yourself know how he is, know what a political and military genius he *believes* himself to be. Isn't it conceivable that he might pull out of his ass more than one of the impulsive decisions he's famous for and act upon our dear friend's advice, literally make it his own? What then, Heinrich? Who among us will have the sand to whisper in his ear, try to talk him out of pursuing such arrant folly? Will *you*, Heinrich?"

*SS*-Reichsführer Himmler's attempt not to appear cowed fell short. "You're exaggerating," he said defensively. "All I had in mind was—"

"To curry favor!" supplied Canaris, biting the words short. "All of us compete for his ear, which is to be expected. But *you* forever shoulder your way to the head the queue, if only when you manage to step around that demented astrologer, Hess, who follows him about like a puppy not yet housebroken. To our misfortune, *Der Führer* has a most unsettling habit of paying close heed to whoever first gains his ear. Your *Endlösung* solution to the Jewish question is an outstanding example of precisely that brand of folly."

"Folly!" Grossly nettled by the remark, Himmler riposted. "Don't tell me you've become a Jew lover, Wilhelm!"

"Nor should you dare tell *me*," declared Canaris, "how your chief butcher, Heydrich, once a Kriegsmarine intelligence officer under my command, and your other scheming vultures have put their heads together and slyly attempted to take over my Abwehr operation and persist, while pretending I know nothing about it. Lifting himself by his own bootstraps, Reinhard is a one of the principal architects of your grandiose scheme to obliterate all European Jews."

"Reinhard," assured Himmler, "has performed remarkably by reorganizing—"

"*Ja, Ja!* He's remarkably murderous. Sometime explain to me how he earned your undying praise for integrating the State Security Police, *SiPo,* and *Sicherheitsdienst* into what is now the glorified Reich Security Main Office. An aide called to my attention the fact that you've put your chop on his scheme to add murder-crazy *Einsatzgruppen SS* executioners to your ballooning list of functions aimed at exterminating millions of Jews. I spoke to Göring about it, but busy as he was juggling his aerial circus, he reacted with graceful indifference. It's my firm conviction that at this critical juncture implementing your Jewish eradication program is an egregious error."

Grossly disturbed by the remark, Himmler cried, "How so?"

"Because it is still early days, Heinrich. Now and then look at the big picture, not merely what's visible inside your *SS* pasture, and you'll notice how the Reich has initiated simultaneous conflicts on more than one front. I grant you the major contests at arms remain a good way over the horizon, making the overall outcome far from decided. I have no qualms about your scheme to target and deplete the ranks of Gypsies, mental defectives, sexual deviates, political dissenters, all others we can do without. But if you and your head assassin, *lieber* Reinhard, insists on initiating your masterful slaughterhouse pogrom as planned and practiced in Poland as well as elsewhere, the Reich will be the poorer for having wasted a valuable asset."

Himmler was incredulous. "You consider the Jews an *asset?*"

"A very *valuable* asset," emphasized the admiral. "Why is it so hard to appreciate what a major aid to our war effort the Jewish labor pool could become if handled properly? Collect the *Juden* to your heart's content, round up every one you can locate! But instead of obliterating the lot, put them to work in the factories, farms, hospitals, and mines. Scrub the plans for your *verdammpt Abschliessende Lösung* until we've achieved at least a partial overall victory."

"Admiral, you amaze me!" cried Himmler. "Organizing a pool of unskilled Jewish laborers would be like—"

"Unskilled, *nein, nein, nein!* You talk foolishness, Heinrich!" Soundly thumping Reichsführer Himmler's desk, the admiral insisted that salting the populace of every major and minor city in Europe were gross numbers of Jewish physicians, nurses, lawyers, scientists, accountants, financial experts, and other assorted professionals, not to mention legions of skilled workers.

"Let the doctors and nurses treat and care for their fellow Germans. Let the scientists' brains be picked, their expertise utilized to the advantage of *Das Reich*. Encourage all competent segments of the Jewish population to perform and earn a stipend, each in his or her fashion, and we shall all be the richer for it."

"What makes you think," demanded Himmler, stung to the quick by the sermon he had no wish to hear, "so-called professional, educated Jews would agree to *serve* Germany?"

"Their willingness or lack thereof," insisted Canaris, "depends on the variety and frequency of whatever fairytales they are told. Talk to Goebbels, solicit his advice on how to spread the word that *Der Führer* wishes with all his heart and soul to protect the poor, downtrodden Jews from further anti-Semitic uproars, wholesale evictions, relocations, and above all the terror tactics of idiocies like *Kristallnacht*. Lean on their patriotism."

*"Jewish patriotism!"* hooted Himmler.

"Sneer if you wish," declared the admiral. "I for one cannot imagine why it's so hard for a man in your position to open his mind part way when I assure you that many if not most Jewish nationals think of themselves as primarily Germans and only secondarily as *Juden*. Haven't they been among us for centuries, and haven't many if not most of them prospered?"

Himmler invariably fell back on the unequivocal mantra he loved. "The Jews are confirmed enemies of the state and must be dealt with!"

"Quite so. But please try to understand how unwise it would be to fail making the fullest possible use of one's enemies before turning about and, as you say, dealing with them."

Stumped by the utterance, Himmler voiced a different rationale for doing anything and everything good, bad or indifferent. "*Der Führer* wills it so."

"Oh, *does* he really? Mightn't Hitler's willful urge," accused Canaris, fire once again in his eyes, his diction clipped, overly precise, "reflect whatever poison you and that imbecile Hess, or the ghost who walks, Borman, whisper in his ear?"

"Admiral, you go too far! Our conversation has strayed into perilous territory. My sincere belief is that the Jewish question *must* be resolved quickly, else we shall be forced to …"

Himmler did not finish his rebuttal. More upset than when he had stormed into the other's office, Canaris turned on his heel, preparing to storm out in a huff, then paused at the door to hurl back a request. "Do me one kindness if you will, Heinrich. Order your alter ego, *lieber* Heydrich, to keep his nitwits from chasing me around every time I leave Tirpitzufer headquarters. What I do, where I go, and who I choose to visit is neither his affair nor yours."

Delivering his exit line, Admiral Canaris slammed the door on his way out.

\* \* \*

Lustmann awoke at daybreak bursting with nervous energy. Blaming his eagerness to get back to the unwelcome task he'd been engaged in when drowsiness overtook him, he made his toilet hastily, sat down in the parlor, and opened the escritoire's writing surface. Scanning the pencil draft of the letter he had worked on until after midnight, he reviewed the gist of the message that had formed in his mind with crystalline clarity, and his enthusiasm waned.

The first draft had given him fits, driving him half mad by writing, rewriting, rewording, and then scrapping the opening paragraph, twice tearing up the text and starting over again, yet again in a determined, haphazard search for an optimum way to frame the message, while adhering to the tone and manner of the first three letters. In the end, judging what he had written unsatisfactory, he scowled angrily and swept aside the legal tablet filled with interlined scribblings.

Thoroughly frustrated by the daunting task after several more hesitant starts and stops, he cursed and charged into the bedchamber, snatched the aluminum carryall down from the walk-in closet's high shelf, and brought it into the parlor. Making sure the entry door was locked, the deadbolt turned, the stout chain affixed, he grounded the taped-together flashlight batteries, produced a tiny spark on the rivet doubling as an anode, and unlatched and lifted open the lid. Taking out the top half dozen pages of flash-paper recounting World War II events, surrounding circumstances, and situations, he concentrated on burning the terse text into his mind:

05/10/40: Per Führer directive, Op Gelb launches 136 Wehrmacht Heer divisions, ≈2,500 Panzers operating w/3- or 4-to-1 Luftwaffe air superiority, opposed by ≈125 French/British divisions & ≈3,600 armored units + support from Belgian forces.

05/12/40: Leeb's Army Group C secures German frontier opposite Maginot Defenses, freeing Rundstedt's Army Group A to negotiate Ardennes Forest hilly fastnesses & allow Bock's Army Group B advance into Belgium/ Holland, drawing most British/French resistance north. With 3 Panzer corps leading,

Rundstedt strikes toward Sedan, Montherme & Dinant w/minor opposition, mainly French cavalry easily thrown aside. Bock's Army Group B effects parachute landings in Netherlands & paralyzes major resistance. Maas River crossed near Arnhem. Eben Emael Fortress falls to airborne glider assault + Luftwaffe strong support. All advances in accord w/Gelb master plan/schedule.

05/14/40: Enemy reaction to Belgian assault causes Allied 1st British Expeditionary Forces Army group + French 7th Army to advance on Dyle & Meuse Rivers above Namur & join Belgian forces linked w/Dutch on left flank. By evening, much of Dyle Line occupied w/Wehrmacht reserves sent to reinforce position. Advance force French 7th Army engages in southern Holland & is handled roughly. Churchill visits king to be officially named PM. British troops land in Iceland, w/advance elements setting up destroyer/scout-plane base to halt/harass enemy Atlantic convoys to Europe, w/U-boat campaign to come.

05/16/40: Guderian's fast Panzers cross Meuse, open ≈80-km gap in front & due to reach Channel coast in ≈six days. Churchill orders Op Dynamo evacuation of troops/equipment stranded on beaches vicinity of Hauts-de-France Dunkerque Port. Leery of Guderian's overly aggressive advance, von Rundstedt orders halt of his Panzers busy closing trap till mobile infantry brought up

```
to assault Allied positions. H agrees, val-
idates order to hall G's armor & prevents
cut-off of retreating British BEF/French
forces, allowing escape of ≈330,000-plus
Allied troops.
```

He paused, deep in thought. Composing narrative of any kind was a foreign endeavor, making him struggle mightily with draft after draft of the Dunkerque letter, toying with a notion to insert a sentence alluding to a rumor that had circulated in the *SS* academy implying that Hitler was disposed to regard the stubborn, wrong-headed Britishers as more than fellow Europeans, but strayed members of whatever the Aryan brotherhood was thought to be, and one day might conceivably be persuaded to aid the Reich's struggle against Communism.

Lustmann had often wondered if that misguided view might have influenced Able Adolph to hold back and permit the British to consummate the infamous Dunkerque rescue. If so, would it be appropriate to hint that such an absurd notion, valid or not, might have induced his dereliction to hold back on ordering the *Panzer-gruppen* waiting in Calais for the invasion to halt the escape of defenseless, stranded Allied forces? It was difficult to take that idea seriously. After all, the enemy was the enemy, a conclusion no one could argue with.

He frowned and resumed reading:

```
05/18/40: Hours later, H rages/worries
about endangering southernmost offensive
flank, and insists on continuing the drive
westward over a fear that a secondary push
southwest might trash the entire western
campaign & clings to following the original
Gelb scenario.
05/24-26/40: Wehrmacht left wing Panzers
```

```
& mechanized infantry halted in place per
Führer directive, while Luftwaffe ordered to
finish-off stranded Dunkerque enemy forces.
Von Brauchitsch & Rundstedt beside them-
selves over "senseless, contradictory"
orders to attack enemy in full retreat in
one sector, but fall back in orderly way
elsewhere, thereby freezing forces in rear
while massed enemy personnel vulnerable to
decimation or capture avert either fate via
seaborne rescue.
   05/27/40-06/04/40: Bad weather grounds
Luftwaffe & 700-vessel hodgepodge of destroy-
ers, minesweepers, trawlers, yachts & other
types small craft cross Channel & evacuate
≈330,000+ BEF/French troops from Dunkerque
beaches, with most military vehicles &
equipment abandoned on strand. Major Weh-
rmacht Heer forces + Panzers stand fast &
rage as more than third of a million enemy
combatants flee to live and fight again.
```

The accompanying flash-paper tutorial advised him the Dunkerque letter would also have to be salted with astrological tidbits and arcane starry gibberish to augment and reinforce the validity of his "visions." *An odd instruction,* he thought, *and damned difficult to follow.* All he knew about astrology was that it amounted to idiotic nonsense. Buying a book on the moronic subject and cribbing from the text seemed the simplest way to solve ODESSA's directive. Again, he revolved the stray notion to include a reference to Hitler's peculiar penchant for pro-British sentimentality, but again scrapped the idea. Daring to mention *Der Führer's* susceptibility to such a weak, false romantic view of the British could not help but be a wholly counterproductive reminder of Hitler's personal foibles, fancies, follies, and cants.

Better by far would be to propose doing everything humanly possible to effect a head-to-toe turnabout in the disgraceful Dunkerque outcome by focusing on how damaging Hitler's failure to act would be ... No, he corrected himself, call it *OKW's* failure to act, accompanied by a vivid word picture of the disastrous rescue vision only he himself reports.

In the vanished Argentine 1960 timeline, Colonel Stoltz and his ODESSA helpmates had stated, restated, and pounded into the half dozen mission candidates the fact that it would be imperative to retain a strong positive note in each letter as the most essential of essentials. In other words, to furnish positive warnings, positive statements, keep every written statement positive, positive, positive! If that tack were to be stringently pursued, the gist of the Dunkerque letter would by necessity consist of carefully worded, positive declarations citing actual "facts" drawn from his native timeline that would hopefully encourage Hitler to return to the real world, revise his thinking, and miraculously become *convinced* looking the other way would ensure disastrous consequences, with no mention of Churchill's "Miracle of Dunkerque," Operation Dynamo.

*And a positive message it would be!* Filled with sudden purpose and determination, what the letter had to say became clearer in his mind, as well as how to best say it. Taking up the fountain pen, he filled it from a bottle of green ink, flattened a sheet of unwatermarked stationery on the escritoire's level, folded out surface, and hesitated when a recurring thought stirred certain misgivings. Was accomplishing the onerous task before him at all worthwhile? To date, had Hitler or any ranking member of the Nazi hierarchy viewed a single laboriously hand-lettered word of the first three missives? What if all his agonizingly difficult work blindly posted to the Schöneberg address had been considered the outré rantings of an anonymous crank and consigned to the trash bin? He had no way of learning the answer, nor would he until, or if and when, the results of his warnings, guidance, and redirections cropped up as newsworthy realities.

He sighed, put aside the fountain pen, seized a pencil, and wrote haltingly, frequently striking out a line, swearing as he crumpled the sheet and started over. Twice more he ripped to confetti what he had written, loosed a hailstorm of lurid curses, and jammed the scraps in the wastebasket. He wrote and fidgeted, clenched his jaw and wrote further, obliterating a word here, revising a sentence there, breaking off more than once to pace the parlor in a fit of pique while angrily chain smoking and condemning his own ineptness.

Lost in the task, he was startled to hear a light tap on the door to his suite. A glance at his wristwatch told him prompt, super-attentive bellman, Hans, had arrived with coffee and the early bird newspaper editions. Hurriedly closing the carryall's lid, he left it unlatched, turned the working papers upside down on the escritoire, and cautiously opened the entry door a slit.

Holding a silver coffee service tray shoulder high in the splayed fingers of one hand, with *Morgenpost* and other newspapers tucked under his other arm, a uniformed bellman he had never seen before dipped his head deferentially. *"Guten Tag, Herr Klasse."*

"Where is Hans?"

"Your pardon, sir. Hans is indisposed, and I have been directed to serve you. The desk also asked me to inform you the manager would like a word with you at your convenience."

Lustmann's pulse rate quickened. "Why does he wish to see me?"

"I was not informed, sir. The desk wanted to phone earlier and request permission for him to visit you, but it was felt that disturbing you at an early hour would be inconsiderate."

"I see," said Lustmann, who saw only potential complications connected with staying on at the Adlon. Concerned about the switch in bellmen, he motioned the fellow inside. "Tell the desk I will gladly make myself available to the manager only if he calls first."

"Certainly, sir." Setting his burden on the table, the bellman's gaze darted around the parlor, came to rest on the closed lid of the aluminum carryall. Dipping his chin, he accepted the more-than-generous gratuity with outward equanimity. *"Viel Dank, Herr Klasse!"*

Lustmann locked and rechained the door, righted the overturned working papers, replaced them in the carryall, latched the lid, and stowed the container back in the bedchamber. From beneath a folded towel in a bedside table drawer, he lifted out a Walther PPK automatic pistol, ejected and checked the clip, jammed it back in place, and screwed a silencer into weapon's muzzle. Working the slide to inject a round into the chamber, he was in the act of slipping off the safety when he decided against doing so, and carried the now cumbersome, too-long, silencer-equipped weapon into the parlor, where he concealed it beneath an armchair's deep upholstered cushion.

Eleven minutes later by his wristwatch, the telephone jangled.

\* \* \*

"Herr Steyr!" The widow Kraven called upstairs again from the second-floor landing. "Yoo hoo, Herr Steyr!"

James left off two-finger typing, got up, and eased open the door. "Yes, Frau Kraven?" Nosy Nellie or not, he appreciated how impressed his landlady must have been by the aristocratic gentleman who had visited her Austrian boarder the previous week. Herr Meisinger's appearance had inspired a marked change of attitude; she had begun treating James like the star lodger.

"Phone call for you, Herr Steyr."

He quailed, jarred by the unlikely response. "Thank you. I'll be right down." *A phone call from whom?* To the best of his knowledge, no one outside the boardinghouse except smooth-talking Herr

Meisinger knew of his presence, so the caller had to be his inquisitor. Curious and apprehensive, he descended the stairs two risers at a time. The antique black wall telephone had been installed across the hall from the entrance to the parlor, where an elderly boarder was using an ear trumpet to listen to a radio already blaring at ear-bending volume.

Lifting the cabled earpiece from where Frau Kraven had perched it atop the telephone box, he cleared his throat and spoke into the cone-shaped mouthpiece. "Herr Steyr here."

Someone at the other end of the line announced himself as "Herr Stampfl" in a reed-thin baritone. "Herr Steyr, I'm calling from the Reich Ministry for People's Enlightenment and Propaganda. I have the pleasure of inviting you to an interview here at the ministry in order to discuss your very interesting article. Can you possibly arrange to come around ten o'clock, should that hour suit your convenience?"

"The, uh … today? Why, yes, thank you. That will be … fine," faltered James, not sure what he had heard due to radio gabble coming from the parlor. Stretching the phone cord, he used his free hand to grab the knob and swing the door shut, halving the noise. "I don't … happen to, uh … that is, I'm a visitor here in Berlin, sir. May I ask the whereabouts of the, er . . ?"

"Our building is difficult to miss, Herr Steyr. The ministry currently occupies office space in the old Wilhelmplatz Leopold Palace. Announce yourself to the receptionist and explain your appointment is with Executive Editor Stampfl, who is eagerly looking forward to meeting you and discussing your work. We shall be expecting you, Herr Steyr."

In the act of requesting something more in the way of an explanation, James heard a faint click as the line went dead.

*What the hell was that all about?* he wondered, groping to replace the earpiece in its pronged hook. The call had to do with the article Herr Meisinger had asked to show to a … Had he said a professional acquaintance, possibly this Stampfl? Wary of rubbing elbows with officialdom, he realized failing to keep the unsought appointment might well be suspicious, so …

At nine twenty-five, after partaking of Frau Kraven's standard breakfast, he buffed his worn second-hand shoes, adjusted the knot in his one and only necktie, donned his brown fedora, and adjusted the wide brim. Leaving the boardinghouse in a mildly nervous state, he turned into Wilhelmplatz, a short walk from Potsdamer Strasse, and realized the caller had been truthful; the looming façade of the Leopold Palace would indeed be difficult to miss. Set well back from the street, he did not remember noticing it while strolling Wilhelmplatz in 1784 while atemporizing prior to the research venture in Potsdam.

On the far side of a cobblestone plaza fronting the impressive building, the bronze figure of "Iron Chancellor" Otto Eduard Leopold von Bismarck-Schönhausen absently studied passersby with sightless metal eyes, his expression one of mild skepticism about the world at large and its denizens. A universally esteemed statesman born during the final years of the Napoleonic Wars, in maturity Bismarck was credited for his nation-building struggles to semi-unify Germany's provinces, and he became the nation's first, most revered chancellor.

Minutes early for the appointment, he roved the plaza to work off a surfeit of nervous energy over the uncertain nature of the coming interview and its potential ramifications. Roman numerals chiseled in a granite cornerstone informed him construction of the palace had been begun in 1880, more than a century after his retro-temporal visit.

The receptionist, an officious, bespectacled woman behind a large walnut desk in the ornate, high-ceiling lobby, appraised James's far-from-new, much-less-than-stylish apparel, and listened with little interest to him explain that Executive Editor Stampfl had invited him to come in at ten o'clock. She squinted at an appointment list through her bifocals. "Ah, here we are, Herr Steyr. If I am not mistaken, he isn't in his office at the moment. I believe he can be found in the Garden Room." She gave directions.

Halfway down a hallway, James tapped on a set of double doors with enameled cloisonné panels. Soon a gold-flashed handle was turned by someone in the chamber, and a balding gentleman of middle years offered a perfunctory greeting. "Ah, Herr Steyr, yes, yes. Do come in and have a seat." Apparently the busiest of busy individuals, Executive Editor Stampfl ushered his guest into the Garden Room, motioned him to a chair, and without another word reclaimed his post behind a massive, ornate desk, where he resumed leafing through a sheaf of papers.

Left to his own devices, James turned his hat brim slowly in his fingers. The telephone rang twice while he waited for whatever might happen next. Overhearing a pair of one-sided phone conversations, mainly consisting of grunted responses by Herr Stampfl, another quarter hour elapsed in a silence broken only by the sound of shuffling papers.

A Garden Room door opened suddenly, and Reichsminister Josef Paul Goebbels bustled into the large, lavishly appointed chamber. Attired in a tailored tan uniform, his upper left sleeve decorated with a red swastika armband, he offered James a quick glance and began pulling off leather gloves one finger at a time. His master's entrance caused Herr Stampfl to rise and scurry away from his temporary seat behind the desk.

Hat in hand, James rose uncertainly.

"Herr Reichsminister," announced Stampfl, "this gentleman is Herr Steyr, the Austrian journalist you requested to see. He authored the article recommended to us by that Abwehr gentleman, Herr Meisinger."

A glance of stony indifference swept over James. "Ah, good of you to come, Herr Steyr."

*Abwehr!* Learning Meisinger's affiliation with the Reich military counterintelligence agency splashed in Silverthorne's consciousness like a douche of ice water. Dismissing his apprehension, he bowed to acknowledge the great man's status. "It's a great honor to make your acquaintance, Herr Reichsminister."

A lukewarm smile accompanied Goebbels' curt nod. "Your article appealed to us very much. A most impressive propaganda tract, I must say." Laying his billed cap and gloves on the desk, the Nazi propaganda minister used both hands to smooth back his sleek black hair and slumped into his high-backed executive chair. Not of impressive stature to begin with, the fortyish, pinch-faced man who looked as if he was wearing some stranger's uniform, seemed to shrink further when seated.

Head cocked to one side, he sized up James candidly. "I suspect my use of a term with pejorative connotations prompted a negative reaction on your part. You may take as gospel the word of a fallen Catholic that the term 'propaganda' was originated by seventeenth-century friars who issued grossly exaggerated treatises promoting their faith.

"During the Great War," he continued, "propaganda per se fell into disrepute when various antagonists tended to propagandize everything from soup to nuts to battleships. By their own admission, the British are adept at dispensing skewed information, especially since falling in league with America's President Roosevelt, who claims neutrality for his nation but dearly loves his mislabeled Office of Facts and Figures headed by a spinner of fables with the unlikely name Archibald MacLeish. Our ministry, you see, conforms to a policy of keeping the enemies' competitive doings in the forefront of our consciousness at all times, hence on either side of the Atlantic the war of words proceeds hand-in-glove with the shooting war. We intend to win both engagements."

"I am certain it will be so, Herr Reichsminister."

Having finished what James supposed was his standard pedantic sermon, Goebbels changed tack without breaking stride. "Frankly, as one scrivener to another, the opinion editorial you penned for Austrian consumption leads me to believe you enjoy total confidence in the Reich's cause and leadership. As a foreigner, can this possibly be true?"

"Heart and soul, Herr Reichsminister," declared James with what he hoped was a depth of feeling the other would appreciate. *"Der Führer,"* he added on inspiration, "is a statesman second to none, a second Frederick the Great one might say, though on a far greater scale."

"One might indeed!" applauded Goebbels. "A noble comparison, I must say. You sound like a student of history, Steyr."

"A most ardent student, Herr Reichsminister.

A slow nod, a glance at the clock on the desk. "I fear little time is available for more discussion this morning, so I shan't bandy words. I asked Stampfl to invite you in this morning to learn if we might commission additional work. How does that notion strike you?"

"Why, I'm ... speechless and flattered beyond words, Herr Reichsminister."

"Excellent! Other than a mild penchant for understatement, you demonstrate a genuine flair for inserting precisely the sort of aggressive, read-between-the-lines message *Der Angriff* yearns to publish regularly. No polemics, diatribes or asides, merely a deft, straightforward word picture of things, not necessarily as they are, but as our government urges the public to believe them to be. In view of your obvious talent, we shall spare you a lecture about how to perform prospective work on behalf of the ministry should you choose to undertake such a duty. If I correctly recall the words of the gentleman who brought your work to our attention, nothing I foresee will prohibit you, a freelancer we were told, from also having your work published in Austria."

"Why, thank you ever so much more than I can say, Herr Reichsminister. You are most gracious. I truly appreciate the opportunity and will do my best to satisfy your interest and trust."

A dismissive wave. "Good, good! One last thing, then I must get to my duties. When forwarding your article, my acquaintance mentioned how he found you living in some dreary boardinghouse. Would it suit you if suitable quarters and an office could be found for you here in the palace?"

Rather than suiting him, the invitation shocked Silverthorne to the point of stuttering, "You're, um … very kind, Herr Reichsminister. I will of course be delighted to show you every word I manage to put on paper, but, uh …"

"But what? Would living and working here with us make you unhappy?"

"Not in any way, Herr Reichsminister. Please take no offense, it's just that I … What I hope to do, and have been doing is, uh … To put it bluntly, my sources are out among the people. I roam the streets for hours and casually engage strangers in conversation. Dressed as I am, speaking with a perhaps unfamiliar accent makes me an obvious foreigner, and those I approach accept me as other than one of them, which makes my rather ingenuous efforts to solicit opinions seem fairly reasonable and proper. Were I to furnish any hint of an association with officialdom, I'm certain those with whom I come in contact would be less eager to confide their actual opinions and observations. Comfort and convenience aside, I prefer to remain anonymous for the present."

*Herr* Stampfl and his master exchanged meaningful glances. "Better and better," intoned Goebbels, sounding more pleased with himself than his ministry's newly acquired journalist. "Steyr, you demonstrate a higher degree of cleverness in person than one finds in your work. Cloak your identity and purpose any way you choose. The results are important, the means of achieving them immaterial. Now then, when will we be privileged to see another think-piece?"

"Quite soon, Herr Reichsminister. Only yesterday I became intrigued by a very opinionated truck driver whose outlook and fiery responses made him a splendid sounding board."

Goebbels nodded and said dismissively, "Precisely what I had hoped to hear. We shall look forward to seeing more of your work." Turning to the editor, he said, "Stampfl, see to it that Herr Steyr is provided with credentials identifying him as one of our stringers."

The telephone clanged, and Stampfl hastened to pick it up. *"Ja, ja,* one moment, *bitte."* Covering the mouthpiece with his palm, he said softly, "Leni Riefenstahl, sir."

"That bitch! Finally returned my call, did she?" Goebbels snatched the telephone.

Executive Editor Stampfl escorted James down a long branching hallway floored in marble, and into a spacious, high-windowed office, where he was handed the stapled-together foolscap pages of his article, as well as a freshly printed copy of *Der Angriff,* and told the issue included the edited piece he had written. A fat envelope was also clipped to his manuscript.

"Please be so kind as to leave your mailing address and phone number with the receptionist, *Herr* Steyr. A card identifying you as a ministry associate will be posted to you." Forever harried and hurried, the other extended a damp hand to be shaken, offered hasty well-wishings, and rushed James to the door with an air of unburdening himself.

Outside in the plaza, a reaction to the nerve-wracking experience made it difficult for James to relax. Delighted in one way, but also leery of what he had unwittingly become involved in, he took the long way around, walking blocks out of his way in a slow-paced return to the boardinghouse. Closeted in his dreary attic room, he unsealed the envelope, peeled back the flap, and upended it over his bed. A thick wad of Reichsmarks fell out.

Too elated by the windfall to count the money, he unfolded *Der Angriff,* learning that his article had been rendered unrecognizable due to a sea change in the propaganda tract now bylined to none other than diminutive, weasel-faced Reichsminister Josef Goebbels. All vestiges of what that gentleman had referred to as "your mild penchant for understatement" were gone, replaced by lurid "Rally round the flag!" diatribes sprinkled with Nazi clichés inserted not to invite, but *command* loyalty and dedication to the cause by each and every German worker with the ability to read and understand the message.

James chuckled, then threw back his head and loosed an uproarious bellow of laughter. The money problem had solved itself with the aid of a principal figure in the Nazi hierarchy, no less than a member of Hitler's inner circle, who had unwittingly helped finance a venture aimed at not only ensuring the demise of *Dritte Reich* in the redux war in progress, but the preemptive obliteration of the never-to-exist *Tausend-jahr Deutsches Weltreich* it might otherwise become.

The ironic assignment Goebbels had handed him inspired James to vow that he would spend each Reichsmark gleefully and faithfully accompany each and every expenditure with silent, yet sincere internal hilarity.

* * *

"Please come in," said Herr Klasse coolly.

In his late sixties, the Adlon's balding manager peered guardedly at the guest before hesitantly entering Suite 204. "I do hope you will forgive me for disturbing you at this hour, sir."

Wordlessly closing and locking the door, Lustmann gestured toward a leather armchair.

The manager settled down, looked up, and gasped upon finding himself staring into the round eye of a tubular silencer attached to the muzzle of a *Polizeipistole Kurz* Walther semi-automatic pistol in his host's rock-steady right hand. "P-please, sir," he quavered, frightened more by the menace in the guest's narrowed eyes than the weapon, "why are you—"

"I mean to ask several forthright questions you are to answer forthrightly," intoned Lustmann. "Choose to do otherwise, and it may not be possible to let you walk out of here. *Verstehen Sie?"*

The manager murmured something that was not quite a word.

"Why did the deskman send a strange bellman here to snoop about in my suite?"

Perspiration filmed the manager's high, balding forehead. He licked his lips. "The, uh, woman, sir ... we w-were requested to ascertain if and when she again visited your—"

"What woman?"

The other had difficulty swallowing. "She, the lady you have, er ... entertained on more than one occasion, sir. I was not told her name."

"Not told by *whom?"*

*"Die Polizei.* Chief Inspector Fürstenburg came to my office and urgently requested to be called immediately if the woman in question were to appear again at the Adlon. Judging from what little he had to say, it has to do with a ... well, a counterfeiting investigation of some kind."

"You will have to be one hundred times more specific than that."

"Please, Herr Klasse! I know nothing of the circumstances except for the detective's repeated mention of a large denomination banknote with an unbelievable ... actually, an impossible issue date." Lifting his hands helplessly, the hotelier let them fall in his lap.

*That verdammt nineteen forty-two banknote again!* Sensing a need to soften his treatment of the manager, Lustmann lowered the silenced Walther PPK, then decided to further diminish the threat by laying the weapon aside but within easy reach. "I pray you to forgive my belligerent attitude, sir. It seemed necessary beforehand, but no longer. Please accept my apologies. What I tell you next must be held in strict, unconditional confidence. Will you—the Adlon— agree to remain silent with regard to the sensitive information I am about to disclose?"

No longer facing a presumably loaded weapon, the manager nodded mutely.

Lustmann frowned, retrieved the weapon as if having second thoughts, and held it loosely. "I'm forced to demand that you instruct the hotel staff to abide by my wishes, sir. I fear a positive response to that demand is all I am able to accept."

"Why, I … yes, surely," blurted the manager, his attention again fixed on the weapon.

Knowing he now commanded the other's undivided attention, Lustmann cleared his throat and launched into a tale larded with intrigue, subterfuge, and implied cloak-and-dagger activities he stated to be of vital importance to the Reich. Revealing no particulars connected with the few clandestine activities mentioned, he declared that in carrying out his specific assignment he reported directly to the office of Reichsführer-*SS* Himmler. Any further snooping into his personal activities, he explained sternly, would open the Adlon's management and ownership to an in-depth investigation by officials not known for being kindly disposed toward anyone who thought to question them, or meddle in their affairs.

"In the future," he concluded, "and for the remainder of my stay in your splendid hotel, I must insist that absolutely *no one* other than chambermaids, room service personnel, and your bellman named Hans be permitted to enter my suite. Have I your pledge to observe that firm rule?"

A jerky nod signified the manager's emphatic guarantee to acquiesce with any demands within reason the guest might make. "Everything shall be just as you wish, Herr Klasse. Your stay with us will be totally in accord with your express deman—that is, your wishes."

"Agreed! Thank you for your patience, sir. You may leave now."

Visibly shaken, the manager bobbed his balding pate, rose, and exited the suite on the fly.

Lustmann relocked the door and attached the security chain. Lifting the telephone, he requested an outside line from the hotel operator, giving her Gerda Sharpe's Deutsche Reichsbank number. After a third ring, someone speaking in unctuous, pear-shaped tones answered and informed him New Accounts Manager Sharpe was occupied elsewhere, then asked if he might be of assistance.

Scowling, Lustmann cradled the handset without responding. Suspected counterfeiting of all things! One lonely, never-to-be-sufficiently-damned-but-*yet-to-be-issued* banknote had once again jumped up to bite him. Still, the simple-to-pose question he asked himself was all but impossible to answer. Would it be wise to quit the Adlon forthwith, or could he hope to stay on, bluff his way out from under an investigation that might already be in progress? Fleeing would be chancy and, worse, could not help but draw unwanted attention to him. Go or stay? Whichever course he chose would make it mandatory to first learn from Gerda exactly what had transpired since they had last spoken. He had to find out why the authorities had purportedly initiated a counterfeiting investigation and suspected that it might involve him.

Muttering an oath, he poured coffee, decanted a stiff dollop of brandy, and stirred vigorously before lighting a cigarette. He stared at the rising curl of smoke, his features twisted in the wry expression, and silently cursed the careless ODESSA scroungers who had rounded up the cache of then-defunct, high-denomination banknotes. The complication accidentally introduced into his treasure trove had redoubled his mission's difficulty simply by raising its unlovely head!

The unique situation in which he found himself could only be termed *ausserördentlich!* With the future of the world literally hanging in the balance, the ingredients and potential consequences connected with a decision to stay or flee the Adlon sliced through his mind like a sharp razor cut, deepening the quandary resulting from a single ironic obstacle to the smooth, ongoing conduct of his mission consisting of one miserable, supposedly misdated banknote, its provenance inexplicable to another living soul on the current timeline.

A disgusted glance at the masthead of the Friday, May 7 *Morgenpost* informed him it was a week later than he had imagined. First, foremost, and above all else would come the mandatory task of finishing and posting the *verdammt* Dunkerque letter that had plagued him like an open, festering wound that refused to heal. Crowded into a tight corner calendar-wise, he was determined to sit down, finish the detested task, get it out of his hair forever, and rush to the nearest postal substation, where he meant to address the envelope and post it then and there.

He reconsidered, feeling it a mistake to worry about the pressure of passing time. Doing the job hastily and haphazardly would violate one of his firmest self-imposed rules. Upon completion, he made a decision to post the crucial letter in exactly the same fashion as all the others, by casually dropping it into the slot of any random sidewalk letterbox he happened to stroll past.

Draining the dregs of brandy-laden coffee, he squashed out the cigarette in a silver ashtray, and with unswerving determination stepped into the bedchamber, took down the carryall, and opened it after impatiently undertaking the electrical fail-safe procedure.

Concentrating intently, his head bent over the task at the escritoire, Lustmann was soon totally absorbed in the effort and detesting every second of it.

# TWELVE

## THE HELPFUL POSTMAN
### *May 1940*

His psyche at low ebb despite semi-employment as a propaganda ministry stringer, James felt himself sliding into the slough of despondency. At the end of the first week in May, he had fruitlessly searched Berlin indoors and out daily, month after month, between times soliciting the opinions of strangers pegged as meat for future articles.

Two-finger typing the piece he had last submitted reminded him of Goebbels' critique of his work as being guilty of "mild understatement." He had changed tack, luridly parroting the optimistic outlook of the truck driver who had picked him up shortly after dropping from the sky into Württemberg. A loquacious fellow, the garrulous trucker had gratuitously voiced glowing predictions that the war would last only a short time before everything returned to normal.

Vowing to stay away from the Leopold Palace unless summoned, on this sunny morning he had stopped in a favorite haunt, his postal substation "office" several blocks north of Unter den Linden, where only pennies were needed to purchase the postage necessary to mail the truck-driver manuscript to hard-charging Executive Editor Stampfl.

Seated at a low counter in the writing room, he had been consulting the *Berlin Von A Bis Z* guidebook in desultory fashion, and was in the act of getting up to leave, when a tall figure filled the writing room doorway. Electrified, he choked, looked away quickly, forgetting to breathe. Seconds elapsed before he could bring himself to dare a second peek. Seating himself in a cane-backed chair directly across the counter, the newcomer bent forward in a posture that partially obscured his features and was busily writing something.

Was it Lustmann? There was no way to be sure; being intent on what he was doing made definite recognition too difficult. James quietly pushed back his chair, rose, and stepped around the end of the counter. Passing behind his suspected quarry, a quick glance returned the impression of an envelope being addressed in green ink.

Fearful of letting the writer react to his presence, James fled the substation, hurried to the far end of the block, and waited to cross the side street with other pedestrians. His scalp tingling in anticipation, he rushed back to a point on the sidewalk opposite the postal substation, waiting there in a state of intense agitation, arms folded to still his palpitating hands.

A tall, hatless figure in a thigh-length tan topcoat emerged from the substation, and all doubt vanished. *Erich Lustmann in the flesh!* The aquiline nose, prognathous jaw, and full head of long blond hair firmed his conviction that it was his quarry.

Unable to contain himself, his heart threatening to erupt from his sternum, he stumbled in his haste to follow his quarry's progress from across the street. His gait loose-limbed, striding leisurely, Lustmann turned the corner toward Unter den Linden, paused there to cup his hands against the breeze and light a cigarette. While his head was turned, he furtively scanned the pedestrians behind him reflected in a storefront window.

*Caution is always provident,* thought James inanely, but for a total stranger sent to reprise a later, wartime era of his native timeline in order to change it, why bother? He tried to imagine why Lustmann, the living, breathing picture of the hero celebrated on his own time-line, was concerned about something so unlikely as having grown a tail. In a state of heady exhilaration, he trailed the once, but-now-hopefully-never-to-become DWK's hero of heroes. James lost himself in the stream of pedestrians screening him from Lustmann, when two words jarred his consciousness: *Green ink!*

A then-meaningless question posed by Herr Meisinger, the polished gentleman characterized later by Stampfl as an associate of the Abwehr counterintelligence agency, reverberated in his mind like a clarion bell. Twice had Meisinger asked if on occasion, rather than being called "Herr Steyr," he might like to be greeted as "A friend of the Reich."

In the postal substation, Lustmann had been addressing an envelope using green ink! The bits and pieces left over from his inquisitor's unexpected visit had taken on a definite, substantial meaning. Apparently, his wariness about being tailed had been compounded by an awareness of some hidden threat here in Berlin, inferring that officialdom might be actively engaged in trying to run to ground any and all those suspected of … *what?*

Blocks farther along the side street, James halted when his quarry stopped to casually pull open the access slot of a bright-red letter-box, one of thousands scattered throughout the Berlin streets, and slip in an envelope. Making a mental note of the adjacent cross street, James was coping with another quandary. Why had Lust-mann addressed an envelope in green ink at the postal substation, but neglected an opportunity to post it there and facilitate delivery?

Shadowing the other discreetly, he stayed well out of sight upon reaching Unter den Linden and saw his quarry cross the broad thoroughfare with a small group of pedestrians. Breathing fast, he matched strides with Lustmann on the other side of the divided artery leading toward Pariser Platz and watched him turn into the small plaza fronting the …

Why, the swank Hotel Adlon, of course! The never-to-become—

knock on wood—premiere *Weltreichsheld,* a living legend universally venerated on that other timeline, had to be endowed with
suave sense and sensibility and could hardly be expected to lodge
just *anywhere.*

Hanging back on his side of the thoroughfare, more excited than
ever before in his life, James watched Lustmann ignore the uniformed doorman's deferential head bob and enter the hotel.

Too impatient to go back to the corner and wait for the white-
uniformed traffic *Schupo* to blow his whistle and beckon the pedestrians an invitation to cross, he trotted to the middle of Unter den
Linden, dodging the light flow of passing vehicles, and stood
behind the base of an ornate bronze streetlight until a break in
eastbound traffic allowed him to trot on across.

Self-conscious over the uniformed doorman's mute appraisal of
his less-than-fashionable attire, he entered the sumptuous lobby
knowing how out of place he looked and slumped on a padded
bench next to a marbled pillar supporting the lofty ceiling. As if
consulting his guidebook, he covertly peeked over the open pages.
His back turned, Lustmann waited for the deskman to reach up and
lift an Adlon latch key from a polished ebony pegboard on the
marbled wall behind him and hand it over.

When the elevator doors rolled closed, cutting off his view of
Lustmann, James sauntered past the desk. Few guests were apparently out of the hotel at this early hour, and the deskman, busy
sorting mail, took no notice of James as he scanned the quantity
and distribution of keys missing from the pegboard. Three keyless
pegs protruded just below the uppermost row, a pair on the left,
and one on the right, from where the clerk may have taken Lustmann's key.

Silverthorne emerged from the Adlon walking on air, secure in
the knowledge that his quarry was undoubtedly a second-floor guest
at the Adlon. Locating him and his living whereabouts was an enormous plus, vastly reducing the former imbalance of probabilities

that affected and influenced his mission, and also drastically lessened the abortive odds formerly arrayed against any chance of success.

His optimism soaring, James hurriedly retraced the route to the red letterbox where Lustmann had posted the envelope. Mail pickups were made four times daily on weekdays in cosmopolitan Berlin. Quickening his pace, he all but trotted along the sidewalk, dodging around pedestrians, and began trotting after crossing the targeted side street upon seeing a postal worker, the strap of his leather bag over one shoulder, kneel down to unlock the red letterbox.

The postman looked up in surprise when James dashed up, panting to exaggerate a shortness of breath. "Excuse … sir. Just now … mailed letter. I think … No, all but sure … address wrong. Would be … too much to ask for me to, uh … check?"

The pudgy, middle-aged letter carrier straightened, subjected James to a suspicious squint. "It's highly irregular, sir, to let anyone tamper with the—"

"*Nein, nein.* Won't … touch letter. *Most* important is … making sure street number … correct. Letter easy to spot; it's … addressed in green ink. There's an *Emmchen* or two in it if … you let me check." James folded the currency in the palm of his hand.

The other's expression remained dubious. He blinked, made the pair of Reichsmarks vanish, then said pleasantly, "Well now, one small favor for a regular customer should do little harm. Green ink, you say? Ah, here we are! Is this your letter, sir?"

James etched the address in his mind. *"Ach,* how stupid!" Hiding his elation beneath a disgusted exclamation, he added, "I've troubled you for nothing. It is as was intended."

"No damage done, eh?"

"Not a lick. Have a beer on me after work and forget your troubles? *Viel Dank!*"

Headed to the nearest bus stop, Silverthorne plopped down on the bench, seized his guidebook, and scrawled the address on the flyleaf, then unfolded and consulted the fold-out map. The letter had been addressed to one Zoltan, no surname, at a street number in the Schöneberg district. It might mean nothing, and yet … He reminded himself of Herr Meisinger's reference to green ink, and then felt that it could mean a great deal indeed.

Either way, he was in a fever to check out the address and whoever might be living there.

* * *

At dusk, the streetlights came on, illuminating the gleaming Mercedes Saloon parked at the curb in front of a "No Stopping" sign. Sitting erect on edge in the rear seat, Lustmann impatiently willed Gerda Sharpe to emerge from Reichsbank and join him in the leased auto. He had phoned several times earlier, finally contacted Gerda on the third try, and invited her to have dinner with him. She had begged off due to a supposed previous engagement, and he had cautiously gone on fishing for information pertaining to the counterfeiting case allegedly under investigation, but Gerda had declined to discuss it over an open phone line.

Eventually exiting the bank, she paused to scan the passersby. Her heels drumming on the sidewalk, she hurried to the Mercedes as Herr Klasse pushed open the rear door. Awarding him a quick glance, she slid inside and inclined her head toward the driver in a silent inquiry.

"Pay him no mind; just speak softly."

"Ee-rich," she said, giving both syllables an unwholesome drawn-out inflection, "your *verdammt* nineteen forty-two banknote has ignited a fucking firestorm."

"So it seems. Are you aware of how the police became involved?"

"*Aware?* Oh, I am very *much* aware!" A frustrated grimace transformed her delicate features. "An arse-kissing colleague at the bank," she said, biting her words short, "took it upon himself to bring the outrageous bill to the personal attention of Reichsbank's President Funk."

"And in so doing," guessed Lustmann, "probably did himself a huge favor."

Gerda tossed her head angrily. "That can be said. The sorry son of a bitch must rehearse his role as fair-haired boy." She glanced nervously out the tinted window at the stream of passersby. "I can stay only seconds. Being seen with you is begging for more trouble I do *not* need."

"I plan to keep you only long enough," assured Lustmann, "to find out if—"

"That's either too long," snapped Gerda, "or not long enough. A chief inspector came to the bank more than once, and each time he and the director were closeted for a good long while. Not only that, I'm sure our security staffers have been watching my office ever since Herr Schacht was assigned to clear up the mystery of your miserable banknote."

"Who is this … Schacht?"

"Hjalmar Schacht is a former Reichsminister of Economics. His reputation as an expert's expert when it comes to currency was well earned. He's convinced the miraculously dated banknote has to be the work of a counterfeiting genius, which automatically casts a degree of suspicion on me as a possible accomplice. I'm all but certain my desk was searched days ago while I lunched with a client. How did you learn an investigation was underway?"

Lustmann recounted the visit by the Adlon's manager. "I stalled him—that is, frightened him—when he mentioned a chief inspector who requested that the hotel notify his office immediately if and when you next visited me."

"Wonderful! All that attention focused on poor little me! Did the police question you?"

"Not yet," he admitted, "but I imagine it's only a matter of time."

"Good God, Erich! What vile brand of deviltry have you gotten me mixed up in?"

"A simple mistake by some clerk," he said, "what else? You told me the banknote was serialized to show an issue date two years in the future and proved to have been circulated afterward,"

"But that isn't the *real* problem, Erich."

"Oh, dear God! What, if I may ask, *is* the real problem?"

"I know only the bare details," she told him. "What I can pass along *has* to stay between us, so don't prod, not that it would do you any good. Herr Schacht took a personal interest in your *verdammt* banknote after Funk's experts judged the paper and engraving to be letter-perfect, and you're correct; signs of moderate wear and tear provide evidence that it's been in circulation."

"Gerda, I ask you in all fairness how either of us," he added, " or anyone else can be faulted for *one* erroneous banknote in a deposit of a million and one-half Reichsmarks? As I said, a silly error by some clerk may seem strange, but so does everything *else* about the miserable banknote."

Gerda swung around to face him squarely, naked disbelief written large in her luminous blue eyes. She started to say something, then stopped and sighed. "I must go. I'm afraid it's goodbye time, Erich." She pushed open the door, fled from the auto back into the bank.

Lustmann fumed. Lighting a cigarette, he curtly told the driver to get the vehicle moving.

\* \* \*

Silverthorne stepped off the bus at an intersection blocks beyond Landwehrkanal and consulted his guidebook map before walking into a respectable if less than fashionable section of Schöneberg. Few pedestrians were about. The storefronts and walkup flats he passed presented orderly, weathered frontages typical of a genteel neighborhood housing a mixed bag of small businesses and the homes of professional and working-class Berliners.

Two blocks farther along the street he passed a deserted delicatessen. The shattered glass of a boarded-up front window was marred by a crude imperative in yellow paint: *Juden raus!* An inaccurately configured yellow Star of David daubed on the front door told a mute, sad story.

Turning into the designated side street, he checked the number on each frontage he came to in approaching his objective on down the block and across the way. Drawing closer, what could be seen in the front window made him utter a low, self-deprecatory chuckle.

The establishment's opaqued plate-glass window was festooned with zodiacal arcana closely surrounding a mystic Persian all-seeing eye keeping watch on a poster depicting a bearded, turbaned seer peering with heavy-lidded indifference into a large crystal ball. The Great Zoltan's advertisement of himself touted him as a "world-famous" astrologer. Red-bordered golden letters lost in a forest of exclamation points urged passersby to come in and learn precisely how:

!!!!! THE ANCIENT ART COULD CHANGE YOUR LIFE !!!!!

*Ludicrous!* How silly of the retro-temporal, never-to-exist genius venerated as the hero of heroes to waste time on an astrological wild goose chase? Even here, in what the vanished Deutsches Weltreich had boastfully labeled the War of World Liberation, and engaged in a mission designed to radically alter a specific quantum time branch of history, the phantom *Weltreichsheld* could not seem to forgo indulging in his personal fantasy, which after further thought struck James as a welcome, perhaps *excellent* sign of Lustmann's success to date. Wasting time and energy on a frivolous preoccupation with the starry occult meant he would have less time and energy to solicit celestial advice through horoscopes and similar nonsense via envelopes addressed in ...

*Green ink!*

Herr Meisinger had casually asked James if he ever wrote using green ink instead of using the noisy, decrepit Olivetti. It was something to think about, and yet …

Bemused, but also vaguely disappointed with himself for chasing Lustmann's wild geese down a blind alley leading to an astrology parlor in a vacuous cul-de-sac, he twice changed buses going back to Pariser Platz and stationed himself on a bench across from the Adlon. He stayed there for hours, making a show of reading and rereading *Völkischer Beobachter* while keeping the hotel entrance in view above the unfolded newspaper.

Giving up the vigil when darkness approached, he dropped the paper in a trashcan, downed a bottle of beer and a liverwurst-and-cheese sandwich, then straggling back to his lonely attic room. Despite the Great Zoltan astrological fiasco, after months of fruitless searching he had put an end to at least the quest, and that alone was enough to paste a bright, shiny star on this, by far his most productive day in the current timeline. Even so, however happily weary he might be, something still nibbled at the liminal threshold of his subconscious, something lurking just beyond the boundary of logical thought. He couldn't seem to pin down what distantly troubled him and bring it into focus.

Seeking his lumpy bed early to escape the chill, he lay there, hands clasped behind his head, staring blindly into the darkness, scheming about what might be done next, examining then discarding every potential plan of action, endlessly speculating until he fell asleep.

Sometime in the wee hours, James awoke with a start, roused by a searing notion that erupted from his subconscious of its own volition: *Could the Great Zoltan's ancient art be used in any way to change not only one's life, but history?*

Rolling out of the cot that masqueraded as a bed, he ignored the deep chill in his unheated attic room and began tiger-pacing back and forth, repeatedly smashing his right fist into his open palm while uttering short-bitten expletives in more than one language.

It fit! God in heaven, how it did *fit!* The caption in Zoltan's window encouraged all passersby to enter and learn how the "ancient art" could change their lives. He muttered the phrase aloud, then repeated it one syllable at a time. Was it remotely conceivable that Erich Lustmann . . ?

No, that would be conclusion jumping! The entire notion seemed not only impossible, but surreal, much too farfetched and insanely incredible for belief.

Or was it? For some inexplicable reason, intuition enhanced his belief that he might have stumbled on a tentative answer to the biggest puzzle of all. Thoroughly fantastic though it seemed, the ODESSA brain trust may have directed Lustmann to play the role of seer to forward his world-changing crusade.

Preternaturally wide-awake, he dismissed all thought of trying to slide back into sleep, wrapped himself in the frayed eiderdown quilt, and sat on the bed until dawn's gloomy luminescence seeped through Berlin's heavy cloud cover, dimly illuminating the filmed window. After Frau Kraven's usual breakfast of oatmeal, coffee, and toast, he went out to purchase a newspaper and again posted himself on Pariser Platz across from the Adlon. It would not do for his antagonist to tag him as a loiterer, so he avoided any chance of that by shifting his vigil to a public bench farther east along the divided thoroughfare.

By early afternoon, having practically memorized every word in *Morgenpost,* the curious glances of several passersby made him leery about of being tagged conspicuously as a fixture on the street, and he abandoned his vigil. Reichsminister Goebbels was now paying him fifty times more for the propagandistic drivel he submitted than it was worth, and the former need to pinch pennies no longer obtained. He treated himself to a decent lunch in a medium-priced café, then wandered about in thought, wondering what to do next.

Despite their lack of productivity, the morning hours had seemed to slip away swiftly, but the early afternoon dragged monotonously, turning his outlook sour. He had hoped to tail Lustmann wherever he might go and perhaps learn what sort of obscure link existed between the current real-world timeline and the outrageous "false prophet" theory of changing history that had shocked him into waking up in predawn darkness. Although Lustmann was apparently sticking close to the Adlon, it worried him to leave the hotel unwatched. His man could depart unseen for some unknown Berlin destination or *anywhere*, such as an obscure locale where he could stay hidden forever.

Yet there was no way he alone could maintain any sort of around-the-clock watch on the Adlon. Whether his man ventured out tomorrow, next week, next month, or never, he couldn't idly wait for him to do so. He ended up deciding to return and reconnoiter the Great Zoltan's lair and perhaps ferret out a meaningful connection between the astrologer and Lustmann, if one existed.

* * *

"Ulrich," said Admiral Canaris, gingerly holding up a carbon copy of the "friend's" most recent letter between thumb and forefinger as if were unclean, "my faith in visions, once zero, has assumed negative proportions."

"I was sure his letters could never become weirder than they were."

"Nor I, and we were both wrong. Our epistolary pundit has added dollops of astrological twaddle to his prophetic scribblings. Now he advises us his celestial visions afflict him only when Jupiter is in trine with the moon, or being buggered during conjunction with Taurus while the awestruck cow that jumped over the moon stands by calmly and watches. This balmy idiocy not only clouds his current letter, but leaves the question of questions unanswered: How in the name of merciful God could *anyone* envision, intuit, invent, or in some *more* exotic manner even *hint* that a potentially senseless future blunder such as *Der Führer's* presumably hare-brained failure to countermand von Rundstedt's order and halt Guderian's advance would open the door and let a huge, helpless allied army stranded on Belgian beaches escape capture or destruction?"

Ulrich Meisinger had earned his reputation as the premiere Abwehr investigator twice over and numbered among *very* few individuals who had won Canaris's total confidence and trust. Called upon frequently to act as the admiral's sounding board, he felt the only logical response to what he'd heard would be mentioning that the morning intercepts had included a recorded telephone conversation between some unidentified British field-grade officer and the presumed BEF command center. "The translation," he said, "described the discussion of a potential necessity to evacuate just such an allied force from the continent."

*"Ja, ja.* That tidbit at the briefing also sparked my interest." Duly vexed, the admiral wagged his head sadly. "Not that I'm about to become a true believer, but coupling that intel gem with our friend's prescient warning punched more than one of my alarm buttons."

Meisinger stroked his jawline. Stepping closer to a wall map of northern Europe, he studied the line of small pinned flags signifying regularly updated Wehrmacht advances and positions. He ruminated, tapped the map, "Here in the north, Reichenau's Sixth Army has overwhelmed Antwerp. To the south, Guderian has apparently taken Cambrai, then halted most of his *Panzerwaffe* formations between Peronne and St. Quentin to regroup. Rommel's Seventh Armored Corps met fairly stiff resistance roughly … here, slowing his advance toward Arras. Trading off our current military situation against the French, Dutch and Belgian geography leaves little choice but to think our prophet's caveat appears to be quite reasonable, perhaps even likely. Another few days of conflict could result in a portion of the massive allied defense forces being thrown back to the Channel coast."

Irritably fluttering the carbon-copy letter in his hand, Canaris let it fall to his desk. "Have our friend's childish ramblings made a believer of you, Ulrich?"

"Not by any means, sir. It's just that. . . whether childish ramblings or Socratic wisdom, can we afford to ignore the caveat? Ardent believer or arrant scoffer, his latest vision, salted though it is with astrological mumbo-jumbo, pictures the mass rescue of stranded enemy forces. Some rationale *has* to exist for our friend's ability to realistically report events that prove valid later."

Canaris smacked his lips, grimaced as if tasting something vile. "Nattering oracular visions larded with starry froth notwithstanding, the bare notion that he would, or *could,* be taken seriously is … *Ach!* Your point is well taken, Ulrich. But if the warning sent by this modern Nostradamus holds the least smidge of validity, it adds up to … well, useless information."

"No argument, sir!"

"Daring to warn *OKW* about Hitler's prospective reversal of von Rundstedt's order and halt *Panzerwaffe* forces advancing on an entire pinned-down allied army near Dunkerque could easily become the end of Abwehr. But it's a sidelight in this latest, most outlandish letter that disturbs me as much or more. To your good fortune, you've had limited personal contact with our glorious leader, whereas I'm forced to answer each imperial summons and be subjected to another severe dressing-down. I know the man, know his heart, his soul if he owns one. This letter hints at Hitler's sentimental belief in the Aryan brotherhood of our British foes."

"When I read the letter, that particular inference caught me unawares, Admiral."

"Months ago," said Canaris, "selected members of *OKW* and a few others were invited to Hitler's *Berchtesgaden Kehlsteinhaus.* A captive audience, we were presented with a grand view of the Austrian Alps looming in his huge picture window while pretending to pay rapt attention to Himself lecturing us on the future of the 'Aryan race,' whatever that is. Strange to say, his *Weltanschaung* credited the tea-and-crumpets gobblers with occupying a separate niche in the Aryan ethnic fairytale. He ranted at length about the likelihood of one day finding common ground with the British, driving home his senseless theory that the islanders might be brought around to his way of thinking and possibly throw in with us by taking part in the battle against Communism."

Meisinger's high forehead creased. "It isn't fitting for me to comment, except to say the concept is so strange that it had never occurred to me. But don't you think warning *Der Führer* of a potential failure to act would be more important than—"

*"Lieber Gott!"* cried Canaris. "Daring to warn him of *anything* would be like picking the scab on a raw, festering wound, then pouring salt on it. That bespectacled, horse's ass Himmler risked his life warning *me* not to mention von Rundstedt's supposed order to halt Guderian's advance toward the stranded Allied forces, or *Der Führer's* presumptive failure to override the order and order their decimation or capture, his rationale being that doing so would infuriate Hitler beyond all bounds. He told me that upon reading one of the earlier letters, Himself had dropped down on all fours and literally chewed the carpet in a red-hot tantrum."

Feeling some sort of response necessary, Meisinger said, "Understandable, I suppose."

"No, it definitely is *not!*" denied the admiral. "What has happened, and persists in taking place, surpasses all degrees of understanding. The privileged who know the content of this latest letter agree that our friend *must* be collared without delay, and the truth wrung out of him by any—and I mean *any*—means to bring closure to these insane, melodramatic missives."

Rising abruptly, he confronted his star investigator and said very softly, "My worst fear is being realized, Ulrich. The inmates *have* taken over the asylum. Our valorous leader pummels Himmler hourly, daily, demanding to be told a new letter has arrived, then in the same breath demanding to be told why *no* letter has been received, and why the writer himself has not been arrested."

Aghast, Meisinger said, "You don't mean to say he is—"

"I meant exactly what you've inferred. Germany's exalted, self-styled Führer is beginning to give *credence* to the predictions of this ... this charlatan."

In vain, Meisinger attempted to placate his superior. "We're doing everything possible to find him, sir. My team leader, Kurt, and I mean to visit the astrologer again this afternoon, not that we think he'll be able to tell us anything new, because the original of the copy on your desk was postmarked at a substation a few blocks off Unter den Linden. Knowing where our prophet had been yesterday could be helpful in locating where he lives. The postal authorities Kurt spoke to said that the letter could have been dropped off in any of ten or more sidewalk letterboxes scattered through mid-Berlin. By now, every postmaster has given his people the word to keep a sharp eye out for anyone with an envelope addressed in green ink."

Canaris pouched his cheeks, splayed his fingers, and held his hands shoulder high, wearily plopped down behind his desk and leaned forward. "I realize your team's been running itself ragged around this ... squirrel cage ..." He hesitated, as if reconsidering what he meant to say. "Here's a thought to chew on. You and your team have been attacking the problem in typical straightforward fashion, by attempting to backtrack the letters sent by this stargazing fraud. Ordinarily I'd be the last to fault you for using standard investigatory methods, but in this singular instance, the trail you've worn yourself out searching for has all the earmarks of an invisible path leading nowhere. This entire affair is so strange, deviates so far from the norm that attempting to solve its puzzle in a roundabout way could be more fruitful."

Meisinger frowned. "Roundabout?"

"It's been my experience," clarified the admiral, "that our peculiar way to search for needles in haystacks often breeds still more peculiarities and often more needles. Why not change venues, play the game a touch differently, and see where it takes us?"

"Not sure I follow, Admiral."

"Order your team to stay in constant touch with the street police, perhaps even liaise casually with Heydrich's Gestapo misfits. Urge your ops to discreetly pulse either of those groups for strange occurrences, anything odd, any inexplicable outliers that happen to surface, any unusual events a tad out of the ordinary, or whatever else doesn't quite fit the normalcy template and perhaps difficult to explain."

Meisinger returned his superior's stare. "An interesting approach, sir. Is it your inference that an uncommon happening in a blind alley might teach one to investigate in total darkness or a dimly lit passageway leading in the direction it might be profitable to follow?"

"Something like that, yes. A clever way to put it, Ulrich."

"Believe it or not," declared his chief investigator, "your observation struck a chord today. My team leader reported just the sort of oddity you may have in mind. Kurt said a chief inspector he's acquainted with mentioned an outrageously unusual banknote the police are holding as evidence in an ongoing counterfeit investigation."

"Unusual in what way?"

"Much more unusual that either of us could imagine," said Meisinger. "Kurt said a number of experts brought in to examine the evidence collectively verified its authenticity, except for the serialization, which assured them it was issued in … I realize how strange it will sound to say that the large-denomination banknote *will be* issued during calendar year nineteen forty-two."

Canaris looked startled. "Ridiculous!"

"No one can argue with that conclusion, sir, except for an

extremely peculiar sidelight that also came to light. The anomalous, misdated bill has apparently aroused a disproportionate degree of interest in high quarters. I'm sure you were briefed on the scheme to undermine Britain's economy by floating gross quantities of bogus Bank of England currency."

Canaris nodded. "An iffy scheme many believe may be a deft stroke of economic warfare by flooding Britain with false, letter-perfect, oversized 'bed sheet' banknotes the British love, as well as their prestige, twenty-one schilling elite guineas. That aside, the police can handle counterfeiting cases? I want you to adopt my suggestion and chase down the slimmest leads out of the ordinary envelope of could be considered natural and normal."

"I'll instruct the team in the morning."

"Explore every avenue and dimension of pursuit your people come across, and *find* this fiendish friend, Ulrich. Use every tool and aid at your disposal, but for God's sake make it march!"

# THIRTEEN

## *Surveillance*

James spruced himself up, combed his hair, now badly in need of trimming, and rubbed out the worst scuff marks on his worn, secondhand shoes. Mindful of how the windfall Reichsmarks from the propaganda ministry entitled him to a new wardrobe, he toyed with the notion to pawn the handful of jewelry before the items were lost or stolen and decided it wise to do so.

Stepping down from the bus at the Schöneberg intersection, he took his time strolling through the now-familiar neighborhood, crossed the street, approached the fortune teller's parlor, then paused to reconnoiter. Nothing seemed to have changed since his pristine visit—with a single exception. The gleaming black Audi sedan parked at the curb directly in front of Zoltan's establishment had a civilian license tab, but also exhibited a well-maintained aspect that made it look a touch out of place in the middle-class neighborhood. Vaguely troubled by the auto's proximity to his goal, James strolled to the far end of the block. Suppressing an urge to abandon the venture in favor of caution, he was overcome by an even stronger urge to scout the premises, perhaps learn what sort of connection might exist between the Great Zoltan and Lustmann.

He stewed about it, then finally decided he could safely pose as a customer eager to learn of any boons the ancient art might offer. He went back across the street without checking for traffic and had to dodge an elderly man riding a bicycle, who tooted the horn on his handlebars in annoyance.

Cautiously turning the knob, he inched open the entry door of Zoltan's astrology parlor, learning that, unlike many other Berlin shops, it lacked an overhead bell to announce a customer's arrival or departure. Leaving the door unlatched and ajar, he slipped into a vestibule hung with faded crimson draperies emitting a faint, musty odor. A crystal ball centerpiece nested like a giant's teardrop in a three-pronged, polished wooden stand on an otherwise bare thick-legged walnut table. A wall poster half the size of the one in the opaqued front window depicted the "world-famous" seer peering into the crystal ball, his insolent dark eyes open wider than normal beneath bushy, gray-shot brows.

Standing motionless, James discerned a barely audible voice-buzz filtering through the closed door to an inner room. Weighing an impulse to bolt from the premises without a backward glance versus the lure of finding out something about the astrologer, the latter bait seemed too enticing to spur precipitate flight. He edged stealthily across a faded Persian carpet, cautiously pressed his ear against the closed door.

". . . and if so," a hidden speaker said testily, "you're telling us you failed to *read* the letter?"

"Never would I presume to be so bold," promised a rougher voice. "The letter came in the afternoon post two days ago. The instant I saw the envelope's green lettering, I called the number you left with me."

*Green lettering!* The words electrified Silverthorne, rooting him to the door. He tried to guess the second speaker's accent, possibly Hungarian, considering the astrologer's given name.

"Patience, Kurt," advised a softer, more-cultured voice. "He's been most cooperative and will continue to be. Isn't that so, Herr Zoltan?"

"In every way possible way, sir," assured the presumed astrologer.

James reacted to the more sophisticated voice advocating patience by jerking his head away from the door. It hardly seemed possible, but even filtered through a closed door, the intonation and precise diction sounded much the same as the Abwehr's smooth-talking asset, Herr Meisinger. Near panic, he realized what an incriminating coincidence it would be for Herr Steyr, a supposed Austrian journalist, to be snooping around in Zoltan's stargazing parlor.

Torn between a powerful impulse to dash out the door and a tantalizing desire to eavesdrop further, his fear of being discovered was leavened by a sense of having stumbled into just the right place at exactly the right time. Breathing open-mouthed for silence, he weighed the odds of taking a huge risk against learning something true value and re-pressed his ear against the door.

"See there, Kurt," admonished the smooth voice, "we should honor this gentleman's pledge to remain cooperative. Herr Zoltan, we dropped by today to inform you that this entire 'friend of the Reich' madness has gotten far, far out of hand. When you alerted us to the first account of the astonishing visions afflicting whoever penned the letter, his work was evaluated as coming from an acutely disturbed individual, a view that no longer obtains. The content of his messages has changed this unknown author, harmless lunatic, provocateur, whomsoever he may be, into an individual *very* high officials have been led to believe is a genuine threat to *Das Reich*.

"Now you are not to worry, Herr Zoltan," continued the soothing baritone voice. "about your blameless involvement in this peculiar affair. Your candid responses provide valid reasons why you opened and read the first two letters, since both were addressed to you personally. You then forwarded subsequent letters unread, keeping you in the dark about their contents, or so you've assured us. However, in the interest of determining where we are as of this moment, and where we might go from here, I plan to recapitulate a few details from the latter 'unread' missives, only because of a pressing need to learn a good deal more about the author."

The soft voice went on to explain how precisely the friend had defined the terms of the Munich Pact, but after the fact, and envisioned neither France nor England reacting in any military fashion to pact violations, a reprise of their spineless 1938 inaction when Austria had been annexed to the Reich, the Sudetenland and Czechoslovakia were liberated. He'd also foretold Germany's coexistence treaty with the USSR, then predicted the *Sitzkrieg* lull in hostilities beginning the previous fall when the Franco-British Allies were preaching offensive schemes they had neither the muscle nor will to execute.

"What you had no way of knowing, Herr Zoltan, was how our friend foretold, some time *before* the fact, how the Wehrmacht would invade France where and when it was least expected, through Belgium and Holland, and cited names and unit deployments, down to brigade level, with *incredible* accuracy. Then, later, the newspapers reported how, in accordance with another of our friend's predictions, strategically vital Norway and Denmark fell to our forces."

A barely audible wheezing sound was presumably uttered by the astrologer. *"Ausserördentlich!"*

"A monumental understatement, Herr Zoltan. Our friend's prophetic visions have in each and every case foretold future events not only in exquisite detail, but with unquestionable, totally unbelievable accuracy that surpasses all probability, or for that matter all rationality. To date, each of his predictions has been *one thousand percent* accurate, a feat so starkly threatening and painful that those in the highest authority have acquired an unhealthy interest in the oracular genius *and* can't wait to receive his next letters."

"Stargazing nonsense!" James recognized the harsh, grating voice of the one called Kurt.

A note of reproach crept into the smooth-talker's rejoinder, "Ah, but is it?"

Entranced by what he'd been hearing, James again distinguished the faint sound of labored breathing and pressed his ear harder against the door.

"Now as I said, please relax, Herr Zoltan," encouraged the silken voice. "There's been no iota of wrongdoing on your part, and therefore cannot be faulted, so you have naught to fear. Wasn't a formal apology tendered after you were mistakenly arrested?"

This time a muffled grunt signified the astrologer's pleased response.

"Despite that reassurance," pursued the smooth voice, "be forewarned how mandatory it will be to reconfirm your pledge of total secrecy with regard to the matters we choose to reveal today. We now intend to make you privy to selective contents from more recent missives, but *only* to hopefully learn more about this, um ... great art of yours. So, for one last time, let me restate the same stern warning: should your tongue wag loosely and divulge one syllable of what we are about to reveal, your skin will be removed one square decimeter at a time. Do you understand?"

A faint blubbering sound evidenced Zoltan's total understanding.

"Very good! We shall skip the accompanying gibberish about Saturn being in the sun's second house and so forth. You may pretend to comprehend those starry natterings ... Oh, by the way, for the record, does our friend's astrological mishmash mean anything to you?"

"Nothing, sir! Not a single thing! It is exactly what you called it: a mishmash. The astrological terms are childish at best, and at worst—"

"Please spare us the details," interrupted the smooth talker. The sound of rustling paper was barely audible. "Ah, here we are. Allow me to read from a letter you swear was never opened. 'In the early hours of May 10, Army Group B, von Küchler's Eighteenth Army, striking across the Peel Line will push Winkelman's army of the Netherlands back to the Dyle Line, while Reichenau's Sixth Army advances across the Belgian frontier with huge success. Von Leeb's

Army Group C will feint an attack on the Maginot defense bastion, thus pinning down over forty French divisions, and permitting von Rundstedt's Army Group A, led by an arrowhead of armored divisions, to crash through Belgium's Ardennes Forest, a region the French military considers impenetrable by *Panzersgruppen*.'

"Herr Zoltan," he said earnestly, "these cited events and actions were featured in every newspaper account and radio broadcast in Germany, making it a waste of breath to enlighten you regarding their predictive accuracy. The crushing, inescapable fact is that the letter in question was postmarked *weeks* before the described events took place. I must also tell you—and please remember your wish to retain a whole skin—that for some time *Oberstgeneral* von Manstein has advocated that very unorthodox strike through the hilly, wooded Ardennes Forest, a tactic later modified by General Guderian, who refined the details of the prospective campaign, made them his own, and took credit for concepting the entire codeword Case Yellow operation sanctioned by *Der Führer*."

The cultured voice grew more insistent. "Now, attend me closely, Herr Zoltan. The just related extract was not, *could not*, have been mere fortunetelling. It amounted to a feat of pure magic on the part of our friend. You see, only senior OKW officers could have possibly learned in advance of the tactical masterstroke used to launch the offensive. Let me to repeat that: *no one!*

"What we hope and pray to hear from you, Herr Zoltan, is a simple yes or no. Would it be remotely conceivable— not probable mind you, but distantly *possible* in some unknown manner —for the, er ... science of astrology to provide an adept like yourself with the ability to develop such refined, definitive, incredibly detailed, unbelievably *accurate* predictions?"

James heard another wheezing, barely audible sigh. "This ... person claims his gift an affliction that, uh ... He also claims to possess ancient Celtic tracts which profess a refined, less-corrupted method for the stars to reveal—"

"No, Herr Zoltan! No lectures on arcana, if you please. All we wish to obtain is a positive or negative response. In your professional opinion, would the finest astrologer in all human history be able to do what our friend has done and *persists* in doing?"

"I … no, never, sir! I can't begin to imagine how such accuracy could be—"

"God help us!" the smooth voice declared loudly. "What should not be mentioned, but I will tell you anyhow, is that our superiors find this mind reader's uncannily definitive and accurate visions to be an extremely serious threat to successful prosecution of the war—and potentially the future of *Das Reich* as well—by dispensing information officialdom insists simply *must* stay shrouded in deep secrecy. Our leadership regards this friend as a potentially lethal …"

Having leaned forward minutes on end, his ear hard-pressed against the intervening door, James developed a cramp in his left calf. He shifted his weight, causing a floorboard to creak beneath the Persian rug. Mouth dry, he whirled, rushed frantically to close the entry door with a thud, and called hopefully, *"Halloo! Ist jemand hier?"*

Concerted whisperings were escaping from the inner room. Seconds passed, then a pale, bearded man emerged looking decades older than the Great Zoltan in the posters. He pulled the door shut behind him. *"Guter tag, mein Herr!* How can I help you?"

"If you are available for a consultation, I should like to arrange a personal reading. I'm a Sagittarian faced with a crucial business dealing, and it behooves me to—"

"Do forgive me! Another time, gladly, but I'm afraid a reading is simply not possible just now." The Great Zoltan used the sleeve of his brocaded robe to pat dry the perspiration beading his brow. "I'm feeling somewhat indisposed, you see. I was preparing to close up and go home."

James thought Zoltan's robe would have been more appropriate for a sorcerer rather than an astrologer and did his best to sound disappointed. "So sorry to hear that, sir! Would you have time for an appointment tomorrow? I have a rather desperate need to obtain your services."

"Tomorrow, yes, by all means, if the hour is convenient. Can you come around ten?"

"Promptly, sir! I sincerely hope to find you feeling better in the morning." James thanked Zoltan and fled the astrology parlor.

Though exhilarated beyond measure, he was also dumbfounded by trying to believe the starkly unbelievable, yet apparently *true* fact that ODESSA's scheme to reverse the outcome of the real war on this present timeline was already being carried out via the most arcane tactic imaginable. Taking advantage of "prescient" fore-knowledge of what had transpired on ODESSA's timeline during the actual World War II—he could not bring himself to think of as redundantly in progress on the present retro-timeline—the fugitive expatriates had overstocked Lustmann with a surfeit of ammunition for his arsenal. Small wonder that he was succeeding, nor would there be a facile or feasible means and method of hindering or stopping him.

He rode back to *mitte* Berlin in a daze, and for want of anything better to do resumed his vigil on an easternmost bench of Pariser Platz offering a clear view of the Hotel Adlon's entrance. He sat there for hours, thoughts whirling, thinking, making plans that were quickly revised and then dismissed, struggling to devise some practical method of nullifying ODESSA's crusade to ensure global Nazi victory and the "rebirth" of Deutsches Weltreich.

* * *

In the morning, the door chime sounded promptly at nine o'clock. Still in his robe and slippers, Lustmann was sipping coffee laced with brandy while scanning the morning papers delivered by the gratuity-happy bellman, Hans. Late the previous afternoon, someone who announced himself as *Schutzpolizei* Chief Inspector Fürstenburg had sidestepped the never-to-be-disturbed directive Herr Klasse had issued and phoned to politely request permission to visit him.

Readily agreeing to the request, Lustmann had put everything in readiness. Street clothing laid out in the bedchamber promised a fast exit from the Adlon if necessary. The silenced Walther PPK was tucked beneath a chair cushion within easy reach. If complications such as an invitation to "drop by" the police station arose, he meant to ignore the detective, snatch the carryall, and disappear down the service stairs, not that he wished to disrupt the comfortable arrangement he had unless it seemed unavoidable. Searching for a reasonably safe place to stay and assuming another of a half dozen furnished identities would be both burdensome and bothersome.

The chime sounded a second time, but Lustmann took his own sweet time answering the door. Hats in their hands, a pair of sober-faced gentlemen in business suits stood expectantly in the hallway. The shorter *Schupo* hung back diffidently, the older gentleman said, "I'm Chief Inspector Fürstenburg, Herr Klasse. This is Detective Kastel."

*"Hereingekommen!"* Lustmann punctuated the chilly reception with a blink of stony indifference. "Would you like coffee, Chief Inspector, Detective?"

"No thank you, sir." Fürstenburg and his partner displayed their credentials, per Lustmann's request, and were urged to make themselves comfortable on the sofa. "We apologize for bothering you at this early hour. You may be aware of why we wish to ask you a few questions."

"Ah, the counterfeiting investigation." Wishing to control the direction taken by their conversation, Lustmann frowned. "The hotel management informed me of the odd banknote. Curious to learn more about its strangeness, I spoke with Reichsbank New Accounts Manager Sharpe, with whom I've had business dealings.

Tell me, has the culprit been located?"

"That is no longer necessary, Herr Klasse." Chief Inspector Fürstenburg sounded a touch uncomfortable. "The case is no longer under active investigation."

"Really?" Lustmann did not have to feign surprise.

"Experts have tried at great length to determine the origin of the peculiar banknote said to have been included in your cash deposit at the bank, the existence of which is ... The spurious date of issue has puzzled every specialist called in to examine the high-denomination bill, causing each to attest to it as genuine, according to Frau Sharpe, save for the serialization tying it to a most exceptional date of issue. The consensus of professional opinion is that misdating the banknote via serialization had to be a simple mistake on someone's part, since it also had to be printed and circulated during a specific calendar year, though naturally not one yet to come."

As if unfazed by the statement, Lustmann nodded sagaciously. "Chief Inspector, you have repeated exactly what Frau Sharpe told me. I do hope you understand that, well ... the peculiar mistake leaves me at a total loss. I may have given offense by not taking her very seriously when learning the concerted opinion of experts that the serialization had to be the result of a printing or tabulating error, and ... frankly, nothing else seems remotely possible."

His expression neutral, Fürstenburg said, "All other eventualities have been ruled out, Herr Klasse, by everyone concerned. Frau Sharpe assures us the banknote was part of the large sum you deposited in person. May we respectfully inquire how, and from what source, in what manner the deposited monies were obtained?"

Lustmann did not hesitate to say, "No, Chief Inspector, you may not."

Fürstenburg and his partner exchanged glances.

"I have no wish to do so, but your question leaves me with no alternative but to confirm my bona fides." Lustmann rose, pulled up the sleeve of his paisley dressing gown, and held out his left arm to give the detectives a better look. "I'm sure you will both recognize this tattoo."

"*Schutzstaffeln!*" Detective Kastel took a small notepad from an inner jacket pocket and unscrewed the cap of a fountain pen, preparing to record the data.

Lustmann quickly pulled down his sleeve. "That would be unwise, Detective. I make no bones about my *SS* affiliation or that I was directed to use an alias. You may list my identity as *SS-Allgemeine Sturmbannführer* Erich Klasse, whose current assignment calls for numerous sensitive monetary exchanges, each with a direct bearing on state security. I have been ordered to disburse and otherwise handle certain blocs of funding posing as a civilian. The purpose of my activities is of interest only to my superiors. As far as I know, how and where the currency was obtained is … sorry, I confess to being as much in the dark as either of you gentlemen."

Fürstenburg cleared his throat. "In that case, would you object if we were to contact your superiors and attempt to learn the bill's origin?"

"Object? No, not at all." The inspector's roundabout way of asking the identity of his superiors irked Lustmann to the point of pinning him with a hard-eyed stare. "I cannot tell you anything more specific about my assignment except to say I report directly to the office of Reichsführer-*SS* Himmler. However, before contacting and possibly asking any questions of that office, it would be prudent to first gain the approval of *your* superiors. In my opinion, prying into the movement of *SS* funds would be, shall we say counterproductive, and might have rather grave consequences. The Reichsführer would not be amused to learn of someone prying into either overt or clandestine *SS* operations. You gentlemen are obliged to meet the demands of your *Schutzpolizei* superiors, but approaching *SS* headquarters should be entirely *their* decision."

The unsubtle warning earned identical blank expressions from both detectives. Lustmann could not help glancing at the chair cushion concealing the silenced PPK automatic, but he immediately dismissed the lethal notion. He wondered inanely how, in the present *Dritte Reich* milieu, even the most diligent policemen could hope to solve crimes closely shrouded in government secrecy.

Looking flustered, the chief inspector rose. "Thank you, Herr Klasse. You have been most helpful." Not knowing what else to say, he eyed his partner. "If Detective Kastel has no further questions, we shall trouble you no longer."

"Delighted to do what little I could." Lustmann made it a point to shake hands with Kastel as well as the chief inspector before showing the detectives out the door.

Smirking, he opened an ivory-inlaid box, selected a cigarette, clicked his gold-flashed lighter, and exhaled smoke, thinking it would be a frigid day in the netherworld before either cop *or* their superiors gave serious thought to posing questions in the office of the gimlet-eyed, emotionally sterile Reichsführer-*SS,* or perhaps twice more dangerous ace henchman *Reichsprotektor-SS* Reinhard Heydrich, or for that matter any lower-echelon *Schutzstaffeln* functionaries.

# FOURTEEN

## *Audacity*

What to do, what to do?

The quest for Lustmann had ended in a sudden, incredible way, although James had learned only the surface what, where, when, and how details of his fellow time traveler's mission activities. First he had to learn why Lustmann was sending prophetic letters to a silly astrologer armed with access to some outré pipeline directly into the Nazi civil and military hierarchies. Obviously his fellow schemers in Argentina had evolved some wholly unorthodox method of vastly enhancing their prodigy's ability to aid, abet, and coach Nazi Germany on means and methods of prosecuting the war more logically. Unfortunately, that likelihood also made inventing some reasonable way to thwart, rectify, or eliminate Lustmann's tactical advantage of possessing encyclopedic foreknowledge of the war in which he'd participated on his native timeline, a fact turning it into a conundrum all but impossible to solve

Prowling back and forth the previous night in his chilly attic room, he had evolved and dismissed one path after another that might lead to a sound, logical method of inhibiting or reversing the hero's apparent mission successes. He had fallen into bed grossly overtired, then strained to unravel and solve the problem of what to do next that had kept him wakeful into the wee hours. He had lain wide awake, his mind gyrating, his thoughts tumbling over one another, only to wake at dawn feeling groggy from the short night, as well as nagged by the fact that a viable course of corrective action had escaped him.

After partaking of Frau Kraven's less-than-sumptuous breakfast consumed with a less-than-satisfactory appetite, he had gone out and purchased the morning edition of *Beobachter,* then headed directly to his surveillance post on Pariser Platz, doing so more from force of habit than a specific reason. Unfolding *Beobachter,* he scanned the front page and found himself reading meaningless words, so he doggedly went back to the lead article and started over with similar results.

Struck by the pointlessness of taking up station with the Adlon in view, where Lustmann might emerge at any moment, or tomorrow, or next week, or never, he doubted any value would obtain from following the man on foot—assuming he would *be* on foot— just to see where he went, who he might go to see, and began to feel his vigil a waste of time and energy.

He tossed the unread newspaper in a trash bin and meandered about Pariser Platz, concentrating on the complex, multi-sided problem plaguing him, imagining and dismissing one fanciful scenario after another. His dangerous eavesdropping adventure in Zoltan's astrology parlor had convinced him that Lustmann had carried into the past an encyclopedic account of how defeat had come about in the conflict the ex-*SS* officer had survived, plus useful insider information pertaining to individuals, circumstances, situations, and enough suggestions to lubricate his starry messages in enough of a convincing manner to influence the concatenation of wills, endeavors, and military efforts in progress, and affect an entirely different, one-sided opposite to the outcome of the real war.

There could be little doubt that the hopefully-never-to-be Deutsches Weltreichsheld venerated on his own timeline almost surely possessed every document, endowing him with hindsight to

use in proactively advising, counseling, and warning Nazi officialdom and military command, basing his prophetic letters on data
from his accurate, reality-based foreknowledge treasure trove and
the aid of an obscure, unwitting fortuneteller in creating a direct
conduit to the Reich's inner circle.

Unfortunately, after being transplanted to the here-and-now Gregorian 1940 timeline, the tactic was anything *but* absurd, nor was
it laughable, just all too glaringly real. What would ordinarily be
thought of as ludicrous by well-oriented individuals was precisely
the tactic used by Lustmann, and it had to cease now, now, *now*,
had to be exposed as fraudulent, or …

Or *what?*

Walking along the sidewalk aimlessly, head down, only his mind
functioning, Silverthorne's random progress took him into the path
of a hurrying pedestrian with whom he brushed shoulders. Con-
tritely dipping his fedora, he apologized to the glowering gentleman.

The incident made him appreciate a need for some place to isolate himself, a think-spot where he could get off by himself, bring
the quandary he had to deal with into sharper focus, find a way to
surround it on all sides and worry it to death until it was defeated,
or at least expose some elusive path to a resolution. Searching for
reasonably restful surroundings, he considered and rejected Berlin's
Zoologischer Garten, where his wanderings had recently thrust him
into the midst of adult visitors and noisy children.

That would never do; what he needed was a peaceful island of
sanity where he would not be disturbed, someplace familiar like …
King Frederick's summer palace in Potsdam, *le maison de plaisance!*

The destination seemed more than simply pleasing; it was self-
affirming. Frederick the Great's rococo Schloss Sanssouci had
doubtless undergone a sea change over the century and a half since
his retro-temporal visit. Yet even on the Deutsches Weltreich timeline, the palace and grounds had retained elegance as a thoroughly

Nazified shrine to the past. On the current redux timeline, palace and grounds should still be a pleasant haunt where he could feel at home.

Potsdam, on Floss Havel in neighboring Brandenburg, was only twenty-odd kilometers from central Berlin. He caught a bus to the Zoologischer Schienenstation, purchased a ticket on the next Brandenburg train, and not long thereafter stepped down from the railcar in Potsdam Stadt, shortening the route to Sanssouci by splurging on a taxi. Taking in the sights along Strasse Schopenhauer, he told the driver to drop him off farther down the avenue, near the southern entrance to the palace grounds. Tipping the driver generously, he soon learned the summer palace, including King Frederick's Lustgarten, had become a popular park and tourist Mecca.

Walking west along Hauptallee through the landscaped plain below Weinberg Hill crowned by the palace, he passed the smaller fountain and continued on to the larger, grander Grosse Fontäne, the centerpiece of a terrace ringed by statuary. Pausing beside the fountain, he scanned the changeless surrounding gardens, Dutch Windmill, and nearby Neues Palais, its domed *Marmosaal* rotunda modeled on Rome's ancient Pantheon, lastly the Communes once housing the servants' quarters, where for months he had taken his meals and slept.

Looking up from ground level, the "carefree" palace looked different from what he remembered in the late eighteenth century. A half dozen curving *Weinbergterasse* terraces on either side of the long flight of steps leading up to the entrance were elegantly landscaped, but no longer with the vineyards he recalled. Tourists and visitors strolling up and down the steps singly, in pairs, and groups added an impression of otherness, where crowned heads, lesser dignitaries, bewigged gentlemen and their elegantly coiffed and gowned ladies had once arrived at the foot of those selfsame steps in opulent, horse-drawn carriages to be greeted by bowing equerries and, on occasion, the aged monarch himself.

As European palaces went, Sanssouci was much more a petite villa than a palace. It featured an elliptical marble hall bisected by a wide center vestibule, with only six rooms taking up the east and west wings, and a pair of principal adjoining chambers branching off on either side of the entry hall. He ascended the long flight of steps slowly, pausing several times to turn back and enjoy the view of the parkland from each higher riser.

In the vestibule, he was pleased by its impressive state of preservation, displaying only minor differences from what had been familiar during Frederick's final days. Stepping into the library, His Majesty's favorite haunt, he turned round and round, gazing up at the high windows, the rococo furnishings, and rich cedar paneling. Lost in a state of déjà vu nostalgia inducing a gawking reverie, James was started by a conservatively dressed elderly gentleman with a shock of flowing white hair.

"Descriptive brochures can be found on a stand inside the *corps de logis* entrance, sir. Enjoy your visit." Hands clasped behind his back, the docent strolled away.

James paused outside the concert room but did not go inside. As if it were yesterday, he could almost see himself ushering guests in powdered wigs, their bejeweled ladies gowned in finery, into the beautifully decorated chamber to enjoy one of Frederick's intimate recitals and concerts. The monarch had more than once delighted a small, sophisticated audience by playing his transverse flute in one of his own compositions.

Deciding it time to shake off reminiscences and concentrate on his reason for visiting Sanssouci, he ventured on down the central hallway, emerged from the garden entrance, and roved the Dutch Garden pathways in company with a sprinkling of visitors, and began subvocally repeating the name that echoed hollowly in his mind: *Lustmann, Lustmann!*

What could a lone stranger in wartime Berlin do to hinder, thwart, or eliminate the perpetration of an outrageous, world-changing

scheme concocted by a cadre of ODESSA expatriates who had fled
Europe to evade punishment as war criminals? What means and
methods could he actually find useful as the first steps toward redirecting, nullifying, or eliminating Lustmann's ignoble objective? He
reviewed the tentative, previous notions he had evolved, and as on
prior occasions any number of obstacles and outright flaws became
glaringly apparent at once in all prospective scenarios he brought to
mind, and all too soon he came up empty, convinced there was no
practical, feasible method to intercept Lustmann's apocryphal letters
and make changes, which seemed the most appealing tactic, and
promised the simplest, most straightforward path leading to achieving his objective.

A widespread hunt was obviously underway for the vision-happy
"Friend of the Reich," who was apparently giving fits to Nazi officialdom by prophesying with unworldly accuracy events yet to take
place, also warning of coming errors and how to avoid them, as well
as what *not* to undertake as a specific military action. Yet most individuals, if told the truth about who, from whence, and for what
demonic purpose the mysterious friend was bedeviling them with
his visions, they would at once dismiss whoever related the "facts"
as someone stricken with acute dementia and who might well be
authoring the letters.

The more he thought about it, the more he admired ODESSA's
radical, fantastic method of gaining the Nazi civilian and military
leadership's collective ear, and perhaps even that of Germany's tyran-
nical demagogue himself. His eavesdropping venture in Zoltan's parlor had firmly established one certainty: the content of each missive
had been artfully designed to fit tongue in groove into the template
of Hitler's mystic conceptions about Nordic myth, destiny, Aryan
superiority, all of that rot, garnishing it with tantalizing astrological
sauce, and making each letter a virtual guarantee that Lustmann
would sit up and take notice, and possibly succeed in the end to
elevate the Master Race to a victorious *uber alles* pinnacle.

Yet what, he also asked himself for at least the hundredth time, could a lone, friendless history professor in Berlin do to counter Lustmann's mission goal, which meant turning to dust the admittedly ingenious scenario hatched by ODESSA on that other timeline. That question was entirely valid and *demanded* a valid answer of some sort. Glancing about as if searching for a clue to the solution—*any* clue—he realized it was not to be found in the geometric, sculpted greenery and statuary of the Dutch Garden.

Slowly pacing along a pathway, he asked himself what a strong, progressive-minded ruler like Friederich der Grosse would have done to thwart ODESSA's ingenious tactic to have their man in Berlin choose a bearded astrological buffoon like the Great Zoltan to act as an unwitting accomplice by installing a direct pipeline into *Dritte Reich's* Nazi hierarchy? He posed the question reflexively but failed to ignite a train of thought that might lead to an answer. The legendary eighteenth-century Prussian ruler was a thoroughly familiar figure to James, not only due to his prior retro-temporal research junket. His interest in the monarch and the events of his reign had ballooned when he and Omsley had first discussed a potential opportunity visiting late-eighteenth-century Prussia. Study had revealed *the* most renowned Germanic prince in recorded history as an absolute despot, yet benign in many respects, and definitely a soldier's soldier who had earned the title bestowed by his people: First Servant of the State. The major driving force of Prussia's revered monarch, a genuine desire to guide the citizens of Prussia in the direction they themselves believed most beneficial, he had promulgated a number of domestic reforms that encouraged his subjects to move forward into the so-called modern age. Moreover, his deep devotion to Prussia as a model for the entire Fatherland and its peoples had done much to shape Germany long after his reign.

A thoughtful hour had slipped away before he again asked himself what King Frederick might have done to disrupt or terminate Erich

Lustmann's world-changing mission. But no matter how the monarch himself might have acted, it would not have been done by the use of timid, halfway measures. A candid, enlightened ruler, Frederick had also proven himself an outstanding military commander in the field during the Seven Years War, then later enhanced his repute during the invasion of Silesia and its annexation to Prussia.

Out of the blue, James was inspired by a sterling tidbit of advice tendered during Frederick's reign by a prominent French legislator and on occasion echoed by the monarch himself. James murmured aloud: *"De l'audace, et encore de l'audace, et toujours de l'audace."*

A daring, audacious move to redirect Lustmann's world-changing mission struck him as not merely unavoidable, but all things considered perhaps a critical, inescapable, *mandatory* necessity. There simply *was* no other way! The stark truth had been staring him in the face all along. He would be forced to somehow audaciously take Lustmann's place and audaciously forward his own mission by penning similar "Friend of the Reich" letters designed to negatively influence, badly coach, and misguide the course of the war, thereby obliterating forever in its entirety the lurking specter of a resurrected Deutsches Weltreich.

To do that, he would have to kill Erich Lustmann. No alternative seemed plausible or possible.

Having come to a full realization of the unwholesome, audacious act he had definitely decided to carry out, he was overcome with a sinking feeling that the sunlit grounds of King Frederick's Holländischer Garten had suddenly taken on a darker, more somber hue. The only unanswered question was whether he, a professional academic who had never slain anything higher in the chain of life than a deer or elk with his longbow, would be able to summon the resourcefulness and courage—the *guts*—to actually commit a truly audacious act of murder.

Catching the train back to Berlin in a deeply worried, introspective frame of mind, his thoughts were clouded by a frightening premonition of his failure to prevent a cataclysmic disaster like the potential victory of Nazi Germany. No, he couldn't wait; it had to happen soonest, not later!

Making his way back toward the boardinghouse, he stopped and purchased a bottle of schnapps and put it out of sight with the cap still sealed on the floor of his room's freestanding wardrobe. The liqueur would be reserved for a special evening when he meant to swallow just enough to make him sufficiently glib to get through what might well be the toughest night of his life.

And quite possibly the last.

\* \* \*

Lustmann had worked until two in the morning drafting a letter aimed at correcting Luftwaffe bombing objectives during the air war soon to erupt with fiery tracer slugs in the balmy summer skies over England.

The sound of his suite's door chime woke him in the manner of an electric shock. Sitting up in bed, feeling as if he had just drifted off to sleep, he wondered if there actually was someone at the door or if the chime had sounded in a dream. Preternaturally wide awake, he dropped his feet to the carpet, decided against switching on the table lamp beside the bed, and sought his robe in darkness. Rummaging in a bedside table drawer, his fingers closed on the Walther PPK pistol and attached cylindrical silencer. Groping his way into the lightless parlor, he used a chair cushion to muffle the sound as he worked the slide mechanism and injected a round into the chamber.

The chime sounded a second time.

*Guter Gott! Who could be calling?* The police wouldn't come at this hour, unless …

Alarmed by a fear of being be arrested, he hoped it was a hotel staffer carrying word of some hotel emergency. Weapon in hand, he speculated about a potential need to use it and edged to the door, feeling for the knob with an outstretched hand. He had to bend down slightly in order to look through the peek-a-boo lens installed at eye level for someone shorter than he himself. Low wattage bulbs in staggered sconces along the hall weakly illuminated a figure standing outside the door.

Silently unhooking the security chain, Lustmann drew back the deadbolt and opened the door a crack. Posting himself behind it, his back to the wall, he peered through the crack between door and molding. Only a dim shoe and trouser cuff were visible.

In a faint, hard-to-hear voice, whoever was in the hall said, "Herr Lustmann, please let me in. It is of the utmost importance!"

Hearing his real name spoken aloud shocked Lustmann almost to the point of letting the automatic pistol slip from his grasp. He muttered, "Wrong … room."

"*Nein, nein!* We must speak, *bitte.* It's a vital matter of grave urgency, Herr Lustmann."

"Who the hell *are* you?"

"A friend of the Reich."

Having his printed sign-off identity from each letter handed back to him stunned Lustmann nearly as much as the thought of some unknown individual being aware of his *actual* identity!

His heart pumping, Silverthorne thought he heard a sharp intake of breath. He searched in vain through the narrow crack for anything faintly visible inside, then began edging gingerly into the suite, holding both hands in front of him.

A violent shove sent him sprawling on the carpet.

Lustmann kneed the door shut, locked it, and secured the security chain. A table lamp blazed alight. Half blinded by the flare of brilliance, James looked up and found himself staring into the malignant eye of a tubular silencer attached to a handgun aimed at his forehead.

"Speak!" Lustmann backed away a step. "Say something!"

James came torso erect to a sitting position, hands lifted shoulder high, fingers splayed. "I have only the best of intentions, I assure you, Herr Lustmann."

Lustmann uttered a sarcastic snort. "I assure you *my* intention, 'Friend of the Reich,' is to make you realize knowing who I am amounts to a death sentence."

"Please, a moment of your time, I beg you." Face to face with the man he'd been told to revere as a legend since childhood, appearing awestruck was easy for James. "I was born June ninth, *Deutsches Weltreich jahr* one hundred and four."

"*Deutsches Welt—*" The Walther automatic pistol wavered, lowered a few decimeters, then came up again smartly. "What crazy song and dance is this?"

"Herr Lustmann, where to begin is, uh ... very difficult. I feel so honored for being able to introduce myself to a *Reichsheld* of your stature that ... I have to find some way to make you aware that in my native timeline you are second only to the memory of our noble *Führer*. It's why I find it so difficult to—"

"*Verdammen Sie!* Keep voicing senseless riddles and I'll kill you just to shut you up. Who the hell *are* you? Speak up, be quick!"

"Three of us were sent back under orders to cover you here in Welthauptstadt Germania."

"World capital of *what?*" sneered Lustmann. "You're running out of seconds, *mein Freund des Reichs.* Nonsense piled upon still more extravagant nonsense! For the very last time, who are you, and as importantly, *what* are you?"

Anticipating a bullet, James was not sure the other had understood a word of his rehearsed spiel.

"S-shortly after conquering the Americas," faltered James, speaking fast, "*Der Führer* renamed Berlin *Welthauptstadt Germania,* the ancient Roman term for a rebellious portion of what was then Germania Magnus. In my native timeline, Herr Lustmann, from the window of the shrine honoring your magnificent feat, beyond the Brandenburg Gate in Tiergarten soars *Der Führer's* magnificent tomb, farther off the Chancellery, and at the far end of a huge, long reflecting pool looms the enormous dome of the Great Hall of the People."

The ice in Lustmann's blue eyes melted only a trifle. "I congratulate you for concocting a smoke screen no one could penetrate, but your fanciful blather has earned only an absolutely last and final chance to make sense. *Final!* In the fewest words possible, explain exactly whatever the hell you're raving about. Reveal your identity, life, purpose in bothering me now, now, *now!* All are dangling at the end of a thin, unraveling thread I haven't snipped, nor will I until obtaining such personal information and an honest answer to one simple question. Is this a waking daydream, or are you daring to hint that the drivel you've been spouting means I may *succeed?*"

"Most gloriously, Herr Lustmann! After concluding your sacred mission, you will be instantly returned to *Deutsches Weltreichs jahr siebenundzwanzig,* where and when you will find yourself welcomed by millions of celebrants and all succeeding generations and become a subject of sublime veneration exceeded only by *Der Führer's* memory."

"Year twenty-seven of Deutsches Weltreich, hah!" The mocking utterance erupted as a caustic accusation. Despite his cynicism, Lustmann grimaced, his lip curled in thought. "Still at it, eh? Well, *mein Freund des Reichs,* one slight flaw in your fairytale was mentioning an instant return to some mythical year, a stark impossibility. I've been condemned to live out my life along what was specified as this present timeline."

James opened his mouth, touched a forefinger to the false molar. "Advancements Herr Doktor Lebe knew nothing about have taken place, Herr Lustmann. Were I to twist this tooth clockwise and bite down hard, my accumulated temporal potential would snap me back to the Carlsbad Caverns reception center in *Deutsches Weltreichs Jahr hundert und zweiundvierzig.* The single drawback would be to inadvertently trigger a return by ignoring the requisite to masticate with care exclusively on the right side of my mouth."

Mentioning the dowdy physicist by name seemed to thaw Lust-mann twice as much as anything else James might have said. Though obviously still overtly suspicious, intense curiosity had been piqued regarding Silverthorne's legitimacy. Smacking his lips, he launched a fishing expedition. "No such magical device is in my mouth."

"Something similar will be furnished when the time is ripe, Herr Lustmann."

"You know this for a fact?"

"A firm, long established fact! Unless my arithmetic is faulty, or I've been misinformed, your retro-temporal transposition was relatively short, approximately two decades. Upon your return, you shall be welcomed in the identical era framed by the timeline in which you departed."

"Argentina," demanded Lustmann, "nineteen sixty?"

An affirmative nod. "Santa Fe in then-Gregorian calendar year nineteen sixty of the Common Era, but with a radically different destination. You will return to New Mexiko Provinz des Weltreiches in DWJ twenty-seven, a calendar year dating from nineteen thirty-three when *Der Führer* became German chancellor and *Dritte Reich* was born." Daring a fleet smile, James went on to say, "You will find things vastly changed for the better, Herr Lustmann. The where-abouts and fate of your ODESSA associates remains a mystery, although many historians, such as me, believe they failed to survive the War of World Liberation waged in South America. If you wish it so, arrangements can be made for transposition to any earlier or later era you may desire."

Overwhelmed by a flood of information he could never have dreamed about ever hearing, Erich Lustmann thought the matter through at some length. *"Mitfreund des Reichs,"* he said slowly, "your demise is hereby suspended pending further examination of the evidence. Sit down, whoever the hell you are, and make yourself comfortable, begin at the beginning, and tell all. You know a thousand times too much to be other than what you say you are, but I must be absolutely certain."

James clicked his heels Prussian style and bowed. "Gladly, Herr Lustmann, but being here in your suite more than minutes places both of us in jeopardy." Speaking rapidly with what he hoped was unmistakable sincerity, he enumerated the time jaunts he had undertaken as a tenured history professor, mentioned his chair of Retro-temporal Research at the premiere university in Colorado Provinz and explained how he and an anonymous colleague at the University of Leipzig were the only individuals vetted by *Reichskounzel* to engage in fanatically and tightly controlled retro-temporal research.

Having listened closely, Lustmann wagged his head. "Extraordinary! Do go on."

James related the manner in which he and a pair of associates purposely kept nameless for security reasons had been serially dispatched from Carlsbad and Leipzig respectively, one to the east, the other west in Brandenburg, while he himself had dropped into Württemberg, a stone's throw north of the Danube. "We three converged on Welthauptstadt Ger—sorry, in the current now timeline the capital is still Berlin—from varying locales, our identities purposely kept from one another until our first contact at an outdoor restaurant in Tiergarten. That way had one of us been arrested and questioned, it would have been impossible to give up the other pair. We worked jointly over a period of months searching for your whereabouts in Berlin."

While slow in coming, the other's nod told James he was by no means out of the woods, though it was clear Lustmann was wavering, leaning toward conditional acceptance of the tale.

"You mentioned being a history professor and a fellow time traveler. Tell me, where and, er … when have you been sent?"

"Most recently to the subjective timeline in the latter reign of

Friederich der Grosse, seventeen eighty-two of the Common Era. My book on that very enjoyable and productive junket was quite well received. While searching for you here in the capital, I gave in to nostalgia and revisited Sanssouci, now a park surrounding the Summer Palace crawling with tourists."

Lustmann's eyes widened in suddenly heightened interest. "Book! You are also a writer?"

"Yes, my real name is James Silverthorne. Here and now in what to me is the old capital, my papers identify me as Hans Steyr, an Austrian journalist."

Lustmann stared at his visitor in openmouthed wonderment. "This is all so fascinating that I ... Wait, isn't posing as a foreigner here in Berlin a chancy business?"

James dared a slightly warmer smile. "As you may recall from 'your' war, Herr Lustmann, roughly two years ago along the current timeline in which we coexistent, Austria was annexed to *Dritte Reich.*"

*"Ach, ja, ja!* Of course! A reporter, history professor, fellow time traveler *and* author. Will my blessings never cease!" The other's lingering suspicions had evaporated. Giving way to overt enthusiasm, he flipped on the safety and laid aside the silenced PPK automatic pistol. "Listen, I've been going stark, raving mad attempting to compose one never-to-be-sufficiently damned letter after another. Can you be of any assistance in that regard, Herr . . ? Again, please, the name you are using?"

"Steyr, Hans Steyr. Naturally I'll be eager to covertly aid your efforts in every way possible. That is precisely what we—the other pair and I—were sent back to accomplish. Wait, I should warn you that assisting you here in the hotel could easily invite disaster."

"Were you seen coming up to my suite?" asked Lustmann.

"I doubt it, but it wouldn't matter much. I met one of my nameless associates at the trysting place we change each week, and he accompanied me to the hotel. With the lobby deserted at this hour, he posed a meaningless question to the security man and a sleepy young clerk on duty at the desk while I slipped upstairs. I mean to leave by the service stair. Now for the good news, sir."

The other leaned forward eagerly. "Good ... news?"

"The *best*. The letters you've been posting to the Great Zoltan are beginning to create an astonishingly deep and valuable impression on a number of major Reich officials."

Lustmann looked startled. "How did you learn of the astrologer?"

"Once we knew where you were staying, it was quite simple." James related how he had trailed Lustmann from the postal substation to the sidewalk letterbox and bribed a postman to let him peek at the green-lettered address on the envelope. He described venturing into the astrology parlor and risking detection to eavesdrop on a hushed, backroom conversation between the seer and what he believed to be a pair of Abwehr agents, one of whom had interrogated him over a suspicion that he himself might be the mysterious Friend of the Reich.

"Your letters," he concluded, "have inspired dozens of investigative teams bent on chasing you down."

"Steyr, the tales you tell grow twice as marvelous every time you open your mouth!" The last vestiges of suspicion had vanished from Lustmann's pale-blue eyes. Nevertheless, he asked why James had been questioned by the Abwehr. "How did you come under suspicion?"

James explained Meisinger's boardinghouse visit, which he himself believed had been instigated by his nosy landlady, adding that it had been accompanied by a totally unsuspected boon. He explained how the Abwehr agent, while awaiting his return, had read a manuscript he had written for the sole purpose of establishing his cover as a journalist, and asked if he could show the article to an executive editor at the Goebbels propaganda ministry, where 'Herr Steyr' was now semi-employed as a stringer. James went on to warn Lustmann that Herr Meisinger, a most impressive gentleman, had asked journalist Steyr if he wished to be addressed as a "Friend of the Reich," a positive indication that the Abwehr was running down every conceivable lead on its crusade to find, collar, and interrogate the mysterious visionary author.

"It's another reason why I risked all by daring to come here tonight."

The revelation did not sit well with Lustmann. "Fortunate," he said, "that your landlady tipped off the Abwehr, not Heydrich's Gestapo clowns. They would not have been quite so gentle."

James glanced at his cheap wristwatch. "I really must go, Herr Lustmann. But quickly, here is the other reason why I disturbed your sleep." He handed the other a slip of foolscap listing his phone number and the boardinghouse address. "Think of my dingy attic quarters as a bolt hole, a safe house should things ever go sour. Have you had any difficulties to date?"

Lustmann grimaced, related the furor caused by the banknote with an issue date of nineteen forty-two, and explained how it had inspired visits by the hotel manager and two detectives seeking an imaginary counterfeiter, and how he had discouraged them from further snooping.

"Carelessness!" James pulled a face to emphasize the seriousness of such a gaffe. "How could your ODESSA associates have been so lax!" he said, shooting another glance at his watch. "Now please listen carefully, Herr Lustmann. Should your telephone ring three times and stop, then only seconds later ring three more times and stop again, seize only the bare essentials and exit the hotel through the service entrance. Get to my boardinghouse as fast as you. If I'm not in my room at the moment, tell the landlady you are from the Goebbels ministry and must see me the instant I return. Chances are she will let you wait upstairs in my attic room."

"Good, very good!" Wagging his head as if it had all been too much for him, Lustmann took James's arm with untoward familiarity.

"More than one sitting will be needed to absorb half the information that keeps popping out of you like gospel uttered by some guardian angel. I owe you and your friends an enormous debt. You've made victory in our battle *vastly* more assured."

"Victory in the war," said James, his mien sober, "is of ultimate importance, while our current battle is merely a preliminary skirmish. Other than in some emergency, please do not contact me; let me call you. May I say what an unimaginable pleasure it has been to meet and serve you, sir. *Wiedersehen.*" James clicked his heels and bowed.

"Until we meet again, Steyr. I really have no way to thank you enough for what you've done."

Cautiously descending the Adlon's service stairs, James breathed a heartfelt sigh of relief. He had entered the swank hotel wondering with good cause if he would be allowed to walk out again. He had managed to pull it off only because never before had he lied so consistently, dramatically, at such length, or for such a noble purpose.

Triumphant over what had transpired, he uncapped the bottle of schnapps seconds after he stepped back into the cold, drab attic room.

# FIFTEEN

## *The Letter*

With visions of missives hand-lettered in green ink dancing in his head like bulletins from a certified maniac locked in the rubber room of an asylum, what little patience remained for finding and questioning the friend of the Reich had almost deserted Admiral Canaris.

Earlier in the day, he had informed Meisinger that Himmler, Heydrich, and that motherless imbecile, Hess, had paid him a visit. "They assured me *SS* experts had deduced our friend's letters to be no less than the work of some Jewish espionage genius. No major surprise, Ulrich. In all their visions, Zionist conspirators are lurking behind every bush. Hess, on the other hand, tried to convince me our friend's prophetic visions simply had to result from what he called 'sound astrological science.' What in God's name are we coming to, with masterful intellects like those in senior leadership roles?"

Meisinger glanced at the office door. "Softly, sir. You can't be sure of every staffer."

"Tell me something I don't already know! But they won't inform on me. A more likely fate will be to find myself left in a doorless, windowless room to rot, a fitting reward for being one of *very* few sane individuals left in government service."

Canaris paused to let his temper cool, then changed the subject. "One thing I *will* say in favor of our phantom seer. His Dunkerque letter could have opened Himself's eyes to the wisdom of now and then loosening his tight reins on most field commanders, and perhaps go so far as allowing the professional military to take advantage of opportunities if and when they appear. But that sounds like heresy, doesn't it? Of nearly three hundred and forty thousand allied personnel waiting to be relieved by sea, at least half are now either casualties or prisoners of war, and Guderian's successful op to guarantee the mass surrender may have been a result of our seer's prophetic counsel. Nowhere is it written that a radically different outcome might have obtained had we lacked the sound, gratuitous advice from our friend.

"But that's looking only on the bright side," pursued Canaris. "Something far less palatable than a Zionist spy plot was buried in the visionary's discussion of Hitler's belief in the Aryan status of our British brethren, a supposed racial bond Himself insists may one fine day unite our separate cultures. That silly bastard Hess apparently took the idiotic notion to heart and discussed what might be done to encourage such a strange alliance by having someone in authority, himself for instance, might sneak into England and gain Churchill's ear."

"He not seriously advocating anything that ridiculous," denied Meisinger.

"Who's to say how a hollow man like Rudolf regards anything as serious. He's Hitler's anointed deputy, and to our misfortune has access to his master's ear at all hours of the day and night. I only wish Rudy would do *exactly* what someone should do. It would rid us of his presence, but I hate to say it would also exchange very bad for very much worse."

"Himmler?"

"Who else? That bland, bespectacled jackanapes believes the personality he uses to cloak himself in benign wrappings fools anyone. At heart he's a conscienceless demon incarnate with naught to discuss more cheerful than his proposed mass extermination of European

*Juden.* He encouraged *lieber* Heydrich in my presence to spare neither man, woman, nor child once the Wehrmacht plows the ground, readying it for his *SS-Totenkopfverbände* animals to march in and commence devouring all inferiors."

"Did you," inquired Meisinger, changing the subject to prod Canaris into sounding off more tactfully in his own office, "mention our nonaggression pact with the USSR?"

"Bah! Ribbentrop's 'pact' amounts to a mutually convenient device to postpone the inevitable. Warring on the Soviet Union is a matter of when, not if, and there'll be bloody hell to pay! Hitler has no iota of respect for *wahrer* Heinrich, but he knows damn well he'll need the craven bastard's slaughterhouses plus Reinhard's *Schutzstaffeln* murder squads to consummate the Jewish cleansing pogrom. I've come to regard the *SS* as a ghastly version of some mythical occult NSDAP religious order, whose adherents pray to their private god, a stolid, bespectacled former poultry farmer who guides them with preachments of loyalty, honor, and most of all undying, personal allegiance to the sacred, sublime person of *Der Führer.*"

His tirade had transformed Canaris into a veritable poster boy for indignation. Meisinger found his vehement ranting and dangerously loose talk greatly disturbing.

"Most worrisome of all," continued the admiral in the same rancorous vein, "are reports filtering back from our assets who've infiltrated Byelorussia, the Ukraine, and near reaches of the USSR. After subtly canvassing random elements of the populace, the general impression we received was that many, if not most, regional Soviet citizens would not only tolerate, but perhaps welcome our invading military. Stalin's mass deportations, relocations, and the intolerable abuses he's visited on his own people has apparently caused gross numbers of citizens to question their allegiance to the USSR. But once Heydrich's SS death angels descend and begin indiscriminately torturing, burning, slaying, and imprisoning civilians, any faint hope of sympathy for our cause will evaporate like the proverbial dew."

The admiral paused to eye Meisinger circumspectly. "Ordinarily I wouldn't dream of saying this to another living soul, Ulrich, but after a semi-sleepless night, I halfway came to a decision about our friend and his letters. I'm seriously thinking of calling off the hunt."

Meisinger had difficulty believing what he had heard. "I don't … understand, sir. With *Der Führer* calling at all hours, demanding that we find and interrogate him, learn firsthand what makes him tick, how he devises his incredibly accurate predictions, we can't—"

"In a nutshell," interrupted Canaris, "you just stated why I believe it might be best to leave well enough alone. Whoever the hell he is, and whatever the source of his visions, I find myself praying our balmy friend stays hidden and keeps sending us foreknowledge, however obtained, of future events, opportunities, and errors. No, strike 'balmy'! Whoever the hell he is, no matter how crazy his ultimate purpose, I can't shake a subterranean suspicion that our friend could well be on our side. To date, his messages have been benevolent, in no way diabolic. I became most curious, went back and analytically reread the copies or transcripts of each letter received to date. Dollops of astrological horseshit aside, read between the lines all his *verdammt* letters and you'll find a crafty lesson not only positive in tone and substance, but pertaining to what he claims to have *envisioned,* which again in most cases could be a more sane, logical, and proper way to conduct specific military matters and political decisions than the amateurs now in charge who bow daily to Hitler's superb guidance.

"The Dunkerque letter," pursued Canaris before Meisinger could comment, "is an excellent example. We were warned what a horrendous mistake it would be to let an entire allied army be sailed away to fight another day. Offhand, can you think of a more sound and sensible piece of advice than what that letter included? Why, our friend counsels us in the voice of logic and reason incarnate. He insists on shouting meaningful, helpful jeremiads and warnings from somewhere here in the capital."

At first perplexed, Meisinger had begun to absorb the admiral's reasoning, if not his motive. "Your rationale is inarguable, sir, but you might reconsider calling off the hunt. Do so, and Himmler will have Heydrich's assign his Gestapo street hooligans to the chase, and you know better how *that* would go."

"Um, quite so, if he hasn't already done so behind our back. I've already reconsidered," he said grudgingly. "All you've done is sway my thinking by mentioning that grim eventuality. Here's what we'll do. To keep up appearances, instruct your team to go through the motions as if the search was not just continuing, but intensifying per a Führer *Richtungweisend.* Have your assets mill about, look busy, but if a serious lead should turn up, direct them firmly to get in touch with you before making any move, or if necessary, ring me directly. Whether its black magic, intuition, witchcraft, or what have you, I truly believe the winds of war may have changed direction a tad due to our friend's letters, and something we had damn well best learn is to appreciate it and him. The last thing desirable would be for our friend to be subjected to Heydrich's 'gentle' interrogations. Someone once said a prophet should never try to be too specific, but by Christ our friend has been specific *plus*!"

Sounding troubled, Meisinger said, "Hope you realize what you're doing, sir."

"In these times, can anyone claim to be *that* self-aware?"

Coming from the admiral, Meisinger thought the question anything but rhetorical.

\* \* \*

From the stairwell, Frau Kraven hailed, "Yoo-hoo, Herr Steyr! Telephone call."

Concentrating on two-finger typing a think piece he regarded as lucrative drivel, the summons did not surprise James. Earlier, Herr

Stampfl had called twice to inquire when the prospective article might land at his desk at the ministry, and twice in the same breath urged him to finish it with all due haste and bring it to the Leopold Palace in person. Rising behind the Olivetti, he tried to imagine a simple way to put off Stampfl.

"Who is it, *Frau* Kraven? Did they say?"

"*Ja, ja,* another gentleman, not the one who kept calling earlier, but a Herr Klasse."

Silverthorne's pulse rate quickened. Having warned Lustmann to contact him only in an emergency, something must have happened to spur the call. He left the attic room, clumped downstairs two risers at a time, excused himself for brushing past the descending landlady, and lifted the hall telephone's earpiece, his knuckles white. "Herr Steyr, here."

"*Guter Tag,* Steyr. So sorry to bother you, but I—"

"What's gone wrong, Herr Klasse?"

"Wrong? Why, nothing," assured Lustmann, "except for my rotten attempt to cope with the, er ... tract I mentioned. I'm in desperate in need of assistance, Steyr. Can you possibly find an hour or two free this evening and drop by the Adlon?"

Relieved, James said, "Yes, be glad to do what I can. But is it practical to meet in your, uh ... where you are? It might complicate publishing the tract."

"*Nein, nein,*" denied Lustmann. "I take your meaning, but not to worry. The publication matter can be handled with usual discretion. There is also something else," he added. "Please take no offense, Steyr, but the other night you were dressed like a ragamuffin. Can't greet you here at the, er ... you know, like that, can we? My driver was given your boardinghouse address. Look out at the street in a half hour or so. There will be a black Mercedes parked nearby. The driver will take you to the haberdashery I patronize. I should admire you much more after you choose a few suits off the rack, some decent shirts, ties, a hat, whatever else you may need.

No fancy apparel, merely togs sufficiently stylish enough to make you presentable here in my, er … habitat. I shall take care of payment."

"Most kind of you, Herr Klasse. You are sure about this?"

"Absolutely. My source material, if you take my meaning, is … I would be uncomfortable carrying my notes and reference materials elsewhere, whereas privacy here is guaranteed."

On uncertain ground, James said, "Right you are, sir."

"Make your purchases, then my driver will bring you here. Have the desk ring me when you arrive. We'll meet in the bar, have a drink together to establish your bona fides."

"As you wish, Herr Klasse. Look for me at, say, a little after five." James rang off, puffed his cheeks, and revolved the development while absently groping to replace the earpiece in the two-pronged hook. He went into the kitchen, explained to his landlady the need to attend an important evening session at his workplace, and might come home late. He requested a latch key to the front door, since Frau Kraven invariably locked up when retiring to her room at the witching hour of seven o'clock, after repeating her standing order to never be disturbed.

Later James cracked open the front door. Glistening in the late afternoon sun, a gleaming black Mercedes-Benz Saloon had pulled up at the curb.

* * *

Despite having left an order that he was not to be disturbed, Admiral Canaris was busy dressing down a senior analyst accused of doing less than was expected of him. Annoyed to be alerted by the intercom's insistent buzz, he answered irritably. An aide announced that Martin Borman was holding on line three.

Canaris lifted the phone, punched a button, and said curtly, "Yes?"

Borman's lifeless, monotonic baritone grated more harshly on the admiral's psyche than his ear. "Canaris, on behalf of *Der Führer,* it is my duty to inform you that Reichsführer-*SS* Himmler has been directed to have his premier intelligence assets seconded to Abwehr in order to augment the search for this mysterious letter writer who has become a cause of enormous concern."

The admiral blanched, closed his eyes tightly, irked by the probability of a monumental disaster in the making. "I see."

*"Der Führer,"* continued the lifeless voice, "also suggested that I encourage the Abwehr to make the best possible use of every scrap of aid believed necessary to resolve with utmost alacrity the strange affair precipitated by this dangerously well-informed letter writer. He also asked me to commend your office for what it has done and doubtless will continue to do in a praiseworthy effort to bring this odd business to a swift, fruitful conclusion."

Fuming internally, Canaris said, "Please thank *Der Führer* for his consideration, and assure him all his wishes will be fulfilled." Caging the phone with enough force to crack the instrument, he turned to glare redly at the analyst he had been counseling. "Get out!"

The middle-aged staffer rose hastily and scurried out of the office.

"What in the name of Christ," muttered Canaris, "is our beloved Fatherland *coming* to!"

Every day, without fail, one or another self-important idiot accorded oversight of the governing menagerie had whispered in Hitler's ear, and the result invariably skewed beyond recognition the proper way of doing any activity that might be involved. *No,* he decided. Whoever and whatever the hell Borman is, he may be self-important, but he's no idiot. The seldom seen figure lurking in the shadows behind Adolph Hitler was an unknown quantity wrapped in an enigma. Yet, if Hess and Himmler had the leader's ear, Borman had gotten his hooks into his master's mind and soul, if indeed Hitler possessed a soul. What could he do to rectify this latest, semi-anticipated fiasco in the making? He pondered at length, unable to think of anything.

When Meisinger came into the office hours later to inquire about another matter, the admiral unburdened himself by rancorously damning the development announced by Borman.

The Abwehr's star investigator wagged his head sadly.

During the wee hours of the following morning, when most Berliners were peacefully asleep, pounding boots and doors ripped from the hinges could be heard in halls and stairwells as senior Gestapo agents led raid after raid after raid. People were snatched from their beds, whisked to somber *Niederkirchnerstrasse* headquarters, where many of the arrestees, mostly Jews whose names and addresses were already lodged in voluminous *Reichssicherheitshauptamt* files, were subjected to close encounters of the worst kind, when numerous civilian "suspects" became intimately acquainted with truncheons, hobnailed boots, red-hot pincers, serial electric shocks, and special, custom-made pliers custom-designed to efficiently crush testicles.

\* \* \*

After dinner in Lustmann's suite, by far James's most sumptuous meal since his retro-temporal departure from his native timeline, his host rolled the room service cartful of china and glassware into the hall, locked and chained the door, and brought the aluminum carryall into the parlor, where he proudly demonstrated the fail-safe method of unlatching and opening the lid.

His first glimpse of the contents forced James to suppress a wild urge to bludgeon the would-be *DWK* timeline hero there and then, re-latch the carryall, and slip away into the night. Stacks of high-denomination Reichsmarks bundled with brown paper straps rested cheek by jowl with what might be sheaves of flash-paper documents that most likely defined ODESSA's lessons on how Lustmann was to conduct his mission.

Casually extracting and handing to James sums totaling three or four times the cost of the wardrobe items he had purchased for his newfound accomplice, Lustmann lifted out a yellow legal tablet filled with a jumble of scribblings, scratched-out phrases, and partial sentences. "Here, Steyr, you see the results of what I labored over half the night attempting to write." Picking up the flash-paper account of World War II on his native timeline, he pointed to a paragraph that called for a letter aimed at firmly encouraging a turnabout in Luftwaffe tactics.

"It seems these, um … sets of coastal towers, whatever their purpose, were installed to somehow alert England's command center of incoming aerial strikes and cue the RAF regarding when and where aircraft should be scrambled aloft to intercept the attackers. Göring has to be informed about how vital it will be to eliminate these towers prior to each aerial assault."

James nodded. "Radar, Herr Lust—Forgive me, Herr Klasse. Radar is a commonly used contraction for radio detection and ranging systems."

"You are familiar with this technique?"

"Only the basics. Electronic pulses radiate, strike any solid object like a ship or aircraft in line of sight and return reflected energy—backscatter, I believe it's called—to provide a visual indication of an aerial threat's elevation, direction of travel and velocity."

"Visually?"

"Yes, by electronically illuminating the object in a cathode ray tube."

Lustmann scratched his temple. "I don't recall ever hearing any such terms while serving in the SS, but let that pass. You make it clear how the Englanders learn in advance when and where our attack is coming in. These towers must be destroyed, not allowed to warn of any Luftwaffe attacks or later weaken a vital endeavor like Übungs-Seelöwe."

"Operation Sea Lion?"

"Codeword for the Channel crossing, a key step toward conquest of the British Isles."

"Ah, I see." James memorized the term and its purpose. He asked his host if he might read the radar data for himself. Lustmann obediently handed over several sheets of flash paper.

Despite hungering to digest each word, James skimmed only the paragraphs aimed at coaching revised conduct of the upcoming air war over England. When he finished, Lustmann was staring at him, a question in his pale-blue eyes.

James reluctantly passed back the flimsy documents. "I'm afraid destroying specific English radar facilities may have to be done more than once, as reinstallation could be relatively fast. It might be best to politely admonish Reichsführer Göring about how mandatory it will be to deal with the radar towers in the path of each specific bombing assault, but an unavoidable negative aspect of that would be forewarning British air defenses where a coming strike might be aimed."

Stroking his cheek in thought, Lustmann grumped, "Not sure I understand," and replaced the flash-paper sheets atop the short stack in the carryall. "Urging Göring to do anything may be a waste of time. Instead, we might concentrate on influencing *Der Führer,* since fat Hermann listens closely to every word that escapes Hitler's mouth. You were quite correct about one thing, Steyr. We must do our damnedest to shift Göring's views to obtain more productive results from the air strikes. Is there any way to put that objective in words?"

"I think so. First, may I read what you've written?"

"Certainly, if you think it's worth the effort. The main impetus of redirection ODESSA suggested was to counsel limiting bombing targets to industrial centers, shipyards, vessels docked or at sea, and airfields, rather than wasting bombs and lives to wreak civilian casualties in the cities. In my opinion, a century of bombing would fail to intimidate the stubborn Englanders."

James did not hesitate to voice agreement, then tried to make sense of Lustmann's scribbles. Even when it came to composing a simple, declarative sentence, his host's effort had fallen below the level of an average schoolboy. Busy trying to make head or tail of the disjointed attempts, interlinings, and crossings-out, he was startled to hear a tap on the door.

Lustmann uttered a sibilant curse. "Could it be one of your associates?" he asked in a whisper, eyeing James with an accusative air.

James whispered, "Never! Neither of them would dare come near the hotel."

The legal tablet was snatched from Silverthorne's hand. "Take the case into the bedroom," ordered his host, hurriedly jamming the tablet and loose flash-paper sheets into the carryall. He slammed shut the lid, but did not latch it before passing it to James, whispering for him to take it into the bedchamber, and reached under a chair cushion to withdraw the silenced Walther automatic pistol.

James did as he was told, eased the bedroom door shut behind him, and pressed his ear to it.

Lustmann peeked through the small lens in the entry door and stepped back in surprise. He did not hesitate to unlock and pull the door open. "Dear Gerda! I can hardly believe it's you."

Frau Sharpe eyed the weapon in his hand. "Thinking to shoot me, Herr Klasse?"

"Sorry, so sorry! I welcome few callers, and doing so armed is second nature. You look ravishing. I was terribly hurt to hear you say you never wished to see me again."

"I'm happy to say I can now." She smiled, primly taking a seat on the sofa. "Our mutual problem has solved itself, Erich. Herr Funk summoned me and related a most peculiar tale. It seems your famous nineteen forty-two banknote has vanished."

"What do you mean?"

"Exactly what I said, *zut,* disappeared! Herr Funk wondered why the police had stopped pestering him with questions he was unable to answer."

"The ... evidence, gone?"

Gerda said, "On purpose, or so Herr Funk believes. He's convinced himself all that tail chasing to investigate the erroneous issue date became so exasperating to the authorities that they put a match to the confounded banknote and slyly disposed of it. He's sure it didn't blow away in the wind, yet thoroughly delighted to have it gone."

"Lord save us!" said Lustmann with feeling. "I echo his sentiment. Here, would you care for a drink, Gerda?"

"No, I can't stay. I dropped by just to give you the good news."

James had heard enough. Taking advantage of the unlatched carryall, he opened it and began avidly speed-reading a flash-paper account of actual wartime events on Lustmann's native timeline with thousands of times more interest than most historians. Entranced by the text, he carelessly allowed the carryall's lid to fall closed with a distinct click.

In the parlor, Gerda Sharpe glanced knowingly at the door to the bedchamber. "I'd love to act surprised, Herr Klasse, but you're apparently entertaining a fresh *Schatze.*"

Lustmann forced a thin smile. "You misjudge me, Gerda. I will always be true to you."

"In your fashion, of course," Gerda said more snidely than she might have intended.

Lustmann's chuckle was meant to lighten the onset of tension. "Lest you think ill of me, I confess that a business associate decided it wise to stay out of sight when you tapped on the door." He called, "Come in, Steyr. I want you to meet an elegant, charming acquaintance."

Figuratively kicking himself for being careless, James left the unlatched, closed-lid carryall resting on the bed. He left the bedchamber feebly attempting to look sheepish.

"Hans, allow me to introduce Frau Sharpe. She and I have had business dealings for some time. Gerda, this gentleman is Hans Steyr, an Austrian journalist."

James dipped his head. *"S'tut sehr gleich,* Frau Sharpe."

"So happy to meet you," said Gerda, examining James analytically. She turned to Lustmann. "My, you certainly do have a handsome associate. I assume Herr Steyr is also of the *SS.* "

His lofty manner that of someone knowing himself above the fray, Lustmann drawled, "Unfortunately, I'm afraid that isn't so. Hans really is an Austrian journalist employed by the Goebbels Ministry. He came to see me in the interest of gathering background material for an article he means to write about a hoped-for rise in Swedish steel production."

"Fascinating," declared Gerda, as if swallowing Lustmann's characterization whole but inwardly conflicted. "Well, you gentlemen must be very busy. I'll be running along."

James was instantly apologetic. "Frau Sharpe, please don't rush off on my account. We had all but finished ironing out what few details remain, and that can be taken care of another time, is that not so, Herr Klasse?"

"Absolutely!" Lustmann had been eyeing Gerda hungrily. He casually slid a possessive arm around Gerda's waist. "If you don't hear from me later today, call me in the morning, Hans. We'll sit down over lunch and hash out the missing pieces."

"Right, sir. I'll ring you around nine thirty, ten o'clock." Lifting his new fedora from an end table, James bent gallantly over Gerda Sharpe's hand and said his farewells.

Descending the service stairway, he readjusted the three folded sheets of flash-paper he'd failed to replace in the carryall and secreted them in an inner jacket pocket. Pilfering the documents had been dangerous, something he ordinarily would never have dared to do, but it had been an on-the-spot decision. He simply *had* to read the material and was glad he had taken the chance. From the way his pale-blue eyes had been devouring Frau Sharpe, he assumed Lustmann would be far too occupied to bother checking the carryall's contents before putting it away.

Alone in his attic room, he read and reread the three sheets, then went back and started over, memorizing the accounts of events during the early stages of what he could not stop thinking of as the real war. Unfortunately, the sheets snatched at random to join those he'd been scanning lacked calendar continuity, offering accounts of happenings in the spring and summer of the current timeline disconnected from those he was reading when interrupted by Gerda Sharpe's visit.

He learned that America's President Roosevelt, of whom he had no prior knowledge, had signed a "Lend-Lease" agreement, whatever that meant, with Great Britain. As a consequence, a number of American minesweepers, destroyers, and other warships had been delivered into Royal Navy service. FDR, as he was known in the flash-paper document, had also approved the overhaul and repair of His Majesty's warships in American ports.

He read of the upcoming Wehrmacht invasion of Yugoslavia and Greece, the airborne landings in Crete, and how Germany's gigantic battleship, the *Bismarck,* had decimated allied shipping by prowling the South Atlantic waters. He learned the Americans had not only moved roughly one quarter of their Pacific Fleet to the Atlantic, but that between thirty-five and sixty ships belonging to what the document labeled the "Axis" had been taken into "protective custody" by multiple American acts of so-called piracy.

Although he managed to absorb only mystifying bits and pieces of the overall puzzle, a start was a start. Yawning, he descended the stairs, visited the second-floor hall bathroom, then went back upstairs and prepared for bed. All but certain he and Lustmann would meet again the next day, he intended to dutifully help the bastard write at minimum one letter designed to improve and enhance the Nazi cause, and possibly a second, and then vowed to change each and every aspect of their supposed collaboration with one swift, final stroke.

# SIXTEEN

## *Schemes and Schemers*

On the fourteenth day of June 1940, after only three and one-half weeks of sporadic, ever-weakening resistance, the Wehrmacht had overwhelmed the forces of France, while all allied forces that had survived the juggernaut were in full retreat. Highly disciplined troops marched into Paris, the jackboots of regiment after regiment pounding in cadence through Place Charles de Gaulle and beneath Napoleon's Arc de Triomphe de l'Étoile, a victory parade that endowed the monument with entirely new meaning for the French men and women sobbing in despair along the Champs Élysées.

On June 22, filled with bitter despair, General Henrí-Phillipe Pétain signed a peace agreement, surrendering the French Republic to the "Boche" invader. Later, the puppet government erroneously called État Français was stillborn in Vichy.

Admiral Canaris also came close to sobbing like other dispirited Parisians, but for an entirely different reason. In a voice laden with stark, unmitigated incredulity, he cried, "Look at it, Ulrich! Just *look* at the damned thing, would you!" The wire photo he waved in front of his chief investigator's nose depicted Adolf Hitler in a tan uniform, a faint smile showing through his signature mustache, as he performed a little hop-stamp of victory alongside the identical French railcar in which the 1918 Armistice had been signed to end the so-called Great War.

"Our friend predicted this artfully staged, unbelievable event weeks ago, *weeks!*" cried the admiral, his faulty diction deriving from abject disbelief. "Nor was it in any way a general, off-the-cuff prediction. He described his vision of Hitler's little dance of elation, *accurately* predicting an out-and-out impossibility, a *miracle*, Ulrich! How in the name of God Almighty can such a thing occur here in the real world?"

"Cause and effect could have been synergistic?" suggested Meisinger. "What this wire photo pictures might be a self-fulfilling prophecy, sir. Suppose *Der Führer* read the letter before the armistice signing and fell in love with our friend's vision of his victory jig. If not for that possibility, it's absolutely beyond explanation, with no means to account for what occurred. As you said, the accuracy of our visionary prophet exceeds all bounds of reason."

"By *leagues!*" Snorting indignantly, Canaris slipped the "impossible" wire photo back in a dispatch case. In an aggrieved tone of voice, he said, "Here we sit, trapped between a gigantic rock and a much larger, diamond-hard wall. Heydrich's Gestapo misfits are prosecuting their anti-Jewish pogrom night and day, and people are talking, wondering what the hell is going on, while our noble Führer bloviates as usual, *never* shuts up long enough to let us do our work. He shouts at me on the phone, and then screams about my transgressions when I'm summoned into his sacred presence. He pounds the table, demands to know why no letter has yet arrived, then in the very same breath demands to know *why* the prophet hasn't been dragged into an *SS* torture chamber and interrogated."

Meisinger started to ask, "Have you told him about the—"

"One does not dare *tell* Der Führer anything at all," declared the admiral, "especially never, *ever* anything he doesn't wish to hear. One listens and pretends to pay rapt attention to his endless, hand-waving monologues, then one nods sagely as if agreeing with the curative hints and suggestive measures he espouses left and right, then right and left. One absorbs, and must commit to memory, his schoolboy lessons on caulking every chink in the armor of Germany's new religion, National Socialism."

"Please, Admiral," pleaded Meisinger, "you owe it to yourself to be more circumspect about voicing acid criticisms. No one knows how many ears have been inserted in Abwehr."

Canaris nodded. "All too true, Ulrich. Were I still in my right mind, I would hand my duties into your care, take my Kriegsmarine uniform out of mothballs and go back to sea. It would be much better to go down standing on the bridge of an honest vessel than trying in vain to do my job while fending off the 'helpful' attentions of Himself, who has surrounded himself with lying, backbiting scoundrels and madmen."

"Softly, softly," urged Meisinger, knowing it useless to try and subdue the other's rantings.

"Oh, get on with your investigatory charade," said Canaris. "My hope is that it will not be an Abwehr asset who collars our friend. In the final analysis, who can say whether the vision-happy scribbler will win fame as Germany's hidden savior or its most lethal enemy?"

\* \* \*

The expected phone call came around four the next afternoon, summoning James. Clad in a new double-breasted gray suit, he entered the Adlon confidently, walking tall, his acting talent stretched to give an impression of owning the lobby. Surprised to encounter Frau Sharpe stepping out of the elevator, they greeted each other pleasantly, and briefly exchanged the meaningless pleasantries relative strangers seem to feel necessary. Finding her again at the Adlon confirmed his supposition that she and Lustmann were more than business acquaintances.

His host had been watching for Steyr, restlessly peeking through the lens in the entry door every few minutes. Admitting him, he went through the lock-and-chain drill, making sure they would not be disturbed. "Have you thought about how to best frame the message in our letter?"

"I slept on it, Herr Klasse." James set his new fedora on an end table, startled to see the open aluminum carryall, its lid tilted back, resting on the escritoire. "At breakfast, something pertinent to the issue occurred to me. During our first meeting, I spoke briefly about my, er … future 'former' life, if saying it that way makes any sense at all, and—"

"Don't bother just now, Steyr; it has no bearing on our present effort." Anxious to get the letter written and posted, the onerous task over and done with, Lustmann lit a cigarette.

"Ah, but I'm afraid it does," assured James. "Born in Greater Denver Gauleitung, educated there, earning a doctorate at Goebbels Institute, I eventually became a tenured professor who—"

"Some *school* bears the name of that rat-faced pipsqueak?"

"A major university," affirmed James. "Not long ago, the Reichsminister interviewed me, said he liked my article, and offered me employment. Since then, four articles have been published in *Der Angriff,* the ministry's propaganda rag. Take no offense, but I sincerely believe it would be a mistake to disparage the work of Goebbels' ministry—or him, for that matter. Influencing how people think," he continued, "is a vital element of our cause, and that is something the Ministry for Education and Enlightenment does exceptionally well. There is much to be learned from their methods. If outrageous half-truths and falsehoods are stridently repeated often enough, for example, people will gradually begin to believe them."

Lustmann floated a smoke ring toward the ceiling. "All well and good," he said impatiently. "I promise to take back what I said about the rat-faced pipsqueak, but stick to the subject, eh? We have to get busy inventing our own outrageous half-truths and falsehoods."

James acknowledged the feeble witticism with a forced smile. "No argument, but first let me explain something pertinent. After the conquest of the Americas, *Der Führer* began distancing himself from the Reichsminister, and their once-close association soured. Pushed back on the shelf out of the way, to understate their curtailed relationship, Goebbels used his newfound leisure to write, dictate, or some said hire someone to ghost write a thirteen-volume set of books entitled *The War of World Liberation.* As an undergraduate, I assiduously studied the wordy, overwritten volumes, each loaded with holograms, flat photos, innumerable footnotes, and references, and then was forced to do so again in greater detail as a doctoral candidate."

"What are holo ... whatever you called them?"

"Electronic three-dimensional pictures reproducible on a flat page."

"Ummm, difficult to imagine. Now hear me, Steyr," said Lustmann. "Before this war we hope to correct ends, we have to rectify a number of errors, and that inclines me to deny you permission to further belabor me with details of your background."

Irritated by the other's sarcasm, James informed him that just before Frau Sharpe's visit, he'd been reading about the coming summer's air war over England and been shocked to learn of it. "What I'm getting at is that in my own *DKW* timeline, a record of the *real* World War Two you yourself fought in, Herr Lustmann, did not exist *merely* a 'factual' account credited to Goebbels, with which I'm extremely familiar, but which deals *only* with what was called the War of World Liberation, *not* the valiant struggle fought by you and millions of others in what from my perspective will always be the long ago."

"Ah, now all becomes clear, especially your motive for bothering me with all this." Lustmann stubbed out his cigarette. "An easy remedy is right before us, Steyr." He lifted from the carryall a larger set of flash-paper documents and gave it to James. "Read only the first pages, then we'll get to work on the aerial Blitzkrieg letter. Afterward, you can steep yourself in the remainder to your heart's content. While you're studying, I'll order dinner sent up around seven. The chef's rouladen is exceptional here, with a decent cabernet to wash it down? How does that sound?"

James smiled. "My mouth's watering already."

While the other was on the phone, his back turned, James flattened the creases in the few pilfered flash-paper documents he had taken home, checked the page numberings, and slipped the sheets into the stack in their proper order. With that scary bump in the road crossed, he began speed-reading the text.

During the so-called Battle of Britain— fifty-seven days and nights of constant aerial attacks from August through October 1940— most Luftwaffe bombs had fallen on London, with one very destructive raid on Coventry and more on Manchester and several other cities large and small. The account informed him that the British had lost more than eight hundred fighter aircraft in defensive aerial battles, costing Luftwaffe casualties of about six hundred difficult-to-replace medium bombers and fighters in what were, if one were to read between the lines, Hitler's first defeats in warfare. American aid to Britain was bitterly condemned for positively influencing British military successes on the ground, especially the defeat of Italian forces in Egypt led by a General Wavell, who capped his victories by taking Tobruk in Libya and other North African towns.

Sensing that he'd missed something, James went back and reread the first paragraphs. The range of Luftwaffe medium bombers operating from airfields in occupied France was described as pitifully limited for targets any distance north of London, although secondary strike capability against the English east coast all the way north to York had been achieved by dispatching squadrons from the Baltic coast or airfields in occupied Norway. What the Luftwaffe very badly needed but did not have, according to the text, was a substantial fleet of heavy bombers, not squadron after squadron of two-engine Dornier and Heinkel mediums handicapped by limited ranges and fairly modest armament payload capacities.

Lustmann caged the telephone, decanted brandy, and lit another cigarette.

"You told me," remarked James after reading further, "how ODESSA provided a rough guideline for correcting the most obvious wartime errors, deficiencies, and potential military disasters."

"*Jawhol!* And a modestly comprehensive set of warnings and suggestions it is." Lustmann rose, lifted a second stack of flash-paper from the carryall, and passed it to James, who reluctantly gave back the priceless record of the actual war.

Speed-reading the how-to documents, he learned that Lustmann's mentors, gifted with twenty-twenty postwar hindsight, had strongly advocated that all production efforts be diverted to long-range, heavy bombardment aircraft, citing the move as imperative due to the vast distances to be overflown in warring upon the hemisphere-spanning Soviet Union. The document insisted that the Luftwaffe be urged to forget civilian London and other English cities and concentrate on constant aerial assaults aimed at decimating coastal radar stations to pave the way for surprise raids on airfields, shipyards, ports, docks, even vessels randomly intercepted at sea. Such redirections of effort were described as mandatory if Operation Sea Lion were to be undertaken and combat-ready Wehrmacht *Heer* forces landed on the English beachheads. How could Germany hope to accomplish Sea Lion's objective—a caveat posed as a question—if Kriegsmarine warships and troopships were decidedly destined to be outgunned in the Channel by the intact, experienced, seaworthy Royal Navy?

Speed-reading a record of the actual WWII, he learned that Hitler had solved the Sea Lion quandary by scrubbing the *OKW* code-word operation in favor of turning the attention of his ground and air forces eastward. Failing to consolidate all Western European holdings prior to invading the USSR was cited in the "correction" document as definitely the most egregious error of the entire global conflict, a paramount mistake contributing directly to Nazi Germany's defeat.

Having plodded through Goebbels' insipid volumes more than once, James recalled page after page devoted to the acclaim showered on Hitler for having the foresight to ensure the total consolidation of Europe—British Isles, Denmark, Norway, the Balkans, Greece, and Yugoslavia, as well as permitting Portugal, Switzerland, and Sweden to retain neutrality prior to loosing his dogs of war on what was snidely referred to as Stalin's Communist Worker's Paradise. That consolidation of conquered territories had apparently not happened in Lustmann's war, a huge difference James decided would need to be fully digested in order to define the where and when of corrective suggestions.

Finishing his brandy, Lustmann chain-smoked while James busied himself learning about the early first year of death and destruction during the "authentic" Second World War. His host interrupted only once to inquire if Steyr knew what role if any the *Juden* had played in the proud, miraculous Deutches Weltreich he had so glowingly word pictured.

Taken aback by the question, James pretended ingenuousness. "Jews?"

"*Ja, ja.* Followers of Jehovah, members of a vile ancient religious sect. Were any still around in the future utopia you praise to the skies?"

As if a light had come on, James said, "Oh, the *religious* order. Yes, I recall reading something about the, er ... *Juden*. In my *DKW* timeline, most religious affiliations had become historical footnotes or were reduced to a few secretive groups and cabals too insignificant for *Reichskounzel* to order eradicated."

Lustmann's pleased smirk inspired James to think eliminating him might not be such an oppressive task after all.

Later, they sat down and spent the postprandial evening working in earnest, with James playing the part of a tyro sounding board, listening and critiquing Lustmann's often disjointed proposals, or occasionally trying to temper one of the other's opinionated notions about the way a prospective "vision" would best translate into a polite redirection suggestion aimed at enhancing the effectiveness of specific military efforts. They labored over the message for hours, and all went well until the topic of astrology arose. Claiming total ignorance of the subject, James explained why his host would have to invent zodiacal mishmash fit to maintaining the theme and tone of the earlier letters.

While scheming a method of fleshing out a vision aimed at changing the tactical plans and self-serving opinions or objectives of Reichsführer-Luftwaffe Göring on how to better wage the air war against England prior to the Sea Lion invasion, James urged it essential to avoid blunt statements, instead emphasizing the power of suggestion as a great deal more effective than direct urgings. He went so far as to propose forwarding an all-encompassing vision of bombing results rather than how-to means of conducting the coming air campaign.

Drawing a word picture of collective British helplessness, he described the value of a Royal Navy seriously weakened at sea or tied up at dock in the wake of wave after wave of bombings, and went on to "suggest a vision" of Wehrmacht armor and mechanized infantry units sweeping through the English shires in practiced Blitzkrieg fashion, with major government officials confined in the Tower of London and huge swastika banners rippling in Piccadilly Circus.

Lustmann absorbed the "enchanting" vision in a waxing fever of enthusiasm that fed on itself to the point of redoubling in the final draft, although James still debated several minor revisions here, or a change of emphasis, a more effective rewording there.

When the amended text finally met with Lustmann's satisfaction, he closed and latched the carryall and put it away in the bedchamber. James twiddled his thumbs, watched his host fill a fountain pen with green ink, and begin to laboriously hand letter the missive.

He had all but finished the letter when James glanced at his wristwatch. "Damn, its after ten o'clock! I won't be able to get into my boardinghouse." At the other's querulous reaction, he related his landlady's penchant for personal privacy and boardinghouse security.

"No matter," muttered Lustmann, completing his painstaking endeavor. "I have … spare blankets, a pillow. Sleep here on the sofa, Steyr. Now let me finish this damned thing before my hand cramps to a point where I can no longer scratch an itch."

James poured himself a brandy without asking permission. Another a half hour passed before Lustmann hand-lettered his pseudo-signature, *Ein Freund des Reichs,* and addressed the envelope.

It was close to midnight when James dossed down on the sofa, his blood stirred by a sudden, fiery notion that occurred to him while undressing. Here he was, alone in a deluxe suite at the Adlon with the once-but-hopefully-never-to-be *Weltreichsheld,* wondering if a more opportune moment would ever come to do away with his supposed accomplice? Now fully aware of all that was needed to rid the world of the as-yet-uncrowned savior of Nazidom's empty promises, why not simply snatch the carryall and its irreplaceable arsenal of ammunition—not to mention more funds than he could ever hope to spend—dash into the night and assume the role of seer?

Throughout the preceding evening, the detested if inescapable need to help Lustmann coach ways and means of *aiding* the efforts of a militant *Dritte Reich* in questing for global domination gave birth to a sense of self-betrayal. Wasn't averting a Nazi triumph expressly why a pair of generations peopled by American patriots had lived and died in an unceasing struggle to send him back across the decades to a timeline not his own? Yet there was also a serious flaw in his wish to dispatch Lustmann in such an impromptu manner. Frau Sharpe had seen him twice at the hotel, as had numerous others in the bar while downing an apéritif with "Herr Klasse," a known hotel guest, simply to assure others that he belonged in the swank Adlon. It was also probable that he had been noticed going or coming from his host's suite.

No, spurred by a stray impulse to do the deed was laden with great risk. He would have to bide his time, carefully plan and prepare for a safe and secure way to ensure Lustmann's demise.

\* \* \*

Herr Klasse woke early and emerged from the bedchamber in a red paisley robe, his bare feet in open-toed mules. Greeting his guest with a yawn, he lit a cigarette, lifted the handset, and asked the operator for room service, requesting that breakfast be sent up at once.

James folded the blanket, rearranged the sofa cushions, and dressed. After coffee, buttered sweet rolls, and fresh fruit, Lustmann sat down at the drop-leaf escritoire, checked Zoltan's name, and hand-lettered the street address on a plain white envelope. Slipping the folded letter into the envelope, he licked the gummed flap to seal it, and pasted on a postage stamp with a sigh. "Good riddance! I never again want to see this *verdammte Zeichen* again."

"I should be on my way." James picked up his fedora, hesitating when the door chime sounded.

"Wouldn't be wise to be seen leaving at this hour," said Lustmann. "Relax in the bedchamber for a moment, Steyr. Likely as not, it's the bellman with the morning papers."

Waiting in the other room, James heard the bellman bow and scrape over the amount of the gratuity, followed by the sound of the entry door closing. He found Lustmann at the window gazing down at the light early morning pedestrian traffic on the sidewalk below. "A pleasant sunny morning," he remarked. "I've a notion to stretch my legs, Steyr. Why not come along? We can stroll toward your boardinghouse, drop the letter into the first mailbox we happen upon."

"I'm all for it, Herr Klasse."

*"Nein, nein!* No more Herr Klasse formality," the other said pleasantly. "As business associates, you are to address me as Erich, and to me you will be simply Hans."

"An excellent idea, Herr Lust—" James pretended chagrin. "Sorry, I meant to say 'Erich.'"

His pleasant expression more a smirk than a sign of goodwill, Lustmann went into the bedroom, dressed quickly, and came out carrying a stylish tan homburg. "Shall we?"

Brilliant sunshine leavened the early morning chill. Concerned that one of very few Berlin acquaintances, Abwehr investigator Meisinger in particular, might see him in company with Lustmann, add two and two and arrive at a dangerous conclusion, James kept his head down, the brim of his fedora pulled low while strolling next to his taller, long-striding accomplice.

Full of himself, Lustmann began chattering about nothing in particular. Gazing at the street scene with a proprietary air, he asked James what future Berlin was really like.

"Welthaupstadt Germania, Erich."

*"Ach,* so you said! But that identity doesn't apply here and now in Berlin."

"True." Fearful of being overheard talking nonsense, James chuckled. "When all is said and done, Erich, you shall be welcomed like a saint arriving in a magnificent metropolis so much lovelier than Paris that the sights will literally take your breath away—broad tree-lined boulevards, innumerable parks and greenbelts, riparian esplanades along the Spree and similar waterways, a skyline dominated by the awesome dome of Speer's Great Hall, and the splendid Reichschancellery, the former palace of Göring, Hitler's tomb, and endless structures, parks, and bridges. I was privileged to visit the capital twice, once as a delegate to the annual *Deutsches Weltreich Historische* convention, then again in *DWJ* one thirty-six for the

Nordic World Games. You'll not believe your eyes at first sight of Speer Stadium. Even larger than the old one in Nürnberg, it seats more than a quarter-million spectators."

"Fascinating! Twice you mentioned the name Speer. I take it he was a relative of the War Production and Armaments Minister I heard praised on my timeline?"

"The same person, Erich. An architect befriended, and in fact all but adopted, by *Der Führer.*"

*"Ah, selbstverständlich!* Our timelines may differ in many respects and aspects, but I recall Herr Speer being famous for putting bombed-out factories back on line practically overnight."

Halfway down a side street not far from Unter den Linden, a red letterbox came in view. Lustmann slipped his hand into the inner pocket of his jacket, preparing to extract the letter and post it, but James reached out, seized his wrist, and tugged him to a halt.

"What are you doing?"

"Look there, ahead of us," said James in a low voice. "In a black leather jacket and derby."

"What about him?"

"Walk past the letterbox with me," urged James. "Ignore the fellow; don't so much as glance his way. His black, thigh-length leather jacket is virtually a Gestapo uniform."

"Nonsense! What brand of Gestapo thug would go around wearing a bowler?"

"One smart enough to be wary of recognition as a Gestapo thug. Look, he's turning, coming back this way, but not losing sight of the letterbox. One of my ... friends warned me of suspicious individuals lurking around postal stations and letterboxes here in *mitte* Berlin."

"You're dreaming, Steyr! Keeping watch on all the postal drops in this city is hardly possible."

"I don't pretend to know what is or isn't possible," said James. "Let's stroll to the end of the block, pause and pretend to discuss something while watching to see what he does."

The man James was leery of slowly approached them on a collision course, causing James and Erich to move closer to the frontage of a building, allowing a few early-rising pedestrians and the man in a black leather jacket to pass in the opposite direction.

At the corner, James glanced back. After ambling beyond the red letterbox, the suspect had turned around, and slowly came back toward the letterbox, passed it and stopped near them, where he turned around close enough to overhear James mouth a few meaningless words to Lustmann, whose aristocratic features had jelled in a stolid mask.

"Let's cross the street, watch from over there," whispered James.

On the sidewalk opposite the letterbox, James faced Lustmann, tracking the suspect Gestapo agent with peripheral vision. His suspicion increased as it became ever more obvious that the fellow tried to remain inconspicuous, but he kept making his way back and forth past the letterbox.

Beginning to lose patience with Steyr, Lustmann said irritably, "It could be as you believe, but there is no way to find out."

"Give me the letter, Erich."

"I'll do no such thing. Mailing it under the circumstances is too risky. I won't have you sacrifice yourself simply to learn whether—"

"Self-sacrifice never crossed my mind," assured James. "The letter has to be posted."

"We can find another, safer place."

James was silent for several heartbeats. "Erich, give me the letter. I'll cross over, wait until he turns the opposite way, follow along behind him, and drop the envelope on the sidewalk between the letterbox and the trash bin next to it and see if he or a passerby spots and picks it up."

Looking at his supposed accomplice with new eyes, Lustmann handed over the envelope.

"Give me one of your cigarettes too," said James, "and matches or a lighter."

"I've never seen you smoke."

"I don't, but I need an excuse to pause near the waste bin and let the letter fall."

"*Ganz gut!* Your ingenuity is most impressive, Hans."

Once he had done as proposed, James strolled back across street.

Lustmann sounded perplexed. "I watched closely but didn't see you drop the letter."

"When your lighter flamed out, I made as if to throw it in the trash bin like a match while sliding the envelope down inside my trouser leg and letting go."

"There's a good deal more to you than meets the eye. You teach valuable lessons."

"Don't stare at him, Erich. Relax and be patient. We may be taught a valuable lesson."

Five or six minutes passed. All conscientious Germans hate clutter. A dowdy middle-aged matron threw a wrapper of some kind in the trash bin in passing, hesitated, and bent over to awkwardly pick up the letter. Holding it close to her nose, she made a myopic inspection of the envelope and was in the act of depositing it in the letterbox when the man in the black leather jacket seized her wrist and snatched the letter away with his other hand.

The woman shrieked indignantly.

"Satisfied, Erich?"

Lustmann nodded. "Eminently! Worried, too. How the devil can we hope to post another *Zeichen* if they have every postal drop in the city covered?"

The woman's shrill protestations were drawing a crowd of gawkers when Lustmann and his prized confederate turned the corner and left the scene at a brisk pace.

# SEVENTEEN

## *Crisis*

At one time or another, Ulrich Meisinger had seen the admiral in an ebullient mood, but never before with his current exuberance.

His eyes alight with mischievous glee, Canaris guffawed. "This time the former chicken farmer Der Führer fondly calls *der treue* Heinrich stuck both feet in his mouth up to the hips, pulled them out and stepped down hard on his own private parts."

Meisinger asked if the woman had been roughed up.

"Ulrich, really! Doubt not that she was subjected to the tender mercies of Heydrich's Gestapo turds. They worked her over diligently, then redirected their attentions to the halfwit who collared her, and he enjoyed still more scathing exercises. The poor woman's confession consisted of repeating the tale she stuck to religiously, screaming again and again how she had seen the letter on the sidewalk and, like a good Samaritan, picked it up and was dropping it in a letterbox when the gorilla wearing a derby hat grabbed her. A truly embarrassing footnote to the incident did not come to light until the next morning. Talk about irony! It seems her only son, a wounded Wehrmacht junior officer presently convalescing in a French hospital, is being rushed home to comfort mummy."

It was Meisinger's turn to chuckle. "You can't be serious."

Canaris grinned. "Never more so! To my everlasting regret, I was elsewhere and missed the glorious sight of Hitler chewing *wahrsten*

Heinrich's arse into raw hamburger. More to the point, the root message in our friend's misdelivered letter is driving Hefty Hermann to
drink, not that he needs urging. By now, the heroic eagle of Luftwaffe
eagles and self-awarded honors has no doubt rolled up his sleeve,
gotten out his needles and little vials of otherworldly delights, and
dipped his wick in more than one user-friendly society lady."

Meisinger had read a transcript of the latest letter. "Less direct
than usual, it only suggests tactical bombing revisions I'm certain
must've ruffled Göring's feathers."

Canaris rolled his eyes. *"That* can be safely said! For the moment,
I doubt if the over-tailored, underbred ace of aces is regaling anyone
with his seditious jokes. The best news of all, in my opinion, is that
Himself has partially swallowed at a gulp the aerial assault revisions
our friend counsels. He's said to have lectured Göring about what
it will be mandatory to do in order to successfully bomb the Englanders to the point of softening their resistance to invasion, and
also made sure he understood what must *not* be done. On the face
of it, I don't believe the tendered advice will matter a whit. For all
his brave talk, *Der Führer* knows even less about directing aerial
warfare than micromanaging every phases of the ground war or the
war at sea."

Meisinger said thoughtfully, "You really believe Göring might
bend, revise his tactical bombing philosophy and stoop to adopt
any of the letter's, er … subtle urgings?"

A caustic snort. "Who can say? For all his grandiloquent bombast,
Hefty Hermann is precisely like the rest of us, or perhaps more so.
When Hitler says jump, he asks, *'Wie hoch, mein Führer?'* Once again,
our visionary scribbler has proven that a sound head rests on his
shoulders. Years of bombing raids aimed at demoralizing the obstinate Britishers wouldn't suffice to pave the way for invading their
precious isles. This last letter assures me it will be critical for our
prophet, seer, charlatan, whatever the hell he is, to stay hunkered
down in obscurity. If left alone to report his astonishing visions, he

could be the sole hope of persuading our faulty leadership to ...

"Wait, let's just say this modern Nostradamus could be the sole hope of persuading Hitler to let go of the reins, stop issuing one intuition-based *Führer Richtungweisend* after another and allow the professional military to prosecute the war in a sane, sensible manner, instead of flying into one of his classic rages if anyone in command shows enough spine to take his life in his hands and voice disagreement with one of his masterful decisions."

The admiral tilted back in his chair, toyed pensively with a fountain pen. "Ulrich, every ounce of competence and ability we can muster is needed to make certain our friend stays anonymous and persists in working his magic glimpses into the future. Our most desperate need is to guard him from falling into Heydrich's hands, where he would be destroyed, and with him every vestige of whatever the hell it is he's trying by some outré method to accomplish."

Meisinger nodded uncertainly.

"I'm deadly serious about that! After subjecting *wahrsten* Heinrich to a near-lethal browbeating," pursued the admiral, "that bespectacled jackass turned about head to toe and put the fear of not God but Germany's Führer into Heydrich's collection of street rabble by ordering them to stay on their tiptoes, be alert for any slight clue to the identity or whereabouts of our friend. What worries me deeply is that rounding up everyone in sight for interrogation could accidentally turn fruitful. After all, even a blind hog now and then roots up an acorn."

Canaris rocked forward in his high-backed executive chair, lifted his hands helplessly. "Oh, what the hell! Leave me to shuffle these meaningless papers, Ulrich. Arrive promptly at tomorrow's staff conference. I added your name to the list, because Gehlen informs us the latest report from assets inside the USSR is ripe for discussion, and naturally it will ignite the usual unending conjecture and argument."

\* \* \*

Frau Kraven had no reason to summon James to the telephone for the better part of a week. He passed the time speculating about Lustmann's failure to call, wrote another op-ed piece based on the "fact" that most German workers should consider themselves fortunate to be earning honest pay for honest labor, doing their wholesome, patriotic duty, in sharp contrast to the members of "counterproductive" unions who voted to receive premium payment for each extra work hour spent in the armaments factories, foundries, and mills. He had also commended the virtuous example of workers employed in the Porschewerk facility, who were allowing deductions from their wages designated to culminate in the purchase of a Volkswagen if and when the small, air-cooled, rear-engine "Peoples' Car" began rolling off an assembly line entirely devoted to spitting out an identical military version of the vehicle known as the *Kübelwagen,* and again condemned the selfishness of unionized and nonorganized workers for insisting on pay increases at a time when the Reich was engaged in an all-out, life-or-death struggle to free those selfsame workers from oppression by traitorous, profit-mad German executives, the stranglehold of greedy, British industry overlords, or the former disdain of industrial executives La Belle France, now an occupied nation sensibly governed in Vichy, not Paris.

Herr Stampfl was so enthusiastic about the latest effort the ministry's Austrian stringer had told him about that he'd called the boardinghouse several times, urging James to drop by the Leopold Palace and be personally anointed with holy water by Reichsminister Goebbels. James had begged off with a fib about some mythical appointment with an iron worker he had previously queried during a discussion of the wholesome effect high-grade Swedish steel imports were having on German war materiel production. Sounding disappointed, the executive editor had nevertheless agreed reluctantly that first things must come first.

Frau Kraven stopped waving the feather duster redistributing the parlor dust to answer the hall telephone and went up to the second-floor landing, calling, "Phone call, Herr Steyr."

He thanked her, descended the stairs hurriedly, and lifted the earpiece. "Hello."

"Erich Klasse here, Hans. Forgive me for not calling sooner. Can you possibly come by this evening? I need your assistance to, uh … line up our ducks for what comes next."

"So soon after the last publication?"

"*Ja, ja!* I really believe it necessary and pertinent to our … I fear the subject isn't appropriate to discuss over an open line."

"I can be there around six, if that's acceptable, Herr Klasse."

"Earlier, if that's convenient. We'll can dine here in my suite, then get right to work."

"Fine! I'll be at your door between five thirty and six."

\* \* \*

The acerbic leader of Meisinger's investigative team, Kurt, had accompanied his superior on yet another fruitless visit to the Great Zoltan's astrology parlor, having learned nothing new, heard nothing worth hearing other than the seer's repetitive vow to dedicate his entire existence toward aiding in every way the ongoing search for the letter-writing friend of the Reich. They stopped for coffee at a sidewalk café, where Meisinger was listening with half an ear to the other grouse about the lack of progress.

"You lectured us," complained Kurt, "about keeping our eyes and ears open for anything unusual, anything a touch out of the ordinary, but when I try telling you of such a happening, you sit there sipping coffee and pay no attention. Has to do with a thief arrested at the zoo for exposing himself to distract a woman, then snatching her purse and dashing away."

"Inventive purse snatchers don't sound all that relevant to what we're after, Kurt."

"Maybe, but … All right, how about this? Over in Wannsee, some halfwit was collared shooting at swimming ducks with a bow and arrow."

Meisinger cracked a smile. "Remarkable! But do try being serious."

"Serious you ask for, so serious you get. Recall the counterfeiting scam I told you about?"

"No, don't believe I do."

"Has to do with an erroneously dated banknote not even expert moneymen can explain."

His mind elsewhere, Meisinger said, "Sorry, doesn't ring a bell."

"Ernst is one of our best snoops. He was chatting up a detective he's known since he was a kid and told me an offbeat tale about the chief inspector and his partner. Seems they went to the Adlon and tried to question the gent who deposited the funny-money bill mixed in with a good-sized bundle of *SS* cold cash. The brassy bastard, supposedly *SS* himself, showed the detectives his tattoo to prove his claim, then clammed up tight and *threatened* the detectives."

"*SS* lizards," observed Meisinger, "automatically fall back on that whenever a breakdown in threats and brow-beatings falls short of getting them their own way."

"Ain't it the truth! But there's more. Ernst said, when asked about the *Hundertkennzeichen* funny-money banknote, the *SS* turd not only refused to open up, but claimed he took orders directly from Reichsfuhrer Himmler's office and invited the dick to pulse *his* higher-ups and learn whether if they *really* wanted to ask questions from anyone from that outfit."

"Begging a favor from those delightful gentlemen," declared Meisinger, "would be like asking a skulk of foxes why they raided the hen house."

"That's for damn sure!" Kurt went on to tell how the *SS* guy irritated the chief inspector to the point of doing it, running the notion past *his* bosses. They didn't just say no, but *hell no!* Probably means zip, but it sort of fits the anything-unusual template you keep holding up for us to keep an eye on." Kurt shrugged and shut up.

Somewhere in the course of the other's narrative, Ulrich Meisinger had begun to give the tale more attention. "When did you say Ernst talked to this senior detective?"

"Oh, three, four … a few days ago, less than a week."

"This *SS* guest, I assume he verified his status, showed his credentials?"

"No idea, except for showing the dicks his *SS* blood-type tattoo. Why?"

"By chance did Ernst mention the *SS* officer's name?"

"If he did, I don't remember it."

*Anything odd,* thought Meisinger, replaying the admiral's words in his mind. *Any outlier beyond the ordinary, anything outside the normality envelope.* Canaris had drummed into Meisinger the notion of watching for any singular, hard-to-explain occurrence or event that crossed the path of him or his team. Kurt was most likely right about it being meaningless in that sense, and yet … "If we're near the Adlon this afternoon, we might stop by and check-out this *SS* guest."

"Can't hurt, if we're careful not to step on too many tender *SS* toes."

\* \* \*

James left the boardinghouse around five o'clock on a pleasant summer evening. Strolling leisurely over the Oberbaum Bridge, he paused at the balustrade and gazed down at the turgid waters of the Spree, speculating about why Lustmann had apparently led a hermit's life for an entire week but then suddenly summoned him. He imagined the answer probably had to do with Frau Sharpe. He found it hard to blame the man he thought of as the never-to-become *Weltreichsheld* for succumbing to the charms of a feline, entirely feminine distraction like Gerda Sharpe. Having been celibate for real-time months, his blood had been stirred a second time during their brief encounter in the Adlon lobby.

Reaching the intersection of Wilhelmstrasse and Unter den Linden near Pariser Platz, hotel, he had to wait in a queue of five or six pedestrians for the white-uniformed traffic *Schupo* to blow his whistle and signal it safe to cross the boulevard with a bent-arm gesture. He had taken only three steps into the street before glancing toward the hotel and slowing his pace, mild alarm triggered at the sight of a black Audi sedan pulling up to commandeer curb space reserved for arriving or departing guests and taxis. Halting upon reaching the sidewalk, he watched two men emerge from the vehicle and approach the Adlon's entrance. The taller of the pair flipped open his wallet, showed the doorman his credentials, gestured toward the parked Audi, said a few words, and led his companion into the hotel.

*Meisinger!*

Recognizing the smooth-talking Abwehr investigator rooted James to the sidewalk. Torn by indecision, several possibilities flashed through his mind, each striking him as possible yet unlikely. He made up his mind and hastily jogged toward a public phone booth near the corner of Wilhelmstrasse. A young woman in the booth was holding the handset to her ear, gesticulating as she talked. Wrenching open the booth's door, he took the woman's elbow and literally yanked her out on the sidewalk, forcing her to drop the phone. She opened her mouth to scream.

"Gestapo!" he said harshly. "Do not interfere, Fraulein!"

Acute indignation fueling her temerity, the woman closed her mouth and scathed the man who had interrupted her call with a look of undiluted outrage.

James seized the dangling phone, popped down the double-pronged hook with a forefinger, and asked the operator to connect him with the Adlon. Politely requesting the switchboard operator to put him through to Herr Klasse in Suite 204, he assured her the guest was expecting his call. After the phone rang three times at the other end, he hung up, then repeated the process seconds later, explaining in agitated fashion he had been disconnected. The phone rang three more times before he banged the earpiece back in the hook and slipped out of the booth.

The young woman had been pouting while glaring at James's non-vocal performance. "Some conversation!" she said angrily.

"Mind you own business, dearie! Here's something for your trouble." He slapped a few Reichsmarks in the young woman's palm and hurried back toward the boardinghouse, walking as fast as possible, hoping his haste would not attract undue attention.

\* \* \*

Silverthorne's evaluation of the Sharpe-Lustmann relationship had been correct in every respect. In late morning, Herr Klasse had called and urged Gerda to beg off from her duties at the bank. She had complained of a minor stomach upset, and they had enjoyed themselves during her impromptu day off, chauffeured about the city in the leased Mercedes, wandering in Tiergarten, lunching at the outdoor café. The afternoon had been spent in a lengthy, satisfying bedroom session, a perfect cap to what Lustmann thought of as a perfect day. Sated, he could not have felt more wonderful, more on top of the world than when saying his lingering goodbyes and ordering his driver to take Gerda home.

Not long out of a leisurely bath, Lustmann was preparing to dress and prepare for Steyr's visit when the phone rang three times and stopped before he could wind a towel around his middle and go into the bedroom to pick up.

*No way could it have been Gerda,* he thought, having escorted her downstairs to the leased Mercedes more than an hour earlier. It had to be Steyr; only he and those infernal detectives knew of him and his whereabouts. If it was important, he was sure Steyr would call back.

The telephone jangled again once, twice, a third time, and again fell silent.

In the sudden deafening stillness, Lustmann sucked in a deep breath of panic, dashed into the bedroom, and dressed with frantic haste. Snatching the aluminum carryall down from the closet's high shelf, he slipped into his suit jacket, unscrewed with fumbling haste the silencer attached to the Walther PPK's muzzle, jammed the weapon into one jacket pocket, the suppressor into the other, grabbed the carryall's handle, and rushed out of the suite.

Descending the rear service stairway two risers at a time, he hastened through the hotel's utility corridor, burst into the kitchen—earning surprised looks from the culinary staff—and charged out the service entrance, emerging in the alley connecting to Wilhelmstrasse at the intersection.

He briefly considered using the nearby phone booth to call for his car and driver, thought better of it due to waiting for pick-up, and ruled out that option. Striding swiftly for several more blocks clutching the carryall's handle, looking over his shoulder and watching the light flow of traffic in his directions, he eventually hailed a passing taxi. He gave the driver Steyr's address and slumped in the rear, panting from the exertion and nervous excitement.

The middle-aged cabbie knew the Berlin streets inside out. Deftly making left and right turns, he negotiated the streets leading to the arched, double-deck bridge over the Spree, and drove onward several more blocks. He then turned into a side street and deposited Lustmann in front of a moderately rundown two-story house where a special swastika banner signified that some family member had sacrificed all through devotion to Germany.

A woman no longer young wearing a faded, blue-flowered dress answered the doorbell. Her frizzy graying hair done up in a bun, she peered at Lustmann with an air of vague suspicion.

"Is Herr Steyr in, *bitte?* I really must see him on a matter of grave urgency."

"Why, nooo, *mein Herr.* I believe he left a short while ago."

"When do you expect him back?"

"That I cannot say. Like my other guests, Herr Steyr comes and goes as he pleases."

"Would you mind terribly if I were to wait for his return?"

"Why, surely, sir. Please come in and make yourself comfortable here in the parlor."

"*Viel Dank.* I wouldn't dream of bothering you if seeing Steyr wasn't so *very* important."

"Think nothing of it, sir." Frau Kraven invited the tall, hatless gentleman to be seated, reassured by the fact that her Austrian boarder certainly worked with a number of mannerly, distinguished-looking gentlemen.

* * *

Hurrying toward the boardinghouse, Silverthorne thought about flagging down a taxi, but had difficulty spotting one in the moderate passing traffic. He slowed his pace across the bridge, turned the corner blocks farther on, dashed up the boardinghouse steps, and was relieved to find Lustmann leafing through a dog-eared magazine in the parlor, the all-important aluminum carryall resting on the floor at his feet. Across the room, the elderly, almost deaf lodger held his ear trumpet and leaned toward the blaring radio.

Lustmann put down a magazine. "What's gone wrong?" he asked loudly.

"Later," cautioned James so softly that Lustmann barely heard him over the blathering radio voice. "Is there another identity you can use, Erich?"

"Yes, several. Am I to assume Herr Klasse has met his fate?"

"*Er ist nicht mehr mit uns,*" informed James. "For the moment, any of the others will do. It will be safer meeting here if I introduce you to the landlady. Otherwise, she might become suspicious of another nameless visitor."

"My papers are in the carryall," said Lustmann. "Can it be safely opened here?"

"No need to bother. Choose a name at random."

Lustmann speculated. "Anders, my best friend as a youngster was a neighbor, Klaus Anders."

"Good. This way!" James led Lustmann into the kitchen. Frau Kraven left off washing pots and pans when they appeared and dried her hands. She smiled at Herr Anders when James introduced him as a business associate. "Klaus and I have worked together for some time."

"*Freucht mich sehr,* Frau Kraven." His manner courtly, Lustmann dipped his head.

All smiles, she fawned coquettishly, told him how pleased she was to meet him.

"Herr Anders and I must go upstairs, Frau Kraven," informed James. "I have some written material in my room we need to discuss."

Lustmann followed James up the creaking staircase. His first glance around the dreary attic room drew a frown. "You *live* in this squalor?" Setting down the carryall, he sank into the sole item of furniture, a rickety ladder-backed chair.

James bent close to explain that a pair of Abwehr agents had come to the hotel.

Startled, Lustmann asked, "You're certain?"

"Positive!"

"And for *that,* you phone in a panic signal, alert me to flee the Adlon?"

"Erich," assured Silverthorne, "absolutely the *last* thing you should want to suffer is being interrogated by Herr Meisinger. He's no ordinary gentleman, but some slick article!"

"What, if I may ask," requested Lustmann irritably, "led you to believe the Abwehr had come to the Adlon in order to discuss the weather with me?"

"Please don't regard my reason for warning you lightly," James said defensively, surprised by Lustmann's indignation. "I had no way of knowing whether the Abwehr came to see you or had other business at the Adlon. The only safe course was to take *zero* risk, none whatever."

"*Ach,* sheer foolishness!" Lustmann shook his head. "Crying wolf for no good reason is simply unacceptable. I'm going back to my suite."

Growing warm under the collar himself over the other's stubborn attitude, James said, "I won't try to talk you out of it, but before placing yourself in what could easily be serious jeopardy, have you no interest in learning what might be waiting for you back at the Adlon?"

"Most likely nothing to worry about," was the other's sharp reply. He grimaced, backed off a hair. "Learning the reason for their visit may be the safest course, but it's too late for that."

"Not necessarily." James described the smooth-talking Herr Meisinger as a genuine threat and truly dangerous interviewer for Lustmann to have words with. "If you must willingly court such a high degree of danger, at least wait until they leave the premises and let me try and learn why they were there."

"Bah! How can you possibly determine that once they're gone?"

"Leave that to me, and my, er ... friends. There's more than one way, Erich. Bribing the bellman you said serves you regularly could be the simplest."

Lustmann mulled the prospect of sitting around in the sleazy attic room with the heavy Walther and silencer bulging his jacket pockets. He withdrew the PPK automatic, laid it and the silencer on the end table beside he Olivetti. Reluctantly doffing the jacket, his expression a blend of unhappiness and uncertainty, he nodded brusquely. "Fine, fine! I admit it to be the smart move, Hans. How long it will it take you and your friends to, er . . ?"

"Hours, more than a few, I'm afraid. We can go out in early

evening to a nearby café, have dinner and you can stay here while I slip over and put a chalk mark on the proper lamp post at this week's trysting place, then shortly after midnight we can ..."

"Midnight!" Lustmann tossed his head angrily and reached for his jacket. "Nonsense! I'm going downstairs to call for my car, escape from this hellhole, and go back to my suite."

James looked his supposed accomplice squarely in the eye. "Your impatience distresses me no end, Erich. Have you no conception at all of how essential your safety is? Do I have to explain how your anonymity and efforts outweigh all other considerations ten times over, including my own? What you were dispatched to accomplish here is not merely important, it's *imperative!*"

"I realize that, of course, but—"

"Except for providing you with any and all varieties of assistance and backup," insisted James, "the task assigned to me and my nameless associates is of minor consequence, while *you* . . Is there no way to talk you out of innocently returning to the Adlon and knowingly placing yourself—your sacred mission—in grave jeopardy?"

The speech swayed Lustmann only a trifle, by no means enough in Silverthorne's judgment to make him think about changing his mind.

"Hans, I know you mean well," conceded Lustmann, "and I appreciate what you are telling me. After what you've already done, how can I possibly doubt you in any way? Yet I've successfully bluffed my way past the authorities to date, and I'm certain it can be done again." Lifting his jacket, he thrust his right arm through the sleeve.

His mind roiling, James felt his heart skip a beat. *The conceited bastard is serious about going back!* The difference of running a bluff on a pair of ordinary police detectives and trying to dupe someone with Meisinger's degree of sophistication and intelligence raised serious qualms. It was something he could *not* let happen! Should Lustmann be allowed to take the carryall filled with priceless documents back to the Adlon, it could at one disastrous stroke write *finis* to his own prospective "Friend of the Reich" role and the vital, anti-success campaign aimed at reversing the course of the war he meant to engage in after replacing Lustmann.

He turned around suddenly, put a finger to his lips, stepped to the door of his room, leaned his ear against it, and pretended to listen attentively.

"What is it, Steyr?"

"Someone coming upstairs," whispered James. Snatching up the tubular silencer resting beside the Olivetti, he twisted it hastily, threading it into the muzzle of the Walther PPK.

"What are you doing?"

"Shhh! Get over against the wall! Stay behind the door if it opens!"

Jarred by Steyr's transformation from an aide to someone in command who issued terse instructions instead of arguing, Lustmann did as he was told.

James made sure the weapon's safety was off, worked the slide to inject a round in the chamber, and cracked the door a slit, then quickly closed it as if jolted by what he had seen.

"Who is it?" whispered Lustmann.

Silverthorne's reply was to raise the PPK. *"You,* Lustmann, that's who it is!" He squeezed off two rounds at close range.

The once but never-to-be *Deutsches Weltreichsheld* slid down the wall to a sitting position, leaving a smeared red stain on the wall behind him. Mouth agape in disbelief, he slumped over on his side and pawed futilely at his chest. In less than a minute, the pale-blue eyes glazed and stared fixedly into infinity.

# EIGHTEEN

## *World War II*

Quaking like breeze-ruffled aspens in hopefully never-to-be Ameri-kaner Colorado Provinz, James Silverthorne let the weapon slip numbly from his hand and thud to the frayed area rug.

Weak-kneed, he sank to the floor breathing heavily, eyes closed, and let minutes pass before he was able to blink repeatedly, draw a deep breath, and struggle to his feet. Moving in the manner of a sleep-walker, he stretched and felt reluctantly for the absent pulse in Lust-mann's carotid artery. Tugging the quilt from his narrow bed, he draped it over the corpse, and with a palpitating right hand opened the stand-alone wooden wardrobe, seized the bottle of Obstler schnapps, uncapped it, swallowed two quick gulps, and then tilted back his head and emptied the dregs.

The plum-flavored liqueur did nothing to calm his palpitating hands. Slumping down, his back against the door to prevent anyone from entering, he tried to think clearly. Killing the would-be hero of heroes had been an unplanned, reflexive response to the dire threat Lustmann himself had posed by preparing to return to the Adlon. Shooting Lustmann had been an act of desperation impos-sible to rectify, second guess, or in hindsight suffer a single pang of regret. He was sure no one downstairs could have heard the sup-pressed weapon discharge twice, but nevertheless it left him with a major problem in his hands: how to invent a reasonable way to dispose of the body without being seen and arrested. Weighing the existing alternatives on the scale of practicality, he decided a straightforward solution was impossible.

The simplest, most direct move would be to twist the false tooth, bite down hard, and abandon his own mission by a cowardly, instantaneous return to the DWJ 142 timeline, but it was in no way an acceptable solution in light of the enormously larger problem he had to solve. His best bet might be to leave the body beneath his quilt, grab the carryall, tiptoe downstairs during the wee hours of early morning, and slip away into the night.

*At best a temporary solution!* he thought. The authorities would have little difficulty rounding up a supposed Austrian journalist employed as a part-time stringer by the Goebbels propaganda ministry. Any plan or derivative involving a firm resolution to the problem would have to be put on hold until the confusion in his mind abated and he was able to think more clearly.

Previous retro-temporal experiences on several timelines had left him conversant with the basic mechanics of transposition, and he realized he'd subconsciously held his breath immediately after eliminating Lustmann, anxiously waiting to see if the corpse would vanish from the 1940 timeline, something that should have occurred the instant his physical essence amalgamated with that of his technically "coexistent" younger self if, in accord with the most rigorous of Mother Nature's rules, the apparent-yet-false temporal paradox had solved itself. To his personal misfortune, James realized the inevitable alternative had beyond doubt occurred when on this timeline youthful *SS* cadet Erich Lustmann had doubtless ceased to exist.

Reluctant to look at the shrouded figure slumped sideways against the wall, he gritted his teeth and gingerly lifted a corner of the quilt. What had once been and would have become on that other timeline the preeminent *Weltreichsheld* of all time, was enduring the first hour of eternity with total aplomb. What James knew *definitely* needed doing was resolving the quandary of how to handle the inevitable consequences of killing Lustmann. It would be imperative to devise a facile means of taking the man's place and learning to hand letter in green ink his own "visions," in this instance aimed at negatively influencing or turning head-to-tail Nazi successes during what he still thought of as The War of World Liberation, to obliterate Goebbels' voluminous history of the Nazi victory leading to the Deutsches Weltreich empire he had known and detested.

With that in mind, he stared numbly at the aluminum alloy carryall resting beside his bed, its lid closed and latched but inspiring a thrilling notion. Here beside him in his chilly attic room was Pandora's box, rendered invalid by a commandment similar to that of Zeus, *never* to be opened. However, instead of releasing all the world's evils, the carryall held a wealth of informative data he simply *had* to read and understand in order to carry out his mission, and therefore it could not remain closed. It had to be opened *now!*

Fired with more curiosity than Hesiod's Pandora could have imagined, and driven by a sudden rush of enthusiasm, James clambered to his feet and went to the wooden wardrobe. Lifting out a shirt gifted by Lustmann, he removed the wire hanger and began bending it back and forth in his hands until it weakened and broke cleanly. Repeating the action at the other end, he halfway straightened the wire, and then burnt his fingers unscrewing the dusty incandescent bulb from the room's one and only table lamp.

Dusk was falling. The filmed attic window admitted just enough light for him to insert one end of the wire into the lamp socket, sending a tingling electric shock coursing through him as he touched the other end to the carryall's off-color rivet. Screwing the light bulb back into the socket, he unlatched and opened the carryall's lid and hungrily eyed the stack of flash-paper that was literally far beyond price.

The door to his attic room had no lock, which had been of no particular concern until it became a necessary aid in hiding Lust-mann's remains. Neither Frau Kraven nor any of the lodgers were liable to bother him, and the opportunity to finally learn the truth, the whole truth and nothing less, was too overpowering for any historian to put off. The scenario concocted by expatriated ODESSA *SS* fanatics and other fleeing Nazis included remedial messages designed to coach the revision of critical wartime errors and oversights, but for the moment that was of secondary interest. His task would be to reverse the advice and counsel tendered by the renegade ODESSA refugees and encourage the self-styled Führer and his Nazi minions to destroy not only the vile global police state they were unwittingly in the process of creating, but if practical also *add* to the mistakes and lapses committed personally by Chancellor Adolf Hitler, thus ensuring a victory by the so-called Allies over Nazi Germany's powerful military machine.

His abiding interest at present was therefore the flash-paper chronicle of the "real" World War Two, as contrasted to its subse-quent early course along the current timeline. He set the Olivetti on the floor, sagged down on the lumpy bed, scanned the first few pages recording events that had already taken place in the now, and then put aside those flimsy sheets and started to voraciously speed-reading the remainder, instantly engrossed in the stark narrative.

The first item to catch his interest, a sidelight pertaining to the terror bombing of London, briefly mentioned a Luftwaffe bombar-dier who had prematurely triggered his bomb release to let high explosives rain down in the city's suburb rather than a neighboring industrial target. The account of Luftwaffe frustration during the Battle of Britain also cited details of a decisive battle at El Alamein in North Africa that hastened the defeat and demise of Rommel's Afrika Korps.

He read a lengthy dissertation pertaining to Operation Bar-barossa, the Reich's rather semi-suicidal plunge into the vastness of the USSR, as well as accounts of ensuing bloodbaths during the sieges of Stalingrad and Leningrad, the truly monumental tank battle at Kursk, and the gradual erosion of Wehrmacht effectiveness due to the awful cold with supply lines stretched interminably in the face of stubborn, increasing Soviet resistance and counterassaults.

Shocked to learn of the atrocious conduct employed by the Imperial Japanese Army during the slaughter and maiming of innumerable Manchurian and Chinese civilians subsequent to invasion and occupation, he read about Japan's sneak attack in Hawaii, a below-the-belt punch on American territory that drew the US into the global conflict and inspired heretofore victorious Nazi Germany to boldly declare war on the United States. The account went on to relate how US armament production and waxing ground and air manpower sent into the field had gradually made itself felt on all fronts and every theater of conflict.

He learned how American and British forces had landed in North Africa, later in Sicily, and later still in Italy, where fierce Wehrmacht resistance had inevitably been overcome. Reading on, he became immersed in a staggering account of the massive Allied landings on Normandy's beaches, the subsequent rampage across France and into Germany, with the Soviet Red Army steadily driving westward like a scourge from the east.

He read about Germany's *U-boot* campaign against Allied shipping, American daylight aerial assaults, and British nighttime raids that transformed many German cities into mounds of smoking rubble. He learned of the bloodbath in the Pacific incurred by America's tenacious, island-hopping Marines and infantry forces that resulted in the reacquisition of Japan's Pacific conquests. He read how American naval forces had turned back and decimated Japan's Imperial Navy in the Coral Sea and Midway battles and later fought suicidal Kamikaze attacks on warships in Leyte Gulf and the seas around Okinawa, and how incendiary raids conducted by American long range, high-altitude bombers had incinerated the

Japanese cities.

Horrified, he read between the lines partially veiled inferences to the *SS* leadership's genocidal campaign dedicated to exterminating millions of innocent Jewish men, women, and children, as well as multitudes of Slavs, Gypsies, mental defectives, homosexuals, and elderly or physically disabled unfortunates, plus numerous other noncombatants.

He also came across brief accounts of attempts on Hitler's life, including a notorious failed assassination by a highly decorated Wehrmacht officer, after which suspected conspirators, guilty or innocent, been hanged or spitted on meat hooks. He read how, with *Götterdammerungen* truly inevitable, Adolf Hitler had not died of cancer after all, but had killed his bride of a few hours and then suicided. He had been joined in death by Reichsminister Goebbels in an underground bunker near the burned-out Chancellery. Göring had taken poison during postwar Nuremberg war crimes trials, which were termed "illegal" in the stark flash-paper document.

He read of the nuclear obliteration of Hiroshima and Nagasaki that had finally pushed Japan's warlords over the edge, paving the way for the emperor's agreement to Allied demands for unconditional surrender. The final eye-opener was a short description of the relentless Cold War that began not long after hostilities had concluded between certain Western European powers and America on one side, and on the other the USSR's ruthless expansion of widespread hegemony led by the steel fist of Josef Stalin.

His vision blurring, James replaced the stark documents in the carryall long after midnight, closed the lid but left it unlatched, and knuckled his burning eyes. The account of WWII, the document's notional term, while explicit and concise, had cited only scattered highlights of the conflict in nonlinear fashion, raising more questions than providing answers by offering only sidelights and details that might once have been common knowledge to the collective authors, but were impossible to piece together and integrate coherently.

Despite the late hour, not to mention eyestrain and an audience made up of Lustmann's remains sprawled beneath his quilt, James retrieved the stack of flash paper, went back to the beginning, and doggedly began speed-reading the entire document again, front to back, striving to assimilate the contents to ingrain as many details and side issues as possible to clarify certain distant acquaintance-ships with those named, and then reconcile them with historical continuity.

Finishing the second reading half blind, the narrative struck him as fantastic and of such a huge, all-encompassing scope that its total impact could not be felt after two quick readings. Much of his adult life had been spent assiduously accessing, examining, and re-examining the published ins, outs, whys, and wherefores of Goebbels' version of the so-called World War of World Liberation. Now, within easy reach, was a unique, difficult-to-dispute chronicle of "actual" WWII wartime events, situations, and circumstances he intended to make excellent use of to ensure that the Deutsches Weltreich obscenity would not see the light of day on his own or another timeline.

Utterly exhausted, he was not surprised to see dawn light dimly illuminating the filmed attic window. After carefully replacing the document a second time, he closed and latched the carryall's lid, fell on the bed fully dressed, and pulled a blanket over himself.

He awoke feeling groggy, more tired than when he had finally fallen asleep, yawned and rolled over, rubbed his eyes, then caught his breath and sat up in bed with spastic haste.

Lounging in the doorway, his expression neutral, Ulrich Meis-inger gazed at him with accusative intensity, and said slowly, "I never believed it could be you."

# NINETEEN

## *Revisionist Doctrine*

The premiere Abwehr investigator agent closed the door behind him, glanced incuriously about the cramped attic room he had visited once before, and silently appraised the closed aluminum carryall. Bending down to the worn, bloodstained carpet, he carefully retrieved the silenced PPK automatic pistol and disarmed it. Lifting one end of the patchwork quilt covering the cadaver with two fingers, he said in a monotone, "I assume this was once Herr Erich Klasse."

In deep shock, the best James could manage was a curt nod. "He's ... *SS*."

"So we were told." Meisinger unbuttoned and pulled up the left sleeve of Lustmann's shirt to examine the *Schutzstaffel* blood-type tattoo inside the upper arm. Taking a mechanical pencil from the inside pocket of his suit jacket, he jotted down the data. "Heydrich's people apparently found you first, Herr Steyr."

"You could, um ... that could be said," faltered James.

"Please, try to see this affair through our eyes and you may begin to understand what has taken place is in the best interest of no one, and could in fact make things worse for all concerned. Were your identity and whereabouts made known to Klasse before he ... turned up his toes?"

"I don't, uh ... not sure," lied James. "May I ask how you found out?"

"Under rather harsh questioning," informed Meisinger, "the driver assigned to take Herr Klasse hither and yon recalled picking you up at this address. My partner and I were lax about evaluating the information. We should have been here hours ago."

James rolled to a sitting position. "Am I under arrest?"

"For the time being, nothing quite so dramatic. Naturally, we expect to sit down with you for a number of heart-to-heart talks."

"There's not ... there isn't much I can tell you."

"Now there I beg to differ, Herr Steyr. I'm *positive,*" emphasized the other, "that there is a great deal you will be able to tell us. First, foremost, and above all else, we wish to know if you are responsible for the preposterous yet incredibly accurate visions described in your letters?"

Fresh out of responses, except for the authentic one that would have gotten him locked up inside the padded cell of some mental hospital ward, James knew better than to try and sell the slick senior Abwehr asset any form of fabricated song and dance, or for that matter to shade the truth in even a minor degree. It would have to be a fairy tale that exhibited at least a semblance of logic, or at minimum enough of a snatch to temporarily hold water.

"Herr Meisinger, all I am free to explain is that certain prominent, influential individuals within and beyond Germany's borders strongly favor the Reich's crusade against the capitalistic, imperialistic allied powers, but they are also abysmally discontented by Hitler's stubborn willfulness and lack of insight, coupled with the tyrannous manner and demagoguery with which he misguides prosecution of the war."

"Intimating that you are in their pay?"

James dipped his head toward the carryall. "Millions in Reichsmarks are inside."

"Very good, Steyr, if that is your real name. I conditionally accept what you've told me thus far, pending added revelations and clarifications on you part. Was the bogus thousand-mark banknote included in your payment treasure chest?"

"Indeed, although I'm unable to imagine the spurious date of issue as being other than an obscure clerical, printing, tabulating error, or something similar."

"Nor I," said Meisinger, his brows contracting slightly. "Exactly who are these, er … influential sympathizers you mention?"

"That I cannot tell you."

"Cannot or will not?"

"Have it either way you wish, Herr Meisinger."

"You are surely aware of the nature and variety of *SS* failure-proof means and methods to inspire prompt, accurate responses."

"Not in my case." James opened his mouth wide, touched the tip of a fingernail to the false tooth which, if actuated, would force his accumulated temporal potential to instantaneously snap him back to his own era's DWJ 142 timeline. "It's laced with cyanide," he lied in a glib falsehood he was not at all sure Meisinger would buy. "All I need do is bite down especially hard."

"And you would willingly do that?"

"It was my solemn promise to the … well, dedicated individuals in question." Figuratively kicking himself for making the statement sound overly dramatic, James added, "Call it their secondary reason for underwriting my assignment with millions in currency."

"I see." Meisinger thought it over. "As a matter of purely academic interest, how in the world did you manage to envision weeks prior to the French surrender something as recondite yet in a sense significant, if superficial, as Hitler's little victory jig at the French surrender railcar?"

"The vision I experienced was quite clear, Herr Meisinger. Despite what you and others may think of as nonsense, I'm actually blessed with psychic powers."

"How wonderful for you!"

Other than that droll, sarcastic quip, James could discern no further reaction by the self-contained Abwehr asset, who after deliberating at length said, "What if I were to tell you we may be willing to help you and your mysterious backers aid in returning the Reich to a more sane and logical prosecution of the war, perhaps even do so much as steer Germany toward ... normalcy."

"I fail to see how that would be remotely possible."

"Well, for now please do try," urged the other dismissively. He then abruptly changed the subject. "We have a mutual problem: devising an acceptable way to dispose of the late Herr Klasse without raising a fuss and attracting the interest of those in questionable authority. Obviously, you felt it necessary to eliminate him or you would never have done so. Had you already given thought to a method of handling his disposition in a reasonable manner?"

James sorted among his imagined, limited courses of action. "Why not call your associates," he suggested, "and have them come here in an ambulance, with the attendants dressed as first responders who roll the body out on a gurney, an oxygen mask over the face, with resuscitation equipment standing by. We can tell my landlady that Herr Klasse was taken ill late in the night."

"Excellent, Steyr! It's a vision with which I heartily concur. I'll go downstairs, call to set things in motion. First, I would like to see what in addition to millions in currency you've secreted in the treasure chest." He began unlatching the carryall's lid.

*Stop!* The imperative crackled in Silverthorne's mind like dry lightning, but he managed to choke back the warning on the tip of his tongue.

Meisinger lifted the carryall's lid and sprang backward reflexively when a brilliant flash and a puff of intense heat turned the nitrocellulose flash-paper documents to ash. Retreating to a safe distance, Meisinger watched residual flames lick and curl around the bundles of currency.

"Close and latch the lid," suggested James. "Starved for oxygen, the fire will snuff out."

Meisinger did so, then turned to regard James coldly with

narrowed eyes, but otherwise looking nonplused. "Was such a drastic precaution really necessary?" he asked calmly.

"No, sir. It was imperative!"

\* \* \*

Grossly out of sorts in the wake of yet another venomous Hitlerian castigation of his fruitless, empty promise to locate and interrogate the visionary friend of the Reich, Reichsführer-*SS* Himmler turned the full force of his bespectacled, owl-eyed glare on a nervous aide. "Beyond doubt, this is the most outlandish report I have ever read."

"The *Klagenfurt SS-Junkerschule* commandant personally attested to the stated facts in his sworn statement, Herr Reichsführer, and every eyewitness questioned has fully concurred."

"Stated facts! If the commandant has let himself go to drink or drugs," sneered Himmler, "his punishment will be severe indeed. People do *not* simply vanish before the eyes of others."

"Herr Reichsführer," declared the aide, "the incident took place in a refectory teeming with dining cadets, including one seated directly opposite the, er … victim. He has sworn that one instant while conversing with the other he looked up and—without warning—the utensils the vanished cadet had been using clattered to the table and the young man was no longer there."

"I can read! What do you make of it?" demanded Himmler in acute displeasure.

"I have no idea what might have taken place, Herr Reichsführer. It appears to be impossible!"

Himmler crumpled the report in his hands. "Instruct the investigators to look into the matter in depth. I want a thorough, definitive report on the results and a deep background check on the commandant and every self-deluded cadet brave enough to testify that he witnessed a fellow *SS* cadet vanish before his eyes. We shall also want every sworn witness to appear before the tribunal when it is convened. No exceptions!"

*"An Ihrer Ordnung, Herr Reichsführer!"*

"And soonest! See to it! We intend to find out precisely what occurred in Klagenfurt, and when we do ..." Himmler let the unvoiced threat dangle ominously. "I also want to know if the relatives of ..." He unfolded and consulted the ball of paper he had wadded up. ". . . Have the closest kin to this, er ... absent *SS* cadet been notified?"

"Not to the best of my knowledge, sir."

"Well, go find out!"

*"An Ihrer Ordnung, Herr Reichsführer!"*

"If his family has not yet been informed," added Himmler, "instruct the commandant and staff members to keep their tongues well back in their mouths until we learn what devious brand of illogic is at the root of this nonsensical business. The cadets are also to be firmly ordered about remaining silent with regard to such a ridiculous happening, or they'll suffer the consequences. The *SS* image could be severely tarnished if a silly rumor like this was allowed to circulate."

*"Jawohl, Herr Reichsführer."*

"Dismissed!"

The aide clicked his boots, snapped a stiff-armed Nazi salute, and fled from the office.

\* \* \*

James had not the slightest clue where they had taken him. After the siren-screaming ambulance had departed with Lustmann's remains in the guise of a stricken patient, two men in dark business suits who did not speak had entered the attic room, escorted him downstairs, and hustled him into the rear seat of a black Audi sedan, where he was deftly blindfolded.

No one had broken the silence during the drive. Although unable to see outside, he recalled a series of familiar sounds as the Audi crossed the Oberbaum Bridge heading toward *mitte* Berlin, but that only hinted at a destination. He was conducted through what might have been a garage, judging from the lingering taint of petrol, into an elevator and up to what he presumed was the bedroom of some Abwehr safe house, where Ulrich Meisinger wordlessly removed his blindfold.

For the better part of a week, he'd become intimately acquainted with one annoying feature of his comfortable prison, the tightly closed shutters over all windows that barred the view from what had to be the second or third floor of possibly an apartment building. Meals were brought in at regular intervals, and all his other needs were promptly taken care of by a pair of stone-faced individuals who spoke only when spoken to, and then only if absolutely necessary. Firmly instructed to make himself at home, he was told that any attempt to leave the premises would be futile, assuring him that others like themselves were stationed in the suite's parlor and downstairs on the street, all assigned to track every person who entered or left the premises.

Unconscious in a drugged state, the tooth Meisinger believed laden with cyanide—actually his return ticket to DWK 142—had been removed. For the better part of a week he had eaten and slept, slept and eaten, between times leafing through magazines, listening to the radio, and wondering what might come next. What came next was actually more than a hint that his captors wished him to engage in visionary letter writing, a notion inspired by a crusty, saturnine associate of Meisinger's, addressed by the others as Kurt, when he had unwrapped a box of unmarked stationery, a new Parker fountain pen wrapped in cellophane, a bottle of green ink, two yellow legal tablets, and enough sharpened wooden pencils to deforest Canada.

Mildly amused by the gifts, James inquired dryly if Kurt would like to wait while he took a nap. "Who knows? Maybe I can rustle up a vision, dash off a prophetic letter for you."

Stolid inattention was paid to his repartee by Kurt, who had refused to comment on the pleasantry, other than with a snide grin and a parting remark. "If you're the smart bird we know damn well you are, you'll shut up and enjoy the decent treatment being handed out, because it won't seem half so terrible if the Gestapo turds catch up with you. Understand?"

Bemused, James spent time reflecting on the encyclopedic insight he had gained into WWII by speed-reading and re-reading the so-precious nitrocellulose documents now turned to ash. Despite recent events, the treasure trove of foreknowledge had also brought to light a serious quandary that *had* to be resolved. His captors were certain the friend of the Reich had been unmasked, was being held in secure custody, and would hopefully continue to furnish pro-phetic letters the Abwehr apparently deemed beneficial to the mili-tant Nazi cause via furnishing prescient, definitive foreknowledge of future happenings salted with pithy suggestions about how to prosecute the war much more advantageously.

A significant flaw in his captors' reasoning had become obvious upon awakening to find Ulrich Meisinger lounging in the doorway of his attic room. *SS Offizier* Lustmann, the "seer" he meant to replace, had intentionally coached only military, political, and civil-ian redirections conducive to wartime Nazi successes. The catch in his plans was that a fairly slack tightrope had to be trod between his own eagerness to preserve the tone and theme of prospective letters aimed at *denigrating* and degrading Nazi actions and purposes by daring to suggest detrimental courses of action, while cloaking his "visions" from all suspicion of his true purpose.

His first opportunity to capitalize on the acquired preview of things to come had been presented on a plate, but in a manner not to his liking. In an earlier letter, he had helped Lustmann cut the legs out from under Winston Churchill's scheme to rescue vulner-able allied forces helplessly stranded on beaches near Belgium's port of Dunkerque. Then later, to his acute distress, he had been forced to stay in character by aiding Lustmann in framing a subsequent

letter designed to correct Luftwaffe bombing tactics, then posting
it with the unwitting aid of an innocent woman passerby. To be
effective, he realized his first visionary effort for the Abwehr would
have to be directed toward discouraging the Operation Sea Lion
Channel crossing as the first step toward aborting the conquest of
England by viewing it as counterproductive due to the overwhelming might of Britain's Royal Navy.

Yet, he recalled Lustmann's remark about the flash-paper wartime
scenario Meisinger had inadvertently reduced to ashes by relating
that his nameless sponsoring confreres had insisted on retaining a
positive note in every letter, although anything resembling a false
positive would defy that approach and make providing discouragement more a conundrum than a quandary. One corrective measure
might be to vividly envision British awesome sea power respectfully,
and capable of sinking many of the ships carrying troops and military equipment to England's beaches, as well as Kriegsmarine warships crucial to protect the troop carriers.

Even an egocentric, willful tyrant like Hitler was certain to be
aware of British superiority at sea. Also something to be tangentially
considered was the astrological rationale he assumed had been
inserted in all of Lustmann's prior letters. He personally knew of
only one such instance, but admitted to being an ignoramus when
it came to astrological lore. How could he hope to inject references
depicting starry influences in one or more missives designed to avert
Hitler's consummate desire to conquer Britain?

Wait! He wasn't thinking logically. Lustmann's reason for sending
his letters to Zoltan no longer obtained. Had not Meisinger inti-
mated that his Abwehr superiors might be sympathetic to the
coaching messages in Lustmann's letters. If true, hand-lettered missives, if any, would be picked up here and perhaps treated as if
posted to Zoltan's astrology parlor in order to keep him isolated.
Assuming that to be the case, would inserting astrological nonsense
be necessary?

Another approach might be to insert selective word play pertaining to Hitler's personal horoscope. Known to be Austrian born in the 1880s, he fell under Aries or Taurus zodiacal influences, indicating that it might be provident to invent a horoscope based on either sign, since framing astrological froth about the consequences of Sea Lion might …

*Silly damn notion!* Stewing about the problem to little or no purpose, he'd begun thinking elliptically. Best perhaps might be to ignore astrology and concentrate on subjects hopefully important only to his captors to boldly undermine the prospective Sea Lion Operation.

Glancing distastefully at the writing materials, he lay back on the bed. A nap seemed the simplest way to evade all conundrums, quandaries, or whatever the hell else was bothering him.

# TWENTY

## *Spy Versus Spy*

With Meisinger's team leader at the wheel, the black Audi sedan negotiated spotty Berlin traffic. Kurt kept shooting glances at the rearview mirror. A block farther on, he announced in a disgusted monotone that they might have grown a tail.

"Again?" asked Admiral Canaris. "Are you sure?"

"Not certain, but I think so. Dark gray sedan two cars back keeps ducking in and out of traffic, then comes on again. We could've been picked up leaving the garage."

Emil, the muscle assigned to accompany Canaris whenever he ventured beyond the walls of Tirpitzufer's Abwehr headquarters, turned his torso around clumsily in the rear seat, craned to look back through the rear window.

"Don't, Emil," warned Meisinger. "It's a dead giveaway."

Emil obediently faced front. "Admiral," he said hoarsely, "those Gestapo assholes like to chase you around just to report they did something more'n play with themselves."

Canaris ignored the huge man's attempt at humor. "Reinhard's people never give up."

"Kurt," suggested Emil, "why don'tcha turn down a side street, pull over 'n wait for 'em. I'll beat the shit out of the driver and we'll be on our way."

The admiral grudged a thin smile. "Go straight to the heart of the matter, you do."

Emil grunted, "Saves time, sir."

"Is our follow-on car tagging the gray sedan?" Canaris wanted to know.

"Haven't seen it for a few blocks," said Kurt, "but it sure better be there."

Their primary escort vehicle was "following" a half-block ahead of them. Meisinger swung around and peeked backward. "Let's chop off the tail, Kurt. Turn right on this next street."

Approaching the intersection, Kurt swung the Audi into a two-lane side street. Halfway down the block, he found a parking space at the curb, pulled in and parked. A minute later, the gray sedan passed by—with both front-seat occupants conscientiously studying the street ahead of them—and found a parking space farther down the block.

Seconds later, another black Audi made as if to pass by, braked suddenly, and double-parked alongside the gray sedan, pinning the vehicle against the curb.

Kurt ignored the honk of an irritated driver blocked by the screening Audi and expertly performed a three-point U-turn, cutting off a taxi coming the opposite way. The cabbie leaned on his horn to no avail.

A quarter hour later, Kurt parked the Audi a half block beyond the Abwehr safe house. While his passengers were getting out on the sidewalk, Emil replaced Kurt, settling his bulk in the driver's seat. Meisinger told Kurt to go back along the route and find out why their chase car hadn't shown up, and then return to pick them up in about an hour.

"Right, Ulrich!"

"Isn't it wonderful," remarked Canaris, oozing sarcasm, "to need a safe house just to avoid being spied on by Heydrich's pipsqueaks?" He led the way up the apartment house steps. "Whatever it takes, no matter how long, I mean to find out what our prophetic genius is all about."

On the third-floor landing, a security officer ushered the visitors into a bedroom and left them alone with the prized guest.

When Admiral Canaris introduced himself, James reacted visibly. After reading Lustmann's flash-paper WWII scenario, he recognized the Abwehr chieftain's name and recalled his reported fate.

The admiral misconstrued the supposed friend of the Reich's flinch and soothed him. "Relax, Herr Steyr. If we wished you harm, would you have been coddled here in comfortable quarters? We've come to speak with you about something extremely unusual which has come to light. I'm certain you will be able to furnish a simple, straightforward explanation. By the way, have you been troubled by any recent visions worth mentioning and perhaps recording?"

"Not … lately," stumbled James, his thoughts gyrating. "I've had difficulty sleeping, sir. Probably a result of being locked up by strangers."

Canaris clicked his tongue. "Regrettable! Suitable sleep medication will be provided. Ridding the world of the *SS* lizard may have also frayed your conscience, kept you wakeful in the night. Is that not so?"

"It was either him or me, sir."

"Oh, we're convinced his life ended exactly as you reported," declared Canaris. "Circumstances often limit one's choices." The admiral nodded to Meisinger, a cue to withdraw a set of photos from the manila envelope he was holding. Slowly and deliberately, as if dealing out playing cards, Meisinger spread the photos on a deal table topped by a polished, inlaid chessboard of light and dark woods. "You may recognize this gentleman, Herr Steyr."

Badly shaken, James tried to give an impression of calmly appraising the half dozen matte prints of Lustmann's naked cadaver stretched out on a steel table. Two entrance wounds were visible, one centered in the lower left sternum below the heart, the second a few decimeters to the left. After a few seconds of introspective silence, he said simply, "Klasse."

"Ah, but *is* it?" the admiral asked himself, his inflection making the question anything but rhetorical. "How are we to be sure, Steyr?" He laid two smaller photographs alongside the others. "A most remarkable resemblance, wouldn't you say?"

Silverthorne's throat constricted. Twenty calendar years, the ravages of wartime, and a decade spent in South American exile had added lines around the mouth and eyes missing in both of the black-and-white glossies depicting the imperious, self-satisfied features of an incredibly young Erich Lustmann. The prognathous jaw, full head of straight, dirty-blond hair, and classic masculine features complemented by an insolent gleam in the subject's eyes would have assured the most unbiased viewer that the photos of both early and late vintages pictured one and the same individual at separate stages of his life.

Transfixed, James stared at the youthful image of Lustmann he had seen numberless times on posters touting the *Heldengedenktag* celebration held annually to honor the hero of heroes' memory in a manner verging on idolatry, and had been reproduced in various books, articles, and documentaries.

Speechless for seconds, he finally muttered, "I don't know … what to say."

"Come now, Herr Steyr!" chided the admiral. "As a true friend of the Reich, with visions of future happenings popping up and dancing in your head and disturbing your sleep, we were counting on you for a response considerably more apt than *that!*"

"In these photos," put in Meisinger, "the deceased was a fortyish gentleman registered at the Adlon as Erich Klasse, an identity corroborated by a number of Reichsbank employees, a chief inspector of police and his partner, and the hotel's management. Fortyish Erich Klasse and the twenty-one-year-old *SS* cadet pictured here, Erich Albert Lustmann, share a resemblance so striking it would be impossible for anyone to believe them *not* the same individual at two distinct periods of life. Also, many leagues beyond understanding is the *fact* that Klasse and Lustmann bear identical *SS* blood tattoos."

"Vision, invention, or accident, have it as you please," put in Admiral Canaris. "How can you or I or *anyone* account for what we have seen and are seeing with our own eyes?"

"I ... can't, uh ... explain it," was Silverthorne's stumbling reply.

"Ah, *cannot!* Hosanna! At long last we are able to wholeheartedly accept the truth of something you are willing to tell us."

"Could this ... Herr Klasse," suggested James, grasping at straws, struggling to keep his voice level, "have been young Lustmann's uncle, half-brother, or—"

Thoroughly vexed, Canaris cried, "Oh, do come off it! In your eyes, are we so incredibly dull that you believe us capable of paying any heed to a stretched-out fairytale of *that* enormity? No, you've voiced the most abysmally lame evasion of all time."

Meisinger broke the ensuing gravid silence. "I'm afraid there's more, Steyr. Reichsbank New Accounts Manager Sharpe swears it was Klasse, not you, who opened an account and deposited very large sums, the first of which included the incredible, yet seemingly authentic, misdated banknote issued ... sorry, serialized *to be* issued and circulated in a calendar year yet to come. Frau Sharpe testified to the fact of meeting you in Herr Klasse's suite at the Adlon, then mentioned crossing paths with you a second time in the lobby. A chief inspector and his partner spoke with this Klasse-Lustmann person, as did the hotel's manager, who swears that he was intimidated by Klasse. What we insist on learning is simply this: were you, a supposed Austrian journalist, actively helping Klasse accomplish whatever he was attempting to do?"

"N-no, not ... really," faltered James.

"Absolutely no one," Meisinger said flatly, "could begin to believe you're being truthful, Steyr."

"I almost hate to tell you," declared Canaris with acerbic intonation, "even more strangeness has sprouted for you to explain, although in this instance it amounts to something so *totally* preposterous and unworldly that everyone who's been made aware of the purported affair was left talking to himself." He tapped a photo of the younger Erich Lustmann. "This youthful double of the individual in question was a cadet taking his evening meal in the refectory of an *SS* training academy. While sitting in full view of other cadets, actually conversing with one at the time, all witnesses swear that he instantly vanished."

"Vanished?"

"Disappeared!" Growing more agitated despite his earlier resolution to question Steyr calmly, the admiral stated that *SS* legal attachés desperate to determine the real circumstances surrounding the inexplicable incident are engaged in putting every single witness through an extremely painful wringer.

"And, oh yes, speaking of coincidence piled upon coincidence," he added, an acerbic sharpness in his tone, "*another* coincidence has lain in wait to confront us with something even *more* bizarre. The inexplicable occurrence at the *Klagenfurt SS-Junkerschule* took place on the *identical* evening at approximately the *same* instant you chose to put two nine-millimeter holes in the chest of a gentleman passing himself off as Herr Erich Klasse."

*Mother Nature,* thought James with a sinking feeling, *had resolved the temporal paradox in the predictable manner he had feared.* Under the pressure of the moment, he wished she had done so while young Lustmann was alone. Further crowded more tightly into a fast-shrinking corner, he could think of nothing to say.

"Now the truth, if you *please,*" demanded Canaris, emphasizing the polite nature of his request. "We *must* learn exactly what the hell has been going on. Was Herr Klasse, not you, responsible for inventing and promulgating this 'Friend of the Reich' craziness we've been struggling to come to grips with month after month?"

"Wh-what … made you think that?" asked James, sorry how weak the query sounded.

"Above and beyond all else, the singular, most outstanding reason," declared Canaris, "is that inside a drop-leaf escritoire in the Adlon suite occupied by Klasse, Lustmann, or any other *verdammt* identity he used, we found a packet of stationery, a near-new Parker fountain pen, and a partially filled bottle of green ink. Our forensic laboratory tested the ink against samples obtained from the original letters written by our psychic friend of the Reich, whomsoever he may be, had once been, and may be *again,* God help us! A forensic analysis has confirmed the constituents of both samples to be as identical as it's feasible to ascertain."

At a total loss for words, James felt the ground slipping farther from beneath his feet. If the determined, inquiring stares of his inquisitors were any indication, he not only had to think fast, but also clearly. He fell back on information gleaned from the flash-paper account of early World War II.

"I'm reluctant to divulge what visions I've experienced pertaining to the coming invasion of the USSR codenamed Barbarossa," he said. "Very little choice exists except to reveal—"

*"Lieber Gott!"* cried Admiral Canaris. *"Where* and *when* did you hear that term?"

James licked his lips. "Never spoken aloud, except when referring to the twelfth-century Holy Roman Emperor, but in more than one vision I clearly saw what I took to be the *OKW* general staff congregated around a long table. A gray-haired officer with red Wehrmacht collar tabs was using a pointer to enumerate bulleted blackboard paragraphs listing manifold units of Wehrmacht *Heer* mechanized infantry, plus a huge *Panzergruppen* column slated to march into the USSR in mid-April, or sooner weather permitting, when the ground in western Russia had dried to the extent that *Panzerwaffe* cleated tracks would not mire in mud. The senior officer was referring to data on a large wall chart captioned with a single word: Barbarossa."

Whey-faced, Canaris sank back in a chair, shot a stricken glance at Meisinger, and turned back to Silverthorne in open-mouthed disbelief. "Of what use," he said, parsing each word delicately, as if it might be fragile, "are we poor deluded Abwehr people who devote our lives to gathering human intelligence to do when *omniscience* can easily replace all our efforts?"

Meisinger had difficulty finding his voice, and when he did, he sounded severely shaken. "What of Klasse? Who was he, Steyr? And as importantly, *what* was he? We really *must* learn!"

"My assigned aide," said James, suppressing an urge to bite his tongue over the false note that crept into his white lie. "He disappointed me."

"How? In what way?"

"Our ... sponsors, the, er ... gentlemen behind our attempt to rectify the conduct of the war, as well as governance of the Reich itself were, uh ... "

"What of them?"

"Klasse and I worked together in his Adlon suite on only one occasion. We wrote and polished the letter aimed at influencing the conduct of the coming air war over Britain."

"Only that particular letter?" demanded the admiral. "Why just one?"

"Because Klasse knew far more about Luftwaffe operations than I do. During the past few weeks, perhaps as long as a month, I'd been growing uneasy about the ... Well, it was my impression that Klasse was getting increasingly nervous by the day about playing his part, mostly I believe because of the notoriety accruing over the discovery of that bogus banknote. After being visited by the Adlon's manager, and later the two detectives, I sensed that he'd begun losing his nerve and was in fact showing signs of being deathly afraid of being found out, arrested, and, er ... interrogated. The carryall had to stay locked in his suite for safekeeping, and I was afraid he was on the verge of snatching it and running."

"So you shot him. Steyr, your latest fanciful tale," accused Canaris, "is riddled with gaping holes. You shot your associate simply because of a fear that he might—"

Canaris broke off when the bedroom door was flung open without benefit of a knock. Hulking in the doorway, Emil said loudly, "We've got one helluva problem, Admiral!"

His train of thought broken by his bodyguard's abrupt appearance, Canaris said dismissively, "Not now, Emil."

"Best for you t'hear me out, sir," asserted Emil hoarsely. "Wasn't any Gestapo turds in the gray sedan that played tag with us through the streets. When Kurt and I got there, we found ourselves in the middle of a dust up. Some guy had jumped outta the gray buggy that'd been tracking us, and he kicked off a shootout right then 'n there in the street. Turned into a reg-lar firefight it did, and one of our guys is a deader. Kurt was shot too. He's hurt bad, *real* bad!"

# TWENTY-ONE

## *The Dragon Lady*

Admiral Canaris prided himself on his semi-legendary ability to retain his composure under pressure, a major conceit none of the individuals among his pet peeves—Himmler, Hess, Borman, and a few other hangers-on fiercely clinging to places in Hitler's inner circle— had ever seen him lose in the heat of some controversy.

Pacing back and forth in Himmler's spacious office, he was exercising the exception that proved the rule, angrily hammering direct questions at director of the Reich main security office, *Gruppenführer-SS* Reinhard Heydrich. Enraged by the unsatisfying responses furnished by the ex-naval intelligence officer under his command, the admiral's harsh questions grew still more harsh, continuing unabated while he paced, trying to keep Heydrich from recognizing how deeply disturbed he really was.

"So you still assert," said Canaris, striving to control the tone and timbre of his voice, "that it was *not* your Gestapo thugs conducting surveillance each and every time I choose to venture away from Abwehr headquarters?"

His head cocked attentively, staying above the confrontation, Himmler watched the dueling pair in pensive, owl-eyed silence.

Tall and ungainly, his long, thin nose the centerpiece of his thin, arrogant features, Heydrich regarded the admiral with haughty indifference. "Twice you've asked me that, and twice have I supplied you with the identical answer. I hardly think a third negative response is necessary."

Taking a firm grip on his temper, the admiral wanted to know if the suspected attackers might have been from the *SD,* or perhaps another *SS* organization or the city police.

"I am unable to either confirm or deny any of those possibilities," intoned Heydrich, his manner defiant, above it all. "What I can tell you with assurance is something I'm sure Reichsführer-*SS* Himmler will corroborate. All personnel serving in the organizations under his comprehensive direction have better things to do than follow you about Berlin."

Deciding the vicious bastard was being partially truthful, the admiral backed off. "Very well," he said, more to soften Himmler's antagonism than for any other reason, "you may think ill of me if you wish, Heydrich, but ever since your outstanding duties as an excellent Kriegsmarine signals intelligence officer, I've had naught but praise for your dedication and leadership. Your word on the matter is accepted without qualification. I hope you understand why the gravity of the situation made it necessary to pose such indelicate, pointed inquiries."

"Your kind words are an inspiration," said Heydrich, making no attempt to mask the snide undertone tainting his diction. "Should further aid in getting to the root of this peculiar affair be required, you have only to request it via the good offices of the Reichsführer-*SS.*"

"I sincerely appreciate that," said the admiral, thinking, *Thanks for nothing, you bastard!*

Himmler sniffled, dabbed his leaky nose with a kerchief. "Sorry to take you away from your desk, Reinhard. I'll join you shortly; the admiral and I have another matter to discuss."

Heydrich lifted his billed cap replete with the *SS* death's-head insignia, insolently dipped his chin to Canaris, again less stiffly to Himmler, and took his leave.

The door clicked shut and Himmler cleared his throat. *"Der Füh-rer* is screaming for action on this friend of the Reich business, Wilhelm."

"So am I," Canaris told him, meaning it.

Reichsführer-*SS* Himmler tolled the known facts. "A dark-gray sedan with two men in it, armed with sound-suppressed weapons, is naught to go on. It leaves us with no leads to follow, since Berlin is awash in dark-gray sedans."

Canaris grimaced unhappily. "I glimpsed the car only in passing. It lacked license tabs."

"So we were informed. Coming out of the blue, it smacks of a foreign attack, perhaps an intelligence operation gone wrong. If so, the British automatically become prime suspects."

"Not really, in my opinion," countered the admiral. "Not one whiff of an SIS operation sullies either encounter. MI6 operations are almost always accomplished quietly, under the rose one might say, and hardly ever violent. The Britishers plant a mole here, another there, and, so to speak, gather information over tea and crumpets, but not a blatant, weapons-free operation in broad daylight, with blood spilt on a relatively busy side street, scads of civilian witnesses about. Such impromptu dustups might occur in a dire, extremely important emergency, but I simply can't imagine a reason for what took place."

Himmler revolved the statement. "I was told your man has failed to regain consciousness."

"True, I regret having to say. The surgeon said privately that he may never come around."

"If so, we shall learn nothing from him. As for the eyewitnesses, all were too far away to provide more than a general description of the shooter." Himmler pursed his lips, removed his rimless spectacles, made a project of breathing on the lenses, and polished them with a tissue. "Don't be a defeatist, Wilhelm. Your man may yet respond to treatment."

"We shall hope so," said Canaris, believing none of it. "I sounded out the physician in charge a second time, and he estimated Kurt's survivability at or near zero.

\* \* \*

No longer in the first or second flush of youth, a petite Asian woman descended the stair's bare wooden risers with measured steps. The steady gaze of her almond-shaped dark eyes settled on the grouped men waiting in the basement of an older suburban house. The seated gentlemen all rose deferentially at sight of her. Securely bound and gagged, another man in the basement was tied in a rickety, straight-backed wooden chair.

The most elderly gentleman of those awaiting the woman's arrival bowed low, his mature Sinic features stolid. "We bid you welcome, Madam Quon," he said in Mandarin.

The woman paused on the stair, gripped the bare wooden bannister, and awarded the speaker a piercing look. "You are not to forget yourself again," she said forcefully. "Were you not instructed that only German was permissible to speak here, either in private or public?"

*"Ihre Entschuldigung,"* said the other by way of an apology. "How was your journey?"

"Long and tiring and necessary." The woman came down, removed her wrap, draped it over a chair. "The Nipponese passport seemed adequate beforehand, but a customs agent appraised me critically before convincing himself I was a misbegotten child of the island race. Several of the shipboard passengers also eyed me curiously, as well as others on the train from Bremen."

"You have arrived safely," remarked the other, "and for that we are most grateful."

"What of him?" She indicated the gagged, half-naked man lashed to a chair.

The elderly gentleman did nothing to temper the venom in his indictment. "His impulsive nature totally overwhelmed Lim, driving him to jump out of our automobile in a frustrated rage and open fire on what we believed were agents from *Sicherheitsbüro* in the auto purposely blocking our pursuit."

Madam Quon's sudden intake of breath gave away the depth of her alarm. "One devoutly hopes and prays he was not using an energy weapon."

"Oh, no! A German machine pistol we obtained. Do you wish Lim to be eliminated?"

The woman pondered. "Disposing of him afterward might be a problem. We have a rigorous obligation to leave no clue of our presence, so I think it best to immediately send him back."

Bound in the chair, the man referred to as Lim sputtered in protest through the gag, and continued to make unintelligible noises until the gag was removed and two sets of eager fingers pried apart his jaws. His moaning attempts to stop them were ignored and his false tooth actuated. He vanished instantly, while the ropes once binding him drooped limply on the chair's seat.

"During the entire exercise now at hand," declared Madam Quon in a tone few would dare to argue with, "laser weapons will be free only if one feels himself targeted, and then *only* if local witnesses are not present. Should any of our people allow a hand laser to be seen in this era, he is to immediately activate a return. I hope we shall all remain quite clear on that mandatory action."

The men nodded in unison, except for a Caucasian gentleman standing apart from the others.

Madam Quon's cool stare raked the tall man. *"Sind Sie der Schweizer?"*

"At your service, Madam Quon."

Continuing her candid appraisal of the *Schweizer*, Madam Quon said, "Your assignment to replace the former team leader was a last-minute decision. Exactly how or why such late recruitment took place was not made clear to me. What drove you to volunteer aid in consummating our critical mission?"

"The deciding factors," he said with what passed for a twinkle, "were no doubt my very handsome, inconspicuous Caucasian features, plus fluency in the odious German tongue."

She said, "How entertaining! Henceforth, you will refrain from repartee of any sort, and you will speak only when spoken to in the manner of an adult, not some witless juvenile. In responding to my question, you either neglected to mention the contractual recompense guaranteed by the Golden One, or intentionally refrained from doing so. Which was it?"

The man smiled. "The exceptional compensation offered is my only reason for being here."

"One sincerely hopes you manage to survive and spend your newfound treasure."

"I shall in one way or another." Despite her instructions, the other again interjected a note of levity. "The trust established in my name is inviolate. Should misfortune overtake me—a truly dreadful prospect—my significant other can look forward to a life of leisure and comfort."

"Only," the woman reminded him, "if our mission proves successful, which is something you might keep in the front of your mind at all times. To put it bluntly, sir, the Golden One described you as an adventurer, not an entirely serious player. Can this be true?"

"Madam Quon, please regard me as a serious adventurer who is very much in accord with the goals you and your team are setting out to achieve."

As if weary of the *Schweizer's* banter, Madam Quon blinked and was suddenly all business. "Now please explain, where are we as of this moment? I take it the subject has been located."

"We have him pinned down somewhere within a four-block radius," announced the white-haired Asian gentleman. "Hoping to track down the specific address, Lim and a second asset were unobtrusively following a suspected *Sicherheitsbüros* vehicle and were apparently spotted. The street was blocked by a second *SD* vehicle, and a sudden confrontation erupted when the impulsive Lim initiated a shootout. Rooftop observers stationed along routes leading into the neighborhood in question signaled the target's approximate location to our vehicle. We have good reason to believe the hideaway was pinpointed when suspected *Sicherheitsbüros* personnel rushed from an apartment building and departed in an unmarked auto."

"Then you've definitely learned where the subject is sequestered?"

"Not the specific floor and room, Madam Quon," informed the elderly man, who went on to describe how, while under surveillance at the boardinghouse, with their team preparing to move in and take him, a rooftop stakeout phoned in to say a vehicle had arrived bearing two more *Sicherheitsbüros* assets, one of whom, a tall well-dressed gentleman, entered the establishment.

"Roughly an hour later," he concluded, "an ambulance arrived and two uniformed paramedics took away a supposedly ill or injured man in a gurney. Later still, the assets hurriedly escorted the target out of the boardinghouse and drove off with him."

"Why were they not tracked to where he was taken then?"

"Our man attempted to do so, but he was alone. By the time he reached his auto, the vehicle and target were lost in traffic."

"Who was responsible for that sloppiness?"

"He who, er … It was Lim, the excitable gunman we sent back."

"I see." Madam Quon sniffed, her displeasure evident. Reclaiming her wrap from the back of a chair, she said, "My journey was long and tiring. We shall sit down together this evening, discuss our prospective moves more fully, and establish a firm plan of action."

"Mei Ling will show you to your room and see to your comfort, Madam Quon."

"Rest well, Madam Quon," added the Swiss gentleman.

Her disdainful glance at the "serious adventurer" still hinted at remaining suspicion.

Once she was safely back upstairs, the object of her suspicion shrugged. "That lady is some specimen! Now I understand how she earned her Dragon Lady nickname."

"Softly, sir! Further impudence would be unwise," warned the elderly gentleman. "I advise you to treat her with utmost respect. Her granduncle happens to be the Golden One himself."

His change of expression made it plain that the serious adventurer had learned of an extremely serious familial connection.

*  *  *

Bored by his lengthy vigil in the Intensive Care unit, Ulrich Meisinger was leafing through a dog-eared magazine when a nurse entered the waiting room. "Sir, you asked to be notified if the patient stirred. The doctor believes he may be gradually regaining consciousness."

Meisinger dropped the magazine. "Thank you, Sister." His rapid strides took him down the corridor to Kurt's private room. Cautiously pushing his way through the extra-wide door, he found the patient looking every bit as pale and immobile as he had earlier, except that his eyes were now open slits. An oxygen mask covered his mouth and nose; an intravenous tube inserted in his left forearm looped up to a bottle of clear solution suspended from a metal stand.

Meisinger bent closely above his team leader. "Kurt, can you hear me?"

The patient's eyes rolled slowly toward the sound of a voice, but his gaze was unfocused.

"Who attacked you, Kurt?"

There was no response.

"Who was it, Kurt? Who did it? Were you able to get a good look at the shooter?"

The patient's mouth worked beneath the oxygen mask. Meisinger lifted the mask a few millimeters, stretching the elastic band holding it in place, and bent closer, his ear next to the patient's mouth. "Who shot you?" Hearing a barely audible whisper, he said, "Again, please!"

The sibilant response was equally tenuous, but a touch louder.

Meisinger straightened with a sharp intake of breath. Kurt's eyes were closed again. He carefully replaced the oxygen mask and turned to the hovering nurse with a look of inquiry. She moved her head slowly from side to side in a subtle negative.

Meisinger charged out of the private room, trotted to the nurses' station, and seized the phone. Obtaining an outside line, he ordered the duty officer at headquarters to put him through to Canaris at once, and to break in if the admiral happened to be using the phone.

When Canaris came on the line, Meisinger told him Kurt had come around long enough to whisper a single word, "Asian."

"Are you certain, Ulrich?"

"Positive, sir."

*"Ganz gut!* Get back here while I'm setting the wheels in motion. If need be, we'll pull in for questioning everyone in Germany who remotely resembles an Asian or Eurasian individual."

"On my way." Meisinger caged the telephone and hurried to the elevator.

\* \* \*

Canaris put through an urgent call to Himmler, then dialed the number of a trusted executive he considered one of the most responsible higher-ups in *Kripo,* the criminal investigation branch of the civilian police organization.

Within an hour, Berlin was fully mobilized and the word spread quickly to authorities of all stripes in Germany. Members of Kripo and all Reich Main Security and Abwehr assets flooded the streets, transportation centers, and seaports, combing the capital's boulevards, streets, alleys, and byways in a concerted search for anyone and everyone of Asian or Eurasian extraction—nor did they over-look the embassies, restaurants, hotels, transit stations, parks, and miscellaneous locales, shops, and small-business establishments.

Dozens of ethnic Asian men and women were rounded up, including a few out-of-towners whose other-than-Caucasian fea-tures made them stand out in a crowd. Heydrich's Gestapo embar-rassed itself by entering an expensive Wilhelmstrasse eatery and arresting four members of a Nipponese delegation and a Japanese charge d'affaires stationed in Berlin who was dining with visitors. Informed of the gauche presumption his minions had demon-strated, Reinhard Heydrich flew into a classic rage, voiced endless apologies, and took it upon himself to soothe the offended diplo-matic entourage by personally escorting them back to the Japanese Embassy.

In a mixed business and residential district, a senior Gestapo asset armed with binoculars spotted a man he thought might be Asian peering down from the parapet atop an apartment building. He led a squad charging up three flights of stairs, flung open a door leading to the roof, and saw the suspect dodge behind a large water tank.

The Gestapo team split and converged from both directions, weapons drawn, but the suspect was nowhere to be seen. The agent in charge rushed to the parapet and looked down. "Gone," he said in amazement. "He couldn't have jumped or he'd be splattered all over the walkway. If not, where the hell did he go?"

The question was never answered.

\* \* \*

Looking distraught, Madam Quon ruminated at length. "Should the media reports be accurate," she said in German, "every corner of the city is being scoured for Asians. The specific shuttered apart-ment building windows and presumed *Sicherheitsbüros* assets posted outside as sentinels tend to confirm the target's whereabouts, yet unfortunately we dare not make a move, though sitting here biding our time waiting for the frenzied hunt to slack off might be equally risky."

After an interlude of pregnant silence, the once casual, at present exceptionally serious Swiss adventurer spoke up. "There could be a way to act safely, Madam Quon."

"I will listen to no wild schemes," she warned.

Nonplused, he explained what he had in mind.

Sudden interest sparked thoughtfulness. She studied *der Schweizer* momentarily. More or less thinking aloud, she mused, "When I arrived, a large white van or panel truck was parked in the garage. Mightn't it suffice, rather than renting an ambulance as you suggested?"

The now-serious Swiss gentleman shrugged. "Don't see why not. If so, all we'll need are a half dozen white lab smocks, some surgical masks, other miscellaneous medical trappings to make the emergency responders look authentic. The *Sicherheitsbüros* assets, or whoever they were, provided a template for conducting the strike by hauling someone away from the boardinghouse in an ambulance. I doubt if paramedics will be questioned for going about their business."

Madam Quon's brow wrinkled. She addressed the aged Asian gentleman. "Damn your man's impetuosity! He was your responsibility and should have been stopped."

The elder did his best not to sound defensive. He explained how the miscreant Lim had leaped out of the vehicle without a word and volleyed the machine pistol on full automatic.

Madam Quon blinked to dispel the image. She straddled the fence, weighing the practicality of the contemplated venture versus waiting out the reported widespread hunt for anyone of Asian heritage. "Days could pass before the chase subsides, which could be more worrisome than getting on with it now when the surprise factor is favorable. Then, too, if the target is moved, we may have to search for him again. Minus Lim, how many of our assets are left?"

"Six here in the house, two on the street, and an eighth on roof-top vigil across from the suspected apartment house, although for whatever reason that one has not been heard from for hours."

Madam Quon made up her mind. "Nine amounts to overkill. You will order all but six to activate immediate returns. Our sole Caucasian is the only one of us able to go into the street without attracting undue attention. Go now," she told the elder, her attitude more cordial than it had been. "Have Mei Ling look up a nearby medical supply store—and take the sedan; the bullet holes in the body and door have been caulked, the paint retouched. Purchase the smocks, masks, and a physician's black bag for yourself, plus a stethoscope and whatever like paraphernalia you think may be needed."

"Fine," he said. "I have one more suggestion, Madam Quon. We'll need every advantage to pull off this operation, so I insist on going in energy weapons-free."

Looking glum, Madam Quon revolved the ramifications of adopting his stated condition. "You," she said, "were elected by default to lead the operation. Since our choices are severely limited, so be it. Once only, on this singular instance, energy weapons will be free, but only if and when you become convinced the situation warrants such an extreme measure. *Only* then, is that clear?"

A bold grin in evidence, the Caucasian said, "Perfectly clear, Madam Quon. You may now refer to me as a seriously adventurous Swiss physician."

The Dragon Lady's lip curled in what, for anyone else, was a reluctant shadow smile.

\* \* \*

The white van rolled up, braked to a stop with a faint squeak of tires, and double-parked in mid-street. Clad in a dark suit and tie, the

Swiss "physician" stepped down from the driver's seat, and with surgical masks covering their mouths and noses, billed caps pulled down to screen their eyes, four white-smocked attendants exited from double doors at the rear of the van.

Alarmed by the sight, the Abwehr asset assigned to sentinel duty bolted from a parked car and trotted to intercept the arrivals. "What the hell is this?" he demanded, one hand on his underarm holster.

The "doctor" slipped a surgical mask over his lower face, seized the black physician's valise from the seat, slammed the door, and in fluent German asked the man who had accosted his team if he had recently been in the apartment house basement.

"Basement? No, I don't live here."

"Have you or anyone else noticed any rat droppings in the basement?"

"What?"

"Some excited person called the hospital and gave this address," explained the doctor with a show of impatience. "Later, a resident was brought in exhibiting symptoms of … well, a not very nice affliction. If you don't live here, why are you interested in our reason for coming?"

"I, uh, work here now and then."

The doctor nodded. "I see. Step to the rear of the van, please. It will take only seconds to see if you've been infected." After surveying the all but trafficless street, he took a small canister from his satchel, held his breath, and depressed the stud. An aerosol spray of concentrated psychoactive medication took the Abwehr asset full in the face. He tried to draw his weapon but was hindered by the doctor. Slumping backward loose-limbed, he was caught by a pair of white-smocked paramedics, who shoved him ungently into the van and closed both doors.

The doctor searched the rooftop parapet of the building directly across the street, but the stakeout allegedly posted was nowhere to be seen. "Go!" he ordered. "If you find any guards downstairs, don't waste time, just take them out." He trailed the four first responders inside.

The bored Abwehr asset on duty in the parlor had no chance to do more than gain his feet before the doctor announced a case of suspected plague attributed to a rat infestation in the basement. What the startled Abwehr asset wanted to say was shut off by a first responder wearing a surgical mask who sapped him hard. Another helped the sapper lift his limp victim and deposit him on the floor behind a sofa.

"Upstairs fast! If anyone should question what you're doing, say nothing, let me handle it." The doctor and his four-man team encountered a fluffy-haired older woman in the second-floor hall-way carrying a Dachshund on a leash and preparing to descend the stairs.

"Medical emergency!" His voice muffled by the surgical mask, the doctor told the lady there was nothing to worry about. "Please stay to your apartment until the patient in this building is taken away. Pending a full examination, we don't know how contagious he may be."

Round-eyed, the woman stared at the medics wearing surgical masks, turned about with the dog in her arms, and hastened back the way she had come.

A pair of medics checked the locked door, backed away, lowered their shoulders and made a concerted bull rush, all but ripping the door from its hinges. An Abwehr asset lolling in the suite's living room sprang to his feet and whirled, weapon drawn, just in time for one of his assailants to sap him while the other seized his arm and weapon.

In the bedroom, Silverthorne came awake with a start, alarmed by the racket of the entry door crashing down. He froze in the act of clambering out of bed when the door burst open and four men wearing white surgical masks rushed in and confronted him. What he took to be a physician following close behind them was carrying a black medical valise.

"Who are you?" demanded James.

"A medical alert, sir! All residents are being inoculated and placed under quarantine."

"That's … Wait, I'm not a resident." James backed away defensively.

The doctor ignored him, withdrew a hypodermic syringe from the black satchel, broke the seal of an ampule, and filled the syringe, squirting a few drops of clear fluid in the air to clear the tube of bubbles.

Instructed to pull up his pajama sleeve and expose his bare his arm, James backed away farther. "What if I don't want to be inoculated?"

"Isn't a matter of choice, sir. The health department has decided it mandatory."

A pair of men in gauze surgical masks seized James, held him firmly by his wrists while a third unbuttoned his pajama top and bared his left arm. Since it did no good to struggle, he stood quietly, head cocked, watching the needle enter the flesh of his shoulder.

Soon the bedroom, as well as everyone and everything in it, grew fuzzy, indistinct. The last thing he remembered was how strange the doctor looked with only a swimming white blob where his face should have been.

* * *

It was like dreaming. Someone seemed to be gently slapping his left cheek, then his right cheek. James felt himself being rocked from side to side by rough hands, opened his eyes, then closed them tightly, blinded by the naked light bulb dangling on a frayed cord from an electrical ceiling outlet alongside a cobwebbed rafter. "Who're you? W-where am I?"

A middle-aged Asian woman bent, observed him closely, her

dark, almond-shaped eyes slitted. "If it matters, still in what you know as Berlin," she said in precise schoolbook German. "Not for long, however. You were awakened in order to say farewell and to thank you for your exploits."

"I don't …" he said groggily. "I, uh . . not sure I … understand."

"It is of no consequence, Herr Steyr, or however you wish to be addressed. After being induced via medication to reveal all, we have been supplied with the necessary basics. The rest will be taken care of later. We have work to do now, and alas, your short stay with us must end."

Lying helpless on a rumpled cot, James tried to sit up, only to learn of the restraints pinioning his torso, arms, and legs.

A low baritone voice spoke from somewhere behind the woman. "Madam Quon, we really should be on our way. All is in readiness. Mei Ling has the van running in the garage."

Outwardly self-contained, yet somehow looking pleased with herself while expressionless, the Asian woman nodded brusquely. "*Wiedersehen!*"

More than one set of fingers pried Silverthorne's jaws apart. Languidly, with the underwater quality of a dream, he tried to lift his hands and fend off the assailants, but the restraints defeated all efforts. The new false molar in his mouth was twisted sharply and pressed down hard.

The convulsive, visceral-crawling sensation of temporal transition surged through him, and he was suddenly falling through an emptiness neither light nor dark, limbs windmilling for balance. Crashing down on a resilient surface, he rebounded and sprawled full length on what appeared to be dim foam-padded covering of some kind.

*Carlsbad!* The searing knowledge was accompanied by a sense of relief. Lifting his head, he searched what could be seen of the vast limestone cavern and its acres of floor space, the recesses lost in Stygian gloom. Far off, he could barely make out the bottom-lit "Lions Tail" stalactite, an illuminated collection of limestone icicles known as "The Chandelier" descending from the jagged ceiling, and an enormous stalagmite called "Rock of Ages."

Managing to sit up stiffly, he tried to reorient himself in time as well as in the familiar Big Room of Carlsbad's temporal reception chamber. He groped and began kneading his aching temples, gradually becoming aware of an alarm klaxon honking in the distant surrounding darkness, then heard the faint, pounding sound of approaching boots.

Lights flared into brilliance on the perimeter of the foam matting. A half dozen armed figures in baggy tan uniforms appeared, halted in a line abreast, and separated to allow a pudgy, balding individual no longer young edge through the cordon. Stepping up on the padded area, he came closer to James, moving cautiously to keep his balance on the resilient floor. He halted and looked Silverthorne over candidly. His eyes narrowed and he said something in Russian.

James responded with a negative headshake.

The portly gentleman snorted a profanity and switched to German. "Don't tell me another run-for-your-life Nazi has fallen into our midst. Did everyone in the so-called *Dritte Reich* seek to escape disaster and hope to save their necks in this same craven manner?"

*"Ich bin ein Amerikaner,"* muttered Silverthorne.

The greeter threw back his head, hooted laughter. Turning to the guards, he pointed at the new arrival disdainfully, uttered a single word: *"Americanetz!"*

Several of the grinning armed guards dared to chuckle.

"No, my newfound acquaintance! It distresses me to tell you creatures claiming to be Americans have not existed for …" He broke off, moved closer, and peered intently at James. "Wait, am I by chance addressing a gentleman named Steyr?"

"It's a … I have used that name, but—"

"Will wonders never cease!" exclaimed the other, clapping his hands. "For many decades we've been led to believe you were

Austrian, Herr Steyr, but not by any stretch of the imagination an *American.* Hmmm, no matter. Permit me to heartily welcome you to the Sino-Soviet Peoples Republic. Our Party's historical technicians have speculated about whether, or for that matter *if* and *when,* you might one day turn up here in the present timeline."

Marched across the Big Room and down a long passageway hewn from limestone, James was thrust bodily into a claustrophobic cell faintly smelling like wet cement; in it, a utilitarian bunk suspended from a jackhammer-scored limestone wall by chains, an integral stainless steel washbasin and commode, and a bare floor of rough, hewn limestone.

An automatic lock clicked, orchestrating the steel-barred door's closure. The footfalls of his tan-uniformed escorting quartet echoed hollowly, diminishing until a thick, all-but-tangible stillness prevailed.

He sat on the edge of the bunk and clapped his hands over his ears to drown the sterile, subterranean silence permeating his cell and surroundings. His mind writhing and gyrating, his thoughts came full circle to a paralyzing realization of what had apparently occurred. He found it like staring into a hall of mirrors where one may view only grotesquely distorted multiple images of oneself endlessly reflected, diminishing in size bit by bit to vanish in infinity.

Rocking back on the thin mattress, he thumped his head painfully on the naked limestone wall and began to laugh. Holding his sides, he roared with hysterical laughter until tears streamed down his cheeks.

What had *Herr Kantzler* Hoffmann warned him about in the vanished, once-familiar neverland of Deutsches Weltreich? In his confused state, he seemed to recall that it had to do with the immense reflexive dangers of promiscuous time travel.

*Immense, indeed! Ever so much more enormous than the world itself or the universe!*

Struggling for breath, James laughed uncontrollably at the futile idiocy of it all until. Choking on the hilarity, he wondered inanely if it might be the last time in his life he ever laughed.

# AFTERWORD

Although far from certain, Silverthorne thought he detected the distant shuffling footfalls of someone approaching his cell. Still clad in the soiled, ill-fitting gray jumpsuit provided weeks or months earlier, he slid his legs off the narrow bunk and slipped his feet into flimsy plastic flip-flops passing for footwear. Keeping his eyes subserviently lowered in the way he had been painfully taught, he sensed that he was not hungry enough for mealtime. But who could tell if it was night or day aboveground, let alone a way to guess the hour?

Surprised to hear the lock click open, he grew apprehensive when unseen hands swung wide the steel-barred door and a taser-armed guard wheeled into the cell a fancy meal cart of a type he had not seen before. On it, was the usual compartmented plastic tray laden with the identical weary staples always served: limp stir-fried vegetables, a handleless stoneware mug of lukewarm tea, and two crumbly lumps masquerading as rice cakes.

The guard took his time retreating from the cell, and the auto-locking cell door closed.

After summoning the courage to look up, James found an emaciated, white-haired Asian gentleman peering at him through the vertical bars with the intensity of a naturalist inspecting a hitherto unknown anthropoid specimen. Clad in a flowing robe of pale gold gathered at the waist by a twisted skein of golden rope, his feet shod in golden slippers, the elderly gentleman shook hands with himself and rattled a phrase in staccato Mandarin.

A much younger man with careworn Sinic features appeared at the elder's shoulder. "The Golden One," he informed in near-flawless German, "wishes you to know your stay with us is about to conclude."

*And a bitter end it will doubtless be,* thought Silverthorne, who had not only longed for his imprisonment to end, but on occasion had *prayed* for it. Perversely glad to hear that he was to be relieved if the necessity to stare for interminable weeks and endless months—however long it had been—at the jackhammer-scored walls of his cell, he once again respectfully lowered his gaze. "May I humbly inquire who it is I have to thank for my deliverance?"

"The Golden One," informed the interpreter, "is burdened with a truly celestial title it would be of no benefit for you to learn. You have The Golden One's permission to think of him as a sort of commissar, an archaic term which in a distant, obscure way is somewhat appropriate."

"Please tell The Golden One I deeply appreciate his consideration, and also that I am prepared to gratefully accept the solace of oblivion."

The interpreter spoke to The Golden One, apparently relaying Silverthorne's words. The elder's wrinkled ascetic features creased in what might have been a smile.

"Nothing quite that barbaric awaits you," assured the interpreter, making no attempt to mask his amusement. "In parting, The Golden One wishes you to know he and his peers wish to repay their indebtedness for the difficult task you strove to accomplish by valiantly opposing the global imperialists in their own home, yet through no fault of your own failed to do so. The Golden One hopes you will enjoy this, your final repast as our guest."

James could not resist a distasteful glance at the meal tray. "Please inform The Golden One," he said with veiled sarcasm, "I sincerely appreciate his kindness, but am not hungry just now. However, please convey my gratitude for his parting display of hospitality."

The interpreter conferred briefly with the Golden One, turned back to James, and declared with mock seriousness, "Had you come as a party of four, egg drop soup, Szechuan lamb, shitake mushrooms, and water chestnuts would have graced your last supper."

"Perhaps I should have made a reservation!"

The Golden One gargled asthmatic laughter when James comment was relayed to him, then proceeded to abandon himself to wizened hilarity.

"Now that everything which we wished to learn concerning your retro-temporal escapade has been catalogued and filed away for the amusement of posterity," declared the interpreter, "The Golden One wishes to bid you a most fond farewell."

With that, the aged dignitary curtly dipped his head, slowly turned around, his golden slippers producing scuffing sounds in the rough limestone corridor that steadily grew more and more faint as he was trailed at a respectful two paces by the interpreter.

A guard reentered the cell, pointed wordlessly at the food tray and performed eating gestures, but did not react to Silverthorne's negative headshake except to take him by the arm and tug him out of the cell. With a pair of guards preceding him and two following, effectively surrounding him in a moving square, he was escorted along the corridor to an elevator bank where on his own timeline tourists had descended after entering the aboveground entrance to Carlsbad.

The elevator compartment grounded with a slight jar. James was conducted through a jagged, arched entrance into the Big Room where on four separate occasions he had returned from one retro-temporal junket or another, each time reappearing in the midair nexus of ultra-definitive fixes that amounted to precisely defined three-dimensional spacetime coordinates.

A dreaded thought seared James's consciousness: *I'm being sent back!* But back to … when, and as importantly, where? Surely not back to the War Years.

A guard gestured impatiently, urging him to climb the wooden steps of a framework supporting a set of circular platform planks elevated two meters above the contiguous foam-filled mats on this, the reception side of the Big Room's vast floor.

Given no choice, he ascended the steps to the platform very slowly and apprehensively, as if a masked headsman or guillotine awaited him at the top. He turned around upon reaching he top, his heart pounding in anticipation of what he knew was coming next. The escorting guards, all but invisible in the dense gloom enveloping the far reaches of the cavern, had retreated past the foam-padded area.

An instant later, the gut-wrenching sensation of retro-temporal transition swept through him like a mildly nauseating tsunami.

Falling through space, his limbs windmilling in a hopeless fight for balance that was in no way obtainable, he plunged to the ground and crashed down in a row of dense, briefly glimpsed vinous growth that scratched his face and arms, landing heavily, bruising his left shoulder and hip.

Gasping for breath, his diaphragm partially collapsed by the impact, he rolled over on his back and massaged his pain-wracked shoulder breathing raggedly, staring up into an empty, cloudless sky, and after a moment struggled to sit up.

Blinking repeatedly, he knuckled his eyes against the unaccustomed glare of either early morning or late afternoon. Less than a meter from the end of his nose, clusters of dusty green grapes appeared ripe for the picking.

Slowly, with considerable effort, he got his feet under him, gradually came erect, and felt his heart skip a beat.

Below the terraced vineyards of Weinbergterasse, an ornate, gilded carriage drawn by a matched pair of clip-clopping grays with bobbed tails approached the foot of the long flight of steps leading up to the entrance of Schloss Sanssouci. The carriage slowed and was halted beside pair of bewigged, liveried servants waiting rigidly at the base of the steps. Facing away toward the carriage, a figure clad in a faded military uniform leaned on his silver-handled cane prepared to greet the arriving guests.

His legs turned to jelly, James Silverthorne swore a lurid oath, sagged down among the vines, and wept.

Review Requested:
If you loved this book, would you please provide a review at
Amazon.com?

CPSIA information can be obtained
at www.ICGtesting.com
Printed in the USA
LVHW111906111119
637016LV00005B/7/P